Thorn Jack

THORN JACK

A Night and Nothing Novel

KATHERINE HARBOUR

HARPER Voyager

An Imprint of HarperCollins Publishers

THORN JACK. Copyright © 2014 by Katherine Harbour. All rights reserved. Printed in the United States of America. No part of this book may be used or reproduced in any manner whatsoever without written permission except in the case of brief quotations embodied in critical articles and reviews. For information address HarperCollins Publishers, 195 Broadway, New York, NY 10007.

HarperCollins books may be purchased for educational, business, or sales promotional use. For information please e-mail the Special Markets Department at SPsales@harpercollins.com.

FIRST EDITION

Harper Voyager and design is a trademark of HCP LLC.

Library of Congress Cataloging-in-Publication Data has been applied for.

ISBN 978-0-06-228672-7

14 15 16 17 18   OV/RRD   10 9 8 7 6 5 4 3 2 1

To my dad, who believed

ACKNOWLEDGMENTS

This book wouldn't have existed in book form without Shari Wentz and Christine Bubinak, who encouraged its journey. The story wouldn't have existed in this form without the advice of my fabulous agent, Thao Le, the patience and belief of my terrific editor, Diana Gill, and the sharp eye of copy editor Laurie McGee. Thanks also to my family, for their support, and to my friends Val Nicotina, Madeline Stark, and Therese Dale, for keeping me grounded and sane.

PROLOGUE

Their creed is "Mischief, Malevolence, and Mayhem."
—From the journal of Lily Rose

Because Jack was always glad to be away from his family, the Summerwoods had become a sanctuary for him. He moved carefully through the trees, the hem of his coat sweeping over fallen leaves and pale toadstools, while things tangled in his dark hair and moonlight illuminated the path and the old rings on his fingers.

He didn't really need the moonlight.

Through a screen of Emory, he saw them, their skin glimmering with pollen beneath the gossamer and velvet tatters of their clothing, their eyes silver in the glow of the fire around which they were gathered. Fireflies and moths swirled in the darkness beyond them, straying toward jewel-knotted hair and fingers scabbed with rings older than the ones he wore.

He should have been afraid.

He stepped forward, into the firelight.

The only way to escape them, the trickster had told him long ago, *is to find the braveheart, the girl, who will make you bleed.*

CHAPTER ONE

But those of aire can easily convert
Into new forms, and then again revert,
One while a man, after a comely maid.
And then all suddenly to make thee start,
Like leaping leopard he'll thee invade.

—"A PLATONICK SONG OF THE SOUL," HENRY MORE

They are not like us. Prick the skin of whoever comes for you . . . if he bleeds, he is human. If he does not, he is from the third kingdom . . .

—FROM THE JOURNAL OF LILY ROSE

They call us things with teeth, Finn's sister had once said, in one of her moods and still wearing her ballerina costume as she huddled on the front porch. She hadn't explained this disturbing statement to Finn. They had argued that night, the night eighteen-year-old Lily Rose had ended her life.

Finn was seventeen when the almost enchanted habit of sleep became a haven for her . . . there were never any dreams and therefore no memories to replay in that vulnerable state of unconsciousness. She lost her appetite. Her body became bird fragile. Her skin bruised easily, as if invisible things were pinching her. In an effort to ward away thoughts of broken glass, she lined her eyes with kohl and left her hair in tangles. She moved through her days like a dead thing, not wanting to be with friends, not wanting anything.

I wake up, she told someone, *and all I want to do is go back to sleep.*

The night before the move, she dreamed.

She wandered barefoot around a pool, past tropical plants and songbirds in cages. Everything was in black-and-white, but her summer dress was green. Girls with flowers in their hair chatted with bare-chested boys and everyone wore metal masks that resembled the faces of frozen children. Throats and arms were decorated with jewelry formed into insects or leaves. There was a buzzing in the air, disturbing and constant.

As a figure in a robe of black ribbons glided past, its identity concealed behind a beaked mask, a voice like ashes and velvet came from behind her, "That is a plague doctor."

Finn turned to find a young man in white jeans and an ivory half mask over his eyes crouched at the pool's edge. A crown of roses the color of blood wreathed his sleek, dark hair. She murmured, "I didn't bring a mask. Why is he a plague doctor?"

"Because he is the Black Scissors and we are a plague."

"Why is everyone else masked?"

"They don't want anyone seeing what they really are."

She looked around. "My sister brought me. Her name is Lily Rose. Have you seen her?"

He slid up and walked to her. He took the rose wreath from his hair and placed it on hers. She felt the wet kiss of petals, the bite of tiny thorns against her temples. He smelled like burning wood, evergreen, wild roses. He said, gently, "Is this too strange?"

"I don't like it here." The buzzing had become loud, unbearable.

He looked at her and a blood drop slid from his left eye, then became a crimson fly that crawled across the scene as if the air were celluloid. "Why are you telling me? I'm dead."

Finn woke at three in the morning. With the exception of the San Francisco traffic outside, the town house was silent. She sat up and switched on the lamp. The dream was still a vivid afterimage.

She rose and walked to the trunk where she kept her sister's belongings, lifted the lid, and withdrew a reel of film. Lily Rose's boyfriend, Leander, had been a student filmmaker who had liked old-fashioned things. He'd given the Super 8 reel to Finn at the funeral, but she'd never dared to watch it. She hadn't been able to watch anything with Lily Rose in it, not recital footage, not digital memories.

She crept down to her da's study, where he kept the Kodak projector he'd purchased at a garage sale. She set the reel into place and aimed the projector at the pale wall. After threading the film through as Lily Rose's boyfriend had taught her, she pressed the motor lamp switch and sat on the floor to watch.

The first image cascaded into black-and-white footage of her sister at a pool party scattered with flowery girls and boys in metal jewelry. Lily Rose stood alone, a tough ballerina in sneakers and a silver slip dress. Finn's throat ached. She wanted to reach in and drag her sister out and scream at her. *Why did you do it?*

The scene scrolled into a jittery shot of a courtyard clotted with briars and gargoyles crouched on stone walls. Lily Rose, spectral in a black gown, stood between two pillars, her head bowed. There was a shadow in the background, the silhouette of a man in a long coat. Finn leaned forward.

The film snapped. The projector buzzed. The wall flashed a wolfish shape, then went blank.

Finn rose and carefully put the projector away. She returned to her room, where she set the film back into the trunk, among her sister's shadow boxes of pinned moths, her ballet costumes, photos of Nijinsky and Nureyev, her iPod containing everything from Belle and Sebastian to Kanye West. She remembered Lily Rose's pale face the night she'd chosen to die. It didn't seem real, still. It was as if her sister had only been stolen away.

She lay back down and buried her face in her pillow, the tightness in her throat as painful as if she'd swallowed thorns. It had been nearly a year since her sister's death.

FINN AND HER FATHER WERE leaving San Francisco because every day in the town house was a reminder of Lily Rose. They had finally packed up her room, where Finn would sometimes sprawl on Lily's bed and pretend her sister was out for the night, that she'd be back late, slightly silly from wine coolers and talking about weird things. They were leaving because her father, despite two Ph.D.s, was still only an assistant professor without tenure, and an assistant professor of world mythology was number one only when it came to budget cuts.

They were leaving because they'd both agreed it was time to start over.

The next day, Finn and her father left San Francisco and the town house filled with memories.

THE OTHER HOUSE APPEARED ON a road lined with Victorian homes and oaks that looked a hundred years old. Finn opened the car window and scowled. Compared to the citrus sunlight of California, the apple chill of New York seemed gloomy and menacing.

Her father, whose shaggy blond hair made him resemble a mad poet, steered the SUV into the drive. This riverside town was his childhood home, and he had been a boy in this house. As a gust of air through the open window flung her hair into her face, she clawed the strands away. "Has the house been closed up since Gran . . . ?"

She couldn't say the word. Her grandmother had last been seen at Lily's funeral, when she had just come from one of her trips to Ireland. Whenever Finn thought of Gran Rose, she pictured a tall woman in an elegant dark suit standing alone on the porch, scowling at the sky. She wished she'd known her grandmother better.

Her father answered casually, "Your aunt Sibyl was looking after it before she moved."

Finn slid from the SUV and stared at the weather-struck house. It looked old, its porch scattered with wicker furniture, its windows dark. She watched yellow and red leaves flutter from the oak on the front lawn. She wistfully thought of texting her two best friends about the house, but she'd scarcely spoken to them in a year. She'd hardly been able to speak with anyone since Lily—

Her eyelashes fluttered and she fought the urge to sleep.

"Da." She used the nickname she'd given her father when she'd been six, after she and seven-year-old Lily had had a fight and Lily had, irrationally, insisted he was *her* dad and Finn was not to call him that. Finn had stubbornly retorted she would call him *Da* from then on. She blinked and quickly wiped a hand across her face before her father could see. "It looks different."

"Does it?" Her da lifted their suitcases from the back of the SUV.

"It looks old."

"Well, you were very young last time we were here."

This time, Lily wasn't here with them.

As they walked up the path, she glimpsed a shadowy figure beneath the oak. She was so startled, she tripped. Her da caught her by the elbow as she peered at the tree, but she saw nothing. It had been nothing.

The porch creaked beneath their steps. The door opened only after her father fiddled with the lock and kicked at the bottom. As they entered the parlor, Finn halted. "Wow."

A chandelier of emerald glass hung from a ceiling painted with stars. The green walls were decorated with framed paintings of fairy ladies. Floor-to-ceiling bookshelves were cluttered with books, seashells, and tiny birdcages. A tribe of Pierrot dolls that looked as though they'd been through a war huddled on a purple divan. The stairway wall was decorated with ornate little mirrors. Behind the sofa, a narrow table was scattered with animal skulls and fossils.

He said, "Your gran was very imaginative."

"You mean *eccentric*." The house smelled like an old church, like candle smoke and sandalwood.

"That's not very nice. Go pick a room." He opened another door. "It still smells like her cigars . . ."

The house was like a forest, dark, with light whispering across dusty wood and mirrors. Finn wandered up the stairs into a hall hung with tiny prints: a frog in gentleman's clothes; a hedgehog reading a book; a rabbit wearing a crown. She moved to a door carved into images of leaping rabbits and opened it. Beyond was a circular room like the inside of a tower, its walls pale green, its furnishings antique. In a tarnished mirror, her reflection revealed a plain, thin face veiled by messy brown hair.

She stepped forward. Above a set of glass doors leading onto a terrace, words had been painted: THE OCTOBER ROOM. She whispered, "My room," and was glad she'd opted out of dorm life, which was ridiculously expensive and a sacrifice of privacy for independence.

When she heard the moving truck grinding and hissing into the drive, Finn hurried back downstairs.

The movers, directed by her father, quickly had boxes and a few pieces of furniture crowding the dining room. As she began unpacking, she chose the precious things first, placing her mother's delicate paintings on the table. Above the divan with the Pierrot dolls, she hung the photograph of Lily Rose with flowers in her hair. Finn's two favorite photographs were of her mother and father when they'd been young—her mother with freckles, her dark hair crowned with daisies; her father a boy with sun-bleached hair and a puzzled expression.

Her father dropped another box onto the pile, stopped, and studied the photographs.

Finn murmured, "You lived here as a kid. Does it always smell like things burning?"

"Only when it's cold." He understood she was avoiding the topic of the photographs.

She sat on the wooden floor and plucked at the strings of the neglected acoustic guitar he'd bought for her after her harrowing attempts at Hendrix and the Smashing Pumpkins on Lily's electric Epiphone. She said, "I've got a million things to unpack. What about lunch?"

"I've made you waffles. Do me a favor? Unpack my office? I can't find anything—and I need my Sharpies."

"Whatever."

"And, once again, the kingdom of Whatever asserts itself." He crouched beside her. "It'll be all right, Finn. This is where we were meant to be. And you've got your first year of college to look forward to. It's a fantastic liberal arts school with a supreme biology department—if you change your mind and decide to go your mother's way."

"Not likely."

It wasn't the first time they'd moved. After her mother had died on a winter highway, her da had taken her and Lily Rose to San Francisco, where life, for a while, had been a world of sunlight and sea. It had been easy to believe that San Francisco had always been their home, that the frigid sorrow of Vermont had never existed.

Finn hated snow. Here, there would be snow. She looked up from the guitar, out the window. The oak there seemed to be leaning close, as if eavesdropping.

"D'you miss San Francisco?" Her da spoke as if he expected her to have a mental breakdown. It was irritating.

"Da. It's been a year. I'm fine. You're right—we'll be fine here. I'm glad we left."

"You can still keep up with Maria and Alex, with all that fancy tech stuff."

The thought of her neglected friends in San Francisco made her feel dark again. "Yeah."

He rose and headed toward the kitchen. "Come get your waffles."

She took her gaze from the oak tree and the overcast sky and scrambled up, brushing off her jeans. "Do we have whipped cream? I'm not having waffles without whipped cream."

IN THE LATE AFTERNOON, FINN dragged artifacts out of cartons and hung prints representing world mythologies on the walls of her father's office. Blue-skinned Shiva smiled next to Viking Odin. A blood-gowned Japanese goddess languished alongside a Celtic youth with blue spirals painted beneath his eyes. She'd grown up with these otherworldly beings whose imaginary worlds were so much more appealing than her own.

She was alone in the kitchen when something struck the screen door to the backyard.

It was a goat. It made a babyish sound and butted the door with its head again. Moving toward it, Finn made a shooing motion. "Go. Go away."

The goat, which wore a bell around its neck, only looked at her. As she pushed at the screen, the nuisance ran away.

She didn't know why she followed it, down a needle-strewn path among the pines, to another house, a rambling fairy tale of towers and gables with a fox-faced gargoyle perched on the roof. Crooked trees clung to the outside of the house as if holding it together. Sounds tumbled from beyond the screen door—the hoarse yells of boys, an insane trill of piano music. A dog barked, and chickens scurried behind a mesh fence near the front. There were five cars parked in the driveway and a motorcycle on the lawn.

As the goat trotted up the steps, onto the veranda, and vanished around a corner, Finn sized up the house, intrigued.

A boy around her age came out, looked around. He yelled something that sounded like "Daphne," and, when he saw Finn, he tilted his head. "Hello."

"Is Daphne a goat? She went that way." Finn pointed.

"She chews through the leash." The boy sat on the stairs. He wore skater jeans and a long-sleeved black shirt. Autumn red hair was tousled around a face that seemed feral and innocent.

"It smells like something's burning." She waded toward him through the leaves.

"It always does. Fireplaces." His tilted eyes were the color of mahogany.

"Your house is interesting."

"Girls tell me that all the time." He smiled with idle charm.

Oh, Finn thought, *he's one of those.*

"It's falling apart though." He folded his hands between his knees. "The roof leaks and squirrels've gotten at the wood."

She jumped when she heard a crash from inside. The boy shrugged. "Six brothers, and I'm not the oldest."

"I'm sorry. I'm Finn. I live over there. I mean, we've just moved here."

"I'm Christie. Christie Hart." He looked mournfully back at the house. "I live here. So . . . how do you like Rose Sullivan's place?"

"It's interesting." Finn's mouth curved. Her smiles were always an effort, but it seemed easier this time. "She was my grandmother."

"D'you have any brothers or sisters?"

The autumn beauty of the world suddenly faded. *Not anymore.* "No."

He sensed something. He pushed to his feet, his face serious. "I'll walk you home."

"No. Show me the woods." She wanted to know her surroundings, to conquer the uneasiness so many trees caused.

"There's not much to see . . . but I'll show you."

As they ambled toward a clot of trees, Finn said, to begin a conversation, "So you have how many brothers?"

Christie talked about his brothers as if they were some outlaw clan from a Clint Eastwood western. As he led her down a trail thick with blackberry bushes, their wine-sweet smell heavy in the air, she spotted a tree hung with ribbons, tiny dolls, and bells. She pushed toward it, fascinated. "What is it?"

"It's a hawthorn, a luck tree." He circled it. "People bring charms and hang them. It's called the Queen's tree because Queen Elizabeth—the virgin with the red hair—came here on a secret voyage when she was young and slept beneath this tree."

"That can't be true."

He grinned. "When she was older, she sent Francis Drake, her sea captain, to build a chapel here in her honor. The chapel's through there, but it's just a shell now."

Finn disapproved of this mucking about with history.

"Behind that is Soldier's Gate Cemetery and the warehouse district. Anyway, kids hang stuff here to get money or a hot date or a Porsche."

"Superstitions are useless and fairy tales are lies," Finn remarked as she touched a silver bell on the tree; the other bells chimed as if the wind was trying to make a song. The hair on the back of her neck prickled. She thought she saw, through the trees, a light. "Is that Drake's Chapel?"

"I see you're an adventurous sort of girl." His smile was crooked. "This way, Finn."

She followed him through weeds to a small ruin, its door gone, its interior dark, the last of the sun reflecting from a pane of glass within. The stone floor was covered with leaves. The broken altar held, creepily enough, a pink cake with mold grown over one side, as if someone had abandoned a birthday party months ago. The air reeked of rotten wood and wet stone, a graveyard smell.

"That's not something I've seen before . . ." He leaned in the doorway but didn't step into the chapel. "Who d'you think left it?"

"Maybe it's an offering."

"To the birthday gods?" Looking down, Christie said, "Look at all this clover. Maybe there's a four-leafed one here." He bent toward a patch of tart-smelling greenery as Finn set one foot over the chapel's threshold.

A wave of dizziness struck her, the kind she'd only felt after stepping off a particularly petrifying roller coaster. She clutched at the door frame as the air began to buzz—

"Finn?" Christie's sharp tone ended the weird noise, which he apparently hadn't heard. He looked uneasily into the chapel. "I think we should go."

"Okay." She backed away with him. The sense of having breached a place of otherworldly privacy made her shiver. They turned and walked back down the path. Finn didn't look back, afraid of what she might see.

"So," Christie said, "you going to school? And be aware that it affects your social standing here, whether you choose St. John's U. or HallowHeart."

She wasn't sure if he was being serious or not. She guessed he wasn't. "My da's working at St. John's, so I'm going to HallowHeart because I don't want him witnessing my awkward attempts at socialization. And it had more artsy courses."

He nodded and said, "That's where I'm going . . . you probably won't like it."

"Um . . . why not?"

"Well, not to put you off or anything—"

"You've already put me off."

"It's kind of cultish."

"Cultish?"

"Like old school, and I don't just mean that in a slangy way—like everybody who goes there had ancestors who went there in colonial times or whatever."

Finn considered this. "That seems interesting though. My mom and da went to HallowHeart and they're not Fair Hollow descendants."

"What will your dad be teaching at St. John's?"

"Mythology and folklore."

"Like Indiana Jones."

"I think he taught archaeology."

"Same thing. Where did you move from?"

"San Francisco."

"You definitely won't like HallowHeart then."

"Gee, way to make a girl feel enthusiastic."

"I always tell the truth, Finn."

FINN'S FATHER HAD ORDERED PIZZA for dinner, and they sat on the parlor floor surrounded by boxes as they ate. Her da had turned on the stereo. Tom Petty echoed through the old house, which was nothing like their town house in the Richmond District. Gran's house was too big. Finn tried not to think of what it would be like if she was ever here alone at night.

Her father poured more iced tea into their glasses—he made the best iced tea, with lots of lemon and sugar. "Where'd you wander off to while I was setting up the TV?"

"I met one of our neighbors . . . Christie."

"A boy?"

She rolled her eyes and said, "Don't look so concerned."

"As long as he's not a ruffian."

"*Ruffian*, Da? Really? Can you use *modern* language?"

"Thug, then. He's not a thug?"

"Never mind. Did you know there's a whole legend here about Queen Elizabeth and Francis Drake having come for a visit?"

"I'd forgotten that. Spooky Drake's Chapel."

"Yeah." She narrowed her eyes at him.

"Well, it's all bullsh—nonsense."

"Yeah." And she wondered if it really was.

AS HER FATHER NAPPED ON the sofa with a local newspaper draped over his chest, Finn attacked the boxes in the dining room, her shadow fluttering over the forest-green walls as she lifted things and set them on the table. She approached another box, opened it, and withdrew a bunch of battered paperbacks. When she saw Judy Blume, Stephen King, and a few romance novels, she realized with a sinking feeling that it contained her sister's belongings—*that* packing up had been done quickly, like cleaning up after a murder.

She turned away from the box. The Tom Petty CD had ended, and the only sounds were the ticking of the grandfather clock and the tinkle of wind chimes on a neighbor's porch. Finn switched off all the lights except for the ones in the front living room and trudged up the stairs, navigating the way to her chosen space.

The tower room looked different at night, desolate and alien, scattered with boxes and the furniture from her smaller room in San Francisco. She slouched in a red plush chair and gloomily considered the mess. The Cheshire Cat clock she'd hung on the wall indicated it was past midnight, but she couldn't sleep because her heart was racing from all the iced tea she'd had.

She curled up, knees beneath her chin, arms around her legs, and gazed at the glass doors leading to the terrace. She hadn't really thought about those doors until now, with the night behind them, peering in.

*W*hat did you do at school today?" Lily Rose sat beside Finn. There were roses in her hair, and she wore a black gown with ribboned sleeves. Her irises seemed too vivid, a lupine blue.

"I'm going to college now, Lily."

"What's the name of the college?"

"I don't remember."

"It is called HallowHeart. It's a very different sort of college. Fair Hollow is a different sort of town. And he is not a gentleman."

Finn turned her head. "What—"

Finn woke to find her room filled with unfamiliar shadows; rubbing the sleep from her eyes, she viewed the picture on the wall opposite her bed, a Leonor Fini print of a red-haired girl peering from a garden of goblets. She thought of her mother, who'd loved the print, and a wistful desire to speak with her made her restless. She untangled herself from the sheets, moved to the terrace doors, and peered out. She wasn't used to leaves crackling past her window, flurrying over the streetlights, making shadows across the walls. The town house in San Francisco had been surrounded by city noises and electricity, a current of safety, not silence and darkness.

She opened the glass doors and stepped onto the terrace to watch clouds drift across the moon. It was mostly woods in back, and, beyond that, Christie Hart's house. Fireflies danced beneath the trees in the darkest part. As more lights swarmed—they seemed to be *big* lightning bugs—she leaned on the railing and felt her throat close up as she remembered how real her sister had been in the dream. She could never tell her father about her recent dreams of Lily Rose, because she didn't want anyone to think she was crazy or grieving unnaturally. The loss of her mom had been immediate, a sharp amputation cushioned by a child's magical thinking. Finn, ten at the time, had pictured her mother in heaven, walking among the clouds.

Lily's death had been deliberate, an ugly severing that had left scars, and Finn knew, now, that her mother's end, like Lily's, had been one of blood and pain and shattered glass, followed by an awful silence that meant a familiar voice would never be heard again.

She stood in the night and listened to the silence.

CHAPTER TWO

It was mirk, mirk night and there was no stern light
And they waded through red blood to the knee:
For all the blood that's shed on earth
Runs through the springs of that country.
                                        —*TAM LIN*

Human blood makes them matter. They have gone through rivers of it,
to see, breathe, hear, taste, become.

—From the journal of Lily Rose

Monday arrived too soon for Finn.

HallowHeart was only three blocks away, so she decided to walk and stall her arrival in yet another new place. Beneath her coat, her legs itched in the new tights, and the collar of the plaid dress she'd chosen rubbed against her neck. The discomfort was not a good omen.

As she rounded a corner onto Birch Street, she gripped the straps of her backpack and looked apprehensively at a massive old building veiled in Emory, its doors framed by an arch carved into leaves and faces, a stained-glass window above them. The other windows came to Gothic points, reminding her of a cathedral. Small gargoyles with the faces of people were hidden in the Emory. The hall, called Armitrage, was one in a collection of buildings that looked as though they'd been imported from old-world Europe. Students were milling around and she felt a swift panic—she wasn't sure where to go for registration because she'd misplaced the map.

The wide stair of Armitrage was scattered with more students, and as she approached she saw Christie Hart crouched on the bottom step, his dark red hair sticking out in tufts from beneath a woolen hat. He had an open book in his lap—Ovid's *Metamorphoses*—and an unlit cigarette in one hand. As she approached, she looked inquiringly at the cigarette. He said, "I don't light it."

"It's an oral fixation." A pretty girl in a black turtleneck, kilt, and purple Doc Martens sat down beside Christie. Her inky hair was wound into two braids, her blue eyes drowned in dark kohl.

"Finn, Sylvie. Sylvie, Finn." Christie rose and gestured grandly toward the entrance. "Finn, welcome to our world."

CHRISTIE, WHO HAD BEEN ON campus before because two of his brothers had gone to HallowHeart, led Finn and Sylvie through the crowds of new and returning students. There were sign-ups for clubs, but no fraternities or sororities. Most of the new students, clutching neon-bright papers being handed out by several volunteers, were filing into the sleek glass building that Christie told them was the Arts Center. The only new building on a campus of archaic architecture, the Arts Center housed the cafeteria and the studios for the Fine Arts. Inside, the walls were covered with murals of art nouveau gods and goddesses. Most of the required classes and the ones Finn had chosen were available. Having no direction yet as to where she wanted life to take her, she'd selected fine arts as her major.

When she found Christie and Sylvie again, Christie looked disdainful and Sylvie, content. As they moved away from the bustling lines, Christie said, "Philosophy's still being taught by Grauman—my brother hated him. I missed out on Gothic Lit with Fairchild."

"Oh. I got that." Finn glanced apologetically at him.

"Well, at least it went to someone who'll appreciate it. And I did get Scandals in Biblical History."

"Is that even real?" Finn peered at Christie's neon-pink sheet and frowned down at her own. "Oh, it is."

"I passed on Interpretive Dance and went for the Mask in Theater. My weird one," Sylvie looked down at her marked-up paper, "is the Study of Symbols in Body Art in Modern Culture."

"Tattoos?" Christie looked at her disapprovingly. "You're studying tattoos?"

"And why do you need Intro to Women's Studies or that scandalous Bible business? Typical candy-ass honor student courses."

"I'll have you know those classes will give me a greater understanding of the human race." He turned to survey the campus beyond the glass walls. "Who wants to sign up for some extracurricular fun? I see someone walking around dressed like a Renaissance fair refugee—that'll be your tribe, Sylv."

She made a face. "Hah." She turned to Finn. "Wanna look for something we can join together? Without him?"

Finn caught her bottom lip between her teeth. "I've kinda got . . . stuff . . . to do. Maybe later."

"You're missing out," Christie solemnly declared, "on a myriad of delightful opportunities."

HALLOWHEART FELT LIKE AN ODD antique. With the exception of the Arts Center, the buildings—Origen, Laurel, Hudson, Armitrage, and McKinley—looked ancient. The two spookiest buildings, located in a grove of willow trees, were Lythewood and Shepherd Hall, the dorms. Wooden faces sprouted wooden leaves in the corners of classrooms and lecture halls. Banister railings were shaped into mermaids, and tables and chairs had the curling feet of animals. The stained-glass window above the entrance depicted a raven-haired girl holding a blood-red apple, while the post of the interior stair was a pewter goddess raising the moon. Everything seemed tarnished by age. The only concessions to the contemporary seemed to be the fluorescent lighting, the sleek Macs in the Comp Lab, and the students themselves.

Christie and Sylvie invited Finn to lunch in the courtyard between Origen and Hudson. Christie had gotten Greek food, which they shared at one of the picnic tables scattered beneath the apple trees.

Christie Hart and Sylvie Whitethorn had apparently known each other since they'd been little. They spoke to each other in a twisty, familiar way and glossed over each other's sentences. At first, Finn felt awkward, but Sylvie didn't seem bothered by her presence. So Finn learned that Christie had once deliberately broken an arm during hockey practice to get out of prom with a girl he couldn't stand anymore ("She was a monster"), and that Sylvie told everyone her mom, divorced from her dad, was a Tokyo actress who only played long-haired ghost women in horror films.

"That's not true." Christie jabbed a plastic fork at Sylvie. "Her mom is gorgeous and only takes the parts of romantic heroines in independent films. She played a ghost lady *once*."

Finn said, "That's kind of impressive."

"My mom is a narcissistic jerk," Sylvie said thoughtfully. "I don't intend to be anything like her."

"You're a performing arts major," Christie pointed out.

"Okay. But am I a narcissistic jerk?"

"Not to me. Finn, does she seem like a jerky narcissist?"

"Certainly not." Finn was poking at her moussaka and trying not to smile.

"Finn's from San Francisco." As Christie randomly tossed that into the air, Sylvie looked up, eyes wide beneath her bangs.

"Why'd you move *here*?" She seemed bewildered.

"My dad got a job at St. John's University. He teaches folklore and myth."

"That seems more a HallowHeart kind of thing." Christie selected an olive.

"Yeah, but St. John's is all shiny and new and hiring." Sylvie looked at Finn. "Do you miss it? San Francisco?"

Finn didn't want to tell them why she didn't miss it, so she said, "Sometimes."

Sylvie's gaze flicked away and she murmured, "Christie . . . ex-monster, incoming."

A trio of girls in perfectly matched dresses and coats approached the table. The leader, golden-haired and curvy, wore a necklace of letters that spelled A.N.G.Y.L.L. Her voice matched her smirk. "Look. He has a *harem* of losers now."

Christie ignored her and continued to devour his pita.

Sylvie sighed. "Oh, God, we're not in high school anymore. Get over it."

"I wasn't speaking to you, weirdo."

Sylvie's eyes narrowed. Finn looked at the golden girl and spoke quietly, "Hey, Angle, were you raised in a cave?"

Christie and Sylvie stared at her. Christie stopped eating.

The golden girl dragged her gaze to Finn. "My name is pronounced *Angel*, moron."

"Misnamed," Christie murmured.

Angyll looked at him. "Why don't you shut up? In fact, why don't you do what *her*"—she jerked a thumb at Finn—"crazy sister did and jump out of a window and die?"

A horrified silence followed. Finn rose and stepped forward. Angyll's legion stepped back. Sylvie cried, "Finn—"

Angyll fell to the ground. Finn, who had never hit anyone before, was shaking. She gazed down at her scraped knuckles while Angyll's friends screamed as if she'd been stabbed.

Sylvie slipped an arm around Finn, Christie was backup, and they were steering her away when Finn saw a black-haired woman watching them. She couldn't have been a professor, not in that sleek dress and high-heeled shoes.

But she was. "The three of you come with me, please."

FINN SAT IN THE DEAN'S office with Christie hunched in the other chair, his eyes wide, as if he couldn't believe what she'd done. Sylvie was pacing near the window.

"We're witnesses," Christie said. "Don't worry."

"I shouldn't have . . ." Finn took a deep breath. "I *hit* someone . . ."

"Yeah." Christie's gaze was dark. "You should have. I can't think of anyone more deserving of a fist in the face."

A silver-haired man in a black suit entered and sat behind the desk, behind a plaque that read DEAN ROWAN CRUITHNEAR. His voice was an intimidating baritone. "Miss Sullivan. You should understand how seriously we take physical assault."

She couldn't speak. When Christie cleared his throat, Cruithnear didn't even look at him. "You have something to say, Mr. Hart?"

Christie said, "Angle started the fight."

"Her name is pronounced *Angel*, as you know very well, and her parents are considering legal action against this institution."

Finn winced. Her hand hurt as she recalled the shocked look on Angyll's face. She bit her lip and tried staring at the floor so she wouldn't cry. "I'm sorry. She said . . ."

Rowan Cruithnear spoke quietly, "I know what she said, Miss Sullivan. Professor Avaline witnessed the incident. I've convinced the Weavers to drop the charges. They know of your loss and understand why you reacted so strongly to Angyll's comment."

Finn went cold. She knotted her hands in her lap and whispered, "How did she know?"

"We are a small school in a small town, and your family is newly arrived, Miss Sullivan. What happened to your sister . . . it would be difficult to keep it from becoming the subject of gossip. You must be strong, Miss Sullivan. Now, try to end your first day on a less violent note. HallowHeart might be old, but we are not medieval. No dueling, fisticuffs, or vengeance scenarios allowed."

AFTER HER LAST CLASS, CHRISTIE and Sylvie were waiting for Finn on the main building's stair. She looked at them, feeling lost, and said, "No one is talking to me."

Christie smiled. "We are. We're rebels."

"You probably don't want to go home yet." Sylvie's eyes were dark with sympathy.

"No." She dreaded what her father would say when he found out. "I don't."

NEITHER CHRISTIE NOR SYLVIE ASKED about Lily Rose and Finn felt a warm gratitude toward them as they trudged through the park and into a pretty woods with pale trees and leaves fluttering down like confetti.

"There are a lot of abandoned houses here." Sylvie lifted branches out of their way. "Mansions in foreclosure or just closed up forever."

They emerged from the trees and stepped onto a grassy hill. Below, mist swirled around a once-grand house with a bramble-choked stair and broken windows glowing in the last of the light. Rayed suns had been chiseled into the stone doorways and columns. Tangled in vines, a massive sundial and a statue of pale marble were remnants of more elegant days. There was something about the house's beauty, both menacing and melancholy, that disturbed Finn. It wasn't the wild place that Drake's Chapel had become, but it seemed as if it was under a spell, waiting. She thought she heard a faint strain of music, like a violin. "So no one lives there?"

"Not anymore. No one'll buy it. It used to be called SunStone." Sylvie began walking backward. "A millionaire lived there in the twenties. He built the Tirnagoth Hotel. We'd take you there, but it's past the warehouse district and it's a rats' nest now."

"Probably more of a bats' and foxes' nest," Christie said.

"Is there a story with *that* house?" Finn glanced back at the sun mansion. Due to some trick of the light, it seemed less of a wreck than before, less *ruinous*.

"The millionaire's wife and kids got sick and died—"

"Oh. So he tried to bring them back, and they came back wrong. I've heard that story before—my dad teaches folklore. It's an urban myth. Did they come back as zombies? Or demons?"

"He was murdered. *Someone* cut out his heart." Christie, his hair tousled with leaves, strolled beside her with his hands in his pockets. Finn, kicking at leaves, unearthed a ring of toadstools. Their earthy odor, reminding her of buried things, made her shiver.

"Fairy circle," Sylvie said. "Stay away from those."

"So how did this rich man try to resurrect his wife and children?" Finn resisted the urge to step into the circle of toadstools just to show Sylvie that nothing would happen.

"He made a bargain with the devil, what do you think?" Sylvie's voice became sepulchral. "But the dead don't ever come back right. How could they? After he was murdered, the hotel was left to rot."

Finn idly turned in a circle. "What do you do for fun around here, besides this?"

"Not much." Sylvie pried spongy lichen from a tree. "Christie and I planned to leave after high school, but circumstances prevented that—the circumstances being no money and no real ambitions. The only reason we got into a college with a good rep is because locals get a discount. Even Christie's honor roll status didn't help him much."

"Hey. I have ambitions—I plan to win the lottery."

They walked Finn to her house. The warmth of the sun still lingered, so they took turns on the derelict swing set that had been there since before her gran had owned the property. Sylvie found the remnants of a croquet game near the shed, and they played until violet shadows and chill slid across the lawns and lights bloomed in the windows of the neighboring houses. Finn tried not to think of Angyll Weaver.

Christie tossed his mallet into a heap of leaves. "*'Now it is the time of night, that the graves, all gaping wide, every one lets forth its sprite.'* Walk you home, Sylv?"

"It's okay." Sylvie looked at Finn. "He's a liberal arts major. It's normal for him."

"My da can give you a ride home."

"I don't live far." Sylvie lifted her backpack decorated with silver skulls. "See you tomorrow?"

"You did a fine job," Christie said, walking backward, his finger pointed at Finn, "protecting me from Angle. I'll always feel safe with you near, Finn Sullivan."

Sylvie glanced over one shoulder. "Come with us to a movie tonight? It's at eight o'clock, at the cinema on Main. We'll meet you there, okay?"

As her father's SUV rounded the corner, Finn murmured distractedly that she would try. She would have to tell him now what she had done, and the worst part would be when he learned why she had done it.

"DID SHE DESERVE IT?" WAS her father's first question as he leaned forward on the sofa, hands clasped.

Finn, curled in the armchair, nodded once, but she didn't elaborate.

"I see." He looked down at his hands. "Your first day, and you hit someone hard enough to knock them down. Not a slap—a punch. What if she'd injured her skull? Or bitten through her tongue? *Christ*, Finn."

"I don't know." Finn sat stiffly, her throat closed up because there was nothing as devastating as the disappointment in her father's voice at the moment.

"You're not going to do it again, are you?"

"I was invited to a movie tonight, by Christie and his friend, Sylvie."

"You think I'm going to nix that? I can't ground you now that you're out of high school." He looked relieved as he sat back. Then he asked the question she'd been dreading, "What did she say?"

There was a dull ache beneath her ribs. She didn't want to lie, and she didn't dare fidget because her da could interpret her every gesture as if he was her opponent in a poker game. She whispered, "She called me a bitch."

"Did she now? She doesn't know you well then, does she?" He hesitated, obviously conflicted. "Are you going to that movie?"

Ten minutes later, she was dashing out the door before he could reconsider.

FINN WAS STRIDING PAST THE ancient church on the corner when she heard a clicking sound in the silence, as if something were coming down the deserted street on spindle claws. She halted.

A giant, orange umbrella was tumbling down the road.

She reached out, grabbed the plastic handle, then gasped as the pull of the wind on the vinyl sent her reeling.

"I'll take that, thank you."

She looked up at a boy in a hoodie and black jeans. His hair, spilling from a black top hat, was orange. He wouldn't have been unusual in San Francisco in the Haight, but he was a strange sight in *this* place. She thought he must be in some sort of theatrical production. Silently, she handed him the umbrella. He snapped it shut. His eyes were the color of marmalade. "You've done me a good turn. I'll remember it."

Who speaks like that?

He sauntered away, whistling.

Finn continued walking, looking back over her shoulder once. Then she turned a corner and came to Main Street, where sycamores strung with tiny lights lined the road and the shops and cafés were still open. The mountains called the Blackbirds loomed in the distance.

Christie and Sylvie were buying a tub of popcorn in the theater, a majestic building of crimson stone with eight screens and a chandelier in the lobby. Tiny fairies and goblins clambered in gilt splendor around the interior doors. The movie they'd selected was about a scarlet-haired girl on a violent journey in a mythical kingdom. Finn didn't recognize anyone in it, but Christie pointed out the hero as someone who attended HallowHeart. Afterward, as they stepped out of the dark into the chill, Finn blinked in the brilliant lights and thought of fairy-tale love and how messed up it was.

"We'll walk to my place." Whimsically Gothic in a small raincoat of black vinyl and striped tights, Sylvie took Finn's hand, ending, before it began, Finn's protest that she didn't want to intrude on the rest of their night as friends. Christie pushed a woolen hat onto his curls and whistled the movie theme as he led the way. He said, "I can't believe Gilchriste got the starring role in that . . . his parents are *farmers* . . ."

"Don't be a hater, Christie." Sylvie nudged Finn and told her, "There are theater people and actors on nearly every street here. Some of those mansions on the river were owned by Hollywood stars. It's like a trend for New York City and L.A. people to have a vacation home in Fair Hollow. They think it's *quaint*."

Finn thought of the boy in the top hat. "I can see that."

"It's especially quaint when a blizzard takes out the power for the whole town or a summer thunderstorm knocks out everybody's digital. It's like the goddamn Stone Age here sometimes." Christie walked very fast, and Finn and Sylvie had to hurry to keep up with him.

SYLVIE'S PARENTS' APARTMENT WAS LOCATED above a shop on Main Street. As Sylvie gave Finn the tour, Christie wandered into the kitchen and opened the fridge. No one was home, but the widescreen TV was on and murmuring with CNN. The apartment was bigger than it had seemed on the outside, and very bohemian, the walls decorated with masks from Venice and Africa, fake animal skins draping chairs carved into bears and goddesses. The air smelled like patchouli, basil, fresh laundry. The hallway was hung with photographs, mostly featuring Sylvie at various ages and two people Finn assumed to be Sylvie's parents, a serious-eyed man with brown hair and a young blond woman.

"That's the laundry room. Here's Kim's exercise room—she's my stepmom. This is the *posh* guest room. Mine's up here." Sylvie's room, in the attic, was a den of candles and books, the dresser scattered with seashells and the skulls of small animals, the huge bed covered by a quilt patterned with peacocks and Emory. Finn touched the gorgeous kimono hung on the back of the door, then peered at a framed cinema poster with Japanese lettering featuring a beautiful woman who resembled a 1940s starlet. "Is that your mom?"

"Yeah." Sylvie was folding a sweater. "Sorry about the mess."

Finn looked around—aside from one or two articles of clothing, the room was as neat as a British butler. She admired a wall displaying a collection of ornate swords and daggers and a bleached stag's skull. A curved bow and a quiver of arrows leaned in one corner.

"Renaissance fair stuff," Sylvie said when she saw Finn looking. "Decorative, but made by real blacksmiths. The bow and arrows are real—Archery Mustang. I don't hunt, though . . . I just do competitions."

"She can't kill things, not even spiders." This came from Christie as he dropped down and sprawled in a chair and then began rummaging through a pile of CDs. Finn crouched to read the titles of books piled on shelves beneath the window. She picked out an Arthur Rackham storybook. "So what's with all the little pixies everywhere? Carved into HallowHeart, the theater . . ."

"They were worshipped here." Sylvie snatched a black bra away from Christie, who had bemusedly lifted it from his chair.

"Pixies?"

"Fairy folk. Some of the immigrants from Ireland followed the fairy faith. And the Irish had badass fairies." She shoved the bra into a drawer.

Finn looked down at her T-shirt, decaled with a bombshell image of Tinker Bell.

Sylvie sat on the bed. "You ever read the original play? Tinker Bell was a killer who pined after a boy who could never die."

"*And* she was hot." Christie didn't look up from poking through the CDs. "You've *got* to get a new iPod, Sylv."

"I got one . . . I just like the CDs."

Finn's mouth quirked as she pictured *their* version of *Peter Pan*. "I know about the fairy faith. It's dark. Honor is the ultimate truth, but the divine elements of nature are tricky—so my da says." Her father *hadn't* told her about any of his hometown's spooky legends.

"Kids've seen things in the woods—carvings of antlered men on the trees, little dolls hung in the branches. Ruth Aspen said an owl followed her for seven nights after she lit a candle and read a poem to *them*. The Iroquois wouldn't come near this land because they thought the dead walked here."

Finn glanced at an old photograph on the wall—a black-and-white image of a boy with long dark hair. He wore a T-shirt and jeans from the '70s. His eyes were dark and tilty.

"That's Thomas Luneht." Sylvie followed her gaze.

"*Don't* tell her the Thomas Luneht story." Christie looked at Finn. "Sylv has this hobby of collecting old photos and making up stories about them." He shoved a CD into the stereo, and an eerie violin solo swirled through the room. "D'you want to come to a party Friday night?"

"It's a concert at the lake. It's an annual thing," Sylvie said as she stretched out on the bed, propping herself on her elbows. "So tell us about yourself."

"What?" Finn was startled by this turn in the conversation.

Christie looked up. "You're new and intriguing. We'll tell you some of our secrets if you tell us some of yours. Here's one: Sylvie went out with the captain of the high school football team. Well, he's varsity now . . ."

"Our *own* secrets." Sylvie smiled at Finn. "Christie has a new girlfriend every two months. *Literally*, every two months. Like a ritual."

"Sylvie owns every season of *The Gilmore Girls*."

"Christie's easily confused by Sudoku."

"In my defense, it doesn't make any *sense*. All those numbers . . . you only like it because you're obsessive-compulsive."

"At least I've got a sense of purpose."

"Okay. Stop." Finn realized she would have to tell them some things and almost panicked, because she couldn't think of anything as whimsical as what they'd told her about each other. Hesitantly, she said, "Sometimes, I eat frosting out of the can."

Christie looked grim. "My respect for you just took a nosedive."

She breathed out a laugh. "I watch reality shows late at night. I only buy ginger-and-honey body wash. I pay for my own subscription to *National Geographic*. I've got a quilt, with pink and green butterflies, that I can't sleep without."

"Like Linus from *Peanuts*?"

"Well, I don't carry it around with me."

"That would actually be rather disturbing. Like Sylv's fascination with dead people."

"Like your fascination with Angyll Weaver?"

Christie bowed his head. "That was a very dark period in my life."

Finn, who had been about to suggest she return home, settled back into her chair with a smile and listened to them talk.

CHAPTER THREE

When he had told her his fair tales,
To love him she began,
Because he was in human shape,
Much like unto a man.

—THE DEMON LOVER

Ivory Mask had been born without a face, child of a union between the spirit of a birch tree and the ghost of a highwayman. She was not welcome in the world, but the forest loved her. The birches twined into a house for her, and she rules there now, in the silver shadows. She will trick you to your death.

—FROM THE JOURNAL OF LILY ROSE

Sean Sullivan, scholar of mythology, woke to an overcast morning and found his daughter outside crouched near a ring of vicious-red toadstools that had bloomed beneath her window. Her head was tilted, and she was frowning as if puzzling something out. He squatted beside her. "Have the fairies been here then?"

She narrowed her eyes at him.

Toadstools were a sign of decay and death, but he wasn't about to remind his daughter of this. Death was an enemy he refused to let strike again. After Lily . . .

any artifact he'd owned that had represented a spirit of annihilation, he'd given away to friends and associates.

"Fairies," he told her, with an Irish emphasis on the word. "Toadstools were known as the third kingdom, living things that were neither vegetable nor mineral."

"Huh. They're very pretty."

"They're very poisonous, so I'll be digging them up when I get home."

She looked disappointed.

"Then again, if the sun gets to them, they'll wither and—" He caught himself as his daughter looked at him. She knew the word he'd avoided, and the grief that had once crippled him snatched at his breath.

"Da." She touched his hand. "I tried to make waffles. I think I've ruined that shopping-network grill."

"I was wondering what that burning smell was. I'll make omelets." He smiled and rose.

"MAKE MINE WITH MUSHROOMS!" AS her father walked away, Finn looked down at what she'd found in the toadstool ring . . . a box of beaten tin. Carefully, she opened it to reveal a key of blackened silver shaped like a moth. She lifted it out, admiring the art nouveau detail, the wistful shape of a face engraved in the moth's head. When the key quivered in her hand, she almost dropped it. She murmured, "Where did *you* come from?"

AFTER CLASSES, FINN SAT IN the courtyard between Origen Hall and Hudson, waiting for Christie and Sylvie. Christie had told her that Hallow-Heart had been shipped over, piece by piece, from somewhere in Germany, near the Black Forest. It could be true, or just another freaky rumor. It was certainly believable.

The sun had almost set when Christie, wearing an anorak over his rumpled clothes, trudged toward her from McKinley. She stood and opened her mouth to say hi when three figures stepped from the shadows to surround him. The three strangers had streaky hair and piercings. One of them taunted, "Your mom make you that hat?"

"Yeah. She did. Jealous?"

A boy with long dark hair and a pale face smiled sharply. "Not really. You just bother me with your existence. Is this the asshole, Hip Hop?"

A girl with black-and-blond hair reached out and flicked Christie's coat collar. Her boots had platform heels. "That's him."

Christie smiled. "The sight of you three pigeons has me shaking in my boots."

Sensing impending violence, Finn strode to Christie and grasped his hand. "Hey, Christie. Come on."

The third member of the trio, a boy with bottle-blond hair and the look of a Victorian orphan, scowled after them as Finn continued to pull Christie away. She said, "Remember what Dean Cruithnear said . . . no 'fisticuffs.' *Who* were they?"

"What were those? They're Rooks. They live in that trailer park in—wait for it—BlackBird Lane. Their whole family's crazy. Anyway, I forgot something in fencing class—I'll meet you and Sylv at Armitrage."

"You're not going back . . . ?" She felt a spark of alarm at the possibility of the Rooks ambushing him again.

"I'll circle around them—they're not too bright." As he gave her a wave and jogged off, Finn looked around at the deserted campus. Then she murmured, "Fencing class?"

"'WANTON EYES, AN ABSINTHE *soul. Hands as fine as sainted sin. Black ink for blood beneath your skin.' Christie* wrote this?" Finn squinted at the text.

Sylvie, walking beside her, swung her satchel. "He appears untroubled on the outside, but I think his soul yearns for the Gothic."

"Huh." Finn handed the cell phone back to Sylvie. "Interesting."

"No, really, it's odd." Sylvie slid the phone into her rubber backpack. "I mean, he doesn't just write it to get laid, either."

Finn's mouth curled. Christie, she'd noticed, was certainly popular with the ladies. This was only her second day and she'd seen him flirting, successfully, with several girls and one leggy teacher's assistant.

As Sylvie and Finn crossed the campus in front of Armitrage Hall, they passed a group of girls singing softly beneath one of the oaks. The girls, HallowHeart students, wore flower wreaths on their heads. Sylvie began humming the tune as she and Finn leaned against the stair railing to wait for Christie. Then Finn told her about Christie's encounter with the Rooks and Sylvie looked fierce.

"Here he is." Finn smiled with relief when she saw Christie walking across the lawn. As he drew closer, her smile faded when she noticed that his wool hat was gone and a bruise was forming red on his jaw. She wanted to hit someone again.

"Those bastards." Sylvie straightened his coat and brushed leaves from his shirt. "It was the Rooks?"

"It's just a hat." He shrugged. "You know, the amount of violence at this 'institution' is appalling."

"Your mom made you that hat. You should never have spoken to their sister." Sylvie glanced at Finn. "He smiled at her, at the drive-in theater, and I guess, in her mind, that meant they were officially married."

Christie shrugged again, his mouth twisted. Beyond him, on Armitrage's lawn, the flower-crowned girls were standing in a circle, heads bowed.

Finn reached out, hesitantly, because she wasn't one for touching people, and tweaked a leaf from his hair. "Three against one. That's nothing to be embarrassed about."

The shame in his eyes vanished as he grinned. "You weren't there to protect me."

Sylvie threw a comradely arm around his shoulders. "We'll walk you to your job, won't we, Finn?"

"Of course." As Sylvie and Christie moved down the path, Finn glanced over her shoulder at the girls beneath the tree. One of them had her hands over her face, and shadows seemed to flutter around her like bats.

Finn hurried after Christie and Sylvie.

"So, Finn," Christie said, rubbing a hand through his hair, "what was *your* high school like? As you've been able to see, ours was populated with Mean Girls and crazy white trash with an unusual fashion sense."

"It was an all-girls school."

He nodded. "Nice." Sylvie's response, "Ugh."

"It *was* nice, even thought it was run by Irish nuns. The Classic Film Club was fun, and I liked Photo Club." Finn shrugged. "It was just a school."

She told them about San Francisco: her favorite pizza place that was open until midnight; evenings spent discussing the movies her mom had loved with the girls from Film Club; being picked up by her da and going for soft-serve ice cream down the block; the general chaos of a big city of hills and culture near the water. She didn't mention Lily Rose. She didn't want to complicate things, and she was awkwardly aware of the fact that they might know what had happened, if what the dean had said was true.

Soon they arrived at Christie's workplace, an electronic games store on Main Street called Parrot Games, which had an inexplicable Caribbean theme, complete with walls painted lime-green and plastic palm trees looming in the corners. As he pulled a green T-shirt over his rumpled shirt, he said, "Remember, my shift ends at nine. Be here or you lose your ride to the lake."

"First, we've got to change out of *these*." Sylvie tugged at her school clothes. "We're going to Hecate's Attic now." She led Finn out the door. "I need stuff."

Christie called after her, "If you see Angyll, ask her 'How's the eye?'"

Outside, as they walked down the street, Finn said, "Why'd he say that?"

"Hecate's is owned by Angyll's parents—don't worry, they're never there."

"I don't think—"

"I won't lead you into danger, Finn. Promise." And Sylvie led her to a storefront painted an alarming black and pink. The display window was decorated with Buddhas, dancing Shivas, expensive candles and chimes, and books about fairies, souls, and Middle Eastern religions. "We're doing *Macbeth* and I said I'd pick up some witchy props."

"There are a million of these places in San Francisco." Finn felt the pang of homesickness ease as they stepped into a luxurious atmosphere of harp music and patchouli incense. A stag's head cast from bronze hung behind the counter, which held an old-fashioned register. Miniature fairies swayed from a crystal chandelier, and there was an entire wall display of scented candles. Everything looked expensive.

A young girl sat at a table, a centerpiece of glassy branches casting shadows across her face and bright hair. She wore jeans and a pink T-shirt with an image on it of a white rabbit checking a timepiece.

"Anna"—Sylvie began selecting black candles—"this is Finn. She just moved here."

The girl couldn't have been more than fourteen, but her serious gaze and voice seemed much older. "I know."

"Hello, Anna," Finn said, then clumsily added, "I'm sorry I hit your sister."

"My sister isn't nice." Anna touched a deck of cards on the table and flipped one over. They were Tarot cards, gorgeously illustrated. The first picture was of a naked girl holding a giant sunflower.

"The Day Girl." Anna tilted her head.

"Let her read your fortune." Sylvie picked up a doll of black cotton. She murmured to herself, "Maybe we can do an exotic version of *Macbeth*, like, set in New Orleans. With voodoo."

Finn was watching the girl named Anna place a pattern of cards on the table. The next card she turned up was illustrated with a slinky, black beast.

"The Beast. Occult things. The Empress of Air and Darkness. These things will seek to harm you." Anna flipped up several more cards. "The Hawthorn. The protector." Her brow wrinkled. She set down a card painted with the image of a pretty boy holding a heart. "Page of Hearts. And the Flower Dagger. There will be a sacrifice."

Anna looked up, troubled. "Betwixt and between. They live in the abandoned places. They are shadow and light. They are the children of nothing and night."

Finn stared at the girl, unnerved by her strange words.

Anna bowed her head and whispered, "Serafina Sullivan, you will die on All Hallows' Eve."

"IT DOESN'T MEAN ANYTHING, FINN. It's just a *game*. Finn, stop walking so fast."

"Telling someone they're going to die isn't a *game*, Sylvie. And how'd she know my full name?" Rotting leaves swept across the pavement as the sun faded behind the clouds. It had become bitterly cold. Finn, very aware of the shadows clinging to houses and trees, felt sick.

"She's autistic, Finn. That Tarot is her way of dealing with the world."

Finn sank down onto a bench, rubbed her hands over her face, and drew in a breath. "My sister killed herself last year."

Sylvie sat beside her, hands curled in her lap. She whispered, "That's why you cracked Angyll . . ."

Finn was done with crying. But anger remained coiled in her; a tender, secret hurt.

"What was her name?" Sylvie asked.

"Lily Rose." Finn stared at the trees before her, the lavender sky beyond. She could smell rain and gasoline. Then the world suddenly vanished in a haze and she couldn't breathe.

"*Finn.*" Sylvie squeezed her hands. "My mom isn't even dead and when she left my dad and me, I cried for a week."

"Is she really a narcissistic jerk?"

"Not really." Sylvie sighed. She stood, tugging Finn to her feet. "Come on. I'll walk you home."

Finn tucked her hair behind her ears. "Won't it be out of your way?"

"We'll take a shortcut."

Sylvie led her on a clambering journey through the woods near the park. As they pushed through a scrim of bushes, berries burst and smeared their legs and thorns scratched their skin. When they reached a derelict wooden bridge arcing over a pond scummed with leaves, Finn said, "Can we go around it?"

"This way." Sylvie looked at her sidelong. "Water phobia? Or bridge phobia?"

"Both. I was stupid when I was a kid." They stepped from the trees and stood on the slope sweeping down to the abandoned house called SunStone in its veil of autumn-rusted creepers. The windows glinted with reflected light. The garden statue, a beautiful youth crowned with a sun, could have been the Greek god Apollo. "It's so lovely. How could anyone not want it?"

Sylvie, undeterred by Finn's observation, said, "Well? What happened when you were a kid?"

"I fell in a pond and couldn't swim. Someone pulled me out. How do we get back? I'm totally lost."

"This way. So you fell off a bridge?"

"I was trying to get something I dropped in the water . . . I don't even remember what it was."

To navigate around the bridge, they waded through the weeds, and slowly the chill air and the astringent fragrance of broken greenery cleared Finn's brain of fog. As they approached a field of grass and dandelions, Sylvie whispered, "What's that?"

"*I* don't know . . ."

In the center of the field stood a group of people dressed in white and holding ivory umbrellas over their heads. They surrounded a stone table on which was set a black cake. Someone seemed to be chanting. When one of them turned, the last of the sun shimmered silver across his eyes and his brown hair swirled. Music, old and lilting, ghosted the air as the shadows of antlers seemed to crest from his brow.

Finn felt as if she was under a spell. The air buzzed around her and Anna Weaver's words returned to her: *They are shadow and light . . .*

"Finn, we need to go. That looks like some sort of wake . . ." Sylvie touched her arm and Finn returned to the true world. She had almost fallen asleep . . .

The sun had dropped, and gloom veiled the meadow. Dead leaves scattered, crackling through air scented with rust and wet earth. The people in white had gone, but the stone table remained, shadows skittering across its empty surface. "Sylvie . . ."

Sylvie whispered, "Where did they go?"

"You saw them too." Finn brushed a hand across her nose—it had begun to bleed.

There was a sound, similar to wind chimes, and, beneath it—what she had mistaken for the wind—was the moaning of a violin. A deep voice was singing in a lazy, hypnotic language that sent prickles across her skin.

Then a ghost stepped from the shadows beneath the birches, a young man in a black coat, silver hair falling across a perfect face. His eyes were pale, and his breath exhaled from him in a vapor. He was like something that had stopped pretending to be human.

"Sorry," Sylvie said as she and Finn backed away.

They turned and strode quickly from the darkening field and the smiling young man who resembled a tombstone statue come to life.

"ARE YOU LAUGHING AT US, Christie Hart?" Sylvie, her cheeks red from chill, scowled across the counter of Parrot Games. "You should have seen that white-haired . . . person."

Christie quickly arranged the used games on a rack. There were scrapes across his knuckles from his scuffle with the Rooks. "A lot of actors come to stay here—"

"No." Sylvie shook her head. "He wasn't an actor."

"Maybe he was a robot. Maybe Fair Hollow's a secret robot community. We're not on any maps."

"The uncanny valley effect," Finn said, gazing at a game with a cyborg on the cover. She and Sylvie had returned to their homes to change for the party, but the whole evening had gone weird because of that wake and Finn felt a little off-center.

They looked at her. She blushed. "My mom was a biologist. The 'uncanny valley' is what it's called when we see something that looks like us, but isn't, and it freaks us out. Something that's flawless and threatening to us as human beings."

"Robots." Christie nodded sagely.

Sylvie murmured, "He wasn't a robot. Halloween is coming. When the dead return."

"A ghost."

Finn narrowed her eyes. "You two don't really believe in ghosts and robots, do you?"

"Maybe not robots," Christie said. "That *is* a little crazy. Were you near the birch forest?"

"Don't start with that." Sylvie glared at him.

Christie grinned at Finn. "She's scared of ghosts."

Sylvie pointed at him. "It's not a ghost in that story."

"Um . . . what story?"

"In the birch forest"—Christie sat on the counter—"a man was hung in the 1700s, for robbing people on the road. And the tree from which he was hung, the birch tree, it had a spirit. A girl spirit. I'll be delicate and let you guess what happened between them."

"I can fill in that blank." Finn nodded.

"Okay, so I'm not listening to this?" Sylvie walked to the Wii console and picked up the controls.

Christie solemnly continued, "So they had a kid who was nothing but tree bark and bones, with no internal organs, just a mess of malice. But sometimes the story changes, and it's just a human girl, born without a face, who was left in the birch forest to die but who learned to speak to the spirits and fell in love with a dead man's ghost. To be with him, she took out her insides, and still searches for him, hidden behind a mask made of her lover's bones."

"That's lovely." Finn leaned against the counter, skeptical. "I haven't heard one like *that* before."

"The birch girl's a popular Halloween costume around here."

Finn remembered Anna Weaver's words about Halloween and death and, as the languid spell of sleep threatened, she pushed her short nails into her palm and hoped no one would notice.

"I'm gonna go change in the bathroom, then we'll go," Christie said, glancing at Finn as he passed her; he looked concerned. She forced a smile, which only made him frown. As he snatched up his backpack and moved toward the restroom, Sylvie called, "What're you going to change into?"

"Gorgeous." He shut the door.

Sylvie muttered, "He has way too high an opinion of himself. It's a problem."

Finn, who had just defeated the enchanted sleep that had plagued her since Lily's suicide, shoved her hands in the pockets of the green velvet hoodie she'd chosen to wear because it reminded her of the Renaissance. Beneath, she wore a dress of brown silk, with calf-high boots. "We could leave without him, but he has the car."

MUSIC THUNDERED ACROSS THE LAKE dyed black by evening, the water glimmering with the reflections of bonfires as flames streaked the eyes of the revelers, painting skin orange and gold. The fragrances of lake water, wood smoke, hot dogs, and beer smudged the air.

Finn followed Christie and Sylvie down a stone stairway to the lakeshore, where a rock band bashed music from their instruments on a makeshift stage. Sylvie, in a little plaid dress and clunky Mary Janes, led Finn by the hand while Christie strutted beside them in jeans and a long-sleeved black shirt blazing with the silhouette of a bull. He idly greeted nearly everyone they passed and accepted a bottle from a boy with a mohawk. Sylvie took it from him and tossed it into a trash can. "No blackberry wine. Remember what happened last time?"

"That was tequila." Christie tossed his head, then became diverted by a girl in white gossamer. He strolled toward her. As Finn and Sylvie sat on the sand and watched him begin to charm, Finn smiled. "Does he know that girl?"

"He knows lots of girls." Sylvie leaned back on her arms. "*Lots.*"

"Hey, pretty ladies." A lanky boy with a lotus tucked behind one ear dropped a bottle of wine into the sand next to Sylvie. "Sample the Fatas' finest vintage."

Sylvie made a face, but Finn boldly took the bottle by the neck, pulled off the cap, and drank. It tasted like berries, night, and chill. "Wow."

"Oh . . . *that's* the blackberry wine." Sylvie took it from her, dark eyes wary. "You probably shouldn't have done that."

Finn wanted to ask *Why not?* But the wine was immediately giving her a pleasant buzz.

On the stage, a girl in a pink dress, her hair a dandelion puff, walked to the microphone and began singing a Celtic-punk song as the guitarist and the drummer thrashed their instruments.

"Where's Christie?" Finn looked around.

"He'll find his way back. He always does. Isn't her voice amazing?"

As the song ended on a wailing note, a straw-and-flower manikin on the lake burst into flames. The whooping, shouting response that followed from the crowd was wild. The dandelion girl and her band began a savage reel of fiddles and drums while a bare-chested young man wearing horns lifted his arms in the air. A bald girl in an emerald gown solemnly watched the burning manikin as a white-haired boy in black bowed his head.

Finn's skin prickled as if lightning threaded the air. There was something sinister about the concert's pagan element, as if she were only seeing part of what was really happening. It felt like a rave that had been given a Hollywood special-effects budget and moved back to ancient times.

When the band's music descended into something dark and slow, a hush fell over the crowd. Finn looked away from the burning scarecrow on the lake and saw a willowy girl in a slip dress of crimson satin and platform sandals moving through the revelers. Sleek black hair framed the face of a young queen. Golden bracelets decorated her arms. As the crowd languidly parted before her—noticing her, it seemed, only in some dreaming part of their brains—the music thundered.

The dancing bodies closed around the girl in red.

Shadows caused by the dancers and the bonfires swirled as Finn and Sylvie rose. Sylvie said, "I'm going to find Christie. Wait here."

Before Finn could open her mouth, Sylvie had vanished.

A darkly dressed young man carrying a staff topped with a stag's skull, red ribbons swirling from the antlers, glided past. *Come with me*, she thought he said, and she hesitated, her eyes downcast.

Then she followed the stag skull and the scarlet ribbons through the crowd. She didn't know what drew her after the stranger, only that there was a glitter of danger in the smoky air, as if the border between reality and an otherworld shimmered.

Finn slid through a group of girls in black and saw the young man holding the staff swagger to a pair of high-backed chairs, where he rammed the staff into the ground. Then he dropped into one chair where he sprawled to watch the concert. Pretending to admire the band onstage, she studied him with sidelong glances. He wore a long coat and jeans, a black shirt, and old-fashioned boots. Dark hair tipped with red fell over one eye to his shoulders. The firelight made a striking portrait of his face, glinting from the tiny ruby piercing the side of one nostril. His careless manner intrigued her—she'd never seen anyone like him off a movie screen, and he certainly didn't seem from this century. Shyly, she glanced at him again. He turned his head, his dark gaze meeting hers, brows slanting—

Then the dark-haired beauty in red came striding across the grass and leaned toward him and whispered in his ear. As she sat next to him, Finn looked away, then back again.

Sylvie returned, following Finn's gaze to the couple. "Jack Fata. Reiko Fata. Straight out of an Edgar Allen Poe story. I'm talking 'Fall of the House of Usher,' possibly with some incest issues. She's a model, I think. He might be, too. Isn't he lovely?"

"I think I've seen her in perfume ads."

"Probably. They're rich as sin. You think she's wearing Dolce and Gabbana? Or Prada?"

"I'm wearing Target." Finn, hands still in her pockets, opened her hoodie jacket. "Where's Christie?"

"He wandered off with that girl."

"So"—Finn shivered a little in her thin silk—"this is what you do for fun."

Sylvie regarded the dancers. "This is what we do for fun. It's the rich kids who keep us entertained. The bastards."

As the band bashed into another fiddle-crazed reel, a figure in a mask of green leaves grabbed Sylvie and pulled her among the dancing bodies. She yelped, "Aubrey!"

When a hand closed over Finn's wrist, she whirled to snap at whoever it was and met the dark gaze of Jack Fata. "Would you like to dance?"

"I'm not a good dancer." She pulled her hand from his, mostly because her palm had begun to sweat in his grip. He had calluses, like a gunslinger or an auto mechanic.

"Neither am I." His gaze languidly drifted from her eyes to the moth key she now wore as a pendant. She thought she saw a pinch between his brows, then those eyes lifted to hers and he smiled. "Maybe it's just the music."

As if on cue, the Celtic-punk rock band ended their set and three other musicians stepped onto the stage—two young men carrying violins and a girl with flowers in her hair. As the music soared over the crowd and the girl began to sing in an eerie, wistful voice, Jack Fata unfolded a hand in Finn's direction. She found her own hand drawn back to his. He took her other, and, as they spun carefully on the grass, he said, "I'm Jack."

"Finn," she whispered. Her feet seemed to magically know what they were doing.

"Finn. Like Huck Finn or Finn the king of the Tuatha Dé Danaan?"

Her gaze flicked up to his face, because she was surprised someone her age and without a folklore professor for a father would know that. He'd even pronounced Tuatha Dé Danaan right. "The second one."

"And why haven't I seen you, Finn?"

"Because I've been in San Francisco."

His smile faded slightly, and that shrewd look returned. "And is it just you that's come here tonight?"

"With friends." She couldn't look at him too long, so she focused on one of his hands twined around hers. His rings weren't chintzy or cheap—they looked old, like something a medieval prince would wear. She recognized a symbol on one of them and smiled crookedly. "The seal of Solomon. Are you a witch?"

"Maybe." His mouth was lovely as it curved. "Are you?"

"Do I look like a witch?"

"I don't know. I've never met one." He said, " '*Who is she who looks forth as the morning, fair as the moon, clear as the sun, awesome as an army of banners?*' "

No one had ever recited poetry directly to her before. She refused to let him see that she'd become breathless. "'The Song of Solomon.' Are you a literature major or studying religion?"

"I don't go to school. You're sure that didn't impress you, what I just said?"

"Have you said it before?" She gave him what she thought was a fierce look. "To others?"

"No, Finn-named-after-a-king, I have not." He politely guided her in a swirling circle. The others dancing nearby might as well have been leaves fluttering around them in a wind scented with fire and smoke. "You sure you're not a witch?"

"I'm not a witch."

He lowered his head, and her eyes closed as his warm breath slid across her neck like a kiss. "I think you are, Finn."

They had stopped dancing. They stood still, his mouth near hers, her heartbeat hummingbird quick, her eyelashes flickering.

"Come with me," he whispered, and her reason and common sense folded into the radiance of his smile. She wanted to curve her body against his, twine her fingers in his raven-silk hair—

Something pinched her collarbones. She stepped back, pulled her hands from his, stared down at the moth key hung on a silver chain around her neck. "I think it *bit* me."

"How unusual." His voice had an edge. She glanced up, frowning when she caught the shadow of something crossing his face, the glint of silver in his eyes, as if what he really was had broken through for a second.

She stepped back. "I need to find my friends."

Jack bowed to her, and it wasn't stupid or silly, but an elegant, practiced motion. His voice reminded her of ashes and velvet as he said, "Alas, my love, you do me wrong . . . bye, Greensleeves."

She watched him turn and saunter toward a line of shadowy trees that closed over him like an army. Lights moved among the leaves as if some people were leaving the concert with lanterns. Suddenly regretting her reaction, she headed after him, among the birches. She could smell clover and damp earth and a fragrance like molten metal.

Finn hadn't walked far when she realized the stand of woods she'd entered was completely silent. She was now surrounded by trees with no opening between them. In an instant, she'd become lost. A sudden rush of panic held her still. She thought, *The way out is right in front of me.* Moving carefully through the violet evening and the endless columns of trees, she listened for any noise that might lead her back to the lake. When something cried out in the distance, she flinched and turned in that direction.

Someone called her name. She halted, looked around, tentatively said, "Hello?"

In the gloom beyond a screen of brambles, she thought she saw a white mask, a glint of eyes and teeth. Something in her knew it wasn't one of the concert crowd. She backed away, stepping on a ring of toadstools, but she didn't take her gaze from that sly flash of ivory moving through the night. Leaves rustled as branches bent before a barefoot shadow. Something began to hum a childlike tune, then laughed, a raspy sound that seemed to scrape at Finn like thorns.

Finn ran. Things scratched at her skin, her face. Her noisy, thrashing flight through the trees didn't disguise the presence of whatever pursued her, gliding along without rustling a leaf or snapping a twig.

She dashed into music and light and the shock of it made her cry out. She twisted around, clawing her hair from her face, staring at the dark woods. Nothing came out after her—there was no girl-thing that had taken shape among the birches.

She turned back to the lake concert, loud and bright and worldly. She took a deep breath, composed herself, and moved into the crowds.

Sylvie and Christie found Finn where she sat on the wooden stairs near the lake, as far from the woods as possible. Aware of her scratched skin and tangled hair, she pointed to the trees. "I got lost. In there."

"There?" Christie looked wary. "Finn, that's someone's backyard. Hey, your nose is bleeding."

She dabbed at the blood, wincing at the slight pain that pinched behind her sinuses. Sylvie and Christie looked worried . . . like they thought maybe she was losing it. She wondered if she was. A numb fatigue descended over her as she said, "Let's go home."

ONCE THE INDUSTRIAL CENTER FOR a steel company, the warehouse district was now a neighborhood of shabby brownstones, bars, and rundown buildings. Across a field of weeds bordered by a wild wood and a fence of black metal was the Tirnagoth Hotel. On the other side was the cemetery.

Jack Fata crouched on a balcony of the abandoned hotel, a bottle of wine between his knees as he observed the revel in the courtyard below. The pumpkin flare of bonfires mingled with the glow of the hotel's stained-glass windows as slender figures danced or played instruments. Teeth and old-world jewelry glinted, and music pulsed through the stones. A savage scream was followed by the sound of shattering glass. At least they'd left the lake concert before reverting to their true natures.

Pain splintered through his fingers. The bottle had broken in his hands.

He rose, glass and beads of wine shimmering over his black coat. Gripping one of the gargoyles, he slid over a windowsill, into a room as red as the inside of a heart. The two scarlet-haired youths who guarded the chamber didn't even acknowledge him as he stepped into a bedroom, its chessboard floor strewn with rose-red furniture, a life-size wax doll with a prince's face and an aura of *awareness* standing in one corner. Above the bed with its treelike posts was a large photograph of a dark-haired girl, her green eyes made even more exotic by black and gold kohl, her glossed lips curving over the logo "Bebe."

Reiko Fata, his only reason for existing, wore a dress of red silk tonight that revealed her legs to the thigh. She leaned against a window of stained glass, her black hair glistening. "Jack. What did you do tonight? Did you do as I asked?"

He dropped into a chair and propped his booted feet on a table. "I played a trick."

"Are you going to behave badly?" She languidly turned and walked over to him; sitting down on his lap, she slid her wrists across his cheekbones. Her fingernails pricked the nape of his neck.

"Is there any other way for me to behave?" His own wrists were knotted with thorny bracelets that glinted as he raised his hands and broke her hold.

She leaned close to him and whispered, "You weren't supposed to scare her. You were supposed to bewitch, bother, and bewilder her."

"I wasn't in the mood for the bewitching."

"Really?" Her lips nearly touched his. "Because it's what our family *does*."

His eyes went dark. He almost said what he really wanted to.

She rose. Something dark and hot twisted in him as she turned and moved to the curtain of vines and flowers that veiled her bed. She looked back over one shoulder. "Jack."

He moved to his feet and took a step toward her because he couldn't help it.

The doors swept open and fiddle music skirled from the courtyard below as a boy in a black top hat and striped suit sauntered in. He bowed gracefully, orange hair sweeping the floor. "You called?"

Reiko, still gazing at Jack, said, "Absalom. What is the penalty for someone who interrupts one of our ceremonies? A wake, for instance?"

"Was the wake for anyone important?"

"David Ryder's girl."

"Oh." Absalom's eyes glowed as he looked at Jack. "Not important, then. My ruling would be the lesser of three evils—mischief."

Jack stalked out. As the doors closed behind him, he pictured the schoolgirl with the tangled hair and sweet mouth, the one he had led into the birch wood. His predator's instincts had caught her scent of sorrow and damage, but it was her resemblance to someone he'd known that had intrigued him. Maybe she would be different. Maybe, unlike all the other girls, she could make him bleed.

CHAPTER FOUR

*Are the dancing girls sleeping or are they dead? The flower fragrance
says they are corpses—the evening bell rings for the dead.*

—*THE SNOW QUEEN*, HANS CHRISTIAN ANDERSEN

*A girl named Maude Clare followed a hare
To a black metal house that is no longer there.
And what did she find in the dark of that place
But a prince with no heart and a beautiful face.*

—FROM THE JOURNAL OF LILY ROSE

After the strangeness of the previous night, the daytime seemed a disappointment. Slouched at her table in Botany, her mind too fuzzy to absorb plant classifications in one of the two classes she'd chosen for their nonartsy value, Finn wondered if she was going crazy. *There is no such thing as the birch girl . . . and who is Jack Fata?*

LATER, IN ORIGEN'S COURTYARD, CHRISTIE dropped down beside her and unwrapped his sandwich. "What a bitch of a day. I was late for metalworking, so Wyatt just ignored me. Then I burned my finger when I was soldering—is that Nathan Clare?"

"Nathan Clare?" She followed his gaze to a boy walking across Hudson's lawn, who was accompanied by some of HallowHeart's elite, including Kevin Gilchriste the actor, and Aubrey Drake, the captain from the school's varsity football team. Nathan's bronze curls shone, and the threadbare sweater and jeans he wore didn't diminish his looks.

"He's a Fata." Christie's mouth curled, and, since she'd never seen him react with scorn to anything—even Angyll Weaver—she became intrigued.

"Are they all genetically blessed, the Fatas?"

"A fire killed his family in Europe a while ago. He grew up with the Fatas. They're his cousins."

"Is that Nathan Clare?" Sylvie had arrived. She sat on the picnic table, opened her bento box, and popped a rice ball into her mouth. "He's lovely, isn't he? Like the whole damn Fata family—I suspect genetic engineering."

Finn, gazing after Nathan Clare, couldn't imagine losing both parents at once.

"TERROR AND AWE." PROFESSOR FAIRCHILD, who taught Gothic Literature, leaned against his desk, looking as if he'd just gotten out of bed. He had the face of a poet and a British accent and didn't seem to notice the avid gazes of some of his students. With his constant air of distraction, he didn't seem to notice much outside of a book. Finn suspected he didn't even have a TV.

"These emotions, combined, create the sublime, something sadly absent in modern life. Can anyone describe the sublime in other terms?"

Nathan Clare, it turned out, had also chosen this class, the last one of the day. So had his friend Aubrey Drake, but Aubrey seemed to be paying more attention to the leaves fluttering past the windows. Nathan looked up from his notebook, the lecture hall's fluorescents shining in his curls. "The sublime is a terror of something you love, something that could destroy you or save you."

"Thank you, Mr. Clare. And is there anything"—Fairchild addressed the entire class—"that makes us truly feel such nowadays?"

"Religion?" someone said.

"Drugs."

"Sex."

"My mom."

"That's *so* inappropriate, Drake."

"I meant that in a 'something you love that could destroy you' kind of way."

"You see"—Fairchild's gaze fell upon Finn, who had not said a word—"we've become a race of cynics. How can the dreadful, the venerable, the sacred and sublime, reveal themselves to our dulled minds? We are no longer capable of experiencing the possibilities of otherworldliness. Cynicism, not science, has killed our divinities."

"You mean our being snarky has shot down our gods?"

"Thank you, Mr. Drake. You have, just now, made my point."

THE SUN HAD DECIDED TO make an appearance, red and sullen and descending, as Finn walked home with Christie—Sylvie had biked to work at her parents' shop. Beneath a scarlet hoodie, Christie's clothes were more rumpled than usual and he seemed distracted. Finn began to approach the subject of his messiness when someone hollered at them from across the road.

Christie turned. "Fantastic."

Three figures were walking steadily toward them: a pale-haired boy, a girl with black-and-gold hair, and a tall boy whose long dark hair was streaked with blue. The Rooks. As they drew closer, the girl smiled. The blond boy was expressionless, hands shoved in his pockets.

Finn sighed, annoyed, as the tall boy stepped forward. He wore Christie's woolen hat, and his coat was lined with black feathers. The slighter boy wore a necklace of them, and the girl's hair was plaited with more plumage—they seemed to take their birdlike family name very seriously. Finn could see the crazy on them now.

The tall boy jabbed a thumb at the girl, who pouted. "Hip Hop has issues with you, Hart."

"Really?" Christie tilted his head and Finn sighed as he continued, "Maybe she shouldn't assume things."

The tall boy smiled, revealing a diamond in one tooth. "You've made my sister feel bad. Now, I'm gonna make *you* feel bad."

Christie tugged on Finn's hand. "Let's go."

"Bottle," said the tall boy.

The slight blond grabbed Finn by her coat. Astonished that someone had actually named him "Bottle," she yanked away. The boy frowned at her.

"Trip"—Christie stepped toward the tall boy—"knock it off."

"Make me."

Staring at the outrageously named trio, Finn felt apprehension turn her cold—they were facing down fashionable lunatics on a road that was pretty much deserted. She murmured, "Did we just time-travel back to high school?"

"Go on, Finn," Christie said, the wind pushing at his dark red hair. He didn't look away from the three Rooks. "Go. I can deal with them."

"No." Her voice shook with anger. She met the chilly gaze of the tall boy, who stared at her. "They're just bullies."

"Girl." The diva with the face of a Victorian doll took one gliding step forward. "You should *respect* your elders."

"Are you *serious*?" Finn looked at Christie, then back at Hip Hop, who bared her teeth and took a step toward them. For a hallucinatory second, Finn thought her eyes went the mercury-silver of a dead possum's.

"Car. *Car!*" Trip's voice halted the potential violence.

The three drew back as a crimson Mercedes appeared on the road, slowing as it approached, pulling to one side.

The Mercedes's door opened and a girl slid out, auburn hair tumbling from beneath a chauffeur's cap. She wore rock star jeans and a black T-shirt with a Rolling Stones decal. She leaned against the car as Reiko Fata emerged, willowy in a plaid kilt and red blouse.

The older girl moved with an unsettling grace toward the Rooks, who had gone quiet. Gently, she said, "What are you doing?"

Trip ducked his head. Hip Hop was white. Pale-haired Bottle hugged himself as if he was cold. When none of them answered, Reiko Fata turned her attention to Christie and Finn. Snow-skinned, her black hair in loops, she looked as if she'd stepped from a fairy tale. "I'm apologizing for them. My cousins are morons. Christie Hart, isn't it? And Serafina Sullivan."

Finn was processing the information that the Rooks were, in fact, from the sterling Fata family, while Christie seemed to have lost his ability to charm and was mute.

"We were on our way home—" Finn spoke hesitantly, and the Fata girl's electric-green gaze slid to her.

Christie interrupted. "Actually, we were on our way to our *jobs*. See, *we* have to work for a living."

Reiko Fata was still studying Finn, who felt as if she stood before an empress—the Fatas, she decided, were like the descendants of some regal, electric-eyed race that hadn't been discovered yet. When Reiko smiled, it made Finn feel even more inferior. Then the regal young woman addressed the three troublemakers. "Go home. Now."

The Rooks backed away, then turned and strode off down the road and didn't glance back.

Reiko Fata's attention fell upon Christie, who looked as if he'd been hit. "They're uncivilized, the Rooks. But they're family. I apologize, Christie Hart."

Christie blushed and became wordless again.

"And you, Serafina?" Reiko addressed Finn again and Finn felt uneasy that this glamorous girl knew her name. "Did they place hands on you?"

Maybe that's how rich people spoke in Fair Hollow. Finn murmured, "I'm fine."

"I'll make this up to you. Phouka, get the invitations." Reiko pronounced her companion's name as a breathy *fuua*.

The girl chauffeur ducked into the Mercedes.

"There's another one of you." Reiko turned to Christie. "A pretty girl with blue eyes and black hair."

"Sylvie." Christie suddenly found his dirt-smudged hands extremely interesting. Finn stared at him because she'd never seen him without his confidence and easy grace.

"Three invitations," she called to the chauffeur who returned with three envelopes.

Reiko handed the envelopes to Christie. Black, Gothic writing snaked across the crimson paper: *Fata*. "The autumn revel has a Shakespeare theme this year. Welcome to Fair Hollow, Serafina Sullivan."

She walked back to the Mercedes. As she slid in, Phouka winked at them before getting behind the wheel.

Christie and Finn watched the Mercedes crunch back down the road. He said, "Finn . . . are you paranoid? Because I know *I'm* not, but I kind of feel . . ."

Gazing after the Mercedes, Finn tasted bitterness, as if she'd eaten one of those venomous red toadstools beneath her window. "Like this was planned?"

"So. You're paranoid too . . . I'm going. You?"

She felt a fizzy whisper across her skin as she remembered Jack Fata. "I wouldn't miss it."

FINN HAD FOUND A JOB over the weekend, at BrambleBerry Books, which was owned by a friend of her gran Rose. At six o'clock that night, the shop's three resident cats watched Finn as she was taught how to use the register and the phone. Later, the owner, Mrs. Browning, worked in the office while Finn explored the store, admiring the old paintings hung on the walls, and the front window display, which was a screen of black metal shaped into fairies. She selected an interesting-looking book on American history and sat behind the counter to read it. Early American History was her first class tomorrow, and it was taught by intimidating and model-sleek Professor Avaline.

When she heard a horn blare, she looked out the window and saw a red Mercedes halt in front of the building across the street. The narrow building, made of dark stone, had black-shuttered windows and child-faced gargoyles crouched on the roof. A girl in a white chauffeur's uniform slid from the car, auburn hair rippling from beneath her cap. She sauntered to the driver's side and opened the door and Reiko Fata emerged, her black hair looped into plaits, strappy sandals, and a slip dress of wine-red silk emphasizing her long legs. She seemed oblivious to the chill air.

A second figure slid from the Mercedes—Jack Fata, who straightened the cuffs of his black blazer before leaning to say something to Reiko. Together, they sauntered toward the building. The doors opened, then closed behind them. The chauffeur remained, leaning against the Mercedes and lighting up a cigarette.

Finn couldn't figure out why Jack Fata fascinated her. He moved like a martial arts star and dressed like a modern-day Victorian gentleman, and those were interestingly eccentric qualities, but she'd only spoken to him once, and she couldn't figure out that look in his eyes when their gazes had first met . . . mischief that had become a shrewd assessment that had darkened to confusion. Maybe the familiarity she'd felt was because she'd seen him somewhere else. In a magazine maybe, or a film . . .

A battered Corvette pulled up to the curb, and a silver-haired boy hopped out of it, followed by two girls in gauzy gowns. Once again, the building's doors opened and closed. Music now pulsed from behind the stone walls, and red light simmered beneath the black shutters.

Finn forgot about the book in her lap.

The bell over the door chimed and Finn saw Christie enter, his red hair sticking out in tufts from beneath his woolen hat. "Hey. I'm done. How about you?"

She thought then about how Christie, with his pack of brothers and his interest in Shakespeare and Greek literature, was reassuringly familiar, because he'd reminded her of the boy she'd left in San Francisco, Alex Mckee. That's why she liked him, and she wouldn't ruin *this* friendship with a kiss. She set aside her book. "You're early."

He shrugged. "I wanted to look around. Do you get a discount?"

"Fifty percent. Mrs. Browning is very generous."

ABOUT A HALF HOUR LATER, Finn said good-bye to Mrs. Browning, and she and Christie stepped into the night rumbling with music from the gargoyle building. As they walked past cars jammed in tight rows along the curbs, she looked back at the building. "What *is* that place?"

"It's a nightclub. It's called the Dead Kings. Let's go; I'm hungry."

Finn, whose small, gypsy world had included few boys, wondered why Christie was always hungry. She thought of Jack Fata again and pushed her hands into her coat pockets. "So . . . what do you know about Jack Fata?"

He gave her a careful look. "Well, he's Reiko Fata's. And she's the great-granddaughter of Malcolm Tirnagoth—the devil worshipper? The one who tried to bring back his kids, they were the walking dead, et cetera?"

She kicked up leaves as she walked. The street wasn't well lit, but the reflection of the traffic lights on chrome was dazzling. "No wonder my da got into folklore, growing up here."

"Mr. Redhawk, my neighbor, thinks a ghost lives in his attic." Christie had decided to wander away from the topic. "He says it followed him home after he took some roses from the garden of an abandoned house. I mow his lawn, and once, I thought I saw something up there when he wasn't home. My brother Liam said a big black dog followed him around the cemetery—he works there. And a friend of mine who lives near the woods says she can hear a violin playing at night. The Fatas give me the same spooked feeling as everything I've just told you. Why're you asking about Jack Fata?"

"Why're you telling me about spooky things that obviously aren't true?"

He grinned. "Superstitions are useless and fairy tales are lies."

Finn sighed as he quoted her words back at her. Then she said, "Mr. Redhawk sounds like Beauty when she took roses from the Beast's garden; the black dog belongs in Ireland; and ghostly violins or fiddles in the woods are a common element in stories about the devil."

"You're a peculiar girl." He pushed the toe of his work boot against a drift of leaves. "Fair Hollow has a creepy past, and the Fatas have always lived here."

Finn glanced at Christie and thought, *Lived in Fair Hollow, or the past?* "Can we get into the Dead Kings?"

His eyes widened. "You are out of control. I'm getting you home."

"Why do you think Reiko Fata would get her poor and crazy relatives to threaten you? Why not just *give* us invitations?"

"They don't think like us, Finn. They're different. They're rich."

As they continued walking, Christie asked why she didn't have a car. She'd almost had a car—Lily's snub-nosed and gunmetal gray Hyundai, the recipient of three speeding tickets. But her da had sold it because he didn't want her driving. She looked away from Christie. It was awful how such an innocent memory could rip open a half-healed wound. It had just been a stupid car. "I can't drive. I fall asleep when I'm not supposed to."

He didn't say anything more and she liked him for that.

SITTING ON THE HOOD OF a car outside of the Dead Kings, a lean, silver-eyed young man watched the girl and the boy walk away. His angel face and the pale freckles dusting the bridge of his nose didn't disguise an air of wickedness. He slid lazily off the hood to his feet and followed them. He wore a long soldier's coat, and his boots had spurs.

A girl in a chauffeur's uniform stepped in his path. "What are you doing, Caliban?"

"Don't say my name unless you mean it, Phouka." The young man smiled, vicious.

"You're a guest. Don't abuse the privilege."

His perfect face was a mask over something hungry and feral as he said, "I won't." Then, "Say, how did David Ryder like his present? The lovely dead girl?"

The girl chauffeur didn't move. She said coolly, "He would have preferred her not dead."

"Well, Lot stitched her up nice and new and filled her with daffodils. And she wanted it."

"Get out of my sight."

Caliban bowed like an actor in a play, and swaggered away.

THE AROMA OF BREAKFAST ALWAYS reminded Finn of nights with her mom and Lily Rose. Whenever her da worked late, they'd make omelets or pancakes and watch *Breakfast at Tiffany's* or *Gigi* or something classy and fall asleep on the sofa until he returned. After they'd moved to San Francisco, whenever their da worked past six, Finn and Lily would order delivery—dim sum and cherry Cokes from the Purple Peony or veggie quesadillas and mango smoothies from the Green Knot on Divisadero. They'd watch one of da's westerns because Lily couldn't look at their mom's favorite classics anymore.

Determined to establish another tradition for herself and her da, Finn had chosen home-cooked meals and was attempting a casserole from scratch, trying to decide whether to watch old TV shows or history specials, when her father walked in. She smiled and gestured like a game show hostess. "Look. I made a casserole."

He considered the gummy results on the counter and pushed a hand through his hair. "We've been ordering dinner for a while now. Why mess with tradition?"

She sighed with relief. "I agree."

He picked up his phone. "What d'you want on your pizza?"

"How about Chinese from Fox Lane?"

FORTY MINUTES LATER, THEY SAT on the porch, cartons from Lulu's Emporium on the table between them as Led Zeppelin's "Immigrant Song" thrummed through the house. Her da, sprawled in the wicker rocking chair, watched her eat. "Finn . . . do you think this was a good idea?"

She looked up, wide-eyed. "I like Chinese."

"Don't pretend you don't know what I'm talking about." He pointed his chopsticks at her.

"What're we gonna do? Move back? Live with Grandad and his wife?" She didn't taste the next mouthful of noodles. She didn't want to go back now. Her strongest memory of San Francisco was of sitting on an ugly sofa, in her cashmere coat, listening to the quiet murmur of conversation around her. It had been an hour after Lily's funeral, at her grandfather's house, and she hadn't moved the entire time, sitting with her hands clenched together, her gaze fastened on a bowl of green-and-pink ribbon candy. The car ride back, in the dark and the rain, was only memorable because Guns N' Roses's "November Rain" had been playing on the radio. Her da had quickly switched the station. She'd never been able to listen to that song again.

"Finn . . . we haven't talked about . . ." He frowned down at his carton, and the pleasant world was suddenly replaced by one of harsh absolutes and bitter ends.

"There's nothing to talk about."

"Serafina." He never called her that. *Serafina* was what her mom had named her because it sounded like seraphim, angel. He'd shortened it to *Finn* for a mythical Irish hero known for his wisdom and bravery, Fionn mac Cumhaill. It was a lot to live up to.

"I don't see anything to talk about, Da. Lily's gone. And I'm growing up, so I like things in order now."

He drew back, hurt, but she wasn't going to fall apart pointlessly discussing the details of her sister's stupid decision.

Any death of a loved one was a betrayal. But a deliberate death was worse . . . it was murder, selfish and monstrous. And Finn would never forgive her sister for what she had done, no matter how much Lily haunted her dreams.

"Okay, Finn. Change the subject."

She inhaled the perfume of rain and smoke and apples. "Has it always been like this here?"

"Quiet, laid-back, uneventful? Yeah. That's why I left."

"No. I mean *weird*. Has it always been weird?"

He peered at her with a touch of hilarity she was glad to see. "If you mean by 'weird,' is it eccentric, yeah. But I never really noticed, growing up." He leaned forward. "Now, I'm noticing."

"You left to travel with Mom. Did *she* like it here, when she came to go to college?"

"No, she didn't really like it here. She was adventurous, and it was a big world. And I was seventeen and I wanted to leave."

Finn pictured her parents, long-haired and reckless, journeying to all the exotic places in those photo albums she'd unpacked onto a shelf in the parlor. It wasn't hard to imagine the couple in the photographs as two young students in love, but it was difficult to see them as her parents.

"I think," she said shyly, "I think *I'll* like it here."

FINN'S ORGANIZATIONAL SKILLS WERE HAPHAZARD at best and resulted in piles of things with uncertain destinations. Lily had hated what she'd called Finn's "lolling around"—slouching in chairs, sprawling on sofas, and generally being messy. A ballerina to the bone, Lily had had lessons on posture, had always been graceful despite her tomboyish swagger, and had also been almost obsessively neat. She could look perfect with only cherry lip-stain and Pixi eyeliner and her hair sleeked down her back.

Content and settled for the first time since the move, Finn sat on the floor of her room, unpacking. She lifted up a velvet Mad Hatter hat and set it on top of boxes containing acrylic paints and brushes. She found her favorite sweater wrapped around the funky old Leica camera she'd bought last year.

When she plucked a Nancy Drew novel from a box, she sat down on the bed. It was one of the old hardcovers that had belonged to her mom. The one she held, *The Scarlet Slipper Mystery*, had been Lily's favorite and still had a wilted bookmark in it.

All Finn's happiness drained away. The book in her arms, she curled on the bed and closed her eyes.

SHE JERKED AWAKE IN THE dark, cold to the bone.

The terrace doors were open. That scared her, because she thought she'd locked them. For a moment, she couldn't move. Above her bed, the Leonor Fini print of the red-haired girl in her garden of goblets was crooked. Leaves had blown across the floor.

Finn really didn't want to get up; she wanted to pull the quilt over her head.

She slid to her feet and crossed the room to gaze out at the little woods behind her house. The sound of creaking metal drew her gaze down to the swing set.

Her heart jumped. A slender figure stood on one of the seats, swaying back and forth.

You can ignore him and be safe, she told herself, *or you can live a little*.

Trashing common sense, she stalked down the terrace stairs, across the lawn.

Jack Fata didn't look at her, but she thought he was smiling. His black coat billowed around him.

"You'll wake the neighbors," she said, and wondered if he was crazy. But he wasn't the one who'd left the safety of his house to speak with a stranger.

He bestowed that dark, lavish gaze upon her, his cheek against his wrist. He said, "Do you remember my name?"

"Jack Fata. Do you know mine?"

He smiled and said, "Serafina. Finn Sullivan. A proper Irish name."

"Don't make fun of me."

Rose petals drifted from his hair. "Look." He caught one in the palm of his hand. "I'm bleeding."

She breathed carefully. "I've got coffee."

He stopped swinging and looked at her. "Are you inviting me in?"

She thought of those stories of wicked things that couldn't cross thresholds unless invited. "Well, it's cold out here. And my da's asleep."

He laughed, and the drowsy, dangerous look went from his eyes.

JACK FATA DIDN'T BELONG IN her yellow kitchen. He sat on the counter, gazing warily at the rooster clock on the wall. He had refused the coffee, claiming he only wanted to get warm. His fragrance of burning things and wild roses confused her. His fine-boned hands were decorated with tarnished rings. Dark, red-tipped hair brushed against his neck as he lifted a pewter goddess she'd placed on the windowsill.

"You live here with your father?" He peered at the goddess. "Is this Isis?"

"Yes, I told you he's asleep. And, yes, that's Isis. And where are *your* parents?"

"No father. No mother." His mournful look seemed mocking.

"Oh." She thought he looked like someone who'd been raised by wolves or ravens. She was startled by a wistful desire to touch his wrist, where skin curved over bone. She knotted her fingers together. She was still doubtful about having him in her kitchen. "Where do you live?"

"I've a place." He slid from the counter. He was so lithe, he made her feel clunky. His gaze scanned the things around him as if he were memorizing them. He was pale, and she wondered if he was sick, but he didn't seem so, with his curvy smile and long muscles. Finn studied different parts of him: the drowsy eyes, one of which seemed lighter than the other; the graceful throat; the curve of dark hair against his cheekbone. He had little scars, she noticed, on his hands.

"You've got a lot of books," he suddenly said, looking at her.

"That's my da's fault. He got me addicted."

Jack tilted his head. "I've got a fair amount of books."

"Who are your favorites?" She watched him secretively, still wondering why someone like him was interested in someone like her.

"Arthur Machen. Angela Carter. James Branch Cabell. Kipling."

"I like all of those. Why are you *here*?"

"I wanted to show you something." He took a pewter locket on a chain from around his neck and handed it to her. "Open it."

She thumbed up the lid of the locket and saw an old painting of a pretty, thin-faced Renaissance youth with long brown hair, his eyes large and soulful, his sleeves decorated with green ribbons.

"It's why I noticed you." Jack watched her. "Because you look like him."

"You think he's an ancestor of mine? What are the odds?" But she was pleased . . . She didn't think the young man in the painting looked like her at all. He was gorgeous.

"Actually, he was a friend."

She gazed doubtfully down at the locket. "This looks old. He liked to play dress-up?"

"Most of my friends do."

She said mischievously, "So d'you have a thing for him or something?"

His smile was breathtaking as he leaned toward her and whispered, "Not for *him*."

"You don't even know me," she whispered back.

"Why did you invite me in, Finn Sullivan?"

"Because . . . you know things." She took a step back—being so close to him made her brain stop working. "You're different."

"That's a terrible reason." He smiled again.

"You looked cold."

"Did I? I'm used to being cold, believe me." And she saw the bitterness like a shadow to the lightness of his words.

"Jack . . ."

He straightened as if shrugging off the shadows, then bent his head to her as he passed. "Don't invite anyone into your house again unless you know them well."

She turned as he flung the back door open. "Hey. What kind of conversation was this?"

"A telling one." He stepped into a swirl of leaves and was gone.

JACK FATA LEFT FINN SULLIVAN to visit his friend Absalom for advice.

Tonight, Absalom seemed all that he pretended to be. His orange hair was pinned up, his slim body camouflaged in skater jeans and a red T-shirt with a lotus emblem. He lived in a one-room apartment with an old television, and '60s rock band prints on the walls.

Slouched in a big chair, his head tilted back as he listened to Bob Marley on Absalom's monster stereo, Jack said, "I've a terrible broken heart, Absalom."

Absalom nodded as he lounged on a chaise of red velvet, a lollipop between his teeth. "And who's broken your nonexistent heart?"

Jack tapped inky fingernails against a Hula girl lamp. "A girl. I don't think I can convince her that I'm harmless."

"Maybe you should try not wearing black."

"I like black." Jack opened the lid of a porcelain teapot. "It hides things and looks clean no matter what you do." He paused. "Unless it's something to do with chalk. Or white paint."

Absalom sighed, exhaling through his nose. "You are no gentleman."

"You've got experience." Jack raised his head. "Tell me how to court her. Properly."

"Jack . . ." Absalom slid forward. "D'you remember the others? The three girls before this one?"

Jack tilted his head.

Absalom frowned. "You don't. Well, those three girls pissed off Reiko and, for some reason, she's got her sights set on this one now."

Jack slung one booted leg across the chair arm. "What are you going on about? Reiko wanted me to smile at this girl. I decided to scare her instead. But she didn't scare easy, and now I'm interested."

"Interesting. Now, did you do that because you like being contrary to Reiko or because you knew that smiling at that girl would be the end of her?"

Jack stretched out his booted legs. "I never get to have nice things. I want her."

"My advice, Jack. If you like this girl, keep away from her. In our family, the fairy tale never ends happily for the pretty maiden. The prince is always mad, or pervy, or a beast."

Jack had found a book and was scrawling in it with a red pen. "Are you calling me a beast, Salome?"

Absalom's sweet face became a mask over something burning and bright, and flames shimmered in his feral topaz eyes. "Don't call me that." He curled up, an innocent boy again. "Or I won't talk to you anymore."

"How do you manage to convince people you're not older than the hills?"

"I don't know what you're talking about."

Jack tossed Absalom the book. Across the pages he'd scrawled *Will Scarlet, Crimson Fool, Puck.*

"I'm just a boy." Absalom shut the book. "And you just defaced Coleridge."

"A real boy wouldn't care about that."

"Jack—" Now Absalom looked guarded, and Jack sensed a grim piece of news about to be slammed in his direction. "Nathan Clare has returned."

Jack pretended indifference. "Has he?"

"He wanted to know if you were still here."

"Shouldn't he be more concerned with why *he's* here?"

"You should talk to him."

"And why should I do that?"

"I realize your falling-out with him was quite spectacular, but he deserves our respect. He is going to die, Jack."

"Then he's one of the lucky ones." Jack rose, his smile bitter, his eyes dark. He pulled something out of his coat and tossed it onto Absalom's table. "Payment for your advice, Absalom."

"Jack. Caliban's the one who brought David Ryder's girl, the one we had the wake for."

Jack halted and the air practically growled around him. "He's *here*?"

"Caliban or David?"

"*Caliban*."

"As I said, *Caliban* brought the girl—"

"From Lot." Jack didn't turn. "With her insides scraped out and filled with flowers. Caliban. So now we've got that bloody lunatic to deal with."

The door slammed as he left. Absalom picked up the object Jack had discarded as payment.

A nice, human tooth. It didn't even have any cavities. Absalom smiled.

CHAPTER FIVE

This night, they dance with the ghosts, and the pooka
is abroad, and witches make their spells.
—*IRISH FAIRY AND FOLK TALES*, W. B. YEATS

They mingle with the dead, who become their servants and who are
mostly their victims. I don't think that they can murder, or affect the true
world unless they have a mortal companion. But they've found ways
around that.
—FROM THE JOURNAL OF LILY ROSE

Finn didn't have her last class until later in the day and it was Math for Life, so she slept until eleven, then slouched downstairs in her pajamas and ate pancakes while watching cartoons. When she passed the glossy red invitation she'd placed on the dining room table cluttered with the miniature glass animals she and Lily had used to buy their mom on her birthdays, she paused.

The autumn revel was tonight. She expected majestic weirdness.

SYLVIE WAS PERCHED ON THE stone fountain in Origen's courtyard when Finn met her after her Basic Photography class. "Christie told me about Reiko Fata's last-minute invitations."

Finn leaned against the fountain shaped into a girl with butterfly wings. "Why d'you look so grim?"

"There'll be hell to pay. You got an invite. Angyll Weaver didn't get one."

The revel, Sylvie explained, was flung by the Fata family every year. The invitations were exclusive—now other HallowHeart students had discovered Finn, a newcomer, had gotten one and were being stupid about it. Finn, who wasn't used to being envied, touched the invitation she'd tucked into her backpack, along with the moth key left beneath her window. She carried that key with her all the time now, because someone unknown had left it for her in a fairy circle and the mystery of it made her feel the world was a bit more full of possibilities. Maybe that's why she'd never asked Christie or Sylvie about it.

"I'm more concerned with English Comp . . . I didn't think it would be so detail-oriented. Does Professor Misaki really want us to read all of Strunk and White?"

"I believe so." Sylvie looked grim again.

"Hey." Christie swung around the fountain and tucked the third invitation into Sylvie's black bag. "For you."

"Reiko Fata just *gave* them to you?" Sylvie pulled the envelope out, holding it between two fingers as if it contained anthrax. "Maybe you should let the Rooks beat up on you more often."

"I think Reiko's got a thing for me and she set them on me, just to 'meet cute.' You know, like in the movies."

Sylvie looked at him with pity. "Do you really think that, Christie? Do you?"

The smile left his face, and as Finn followed his gaze, she felt her whole body heave in a resigned sigh. "Goddamn."

Angyll Weaver and her cabal were moving across the lawn. Sylvie began to whistle the Wicked Witch theme from *The Wizard of Oz*.

Angyll halted a safe distance away and stared at Finn. "*You.* You're nothing. At least he's pretty and the Goth girl is interesting in a strange way, but *you—*"

"I'm not a Goth—" Sylvie began.

"*You.*" Angyll's gaze was venomous. "Sullivan, you're just trash."

Finn was mute. She couldn't hit Angyll again, not without the anger that had fueled her the last time. As she remained silent, it was Sylvie who rose and glared ferociously at the golden girl. "I've seen trash and it looks a lot like—"

"Ladies." Christie slid in front of Sylvie and said to Angyll, "Get gone. We don't like you and your perfume is making me gag."

Angyll and her two companions flung themselves around and stomped away. Angyll looked back once, a glance promising vengeance.

"She's a spiteful beast," Christie said lightly. "Crazy's only hot for a while. Would you believe she's an economics major?"

Finn gazed after Angyll. "I feel sorry for her sister."

FINN REALIZED CHRISTIE AND SYLVIE had their own lives apart from her own, but she still felt a little neglected when she had to walk home alone later that day. She chose the shortcut through the tame woods, her landmark the Ogun Metalworking plant, a fortress of towers and chimneys on a slate hill. As she walked, she thought about how old Fair Hollow must be. San Francisco's Wild West history had been glamorized by a modern edge, and Vermont had been quaint, like an old-timey Christmas card. But this place . . . this place not only seemed haunted by its past, but occasionally still living it.

The sun was already setting, its pale light bleeding through the trees, when a violin solo suddenly twisted through the air, the music so beautiful, it didn't seem human-wrought. Finn halted, intrigued and wary; then she saw lights twinkling through the trees—more fireflies.

She followed the music to a place thick with berry bushes as tall as she was. She saw beyond them a group of people seated around a small bonfire. She was glad she'd been quiet in her approach, because they hadn't seen her.

A man with long silver-black hair sat, shirtless, on a tilted stone, a live python around his neck. A girl in a black dress and tattoos, golden braids shimmering around her face, chatted with a boy who held a staff topped with the head of a porcelain doll and wore his tawny hair in loops. A shadowy figure was playing the violin and it was difficult to tell whether the musician was male or female, because he or she wore a Victorian coat, the hem of which dragged on the ground. Another boy sat nearby, red ribbons knotted around his arms, flowers wreathing his black curls.

She wondered if they were drama students, or just high. They made her remember her da's romantic word for San Francisco's vagrant population: *vagabonds.*

Jack Fata, in a coat of black fur, sat among them.

The music wavered, became plaintive, ended. The musician bowed. The boy with flowers in his black curls called out, "Do 'Ivory Mask and the Lily Gentlemen.'"

"No. Do 'Satyr's Lament.'"

"'The Churchman's Shoes'!"

"Jack." The violinist spoke, and his gender was no longer a mystery as he stepped from the dark. Scarlet hair framed a narrow face almost alien in its beauty. "You choose."

The man with the python growled, "Why does he get to choose?"

"Because, Atheno, he is lovely and was once so warm."

"Aurora Sae is lovely, although she was never warm." The youth with the black curls laughed.

The golden-haired girl scowled and stretched out one bare leg. Her toes glimmered with rings. "David Ryder does not mind that I am cold."

"Hush." The violinist turned to Jack. "Jack?"

Jack Fata said, "Play 'Greensleeves.'"

And his gaze idly drifted to Finn's hiding place.

She flinched back and was suddenly very certain she must not be seen by the others. It was a crazy thought, but she felt it as keenly as the blackberry thorns now pricking her skin.

"'Greensleeves' it is—what is that?" The violinist's coat rustled as he turned his head, the quicksilver glint in his eyes making Finn think of buried things. When he murmured, "I do not like it when they see me," the air began to buzz faintly as he looked down at his bare feet peeking from beneath the hem of the black coat. Beneath his toes, half hidden by leaves and dirt, was a pale curve of something that looked like a skull . . .

The golden girl began singing softly, "*The lily she grows in the green wood. Maidens, maidens take care. Her sweet-scented breath do tell of your death. Maidens, maidens, beware . . .*"

Jack rose and said to the musician, "Farouche. No."

Finn backed away as the red-haired musician fixed his gaze on her. She felt faint.

She whirled and ran, away from the fire and the vagabonds, away from Jack Fata.

She finally had to stop, to catch her breath, her back against a big tree. The moonlight that illuminated every leaf and branch and the strong odors of dark earth and toadstools . . . all of it made her feel ghostly, as if she had stepped out of the true world. She pressed one hand against the bark of a tree just to feel something. *What is wrong with me?*

She felt a secret, biting fear that she might be going crazy.

Someone called her name from a gap in the trees and it sounded like Sylvie. It *was* Sylvie. Finn lunged forward, out of the woods—

—and found Drake's Chapel, its details exquisite in the cold light that traced the sea dragons carved around its doorway and the old-fashioned cross on its peaked roof. From inside the building, where darkness had gathered, she heard a faint sobbing. She stepped forward and whispered, "Sylvie? What are you—"

The rotting cake on the altar had been replaced with broken dolls, bottles, candles, and tattered books. A cracked teapot sprouted toadstools. Nearby, a rocking horse missing one ear was tangled in Emory, and an angel of pale stone, its wings black with decay, streaks of rust beneath the orbs of its eyes, regarded her from a corner.

She felt a twist of nausea when she heard the girl sobbing again. She backed slowly out of the chapel with the stone-cold realization that she'd been *lured* here.

Then the dying light splashed a wall and the words spray-painted there:

HE IS NOT A GENTLEMAN.

She stumbled out of the chapel. She was shaking and angry and had had enough. The sobbing came from all around her now, descending into hysterical laughter. She shouted, "Stop it!"

The laughter faded.

The air shivered, and from the trees came a girl in white, pale hair drifting over her face. Her bare feet were speckled with red, and something about the look of her reminded Finn of hippie girls from the late '60s.

Finn closed her eyes, opened them again, but the girl remained. Finn whispered, "What do you want?"

The girl wasn't beautiful, but her curvy grace was almost achingly sad and Finn felt as if it was that grace that had caught unwanted attention, that this girl was not . . . not like her, anymore. In a human voice, the girl said, "He will kiss you too, like he did all of us. And to the grave you will go."

Finn stood there, hands curled into fists at her sides as she fought the enchanted sleep threatening to drop her to the leaves. "Why are you . . . ?"

But she spoke to air. The girl was gone. She hadn't been a ghost. She had not. Because, if she had been, then Lily . . .

Finn backed away, turning toward Drake's Chapel, where the glitter of broken bottles on the floor suddenly made her queasy. As the sleep rushed at her, she stumbled against the door frame, catching at it—

When she opened her eyes, Jack Fata sat on the altar steps. He said, "I figured it wouldn't take you long to find this place."

Finn, who didn't like people figuring things about her, was suddenly very awake as she stepped inside, out of the cold. She curled her hands in her coat pockets, resentful of his looks and his casual appearance. "Did you see that girl?"

"What girl?" He narrowed his eyes. "You've been asking questions about me."

"No, I haven't."

"The tip of your nose turns pink when you lie."

Angrily, she touched her nose, then snatched her hand away. She was tired and confused and in no mood to be mocked. "You followed me. Stalker."

He stretched out his legs and tilted his head, and Finn began to feel mutinous. "You're an unkind girl."

Who speaks like that? she thought as a wind swirled through the chapel.

He rose so quickly she flinched and stepped back. Gently, he said, "What do you think I am, Finn?"

As leaves fluttered into the chapel like oversized moths, clinging to the stones, she replied carefully, "I think you might be a little crazy. You didn't see that girl?"

He began to look annoyed. "What *girl*—"

Something struck Finn, tangling in her hair. She yelped, yanked at the object, then gaped at the crumpled thing in her hand—an origami bird of black paper.

Jack snatched it from her and smashed it in one fist. Hoarsely, he said, "I'll take you home. Don't come here again."

"Where did it come from?"

"Someone playing tricks. Maybe the girl you saw."

She tried another question as they stepped outside: "Was this chapel really built by Francis Drake?"

"How should I know? I'm not that old." He began walking and she hurried after.

"I saw your friends," she said.

"I know. They're very touchy about being spied on."

"I wasn't"—he made her feel so prickly—"*spying.*"

"You were very quiet."

As she followed his lithe shape through the woods, she began to wonder why she'd been so afraid of a bunch of theater majors. "So . . . who are they? Your friends? Drama students?"

He looked back at her, and his smile reminded her of something bright and edged. "They *are* very dramatic."

She pushed aside another leafy obstacle, ducked beneath a branch. How could he see in the gloom? He gracefully dodged trees and avoided roots and stones. Finn said, "And you? Are you into theater, Jack?"

"My *family* is very much into theater."

Sylvie had told her some of Fair Hollow's residents had been in films, others had been musicians, and some had become famous on Broadway. Sir Ian McKellen had a vacation home nearby, and one of the mansions on the river had belonged to the 1920s actress Lulu, whom Finn only knew about because of her mom's love of old movies. For decades, Fair Hollow had been a haven for the artistic and the eccentric, for old and new money.

Other than Reiko Fata and the young man beside her, Finn had seen very little glamour in Fair Hollow. She suspected that most of the people her age here fell into one of two categories: small-town and somewhat normal; or New York City teens and college students—emancipated and overindulged.

A few silent minutes later, they reached her house. She turned to thank him.

Jack was gone. For a wild moment, she thought she'd been talking to a ghost. Then she heard his voice, echoing back through the trees, "I'll see you tonight, Finn Sullivan, at our little revel."

She trudged into her house and locked the door. She glimpsed herself in the hall mirror—her hair was flecked with leaves, her face scratched, her clothes twisted. She had a run in one black stocking. She slid from her shoes and tried not to think of the white-skinned girl at the chapel, who had either been crazy or high or a ghost.

Finn wandered down the hall. Her grandmother's house didn't seem familiar now. For one terrible moment, she wondered if she'd been led into a replica of the place that had become her home. The fake raven on the hall table watched her with a moist eye. In the front parlor, the antique rocking horse seemed to move slightly, and from the top of the wardrobe in the corner, the crocodile skull someone had given to her father cast crooked shadows.

Stop it, she told herself.

When she tapped at her da's office door, then opened it, she found him asleep at his desk, his head on his folded arms. She gathered up one of the Navajo blankets and draped it over his shoulders before moving soundlessly upstairs. It was only seven o'clock. She had one hour before the Fatas' party.

She raided her closet, flinging everything she owned onto the bed. She upended her jewelry box. She had no idea how to dress for a Shakespearean costume party. Reiko Fata and her Fatas were sophisticated in a fashion Finn couldn't define. Reiko, in a way, reminded her of Lily.

Sitting on her bed, Finn thought of the night she'd awakened to find Lily sprawled in the rocking chair beside her bed. Her sister had been wearing a gas mask and a black, fringed flapper dress and Finn had thought she was a spirit. Then Lily had lifted up the mask and grinned. *It was a sort of World War I rave.* Finn had smelled incense and alcohol and frowned at her sister, who had been so adventurous. She had been so jealous.

AS FINN WAS TUGGING ON a pair of Doc Martens, the doorbell rang. Finn's da answered it, and moments later Sylvie stomped up the stairs.

"I love it." Sylvie walked around her, her gaze critical.

Finn had chosen a small, red dress embroidered with patterns of green Emory and a pair of red-and-black-striped tights. The Renaissance hoodie of green velvet completed her Shakespearean look.

Sylvie pointed. "Your hair."

She slinked around the room, then picked up a wreath of fake leaves and red roses. She set it on Finn's hair, smudged her eyeliner, and chose pomegranate lip gloss. When she was done, Finn, glancing in the mirror, saw a fey creature. "This is not me."

"You're Ariel. From *The Tempest*."

The doorbell rang again and the sound was followed by her father's amiable voice. A light, loping tread creaked the stairs before Christie appeared in the doorway. Dressed in jeans, buckled boots, and a black Renaissance jacket laced at the sleeves, he looked like a modern Prince Charming.

"Did you play Romeo once?" Finn indicated the jacket.

"This? The thrift shops are full of this stuff. Ready?"

"Hold on." Sylvie turned in a circle. "We need to find Finn's fairy wings."

AS CHRISTIE STEERED THE BATTERED Mustang carefully along a dirt road, Finn glimpsed the Hudson River, dark and ancient, snaking beyond the trees.

"There it is." Christie nodded at the sinister silhouette of a mansion beyond a screen of oak trees. As he parked on the lawn with the other cars, they heard music. The house's windows were dark, and there was a notice on the door, which made Finn feel uneasy. The path to the stairway was guarded by statues—Greek fauns with slanting eyes and hooved feet, tiny horns peeking from their curls. Behind the silent house, lights were strung in the trees and the raucous noise of a large gathering came from there.

Christie led Sylvie and Finn to the back, where the pillared veranda had been made into a stage and a banquet table was scattered with hot plates warming food and beverages in tubs of ice. A group of girls, glitter swirling from their gossamer wings, passed them. Young men in horns or grotesque masks rambled around the lawn. There were lots of ribbons. A boy wearing a tin crown strode past, and two others were thrusting fake swords at each other. A girl in a rose-red dress was serving punch from a bowl.

Finn looked back at the dark house. "Is *that* where the Fatas live?"

"No one knows who owns SatyrNight. It's been empty forever. Look—caramel apples." Christie, easily distracted by food, wandered away.

Finn warily regarded the carvings of leafy faces strung up in the trees with the tiny lights. Then the fragrances of fried dough and barbecue drifted over her. She said to Sylvie, "I forgot to eat today."

Sylvie handed her a tiny skull made of pink sugar. "All Souls' night is only a few weeks away. Eat these and honor the dead."

Finn looked down at the candy and wondered how death could be treated so lightly.

Christie returned and gave them each a candy apple on a stick.

He plucked at Sylvie's costume. "Why're you wearing raven wings instead of butterfly wings? Shakespeare wrote about fairies, not angels." In jeans and a black corset, with bracelets on her bare arms, she looked pretty and barbaric. Her dark hair was plaited with loops of ebony beads that draped her brow.

"I'm not an angel. I'm a Juliet of the afterlife. Or maybe Lady Macbeth in hell."

"You look like a crow harlot."

"And who're you supposed to be?—Did you just call me a harlot?"

Christie raised a tiny sugar skull. "'*To die: To sleep, no more, and by sleep to say we end the heartache—*'"

"Stop showing off, Hamlet." Sylvie took a bite from her caramel apple.

A pale-haired boy in tight, striped trousers approached and held out a tray scattered with plastic cups containing a luminous green drink. "Try some fake absinthe?"

Christie and Sylvie each accepted a cup. Finn sipped cautiously. It tasted like licorice and lime and alcohol, and it made her mouth water.

She scanned the costumed creatures around her, looking for Jack as they went past a fountain decorated with candlelit pumpkins. The burned-squash smell of the jack-o'-lanterns made her nose wrinkle. Musicians with pale hair and dark tattoos had taken the veranda stage, and electric guitars and the singer's howling voice soon became deafening.

Finn lost Christie and Sylvie in the crowds when she stopped to watch a magician in a striped black suit and no shirt pulling snakes from his sleeves—she recognized him as one of Jack's friends, Atheno, the man with silver-and-black hair. As he draped what looked like a boa constrictor around his neck and let a pouty girl pet it, he met Finn's gaze and grinned. His eyes reflected light like an animal's.

"Hey."

She whirled to find an orange-haired boy in jeans and a jacket of checkered black and red standing before her. He wore a jester's cap. His pretty face was painted with red tears. "Don't go near the woods. They're roaming tonight."

"Excuse me? I know you . . ."

"Everybody knows me. Aren't you going to ask me who's roaming?" The firelight seemed to glow in his topaz eyes, as if his irises were flames themselves. She took a step back as he murmured, "So it's to be you, is it?"

He was definitely on something, and she didn't trust people not in their right minds. "Okay. See you." She turned to slip away and heard him say, "It's the restless dead that are roaming. Why d'you think none of us are wearing our true faces?"

Finn was distracted from his question when someone called her name. She turned her head to see Nathan Clare from her literature class walking toward her. As he drew closer, he flicked a wary look at the youth in the jester's cap. "Absalom."

"Nathan." Absalom bowed and vanished among the revelers.

Finn looked after him. "He's . . . odd."

"Did he say anything to you? Anything disturbing?"

"Well, no . . . was he supposed to?"

"It's just that he's . . . a dealer."

"A drug dealer?" Finn wondered how Nathan knew that. He was dressed in black jeans, a jacket with laced sleeves, and Converses. There was a flower in his curls. "You've got a flower in your hair."

He grimaced, plucked it out. "Are you sure you're okay? You look a little confused."

"I just got dizzy."

"You didn't eat any of those sugar skulls, did you?"

She must have looked dismayed, because he said, "Let's get you some coffee."

"What was in those skulls?" she demanded as they threaded through the crowd. The music was pulsing and extra loud now and she almost had to yell. He bent toward her and said in her ear, "Pixie dust."

She'd never heard of that drug, but then she didn't know much about drugs. As he guided her, he cupped a hand beneath her elbow in a nice, old-fashioned gesture and continued, "Don't worry . . . the effects will wear off after an hour. Just don't stray."

She wanted to ask him what life was like with the Fatas when three black figures in demon-crow masks stepped before them.

"Rooks." Finn halted. "I don't like them."

The tall one who called himself Trip approached, tilting his head. "Nate, Nate. You got yourself a girl. That's against the rules."

"It's *that* one," the girl, Hip Hop, said. The black feathers on her coat rustled.

Trip's masked gaze slid to Finn. "Nate, Reiko's going to be *pissed*."

Nathan spoke calmly, "I'm just helping her. We're exchanging *words*. Conversation. Like civilized people do."

"You saying we're not civilized?" Trip took a step forward.

Nathan didn't back down but faced him like a prince confronting a villain. "Go away, Victor."

Trip actually flinched. "That wasn't nice."

He spun on one booted heel and stalked off with his siblings.

"I liked that," Finn said, her eyes following them. "I like what you did there."

Nathan looked at her. "You really need that coffee."

"WELL, WHERE DID YOU LEAVE her?"

"Christie. Settle down." Sylvie was beginning to feel a little funny and noticed that the Shakespearean romp was becoming a little wilder. The two bands had been replaced with a mini orchestra, all in glittering white, like fairies from *A Midsummer Night's Dream*. "Listen carefully . . . I think there was something in those candy skulls."

A sweeping wave of drums and violin music drowned out Christie's "f"-shaped reply, but she was pretty sure he hadn't said "fairy."

Sylvie pulled on Christie's arm as she said, "We'll find Finn, then get some caffeine—there's an espresso machine near the Emory."

"I knew we shouldn't have come." Christie followed her through the gaggles of ribboned and flower-crowned revelers. "I saw Absalom here, so is this really a surprise? At the homecoming dance, he spiked the punch with tequila."

Sylvie wished he'd stop bitching. She was trying to concentrate. "Christie . . . d'you remember what Finn was wearing?"

He described nearly every detail of Finn's costume. She halted to look at him. She said, "Okay. Now close your eyes and describe what *I'm* wearing."

He closed his eyes. "You . . . black. You're in black . . . and . . . are you wearing sneakers or . . ."

"Never mind." She wanted to swat him as she hitched up the strap on her fake wings. "Christie, are you crushing on Finn?"

"What? No!"

Oh, he was. She could see the symptoms. She sighed and glanced at the orchestra as the cello music turned sinister. "Don't you dare, Christie Hart, mess with her. You hear me?"

"I wasn't going to—"

"I think you were. I think you saw something new and got all intrigued and decided to charm her, then do what you usually do—be nice and wander away from her after you've stomped all over her heart with your big, stupid feet."

"Hell, Sylv." He looked stunned. "Is it the creepy music or the drugs that are making you say that?"

She was a little surprised at herself, but she'd lost friends because of his Casanova complex. Finn seemed so fragile and lost despite her smiles and clever words, and Sylvie felt worried for her.

"So, if you feel that way"—Christie was moving back from her—"maybe you can enjoy this little soiree on your own."

"Christie—"

But he'd already vanished into the crowds of punk Romeos and sexy fairies.

Turning away, Sylvie nearly ran into a young man in a velvet half mask and a vintage soldier's greatcoat. Beneath, he wore nothing but a pair of jeans. His bare chest was tattooed with silvery Celtic spirals.

"What a pretty fallen Juliet you make." His smile sent a shiver through her. An earth-scented wind fluttered the tiny bones in his shoulder-length, satin-white hair.

As she took a step back, he took a step forward, still smiling. Boldly, she said, "And who are you supposed to be?"

He flung out his arms. "Caliban from *The Tempest*. Don't I look the part?"

He looked savage and unnaturally attractive. She felt a little flare of heat and, before she knew what she was doing, she was reaching up to touch his hair.

His hand flew up and gripped her wrist. She widened her eyes. "Is it dyed?"

"Is yours?"

"No. Let go of my hand please."

His gaze held hers as he tilted her wrist up and brushed his lips across it. He whispered against her pulse, "Why don't you tell me your name?"

"No." What had made her step so close to him? "I don't think I should do that." She reached up with her other hand and snatched the mask from his face.

The ghost from the wake shook his head and caught her other hand, yanking her closer. He looked like something out of a church window, but his eyes reflected the light in a cold shimmer that she found disturbing. He bent his head and whispered in her ear, "What if I told you you could be as you are now, forever. Never change. Never decay. Only lose your mind a little, now and then, but it comes back."

"Let me go." Sylvie's voice was shaking.

"Ah, you'd be such a pretty one." Close to her ear, he said, "What's your favorite flower?"

She was so cold and she'd begun to shiver—

A voice whispered through the air, and Caliban released Sylvie. His mouth twisted and his eyes narrowed. She turned to see what he was glaring at; then she stared as the revelers seemed to part, revealing a shadow beneath a tree. Light brushed against a bare arm, a bare foot, and revealed the hint of a T-shirt and jeans, long black hair . . .

The orchestra burst into a cover of Creedence Clearwater Revival's "Bad Moon Rising," and the shadow vanished in a swirl of icy wind and ragged leaves that swept over Sylvie and the silver-eyed Caliban.

"*Sluagh*," Caliban spat and backed away from her. He turned and vanished into the crowd.

Sylvie slowly turned and frowned at the tree beneath which that unsettling figure had stood and told herself she had *not* seen dead Thomas Luneht.

CHRISTIE REALIZED HE WAS DEFINITELY drugged when the three girls sauntered toward him from an arch of Emory hung with little birdcages. Macbeth's witches, he thought, because their eyes were rimmed with black and their gowns were tattered, their skin smudged with dirt. They were bravely barefoot.

"Ladies." He glanced warily at the dark-haired one, who did not slink up to him like the other two. "I'm Christie."

"I'm Beatrice." The girl with red hair laid cold hands on him. Her green eyes reminded him of a pond covered by lichen. He couldn't move away from her though, and the girl with the pale hair and crown of flowers had set her hands and chin on his shoulder and was gazing at him with blue eyes that had, painted beneath each, a red tear.

"I'm Abigail, Christie." Her lithe body was cold against him, and she wasn't wearing anything beneath the dress. "And that's Eve."

The black-haired girl was silent. He forced a smile this time. "I've got friends who are looking for me—"

"Girlfriends?" Beatrice's smile was a curve of malice.

Christie really couldn't move, as if they held him there, and they stood on a shadowy part of the lawn, near the woods. The dark-haired girl was whispering and a wind had picked up, swirling her hair around her head. She looked, he thought with alarm, a little like Sophia Avaline the history professor—if Sophia Avaline were white as snow with eyes like hollows in her face—

"Ladies." A cool female voice snapped Christie from the trance. The two girls stepped back from him, and, with the dark-haired one leading, they all vanished into the night.

Reiko Fata's best friend/chauffeur/cousin walked toward him. "Don't you know not to give your name to anyone?"

"*What* are they *on*?" He tried to peer into the shadows after the three girls. "They were hot, but ice-cold . . . I'm Christie."

"I know who you are." She spoke to him as if he were a moron. Her skin seemed to glisten and her red hair was in knots on her head, like two small horns. She wore black leather jeans and a black T-shirt with a skull on it.

"I know who you are. You're a girl Hamlet."

She shook her head, her gray eyes incredulous in their black liner. "It was the sugar skulls, wasn't it? Who gave them to you?"

"I don't know." He frowned now and didn't like the confusion he felt. "Phouka, right? That's your name." He pronounced her name the way he'd heard Reiko say it, an elegant *fuua*.

"Why don't I walk you back to your friends?" The punk-elegant girl held out a hand. For a moment, her eyes glinted silver and he was almost more afraid of her than he'd been of Macbeth's witches.

Don't, something in his mind whispered, *take her hand.*

"Christie Hart." Her smile, so sudden and so charming, made him reach out and take her hand.

AS FINN AND NATHAN WOVE through the Shakespearean maidens and strutting boys, she glimpsed herself in a mirror hanging from a tree and saw a fey girl with flowery hair and gypsy eyes. She looked through an Emory arch where Reiko Fata held court in a blood-red Elizabethan gown, surrounded by girls in black gossamer.

Jack Fata, a gangster Macbeth in a fur coat and striped suit, leaned against Reiko's chair. When he raised his head, Finn looked quickly away.

Someone began speaking Shakespeare with an Irish lilt. "'. . . *will lead them up and down. I am fear'd in field and town. Goblin, lead them up and down.*'"

She was about to ask Nathan about the coffee when a platinum-haired young man moved to Reiko and whispered in her ear.

As Reiko turned her head and focused on Finn, the blood red of her gown made her resemble a queen of hell, and her eyes seemed to reflect the light, mesmerizing Finn. She felt Nathan's hand close around hers, pulling her away. She remembered the coffee. Reluctantly, she followed him to a table where coffee and tea steamed in pots. He chose coffee. After a moment, she did the same, hoping it'd dull the effects of the sugar skulls. She said, "Have you seen my friends? Christie and Sylvie?"

"I thought I saw them heading back down the path."

"They're leaving already?" She quickly turned and ran across the lawn.

"Finn!" Nathan's voice faded behind her as she pushed through a scrim of hedges and saw Christie's Mustang.

The platinum-haired youth, the angel-faced ghost from the field, waited on the hood of Christie's car. He raised his head and looked at her with pure, savage joy.

"What are you doing, *girl*?"

"My name is Finn." She began moving back, step by step.

"Is it, *leannan*? But that's not your *true* name." He slid from the car, and she stumbled as he came toward her.

But he continued past her, his pale hair swaying, and said, with contempt, "Your friends are in the house. In SatyrNight."

Finn stood very still. Her nose was bleeding again, as if some unnatural pressure had passed over her, rupturing delicate membranes.

Dabbing one hand against her nose, she flung herself around and strode toward the house called SatyrNight, the dark, silent centerpiece of the party. When she got to the front, she saw the paper on the door was a legal notice of foreclosure. There were cracks in the windows, and the second-floor was boarded up.

Someone stood behind her, breathing so quietly that she hadn't even heard a step. She was alone out here, with the party seeming so distant, and the wind stirring the creepers and leaves that veiled the house.

Frightened, Finn shoved at the door and, as it opened, lunged into the hall. She spun to face whoever had stood behind her. There was nothing on the stairs but windswept shadows thrown by the moon and trees and the stone fauns in their draperies of withered Emory. The dance of light and dark made the fauns' faces, turned toward the house, malevolent.

Sternly telling herself to grow a spine, Finn turned and saw a corridor lit with a red lamp. At the end, in the center of a circular room, was a giant statue of black marble, ram horns curving from its hair, hooved feet glinting against a midnight floor. The museum silence within the house was unnerving.

Then someone whispered, *Uninvited* . . .

Light glanced across the black eyes of the statue. The world wavered. Finn felt dizzy, stumbled back—

Suddenly, someone yanked her out of the house.

She yelped and slammed into another body as the door was kicked shut by a booted foot.

"What are you *doing*?" She staggered back, staring at Jack Fata. His face was in shadow. He glinted with things, bits of jewelry and spikes of menace, but she suspected the menace was not directed toward her. He said, "What were *you* doing?"

"I was looking for Christie and Sylvie."

"In there? Who told you they were in there?" Something in his voice made her scared then, because he acted as if she'd been in real danger. She wanted to tell him about the platinum-haired young man who looked like an angel but didn't talk like one, but her tongue locked.

"Never mind." He swung around and stared at the revel. "I know."

She edged away from SatyrNight. "What is this house?"

"This house?" He didn't turn as he led her back to the party. A leaf-crackling wind lifted his hair from the nape of his neck, revealing a tattoo, a black cross of Celtic knotwork. Something about that design made Finn's throat close. Christie had one like it, but not as intricate or as barbed or as darkly significant. Jack Fata's tattoo seemed to be more of a battle scar than a decoration. He said, "It's not a house. It looks like a house. It acts like a house. But it's not a house."

"Well, what is it then? Are you going to tell me? No, you're not, are you, because you want to be—"

"I can't tell you." His voice was cool. "Because you wouldn't believe me."

"I—" Then Finn saw the platinum-haired young man standing among the revelers, speaking with an arrogant Ophelia in a gown of black silk and a crown of flowers. She whispered, "Angyll Weaver."

Jack turned and followed her gaze. Idly, he said, "*She* wasn't invited."

Angyll was her enemy. But she was also Anna Weaver's sister and that young man with the white hair was bad news. Finn pushed through the crowd toward them, Jack calling out to her as she left him behind.

She lost sight of Angyll and the pale young man. As Finn stood still, looking left and right for them, a girl in a gauzy mask ran, laughing, past her as a hooded figure on stilts lurched around a tree hung with tiny mirrors. A group of wild boys carrying antlered staffs parted around her, and she saw a figure in a leaf mask playing a flute as a woman in black danced, dark flowers falling from her hair. Finn swayed on her feet and wondered what, exactly, had been in that sugar skull. She thought of SatyrNight and shivered. Wasn't Pan, the satyr, a god of wild revels and fear?

"All the world is a stage," she heard someone say and glimpsed orange hair beneath a jester's cap; passing her, the boy murmured, "A stage for what?"

Someone was playing a violin, low and mournful. A girl's laughter sounded like a sob. There were too many people. Finn felt the terrible sleep falling over her—

Someone placed a fur-lined coat over her shoulders, and she smelled ever-green, burning things, wild roses. She turned her head. Jack, coatless, clasped her face in his hands. His rings were cold, but his fingers burned and his eyes were dark. "You need to go home."

"This will help her, Jack." A female hand gleaming with antique rings held half of a fruit to Finn's lips. Finn, struggling with nausea and chills, met the green gaze of Reiko Fata.

"Pomegranate." The beautiful girl's voice was sweet. "It'll get some sugar into your blood."

Finn accepted the halved fruit even though the ruby seeds reminded her of blood. As another wave of dizziness shook her, she bit into the fruit. The seeds burst tartly between her teeth. When Reiko offered her water in a goblet, she gratefully drank it down. "Thank you."

Reiko looked at Jack. "You'd best let Jack take you home now. I'll tell your friends that you've gone."

As Reiko glided away in a flare of crimson, Finn murmured, "This has been a strange night."

"Is it your first?"

"No, I—" Irritated by his way of speaking with hidden meaning, she narrowed her eyes. "What do you do?"

"For kicks?"

"I mean, do you go to college or live on a trust fund or cook meth—"

He contemplated her with amusement. "Do I look like I do any of those things?"

"No."

"Then there's your answer."

"Not really." She tasted a bead of pomegranate on her tongue as she studied him. The tiny ruby glinting in the side of his nose matched the ones on two of his rings. There was a fine ivory scar across the arch of his nose and she won-dered how he'd gotten it. His eyes weren't dark—one was a deep blue, the other more gray, and the candlelight emphasized the difference. "Where do you live? Don't be funny about it either."

"I told you, I live on my own."

"Not with the Fatas?"

"Sometimes."

He was being funny about it. Frustrated, because she was trying to find out things about him and was too socially awkward to go about it with grace, Finn tucked her arms into the coat and frowned at him. The fur collar brushed her chin. The unsettling atmosphere was still affecting her judgment. "Show me where you live?"

He looked at her and something like fear flicked across his face, but it was gone in an instant. Softly, he said, "You won't let it go, will you? All right then. I'll show you."

He held out a hand.

Beware, the rustling leaves seemed to whisper.

Finn clasped Jack's hand as her own self whispered, *Be brave*.

JACK DROVE AN OLD SEDAN, which surprised her. A tiny angel of black wood, its arms broken off, hung from his rearview mirror. She gazed at the armless angel as the young man she scarcely knew drove up a wooded road, toward the warehouse district, where brownstones and old cars were splashed with orange lights and she could see plastic jack-o'-lanterns and cardboard cutouts of witches in apartment windows. They drove past a warehouse with Emory clinging to its roof, the painted words *Greenwald Foundry* faded on its bricks.

He parked the sedan in the weedy lot of an abandoned movie theater with boards across its windows and doors. Above the doors was a stone face spewing leaves and a shattered marquee with three letters remaining.

"You're kidding?" Finn clutched at the car seat, thinking of the idiot victims in horror movies and how she might be about to become one.

He didn't look at her. The streetlights made his profile very white. "Here."

She studied him, realizing then that he was tense and almost ashamed. Quickly, she said, "Who owns the building?"

"The Fatas own it."

"I want to see it."

"Reckless girl."

She wanted to tell him she wasn't reckless . . . she just wasn't going to be afraid anymore.

They got out of the car, and he led her around to the back of the abandoned cinema, to a fire escape.

"Careful," he told her as she followed him up to a second-floor window. He pushed it open and helped her over the sill. As he moved around, turning on lamps, she gazed in awe at a narrow, high-ceilinged room painted black and decorated with cinema posters in plastic frames. A chandelier of red beads glittered over a sleigh bed with rumpled covers. There were hundreds of books, in stacks, on tables, crowding the shelves along one wall. She gravitated toward the shelves. Nearly everything was hardcover. History books. Classics. Greek classics. Encyclopedias. Biographies. Literature. Poetry. She was impressed and intimidated.

"Don't you have any paperbacks?" She shed his coat over a chair. "Beach reads? Suspense novels?"

"I'm old-fashioned."

She took down a volume of Angela Carter's *The Bloody Chamber* and opened it. "Is this a boy's book?"

He leaned against an antique chair—all his furniture seemed to be wrecked antiques. "It's an interesting one."

She read, " '*Now we are at the place of annihilation.*' Do you have a kitchen?"

"I eat out."

"Okay." She touched an armillary sphere set on a table and watched the rings lazily rotate around the metal ball. "You've got a lot of . . . interesting things here."

He moved to her and circled one hand around her wrist. She didn't look at him, fascinated by the rings on his fingers—and how cool and strong those fingers were.

"What happened to you," he said gently, "that makes you so careless?"

"I'm not careless." She had gone very still.

"You are. You're like some mad child flinging itself at things just to feel something."

"*Me?*" Her gaze flicked up to his. "What about the stuff you're not telling me? Those scars you've got, and don't think I haven't noticed how you twist up sometimes."

He released her wrist and looked slightly bewildered. "Twist up?"

"You've got secrets, Jack." She lifted her chin.

"And you'll be lucky if you never meet them."

"See? You say things like that. Like about SatyrNight not being a house, and you live in an *abandoned movie theater*."

His eyes were dark and wide. When his lashes flicked down, she realized she'd lost him and slumped against a bookcase.

"Jack." She took a deep breath and stepped toward him, reached out, and slid her fingers around his, catching *him* this time. He didn't move, but he pressed a thumb against the thrumming pulse in her wrist as he looked down at their clasped hands. When he met her gaze, the anguish in his almost made her step back. He said hoarsely, "I didn't know . . ."

"Didn't know what?"

"Never mind." He slid the fingers of his other hand across her other wrist, up her arm, to her collarbones. His sudden smile made her breath catch. As drowsy desire moved through her, she heard him whisper against her ear, "You smell like sunlight."

His lips brushed the skin there, but his body hadn't come any closer. She curled her hands against his chest—

He stepped back, and she blinked as he said, "Not such a good idea."

She bit back the urge to ask him if he was bipolar as he turned away. She drifted back on slightly unsteady legs and bumped into a chair. Glancing down, she saw a violin case. "Do you play?"

"I go through phases." He sank down onto the sofa and hunched forward. "You can open it."

She unbuckled the case, cautiously raising the lid to gaze at the sleek, dark instrument in its nest of red suede. "That's an expensive one, isn't it?"

"It's a Stradivarius. Now, tell me what *you* love to do, Finn Sullivan."

She gently closed the lid of the violin case and turned, trying to think of something interesting. "I don't know yet. I like science, but I'm not technical. I like English, but I'm not very good at making up stories . . . so, I'm not sure. I liked photography once. But that was before . . . before." She noticed a cat watching her from the mantelpiece of the fireplace. "What's the cat's name?"

"BlackJack Slade."

The cat stretched and jumped to the floor, walked to Jack, and sniffed his boots. He reached out to stroke its head, and Finn, frustrated, moved to crouch near. She held out a hand, smiling when BlackJack Slade meowed at her and climbed into her lap.

"Well, you've bewitched *him*," Jack spoke with approval.

As she stroked the cat, it batted at the moth key around her neck—

—and yowled as if it had gotten a shock, scrambling from her lap and lashing out at Jack's hand before diving under the bed.

"I'm sorry!" Finn pushed to her feet.

Jack sounded stunned. "I'm bleeding . . ."

"He scratched you? Do you have water? Band-Aids?"

He moved to his feet, his face striped with shadow. "I'm taking you home. Now."

"Okay, but, seriously, I'm not afraid of blood—"

"Finn." He looked at her, and his expression had become cool. "You should never have come here."

She was unable to prevent revealing the hurt she felt. She whirled and stalked to the window, shoved it open, and slung one leg over the sill. "Let's go then. Take me home."

"Finn . . ."

She hesitated, sitting on the windowsill, not looking at him. "I won't visit again."

And she slid out.

WHEN JACK RETURNED TO THE autumn revel, it had become wild, as his family's revels inevitably did. Shadows and pumpkin light splashed across his face as he slouched in a chair and thought of Finn Sullivan.

As sharp pain pierced him, he clenched his scratched hand, hidden by the cuff of his shirt. Another pain in his chest tore his breath away. He sat up, opening his shirt. He pressed a hand against his chest and the black tattoo of a serpent biting its tail.

When he saw Reiko weaving toward him through the dancing bodies, her face shadowy, he dropped his hand and looked bored.

"Jack." She knelt and placed her hands on his knees. "Do you still love me?"

"Always. From the bottom of my black heart."

"But, Jack"—she stretched up and whispered against his mouth—"you don't have a heart."

"That's right. You cut it out of me."

She didn't smile. "If that little mayfly makes you grow another one, I'll take that one too."

Then she kissed him.

JACK WOKE ON A BED draped with pomegranate silk, in a chamber where candlelight danced over the belongings of a primitive queen: a black cradle carved from elderwood; an ivory box containing wooden charms from Laplander shamans and Haitian priests . . . trophies, from those who had tried, and failed, to evict her.

Reiko stood at the window. Without turning her head, she murmured, "You're different."

Lazily, without revealing any alarm, he said, "How am I different?"

Her voice held a fragile note. "This is not the same. She is not like the other three. I warned you that this time would be different."

"Reiko." He kept his voice low. The sting in his chest had faded. "She's just a girl. And what other three girls are you talking about?"

Reiko laughed softly. "It doesn't matter. You are stronger. You are wicked. You are mine. And I will not lose you. Have her, if you like."

Jack stared at the curve of her back. Shadows snaked through the chamber as the candles flared a malevolent blue, and he heard wild laughter in the distance, a burst of fiddle music. To divert her, he stretched lithely and slid a hand across his scar-laced body. "I'm the same as always. If she changes me, it will only be for a while."

He slid to his feet and walked to Reiko, folding his arms around her from behind, and whispered, "You haven't told me why you're interested in this girl."

"Her family has been a bane to us before. While we gather for All Hallows' Eve, I'm going to indulge myself."

He stilled, his mouth against her temple. "Is that wise?"

"Am I sensing something, Jack? Concern for a mayfly?" She turned to him, the irises around her pupils flaring poison green. "Remember what we are. We cannot return. We can never return. *And you are one of us.*"

He smiled as if he didn't care. He whispered in her ear and led her back to the bed as he thought, *I will end you.*

CHAPTER SIX

Monster, your fairy, which you say is a harmless fairy,
has done little better than play the Jack with us.
— *THE TEMPEST*, WILLIAM SHAKESPEARE

*He kissed the girls and stole their breath
Kissed them 'til there was nothing left.
Now they are lilies, white of skin,
sown by the lips of a prince of sin.*

—FROM THE JOURNAL OF LILY ROSE

Lily Rose's bedroom window overlooked the avenue sloping toward the distant sea.
It was always bright in her room, the red walls patterned with posters of Vasilov
Nijinsky and Anna Pavlova, photographs of friends and trips, Lily's sketches of
beautiful waifs.

Finn was fifteen years old. She was sprawled on Lily Rose's bed, watching
her sister pace before the mirror. Lily Rose was moody. She was always moody.
Breathing in the room's scents of fresh laundry and patchouli, Finn listened to her
talk.

"... so I told Leander. 'Fine. I won't see you anymore.'"

"Boys"—Finn kicked one bare foot in the air—"are a waste of space."

Lily Rose glanced at Finn. She didn't look like a ballerina in her peasant blouse and denim cutoffs, her fingers glittering with skull and serpent rings. "Finn. You don't know what I've done."

The sun vanished. The bedroom became drenched in gory red. Lily Rose was in shadow now. "I hid it, Finn . . . find it—you brought it with you."

Finn sat up. The room was very cold. The posters of ballet dancers had been replaced by paintings of Gothic ruins. "Lily. What are you talking about?"

But she was alone.

When Finn woke, she slid out of bed, crossed the room, and flipped open the lid to Lily Rose's trunk. She pulled out everything and stared at the bottom—it had been Lily's place to hide things, but she'd found out about it when she'd been twelve. Her heart slamming, Finn tugged at the lining on the trunk's bottom. The lining slid up, revealing the compartment beneath.

She sat back on her heels. With shaking hands, she reached in and lifted out a book, its black velvet decorated with crescent moons and silver ribbons. Carefully, she unwound the ribbons, opening the book to find pages scrawled with sketches and her sister's handwriting. She turned to the beginning. The first words were: *They call us things with teeth . . .*

Finn curled beneath a window with the book and became lost in a land of whispering leaves and toadstools blossoming from black earth, of dark kings, and fairy witches. She became so caught up in the words and images, she didn't notice the shadows branching across her walls, the wind rattling at the glass doors to the terrace. The stories that her sister had written were bizarre and bewildering: tales of twiggy boggarts who lived in trees; flower-wreathed creatures called nisses whose teeth were like thorns. She read about the pale Mockingbird clan and the Alder people, the court of Wyvern, and the Dragonfly tribe. *Be careful of the grindylow, which creep in the shadows. And the Anubi, hounds who patrol the borders.*

She traced the sketch of a wolfish bogie with slanting eyes and spiky hair and wondered why her sister had made this book, if it had been a process of years, or weeks. These stories were a part of Lily Rose that Finn had never known, and they were amazing. What other secrets had her sister kept? It made her throat ache, that she'd found this . . . after.

She leafed through the journal, seeking any sentence, any scribbled entry, that would reveal the reason why Lily Rose had killed herself. But they were just stories, just a world invented by a girl.

Finn had never been able to speak to any of Lily's friends after, not even Lily's boyfriend, Leander Cyrus. She'd looked up "schizophrenia," which had led to the definition of "hebephrenia," a mental illness specific to teenagers. She'd come to realize that it had been an unseen thing, something that could not be fought physically, that had danced her sister through a plateglass window.

Suddenly, there was a crash in the hall below. Finn scrambled up and hurried down the stairs.

Crouched in the hall, her da was carefully picking up the pieces of a Buddha statue Lily Rose had given him. He stopped gathering the broken bits and stared at the floor. Finn couldn't move. She just gaped at the glittering porcelain, which looked like glass.

She snapped out of it. "Da?"

"It's broken. I've broken it."

"I'll glue it."

He was quiet, his head bowed, ink-stained hands folded on his knees. It hurt her to see him so lost. "I should have known. I should have *seen* it."

"How could we know?" She put her arms around him and gazed down at the face of the broken Buddha, which blurred.

"It was the same thing as . . ." He drew in a deep breath, shaking his head, and Finn felt he'd been about to tell her something important. "Her mood swings . . . I should have gotten her help . . ."

"Da." She crouched down, gripped his hands. A fierce protectiveness for him and a frightening anger toward Lily rushed through her. "*She left us.*"

FINN WATCHED SYLVIE BURROW THROUGH her closet as the setting sun rippled over strings of crystals hung across the windows. Three days had passed since the party at SatyrNight, and she hadn't told Sylvie or Christie about Jack; she had only texted Sylvie that night to say she'd taken a cab home because she'd gotten sick. She hated lying, but *she* couldn't understand why she'd left with Jack Fata.

"Finn." Sylvie's voice was muffled. "I can't find the shoes I wanted to give you."

"Never mind." Finn took in the Rackham illustrations on the pink walls. The willowy people in those paintings always made her sad. They seemed so delicate, victims of sinister creatures disguised as trees or shadows.

Sylvie sat back on her heels. Then she opened a box beside her. "Want to see the mask I made for my Mask in Theater class? We're doing Balinese." She raised it and Finn breathed out, amazed by the crimson, papier-mâché face with its fangs and bulging eyes. Sylvie said, "It's a female demon called Rangda, a leader of witches, a creature of darkness and death."

"I know." Finn looked away from the mask and uneasily wondered why it reminded her of Reiko Fata. Just because it was red, her color . . .

Sylvie chatted on. "So it's my birthday today. Christie and me are going out to a Caribbean place. Want to come?"

Finn's mind instantly scanned the room for any ideas as to what kind of present Sylvie would like. "You don't mind?"

"You *do* know Christie and I aren't a couple, right?"

Finn said wryly, "I got that."

"We were going to go out with some friends, but I'm tired of lots of people. I just want something small and fun, and without any Fatas."

THE LAST OF THE LIGHT was draining through the leaves when Finn arrived at the bookstore. Before stepping inside, she glanced at the building across the street—the Dead Kings didn't look like a nightclub now, with its windows shuttered and its silence ominous.

She found the perfect gift for Sylvie on her break. Mrs. Browning even sold gift wrap and cards.

As Finn was struggling to knot the fancy ribbon, she looked up and saw the street lined with cars as music pulsed from beneath the Dead Kings' shutters. She was impressed.

Later that evening, she was rearranging the cooking section when she heard the bell above the door tinkle and the scent of wild roses and burning slid through the air. Cold and hot all at once, she dropped a misplaced paperback with a sexy guy in a kilt on the cover.

A hand gleaming with antique rings caught the book and returned it to her and a voice said, "Not my type of read, but kilts are irresistibly hot."

"Jack." She shoved the book onto a shelf.

He wore a black hoodie and jeans. The Chinese dragon writhing across his long-sleeved shirt was crimson and blue. She wished she wasn't wearing jeans and an old baseball jersey and her red Converses that were fading to pink.

"Did you know," he said, "that this used to be an apothecary shop in the 1800s?"

She faked casualness, ignoring his question as she said, "Are you going to the Dead Kings?"

"Not tonight." He began walking down the aisle, his heavy boots making the floorboards creak. Another lovely aroma drifted through the store as she followed him.

"Did you bring *food*?"

He nodded. "It's my apology for the other night."

He'd indeed brought food, cartons of the finest from Lulu's Emporium. Finn's mouth watered as he set the chopsticks on the counter. "For you. I've already eaten."

She greedily opened a carton of noodles. "I'm going out to dinner tonight, with my friends, but thank you. I forgot a snack."

"Are you alone here?"

"I've got the cats. Mrs. Browning's gone out for a while. Did I thank you for the food?"

"*I* didn't make it." Jack pulled two stools up to the glass counter, which held fancy bookmarks and book lights, and he shed his coat. She wasn't so preoccupied by the food that she didn't notice the way he moved.

Glancing out the window, she saw an ivory Rolls-Royce glide to a spot in front of the Dead Kings. Behind the car's tinted windows, a pair of eyes glinted. The occupants glided out, all in white, and the Rolls moved away. The license plate read "Mockingbird."

Jack murmured, "There are some bad people out tonight."

"Are you going to tell me who the bad people are?"

"No."

"Ah, you're going to be mysterious." She slid a fortune cookie to him and broke open hers. *You will find true love, and lose it, and walk the dark path to find it again.* She didn't read it out loud; the fortunes from Lulu's Emporium were always bizarre. She eyed the bookstore cats, who were winding themselves around Jack's legs.

"They're expecting me back soon," he said—he was watching the Dead Kings.

"Oh." It seemed odd that he had a curfew.

"What book are you reading?" Jack asked, glancing at her book on the counter.

"*Gormenghast,* by Mervyn Peake."

"It's good. The third book doesn't seem to belong though." He bent to stroke the cats.

"Why don't you live with the Fatas?"

He didn't look up from the cats. "These cats don't scratch, do they?"

"Are you avoiding my question?"

"I don't like their house. It's old and drafty."

"My new house is like that."

He looked at her. "You came from San Francisco. It's quite a change."

Finn tried not to withdraw from his unspoken question: *Why did you move here?* "My da used to live here. He got a job at St. John's University, teaching mythology."

"Mythology?"

"Mm-hmm."

"Is that something you like?"

"Well, my mom was a biologist, but I don't want to be a scientist—although I was interested in physics once, because it's crazy. My sister—" She stopped. "My sister liked mythology. When we were little, she was interested in Nordic legends, Odin and Loki and the Valkyries. She called her imaginary friend Norn."

He narrowed his eyes. "After the goddesses of fate?"

"Fate." Finn's mouth twisted.

He spoke gently, "Your sister died, didn't she?"

Her fingers clenched on the counter. "Yeah, she died."

His hand, strong, fine, and decorated with antique rings, settled over hers, and a sweet warmth blossomed within her.

"Finn." He looked away, a muscle twitching in his jaw. "My family . . . they're not good people."

She didn't want to move her hand from beneath his because the breathless ache that choked her whenever she thought of Lily didn't come this time. She felt concerned for Jack, though, because that statement—it made her think of secrets that rotted people from the inside out.

"It's not like they're the Mafia, right?" She watched him for a response. "No one has a perfect family."

His mouth curved, and he looked back at her, laughter glittering in his dark eyes. "Right. Not a perfect family, but a lot like the Mafia."

She wanted to ask him about his parents but decided that might be too much prying. There was one thing she was determined to clarify, however. As she looked down at the rings on his fingers, she said, "Reiko isn't your sister, is she?"

"Not even a distant cousin."

"You're adopted, like Nathan Clare."

"Somewhat."

A horn blared outside, making Finn jump. Jack slid his hand from hers and rose. "I think that's for me."

He was leaving her for the glamour of Fata civilization. She said lightly, "Thank you for dinner."

He sauntered toward the door. The bell didn't chime as he stepped out and dead leaves webbed with smoke and cold swirled in. "Don't look out the window so much, Finn Sullivan."

When he had gone, she shoved her food cartons into the trash before looking for the tiny paper with *his* fortune on it, only to find one of the cats eating it.

CHRISTIE CAME IN AS FINN was switching off the electric jack-o'-lantern in the bookstore window.

"I couldn't park nearby." He shoved his hands into his pockets and frowned at the Dead Kings. "Annoying."

"You're jealous you're not in there, aren't you?" She reached for her coat.

"My soul bleeds whenever I can't mingle with the jaded and the obnoxious."

Finn locked up and grinned as music pounded from the nightclub. "You've never gone in there?"

His eyes widened. "I'm afraid to."

As they left the shop, she noticed that he wore a new wool-knit hat embroidered with Emory. His dark red hair stuck out around his face. She couldn't resist. "Your mom really does make you those hats, doesn't she?"

"Two, every winter. If you come to my house, she'll make you one for Christmas. Sylvie's gotten one with skulls on it, a Laplander hat, and a cherry blossom scarf."

"I would *love* a hat." Finn slid into his Mustang, quickly moving a milkshake cup before she sat on it.

Starting the engine, Christie said, "I'm taking a little detour first."

"Did you forget to get Sylvie a present?"

"I did not." He was indignant. "She's been hinting at a skateboard—yes, a skateboard—and I got her one, customized. The shop's in the warehouse district."

"All I got her was a book."

"Does the book have lots of illustrations?" Finn nodded, and he said, "She'll love it."

No sooner had they left most of the town lights behind than the Mustang decided to seize up, spit gasoline fumes, and lurch to a halt. Christie attempted several starts, with no results other than a sick-sounding car.

"Are you *kidding* me?" He gripped the wheel. "Finn, lend me your phone."

She handed the phone over; Christie frowned as he poked at it. He said, "Did you recharge this?"

"Yes. Let me see." The phone was absolutely dead. "It *can't* be dead. I just charged it." She sighed. "We'll need to walk somewhere. Wasn't there a 7-Eleven back there?"

They slid from the car, their breath misting. As they trudged up a road lined with trees and brambly bushes, Finn tilted her head back to gaze at the stars. When her gaze returned to earth, she saw a large house looming on a bank of slate knotted with ornamental bushes. The silhouettes of palm trees and Egyptian-looking statues surrounded the house. Finn remarked, "That's kitschy. Like old Hollywood."

"That's the Sphinx."

"This house has a name too?"

"Most of them do. Want to see?" He moved toward the steep stairway. "It's kind of interesting—no one's lived in it since the seventies."

Finn thought, *Another abandoned house.* It was a little disturbing, all the decaying real estate around town. She trudged up the steps after Christie because she was curious, soon discovering that the palm trees were actually made of the same dark marble as the stair's sculptures—female figures with the bodies of lions. The windows were hidden by bamboo shutters, and the landscaping had been ravished by weeds. "It doesn't look bad."

Christie said, "It belonged to the Lunehts. They came from Egypt, at least their ancestors did. Their son killed himself, so they left Fair Hollow."

"How do you know all—"

"Sylvie has a crush on dead Thomas Luneht. You never saw that photograph in her room?"

Finn recalled the photo on the pink wall, of the Rackham boy in bell-bottom jeans, black hair framing his face. "What happened to him?"

"He loved a girl. The girl was a bitch. He couldn't live without her."

"That's a stupid reason to die," Finn whispered, thinking of Lily.

"So I should tell you . . . the Lunehts supposedly kept a menagerie of strange animals—"

"*Christie.* There's a light on in one of the windows."

"You think it's a new owner? A real estate agent with a phone? Let's go find out."

"You want to tell me why so many of these big old houses are abandoned?" Finn asked as they continued up the stairs toward the light glowing in a first-floor window.

"They're old. Expensive to keep up, much less modernize. Or weatherproof. Newcomers have money to build their own McMansions." He looked thoughtful. "My mom says the old gods, the spirits, have no groves or grottos, caves or shrines. Now they only have cemeteries, wells, bridges. Abandoned buildings."

"You're trying to freak me out. Stop it."

A voice said something. They froze. Finn thought she saw a silhouette in the doorway of the house. "Christie . . ."

He looked and grabbed her hand as a boy's voice said, clear as ice, ". . . you they want . . ."

The hair stood up on Finn's neck, but she defiantly took another step up. "Hello?"

"Finn, don't—"

The front doors swung open, revealing a lamp-lit hallway. She heard the

Creedence song about a bad moon rising faintly playing within the house, which didn't look abandoned.

. . . don't come around tonight, for it's bound to take your life . . .

A figure moved at the end of the hall with its abstract paintings and chic lighting. It was only a silhouette, but it seemed . . . *wrong.* Finn took a step forward. "We need help—"

She felt nausea roil through her and stumbled back. The air began to buzz, further disconcerting her. "Christie . . ."

He tugged at her, and they fled back down the stairs. He cried out and she twisted around, reaching for him.

"Something hit my leg," he whispered. "Finn . . ."

She looked back at the house—the doors were closed, but there was something else out here with them . . . she heard it breathing.

Someone laughed like a mutilated lunatic.

They ran toward the road and didn't stop until they reached Christie's Mustang. They were breathing like dragons by the time they slumped inside the car.

"Someone threw a *rock* at me. Christ, I'm bleeding . . ."

Finn gazed warily at the Sphinx in its shadows. "Whoever was in the house . . . they were warning us."

"By throwing *rocks*?" Christie turned the key in the ignition. "Come on, baby, work for me."

The engine roared to life. They looked at each other.

As they drove away, Finn glanced over her shoulder at the black bulk of the house called the Sphinx and thought of the boy who had killed himself, the one in the photo on Sylvie's wall, the one whose dark eyes had had the same haunted look as Lily's.

"WHAT IS IT?"

"That's a *kitsune*, a Japanese fox spirit."

Finn sighed when she overheard the conversation between Christie and her da as she was coming down the stairs. Her father continued, "Your father works at the metalworking plant. In Japan, a fox divinity rules metalsmithing. It was always a sacred craft. Ironworkers were said to have connections to the otherworld— Oh, hi, Finn."

In the hall, Christie was holding a fox mask. With its slanting eyes and mahogany spikiness, that particular mask had always unsettled Finn. As she sat on the bottom stair and laced up the black boots she'd selected to wear with her white linen dress, she said, "Put it back, Christie."

Christie set the fox mask back on the wall. "D'you believe in spirits, Mr. Sullivan?"

Her da smiled. "No. Do you?"

"I do now—" Christie grimaced suddenly and gripped the table. "Ouch."

"Are you okay?" Finn rose. "Let me see."

"It's just—"

"Let me *see*."

He pulled up the leg of his jeans and revealed a bloody hole in his ankle.

Finn and her da winced. Her father crouched down to examine the puncture. "Something's in there."

Christie was now very pale. "Like a bullet?"

"More like a splinter. Finn, get the alcohol and that medicinal gauze—and the tweezers."

Christie said faintly, "Does she have to get the tweezers?"

She hurried to the bathroom. When she returned with the items, her da probed the wound as Christie gripped the hall table. While she'd been gone, Christie must have told her father about the Sphinx, because her da said, "There'll be no more wandering around condemned places."

Something popped out of the bloody, darkened skin, and Christie went absolutely white. Her da reached down, picked up the object. "I'll be damned. It's a human tooth."

Christie swallowed. "How did it get in my goddamn ankle?"

"No idea—unless someone shot it from an air rifle. Creative, that. Finn, please don't go near that place again."

"That is *so* wrong." Christie's voice shook.

"We'll patch it up." Her da rose. "You watch it for infection."

"I'll be sure to do that, Mr. S." Christie nodded solemnly, but his eyes were dark with panic. "Finn, did your dad tell you that our little town is filled with weirdos?"

"Like people who use human teeth as ammunition?" She nodded. "I kinda noticed the weirdo factor *long* before this, what with, you know, girls in gowns running around in the woods and theater majors holding bonfire chats."

"What?" Christie and her father spoke at the same time and looked at her. Her father was frowning. He said, "What the hell have you been doing?"

"Getting to know your hometown." Despite her bland tone, Finn felt a creeping uneasiness as she gazed at the gruesome projectile in her father's hand.

CHRISTIE'S FRIENDS WERE MOSTLY GIRLS whom he had dated or an eccentric ensemble of would-be poets and athletes who were into either hockey or football. He had a wide social circle, which, like most popular beings, he seemed to take for granted.

The parents of one of his friends, Aubrey Drake, owned the Voodoo Lounge, a hangout for HallowHeart and St. John's U. students. Lime-green lamps lit murals from Caribbean folklore, and the tables and chairs were painted with images of cockatoos, palm trees, and panthers. The Drakes also owned the game store where Christie worked.

As they sat, it was Christie who brought up the Sphinx and the tooth incident, then displayed the bandaged ankle. Sylvie said it was revoltingly fascinating, then added, "You didn't tell Finn about . . ."

"He did." Finn caught on to exactly what Sylvie was trying not to say. "The boy who killed himself at the Sphinx? I doubt he's the one who shot Christie with a bullet made from a human molar."

"Probably some idiot kid," Christie said, passing out the menus, "experimenting with different ways to mutilate people, living his dream."

Sylvie looked at her. "You thought you saw Thomas Luneht's ghost?"

Finn uneasily remembered the boyish, doll-like figure in the hallway. "You saw it, Christie, didn't you?"

Christie looked down at his menu. "I saw the light on."

"You didn't . . ." Finn couldn't understand how he'd *not* seen it.

"I believe you, Finn."

Sylvie said, "It's weird that your car stalled out, at just that spot . . ."

"Let's talk about something else, okay?" Christie glanced up and around. "It's dead in here tonight."

"Well, they're having an all-you-can-eat shrimp fest at the MooseJaw Restaurant."

"Ah, that explains it."

Finn decided to pursue the subject she wanted to discuss and attempted a casual tone. "Hey, what do you two know about the Fatas?"

Sylvie and Christie both lowered their menus to exchange a look. Christie said, "I know Jack Fata's been in prison."

"Christie, you *don't* know that." Sylvie swatted him with her menu.

"Maybe it was a mental institution? Drug rehabilitation? Anyway, he was away for a long time, a couple years ago."

"It was a year he was away, and Reiko went with him. They probably went on some amazing trip to Paris or something."

"I don't like them." Christie frowned down at his menu.

"You like Reiko." Finn's mouth curved. "You did a fabulous imitation of a stunned deer when she was talking to you."

Christie narrowed his eyes at her as Sylvie asked mischievously, "Is that true, Christie?"

"Yes. It's true. She's a supermodel. I looked like an idiot. And yet Reiko gave us all invitations to her autumn fling. That was probably because of me and my effect on her."

Sylvie rolled her eyes and set down her menu. She slid up from her chair. "I know what I want. I'm going to put on some good music."

"Oh *no*." Christie scraped back his chair as Sylvie walked toward a retro juke-box in the corner. "I'll have to go with her, Finn, or we'll be listening to golden oldies all night. I mean, I don't mind Guns N' Roses and Nirvana, but the one-hit wonders—"

"Stop her," Finn said solemnly, "for all of our sakes."

As Christie and Sylvie wandered to the jukebox, Finn, seated beneath the huge painting of a hooded figure holding a rose in its hands, read the menu and tried to decide which item would be new and delicious.

Someone sat beside her. "Finn Sullivan."

She lowered the menu.

The platinum-haired young man from the autumn revel gazed at her. He wore a black, pin-striped suit and his eyes were colder than moonlight on a knife.

"Serafina Sullivan." There was a faint twist of Irish to his words. "I'd like to talk to you about Nathan Clare."

She glanced frantically at Christie and Sylvie, who were arguing over a song selection at the jukebox and hadn't noticed the new arrival. Fear prevented her from speaking.

"Look at me," he said, and she did. There were pale freckles across his nose. His eyes were so gray they seemed silver, and his gaze held hers as he said, "Stay away from Nathan Clare or you'll see things you'll wish you hadn't. And don't think that Jack will help you—he's a wicked bastard—"

"Finn." Christie's voice broke the platinum-haired young man's spell.

The stranger rose and faced Christie, and Sylvie, who seemed fragile in her black shift and purple Converses, her eyes large beneath her bangs. Christie, lean and sweet-faced, didn't seem any less vulnerable.

"Christie. Sylvie." Finn found her voice. "It's okay."

"Christie." The stranger murmured the name as if memorizing it. Then he smiled at Sylvie. "Sylvie."

He turned and sauntered away. Rings flashed on his hands as he pushed open the door and slipped into the night.

Finn looked down at her menu, no longer in the mood for something new and delicious.

Christie said, "*What* was *that*?"

"That was a Fata." Sylvie sat down. "I met him at the Fata revel. He's the one we saw at the wake."

"He was at the party the other night," Finn murmured, "talking to Angyll Weaver."

"Well, he deserves whatever he gets then." Christie sat back, but his gaze remained on Finn. "What did he say to you?"

Finn had never felt true malevolence directed at her before—the platinum-haired Fata had *threatened* her. "He doesn't want me to speak to Nathan Clare."

"Oh. Maybe they're a couple." Christie flipped open his menu.

"Is that all?" Sylvie glared at the door as if expecting the menacing Fata to return.

"That's all." Finn's hands shook a little.

"Finn . . . you're not going to talk to Nathan again, are you?"

"Oh hell," Christie said, eyes narrowing. "She is."

They ordered quickly. Finn managed the spicy food, the plantains and rice, the jerked chicken. But, afterward, she excused herself from the table and hurried into the dimly lit restroom, where she ran cold water over her wrists, dabbed her face with water, and noticed how her artfully smudged mascara made her eyes look shadowy.

The pale-haired Fata had terrified her.

When something skittered across the wall, she whirled, staring into the corners. Nausea suddenly burned in her throat, and she hunched over the sink, glimpsing out of the corner of one eye something like a black, furry hand retreating into the darkness of one stall.

She dashed out of the bathroom and halted to wipe clammy hands on her sleeves. Either the pale-haired Fata was making good on his threat, or she was losing her mind.

SHE DIDN'T TELL HER FRIENDS what she'd seen as Christie drove them home and Sylvie thanked them for the gifts—an illustrated book about mythical witches from Finn and the gorgeous skateboard from Christie. As Christie pulled up in front of her apartment, Sylvie got out and said, "*Sayonara.* It was a fabulous night. Finn, *don't go near Nathan Clare.*"

As soon as they'd pulled away, Christie looked at Finn. "He's dangerous."

"Who?"

"That white-haired gangster. Just do as he says. Nathan's got plenty of friends."

She laid her head against the window and thought about Jack Fata, not Nathan. "Don't worry about it, Christie."

After a beat, Christie said, "So you've been seeing Jack Fata."

She glanced at him. "Okay."

"And tonight you found out what the Fatas are like—not all that money came from them prostituting their kids as models and actors."

"Christie—that pale-haired Fata doesn't like Jack."

"We've got something in common then."

"You haven't even *met* him—"

"Do I need to?" They'd reached her house. He stopped the car and looked at her. "I could meet him a hundred times and still not like him."

"Thanks for the ride." She got out of the car, angry.

"Finn—"

She slammed the door. Surrounded by neighborhood silence, she stalked toward her house.

JACK FATA SLID INTO HIS apartment and lifted BlackJack Slade into his arms, setting the cat on a table to feed him mouse blood and milk in a teacup. Moonlight striped scattered books and broken things as he let his coat fall and pushed the button on his stereo. As violin music wavered through the apartment, he lay on his bed and touched his hip, his ribs, his collarbone, all of the scars beneath his fine clothes. He counted each year he'd been in the world. There were many.

What would she think of these marks, that girl with the tawny eyes? The one who reminded him of a long-dead friend?

He rose to his feet and left his nest to visit the oracle.

ANNA WEAVER DIDN'T LOOK UP as Jack entered Hecate's Attic. She continued sorting dried herbs and flowers into velvet pouches.

He sat on the table and said, "Your folks really shouldn't leave you alone."

"Why? Because I'm only fourteen?" She shrugged. Straight golden hair made her face seem elfin as she brushed leaves from her clothes and folded her hands on the table. "My mom's in the stockroom. What do you want?"

He smiled, but she was immune to his charm. The blackbird cuff links glinted on his sleeves as he tapped the table. "I want to know my future."

"I've told you." She was solemn. "I can't. You have no future. The bells over the door didn't even ring when you came in."

He bowed his head, the red fringes of his dark hair sweeping against his neck. "Then tell me about love."

"No—"

He reached for her Tarot deck, slid out a card, and turned it faceup, revealing the image of three swords sticking out of an androgynous body. "That tells me everything, doesn't it? Thank you, Anna."

As he stood, he set a fossilized ruby shell on the table. Anna watched him leave the shop, his long coat snapping in the wind as the door closed behind him. She curled her hand over the shell.

LIKE JACK'S PALE SHADOW, A young man walked into Hecate's Attic just before closing. Again, the bells above the door didn't ring, but clanked instead, as if dull with cold. The stranger inhaled, fixed his silvery gaze on the golden girl behind the counter, and used the voice that had lured so many others into his jaws. "Hello."

Anna Weaver stared at the young man in the dark coat and pin-striped suit and immediately knew what he was. She wanted to call for her mother, but didn't dare.

"Hello, oracle." He sauntered toward her, casting her a bauble—his sweetest smile. "Tell me my fortune."

"Get out."

"You've been speaking to dead people, little girl. We don't like that. They tell all sorts of stories."

She gazed sullenly at him.

"Tell me my fortune, and I'll tell Reiko to wait until you're sixteen to recruit you."

The child walked to a round table and sat. She drew large, colorful cards from an ivory box. He took a chair opposite, his head tilted. "Go on, *seanchaidh*."

As she laid a cruciform pattern of cards on the table, she watched him from beneath her lashes. Her voice was cool. "I see a black beast in thorns. I see a grinning crescent moon that draws blood. I see . . ." Her gaze flicked up. "I think you should leave."

"Make me, Anna Weaver."

"Go away." She kicked at him beneath the table.

"All right, all right. If you're going to be that way . . ." Revealing a bit of otherworldly grace, he rose. "What happens to the black beast? Tell me."

She looked at him. "The crescent moon, the laughing god, kills it."

"Good little oracle. Is your sister around? The leggy blonde? No? Pity." Caliban tossed her a coin from a dead queen's tomb and casually walked out of Hecate's Attic.

It had been a long time since he'd been called a god. He found he missed it.

CHAPTER SEVEN

Here once dwelt
A high idol of many fights.
The cromm cruaich by name,
And deprived every tribe of peace.

—BOOK OF LEINSTER

The crom cu, the crooked dog, runs by the light of the moon. Once, he was a brave and virtuous Celtic prince. Now, when the moon is a crescent, he kills for blood. That is his nature. Beware the crom cu.

—FROM THE JOURNAL OF LILY ROSE

College life, veiled in flame-colored leaves, had become a welcome pattern for Finn, whose favorite class was Gothic Literature and not just because Professor Fairchild reminded her of a young poet from a turn-of-the-century novel. It was the way he spoke of the books, as if he knew secret things about the people who had written them. In her other classes, it was how Professor Avaline referred to historical figures, or how Miss Perangelo talked about Frida Kahlo and Dorothea Tanning in Women in Surrealism.

"The imagination is unexplored terrain." Fairchild looked even more tousled than usual. "Coleridge's poems . . . were they the product of opium or the writings of a man under the influence of something else? And what of Edgar

Allan Poe's gaslit nightmares? Goethe's Erl King? Christina Rossetti's Goblin Market? Emily Brontë's changeling Heathcliff? These writers lived in a time when nature and night, the greatest landscapes of the imagination, had not yet been illuminated by the advent of electricity. Science had only begun to explain things."

"You forgot Mary Shelley's *Frankenstein*."

Finn looked at Nathan Clare, who had spoken and was frowning down at his hands. Fairchild nodded. "And *Frankenstein*. The first work in which the other-worldly was—not quite—explained by science. What do these writings have in common? What theme do they share?"

Finn, who'd read most of those writers but didn't want to be a show-off, spoke carefully: "The heroes were taken by violent supernatural forces, by creatures of the dark."

Fairchild's gaze seemed troubled. "Exactly, Miss Sullivan. And all these dark forces—monsters, witches, changelings—*loved*. And, eventually, destroyed what they loved."

Why, Finn thought uneasily, *is he looking at me?*

PROFESSOR AVALINE, WHO RESEMBLED A model from Italian *Vogue* in her sleek dress and heels, led Finn's class through Fair Hollow's only museum, located in a neat and sprawling mansion by the river, a house once owned by the town's mayor.

As they passed the re-creation of a Native American feast straight out of a Thanksgiving storybook, someone asked, "How come there are no arrows in the pilgrims?"

Avaline's gaze skewered the speaker, and there were no more remarks.

They came to a room filled with displays of unusual artifacts the settlers had brought from their countries of origin: a dragon-shaped helmet; a painting of a scarlet-haired knight; an eerie, life-size wax doll; a sword with an ivory hilt shaped into a wolf. Avaline indicated a display of birds' nests. "These were found by the settlers. The natives said they were created by the spirits, who have always been here."

Finn stepped closer to the display. The knots of branches and straw were not birds' nests, but miniature houses or dolls with clay faces. Each was exquisitely made, strung with wooden beads and bits of stone. She thought uneasily that some of the beads looked like human teeth . . .

They call us things with teeth.

They entered the mock-up of a pub, the town's first gathering place, its wooden beams carved into naked fairies and leafy faces, the walls covered with black-and-white photographs of the past, each framed in ornate wood. As Finn walked along the rows of pictures, she thought of Sylvie, who collected old photographs because she loved to discover people's histories.

Finn saw grim people in Victorian clothing standing in front of shacks. Next to a blurry picture of the Ogun Metalworking plant was the photo of a horse-drawn coach. A young man in a long coat stood near the coach, dark hair spilling from a stovepipe hat that shadowed his face. The next photograph was from the 1920s. Poised on the stairs of a large house were a beautiful girl in a flapper's dress and a young man in an elegant suit. Finn read the caption beneath: *Lady Valentine and her husband, Lord Ryder, LeafStruck Mansion, 1922.* She looked carefully at Lady Valentine—who resembled Reiko Fata—an ancestor, then. The next photo was another of the young coachman who stood before the mansion, without his hat.

Gazing at her from the 1900s was Jack Fata.

OF COURSE IT COULDN'T HAVE been Jack.

Finn stayed late at HallowHeart's library, located in the atrium-like part of Armitrage. The floorboards creaked beneath her feet as she wandered the aisles, searching for books on Fair Hollow's history. There were none. There were plenty on New York history, with little paragraphs on Fair Hollow, but that was all.

The sun was already beginning to set as she left. When someone called her name across the leaf-scattered lawn, she turned to see Nathan Clare coming toward her. "Hi, Finn."

"Nathan." She regarded him warily, remembering the creepy, platinum-haired Fata's warning.

Nathan looked solemn, his gaze veiled by his lashes. "Sorry to bother you. But I've been in England for a while and I don't know anyone, other than my family and their friends, so I guess I just wanted to say hello."

She wondered why he was telling her this. She couldn't help thinking about what it must have been like for him, finding out both of his parents were gone. That they'd died in a fire was all the more horrifying.

"Would you like to go for coffee?" He rubbed the back of his neck. "I really need to get away from Aubrey Drake and his crew."

"Coffee. Sure." The hell with the platinum-haired Fata. "So who's the guy with the pale hair and gray eyes? A cousin? Something else?"

Nathan's mouth turned down. "Caliban."

"That's what he calls himself?"

"Yeah . . . Avoid him." As they began walking, he seemed to concentrate on his sneakered feet. Changing the subject, he asked, "What do you think of HallowHeart?"

"I think it's unique."

"Unique." He nodded, and his wounded look vanished into a bright smile. As she decided the Fatas must actively seek out orphaned hotties for their tribe, he continued, "That's a good term. I would say 'bizarre and old-fashioned.'"

"Well, it's not ordinary."

He looked down at his battered sneakers again. "Sometimes, it's nice to be ordinary, to just pretend you're who you're supposed to be."

"Are you pretending to be someone, Nathan?" She cast him a guarded look.

He met her gaze. "No."

"Good. Because, for a second there, I was worried."

As they continued making their way across the campus, he murmured, "You're friends with Jack."

"I know Jack, a little. He's not easy to know. Did you grow up together? I mean . . . after . . ."

"I came to the Fatas when I was younger." He shrugged. "It was a long time ago. Jack and I had a falling-out. We haven't spoken in all the time I was away. You'll be good for him."

"Will he be good for me?"

He was suspiciously silent, gazing at her. Carefully, he said, "Jack thinks he's not good for anyone."

He was being evasive, and he wasn't as practiced at it as Jack was. She would have to find a way around that. *Here,* Finn thought, *is a perfect source of Fata information.*

Nathan hefted one strap of his backpack farther onto his shoulder. "Do you know about the party on Halloween night?"

Her heart jumped as she remembered what Anna Weaver had said about Halloween and her death. "No."

"It's a masque—a costume party."

"Oh."

His attention was suddenly diverted by something behind her. Tracking his gaze, she saw a red Mercedes at the curb in front of Laurel Hall. He waved to the girl who had emerged from the car, her auburn hair tumbling from beneath a chauffeur's cap. Phouka, Reiko Fata's minion.

"I'll be right there," Nathan called to her. He looked pleadingly back at Finn. "Listen, would you like to go to the party? I need to go with another person on Halloween. I don't want my family to know I've got someone. You and I would just be attending as friends . . ."

She was a little worried about the way his fingers kept knotting and unknotting around the straps of his backpack. His fragile desperation made her determined to help as she wondered who the "someone" was he didn't want his family to know about.

"Okay." Impulsively, she continued, "Why don't you come over to my house tonight? Sylvie and Christie'll be there and I have coffee."

The girl driver, walking up to them, heard Finn's invitation and smiled at her. "I'll drive him."

Finn looked frantically at Nathan, who wouldn't meet her gaze. She glared at Phouka. "That's okay. We can pick him up—where do you live, Nathan?"

Phouka answered, sliding an arm through the crook of Nathan's, "LeafStruck Mansion. Seventy-seven Squire Road. I'll drive him, don't worry. Where do *you* live?"

Finn didn't look at Nathan this time. Reluctantly, she told Phouka her address.

"We'll see you tonight." Phouka smiled, and, as they strolled away, Finn wondered what she'd just invited to her house.

AS THE SUN BEGAN TO drop behind the Blackbird Mountains and the yard lights clicked on, Finn, Sylvie, and Christie set up a croquet game on the lawn of Finn's house. Sylvie's father, who owned a salvage shop, had cleaned and painted the old mallets, balls, and wickets free of charge. The croquet equipment was now decorated with chessboard patterns, painted flamingo pink, and lavished with red hearts—an homage to *Alice in Wonderland*.

"Amazing." Christie crouched on the steps, examining one of the black-and-white mallets. "I hope you appreciate Samuel Whitethorn's work, Finn."

Finn, who had forgiven him for his words about Jack Fata, was trying not to look agitated. "Where are they?"

"I can't believe you invited Nate Clare after that Caliban psycho threatened you." Christie toed a ball. "Do you like living on the edge?"

She didn't know what had possessed her to invite Nathan, other than the desire to get information from him about Jack and the Fatas—also, she really didn't like being bullied by Caliban.

Sylvie, experimentally swinging a mallet, paused and looked wistful. "Here they come."

Three figures emerged from the leafy shadows down the street; Nathan and Phouka had arrived—and Jack was with them. Finn felt a bewildering mix of dismay and delight. Phouka didn't seem quite so intimidating in a jacket of crimson fur and embroidered jeans. Nathan wore a short coat and gray corduroys. Jack was all dark hues, as usual.

As he came near, Finn murmured, "Hey."

Then she saw his expression.

"You don't mind that I've come?" he said, his gaze scornful. "We were *invited*, after all."

She glanced at Sylvie and Christie, who looked like the innocents in a fairy tale, as the wolves circled and chose their mallets with careful and cunning skill. She strode toward her friends, her voice low with determination: "We can do this."

"What are the stakes? We won't play without a prize." Jack twirled his mallet and Finn wanted to run from him, hit him, and kiss him all at the same time. He leveled a look at her as he continued, "And invitations don't come without a price."

"You want *money*?" Christie's easygoing manner had vanished—he was watching Jack with hostility. "For *associating* with us?"

"A kiss." Phouka's smile was devilish. Her auburn hair was loose, knotted into braids at the front. She was as pretty as one of those fresh-faced models from the 1960s.

"From each. If we win."

"I'll do it," Christie murmured. To Finn, he said, "But I'm only kissing the girl . . . maybe Nathan. But not *him*."

"What do *we* get?" Sylvie was watching Nathan, who looked guarded, his hands wrapped around a mallet with familiar ease.

"We'll give each of you something precious." Phouka flashed an antique bracelet. "We've all brought nice things."

Finn parted her lips to question them further, but Sylvie said, "Deal. Let's get to it."

Annoyed by her friends' recklessness, Finn accepted her mallet from Christie, who was watching Phouka. He said, as if to himself, " '*She seemed, at once, some penanced lady elf, some demon's mistress, or the demon's self.*' "

"Why are you quoting Keats?" demanded Sylvie, a red leaf tangled in her hair. A ball shot past her, through two hoops, and struck a tree with enough force to splinter the bark. Finn, Christie, and Sylvie looked hard at their opponents. Phouka politely clapped her hands.

Jack twirled his mallet and stepped aside. Finn narrowed her eyes at him.

Christie hefted his mallet as if it were a sword. "Let's begin already."

It was a lunatic game, played with ferocious glee by their opponents—as if Phouka was the Red Queen teamed up with Jack's Mad Hatter and Nathan's gallant White Knight. When Nathan's ball slid through seven hoops, he seemed almost apologetic. Christie knocked his ball through one hoop. As another whistled past his head, he ducked and swore. Finn hadn't thought croquet could be so combative.

"On the *ground*." She pointed her mallet at Jack. "Keep it on the *ground*. This isn't hockey."

As Jack lithely avoided the ball that cracked toward him from Christie's mallet, Finn, standing next to Nathan, murmured, "Did you and Jack make up?"

"When he found out I was coming here, he decided to accompany us."

More whoops and hollers followed as they dove and ran, ignoring slight injuries and leaves in their hair from the surrounding shrubbery.

"They're winning." Christie looked grim, his dark red hair sticking up in twists. "I really don't want them to win."

Finn pushed him aside, smiled at Jack, and raised her mallet to strike her ball.

A black ball sliced hers from beneath her.

Jack lifted his chin and stood with his hands on the top of his mallet as she turned away, silently vowing revenge.

The defeat came as Nathan deflected Christie's ball and knocked Phouka's through three wickets.

Like the bad-guy gunslingers from a spaghetti western, the three Fatas strolled toward Finn and her allies, the glow of new evening settling across their pale skin and silvering their eyes. Nathan shyly claimed his kiss from Sylvie, who was not so shy, and stood on tiptoe to return it. Christie smiled when Phouka, who was as tall as he, clasped his face in her hands and kissed him until his eyes closed.

Then Jack stood before Finn. She didn't know what to say. She whispered, "Are you a gentleman?"

He leaned close. She shut her eyes, her face burning, as his lips brushed her cheek. She kept her hands on top of the mallet, but his hands rose to cup her face. Only an inch away from him, she could smell evergreen, roses, wood smoke. Those photographs in the museum told her he and Reiko were from an old family, with ancestors who had been here since the town's beginning, but they had also made her wonder . . .

He leaned close, his fingertips moving along her neck, to her collarbones. She remained still as a hunted thing. His mouth only a breath from hers, he whispered, "Finn Sullivan, you shouldn't have invited us."

"Jack." Phouka's voice dragged him back.

Without taking his kiss, he spun away from Finn and swaggered after his companions, calling, "Good night, Greensleeves."

"Good night." Nathan glanced wistfully over one shoulder. "It was fun."

Watching them walk into the night, Finn drew a deep breath and realized that her safe world of schoolwork and breakfast and television was now being compromised by *their* strange, not-so-safe reality of abandoned mansions and revels after dusk.

Defeated—Jack's and Phouka's presences had made it impossible for her to interrogate Nathan—Finn turned back to Christie and Sylvie.

"That wasn't weird at all."

FINN SPENT AN ENTIRE LATE afternoon hunched over her laptop researching the Fatas and pretending she might be able to use the results in Avaline's history class. She was soon surrounded by images printed from Fair Hollow's historical archives.

Lady Valentine Fata had been Reiko Fata's grandmother, but Finn couldn't find the name of the Jack-like coachman in the Victorian pictures. She went to another site called Victoriana and typed in *Coachmen. Fair Hollow*, with no luck. She tried simply, *Fata*.

The face of Lady Valentine Fata appeared, raven hair cascading over her shoulders. The caption read *Actress playing Aphrodite. 1827*. Finn returned to Fair Hollow's historical archives and searched every male face in the Fata family photographs.

She found him leaning against a silver Rolls-Royce, his dark hair tucked beneath a chauffeur's cap, one ungloved hand, resting on the car, gleaming with antique rings. The fine features and curving mouth were Jack's. The caption read *LeafStruck Mansion, 1927*.

Unearthly cold now tainted the air of her bedroom. A draft scattered the printed photos over the floor. *LeafStruck Mansion*. Phouka had said that's where the Fatas lived.

When a wind kissed her skin, she looked up to find the doors to her terrace had fallen open. Sharp fear twisted through her.

She set aside the laptop and rose to face the figure who stood there, dark hair swept over his face. He didn't wear a coat now, only jeans and a buttoned shirt of gauzy linen. A wreath of roses circled his brow—he looked as if he'd just come from some pagan ritual. His gaze flickered over the prints on the floor and his eyes narrowed. Softly, he said, "May I come in?"

"Jack." Her voice shook. "Could you maybe use the front door next time?" She glanced down at the printed photographs and sighed. "You can come in."

Jack stepped in, then crouched down to gaze at one of the images. He lifted his gaze to hers. "Why do you have pictures of my ancestors all over your floor?"

She felt as if he was really saying, *What did curiosity do to the cat?* She blushed and felt like a stalker herself. She sat on the floor, her arms on her knees, her toes curled. Her heart was racing. "It's a project."

Calmly, he continued, "It's a small town. It's an *old* town. People sometimes resemble their ancestors."

"Stop," she whispered. "How come I've never seen you *in the day*?"

"Finn," he said, sitting back on his heels, "I didn't think you were the type to get paranoid."

While she huddled, he reached out and picked up one of the prints. He had a new tattoo on the back of his hand, a black Celtic cross. She slid another print toward him. "This is from the 1800s. And this, from the twenties . . . they all look like you."

He crouched before her and she waited for a sensible explanation. Then he spoke, his voice hoarse: "I won't hurt you. I would never hurt you."

She looked away from him, down at the picture of the Victorian coachman with *his* face. She closed her eyes. What she was thinking wasn't possible. Her hands were shaking, and she knotted them together to keep him from seeing her steadily growing panic as a horrifying theory began to form. "Jack . . . why won't you ever tell me about yourself? Like, *real* things?"

When she opened her eyes, she was alone in the cold room, with the papers swirling around her like discarded memories.

Finn had gone often to Golden Gate Park with Lily Rose and Leander Cyrus, her sister's boyfriend. She would feed the red carp in the pond near the pagoda while Leander photographed people. One day, when Leander hadn't been with them, she'd watched Lily Rose speaking with a well-dressed stranger whose hair had been the color of autumn leaves and whose eyes had been as blue as a wolf's. As she gazed at the scattered printouts of Jack's and Reiko's look-alikes, she experienced the same feeling of *otherness* she'd had that day.

Who are you, Jack Fata?

Phouka had told her where the Fatas lived. She grabbed her laptop and googled *LeafStruck Mansion.*

IT WASN'T FAR. BUT IT was seven thirty and it was dark and Finn had to bike because she'd never learned to drive in San Francisco.

LeafStruck was a large, old house covered in Emory, with extravagant stone carvings peeking from the leaves. Its windows were shuttered, its doors of heavy timber wreathed with moss, its towers and walkway clotted with wild clover and gloom. Behind it, she saw a crumbling carriage house floating in a sea of Emory and oaks. There was no way the Fatas, privileged and glamorous, could be living in this wreck.

She left her bike and moved up the steep stairs. *All she had to do was push the doorbell.*

"What are you doing?"

She flinched and swore with delicate ferocity. "Jack."

"Finn." His voice shouldn't have caused a conflict of warmth and dread within her, but it did. She turned and decided to be defiant instead of defensive. "Isn't this where your family lives?"

He was seated on the porch railing, in the shadows . . . as if he'd been waiting for her. "Not anymore."

"Why're you being so evasive about where your family—"

"Only one person lives here." He rose then and pushed the door open. The flicker of scorn she'd noticed earlier had returned. "Would you like to meet her?"

"I'm not going into another strange place with you. You yelled at me about SatyrN—"

"I'm inviting you. Go on. I should think your curiosity is rabid, now that you think I'm some kind of vampire."

She scowled because he was right. "You're trying to scare me. Well, it won't work."

Defiantly, cautiously, she stepped into the shadows of LeafStruck.

It took her eyes a moment to adjust to the moonlight frosting decayed furniture and a floor littered with leaves. As a rancid, animal scent drowned the sweetish fragrance of clover, she turned in place and watched Jack's shadow flock over the peeling wallpaper. She said, "Your ancestors lived here?"

"Once."

"Why'd they leave?" Red toadstools covered a moisture-warped wardrobe. A sapling had rooted through one wall.

"They had bad luck—" He flinched from a wooden rocking horse he'd touched. "Splinter." His next words were quiet, "I'm bleeding again."

She moved toward him. "It's only blood."

He stared down at the drop of red on his finger. Then he smiled, but his eyes were dark, almost scared. "You don't even know what you've done."

"What have I done?" She stepped back.

He moved forward, quick, and bent his head toward hers. His scent of green things and wild roses made her dizzy. She could feel warmth radiating from his usually cool skin. "You've bewitched me. It was supposed to be the other way 'round."

When he turned away, she felt abandoned. To cover her disappointment, she said, "So are you going to tell me who lives here?"

His hair glistened in blackberry tendrils as he tilted his head. "The caretaker. Come."

Hands clenched in her coat pockets, Finn followed Jack into a hall gloomy with stuttering electric light. At the hall's end, she saw a room with a glistening piano and leaves and dead moths covering the floor.

"She's upstairs." He led her up a stairway, its banister carved to resemble vines. Portraits were hung on the ascending wall, pictures of stern, yellow-eyed people. She glimpsed the age-darkened painting of a brown-haired girl in white, her arms cradling an infant in feathers. The painting reminded her of her mother's mysterious figures in watercolor.

"So"—Jack sounded casual as they continued up the stairs—"who told you about LeafStruck?"

"Phouka. But I saw it referred to in a caption on a photograph at the Fair Hollow museum, and it was mentioned in a caption in those old photos I found online."

"Those photographs of my ancestors?"

"Yes. So Phouka lied about your family living here now. Why?"

"She's a contrary sort of person."

Finn wanted to growl at him. The stairs creaked beneath her sneakers, but Jack was soundless before her even though he wore boots. He led her down another hall cascading with the Emory that had grown through cracks in the boarded-up windows and over arthritic furniture. It did occur to her that he really *might* be crazy, that this might be the lair where he placed the bodies of dead girls, like Bluebeard in the fairy tale. She remembered the ghostly girl near Drake's Chapel and hoped she hadn't really been a ghost.

He looked back at her as if sensing her thoughts and grinned. "I'm not going to devour you."

"Jack—"

"Hush." He knocked on a door. Light flickered beneath it. Her apprehension began to crest when she heard a rustling from within. He said, politely, "*Cailleach Oidche.*" Finn, remembering the old Gaelic her father had taught her, thought, *The owl.*

The door clicked open, releasing stale air like a sigh. As Jack stepped forward, Finn reluctantly followed him into a room that seemed constructed of ancient wood and gray gossamer, with a fire burning in a hearth of old brick. A table near the window was scattered with dozens of ornamental eggs—painted, jeweled, or carved from wood, some with illustrations of Russian folklore. Only one lamp was lit.

The chamber's occupant was tall and skinny, and she wore a filmy white dress and a wide-brimmed hat. The hat's veil, covering her face, was stained brown over the mouth. Gloved hands held a porcelain teacup. Finn didn't want to look at her—a sense of *wrongness*, of danger, crawled across her skin.

The woman tilted her veiled head. Her voice was faint, "Jack Daw. Have you anything for me?"

"Not this time," he spoke gently. "Colleen Olive. I need a favor."

"No gift? No mice? No sparrow in a wicker cage? The last time, it was a rabbit."

"Colleen, this is Finn." To Finn, he said, "She's not right in the head. Whatever she says—"

"*Finn.*" The veiled head turned toward Finn, who had listened to the strange list and hoped the woman was only revealing a gruesome sense of humor. When the woman extended one gloved hand and said, "Come, *caileag*, let me have a look at you," Finn walked across the room, almost stepping on a tiny bird skeleton in a heap of leaves. She shuddered. The woman beckoned her closer. Finn delicately clasped her hand, pretending the glove wasn't speckled with stains. "Pleased to meet you, Miss Olive."

"Oh. A *polite* child. Have *you* brought anything for me?"

Finn took a quick, personal inventory. Carefully, she slid from her finger the ring of tiny pink hearts her father had given her. "Could you tell me where the Fatas live—"

Jack was suddenly at her side, his fingers closing around her hand. "No exchanges. *I'm* asking the favor."

The eerie, unformed face beneath the veil turned toward Jack, and Finn shuddered again when she thought she heard the woman sniff.

"*Cro.*" The voice creaked. "You *reek* of it." She snapped to her feet, hissed. "*How?* How did you manage *that?*"

"Never mind, Colleen. I want to know what Phouka has said to you. About Finn. Why did she want Finn to come here?"

"You will tell me why you are ripe"—the faint voice had a crafty lilt now—"my fine Jack? Tell me how you run red."

"Jack?" Finn had begun backing away, because the woman's words were crazy. She wanted out of the hot room and its unpleasant odors of burning wood and dead mice.

"Finn." Jack stretched out a hand. "Don't be afraid."

She shook her head as the woman voiced a laugh that sounded like the hunting cry of an owl and said, "Does the *luch bheag* want to know what happens to girls who run with Jacks?"

"Jack." Finn watched the woman begin to lift the veil. "What is she—"

"Finn." He looked at her, his eyes silvered.

She turned away before she could see what was behind that veil and ran out the door. She clattered down the stairs, out of the house, down the leafy path.

On the street, she halted, and turned to gaze at LeafStruck.

She waited for Jack because she didn't want to walk in the dark alone and because there might be worse things in the night.

JACK KNELT BEFORE THE CAILLEACH *Oidche*, who clutched her veil and murmured to herself, her honey-colored eyes half closed. White-streaked brown hair tumbled around her face, which was still that of a lovely girl.

"I frightened her." Colleen Olive sighed. Her eyes widened and her sharp teeth bit at her bottom lip. "I did not mean to. Oh, Jack, am I such a monster?"

He gazed at her, at the young woman who had been Nathan Clare's governess, and, once, something much more to Jack. Bitter anger coiled through him. His family twisted everything.

"We are both monsters. And I think Phouka meant for you to frighten her."
He gently folded her gloved hands over the veil. "Did Phouka tell you anything
about her?"

"Nothing, Jack. Nothing at all."

AS FINN SULLENLY WATCHED JACK stroll toward her from the
shadows of LeafStruck, he idly said, "So you've met Colleen Olive."

"Are they all crazy? Your family?"

"Not all. And she's more of a distant cousin."

"Well, you succeeded in scaring me, Jack Fata." She whirled and strode to her
bike. She yanked it up and began walking it. "But your other cousin or whatever
already did a good job of it."

He caught up to her, striding beside her. "My cousin . . . ?"

"The one with the pale hair, all *American Psycho*?"

"Caliban."

"That's his real name?"

"That's his real name. So, you see"—his voice was soft—"what we're like now,
don't you?"

"There's eccentric, Jack, and there's crazy."

"And which do you think we are?"

"Your family?" She turned on him and felt suddenly as if she was losing something she'd never find again. She tried not to sound desperate. "Or us? *Why* did
you take me in there?"

"Do you still think I'm a vamp—"

"No, of course not." She clutched the bike's handlebars. "I was stupid, okay?"

He rubbed at the bridge of his nose, and his rings glinted. He dropped his
hand and said, "Would you like to watch some old movies at my place?"

"You mean in the movie theater?" She considered this. "What movies?"

"There used to be a studio here in the 1920s. I've got some reels."

"Silent films? Like on a projector?"

He turned away, as he said, "My car's parked over here. We'll put your bike in
the backseat. Coming?"

She thought she shouldn't. But he was a mystery she desperately wanted to solve, and talking to him was fascinating. She steered the bike toward him and said, "Can we get something to eat first?"

He looked blank for a moment. Then: "Food. Right."

HE DROVE THEM TO MAX'S Diner, a streamlined throwback with a '50s theme. She ordered a hamburger, a shake, and fries and watched as he made origami animals out of paper napkins. She frowned. "You sure you're not hungry?"

He flashed a smile. "I'm good."

"So what are the movies?" There was an unspoken agreement between them not to talk about his family, and she was frustrated by it, but she'd follow his rules.

"They don't really have names. Most were never released; you won't recognize the actors."

"Any westerns?"

"Some."

She narrowed her eyes, curled one hand into a gun shape, aimed it at him. "None as good as Clint Eastwood's."

He grinned. "None of the heroes in silent films smacked women around or spit on dogs."

"But that's what makes spaghetti westerns so awesome." She twirled her straw in her milkshake. "The antiheroes."

"Girls these days." He shook his head. "Being an antihero—would that make *me* awesome?"

"What's attractive in fiction isn't necessarily attractive in real life."

He nodded. "The Wild West was dirty and brutal."

"And knights in shining armor were jerks."

"And pirates were nautical psychopaths."

Finn liked this truce between them. "Let's go watch some old-timey cinema."

THE THEATER BELOW HIS APARTMENT smelled like stone and mold. Two lamps were lit near the doors. The baroque charm had been preserved by Jack, because some of his friends—the vagabond theater majors, no doubt—loved old movies. The plush seats and gilt details were well cared for, and the perennial fairies and gnomes gilded the area where the screen cranked down.

As Finn watched shaky images of raccoon-eyed starlets and actors, Jack occasionally left her to change the reels. When a pretty outlaw in black stalked across the screen, she saw a light flicker in a corner of the theater and thought of the restroom in the Caribbean restaurant and what she'd seen there, that black-furred hand that might not have been her imagination. She ignored the glimmering and wondered if a person could *will* away crazy.

Jack settled beside her. He leaned toward her and began explaining the plots and actors, whom he seemed to know a lot about despite their being unknown. She listened, distracted by his closeness, his voice. She hadn't really told anyone about her friendship with him, although Christie and Sylvie seemed to suspect.

"It was called StarDust Studios," he said, close to her ear. "It was owned by Malcolm Tirnagoth's wife, a troubled soul."

"How come none of these actors became famous?"

"A couple of them did—only not in a good way." He looked back at the screen, where a new melodrama was beginning. She saw an art nouveau room and a young man standing with his back to the camera. He began to turn—

Jack was out of his seat so quickly, she only noticed he was gone when the film cut off. She twisted around to see him fiddling with the projector. "Hey! I was watching that."

"It's broken."

She rose and walked to him. He was setting aside the film reel in red casing and choosing another. She picked up the red reel. "Can't you fix it?"

"No." He didn't look up from fiddling with the projector. His coat was off and his sleeves rolled up. Dark hair swept across his profile and he wouldn't look at her. She realized he didn't *want* her to see what was in the crimson reel. She opened it and examined the strip. "It seems fine."

He looked at her, and his eyes were very dark. "Finn, I said it's broken."

She continued to hold it out. "Put it back on."

"It's 1920s porn."

"You know how I can tell when you lie? You won't look at me."

He was tight-lipped and grim—and he wouldn't look at her.

Quietly, she said, "One of your ancestors is in it, right? A look-alike. I want to see the rest."

He straightened, took the reel from her, and flung it into the shadows.

"Unbelievable." She turned and stalked toward the exit. "I'll bike home."

He called after her, "Emotional blackmail won't work!"

She pushed through the doors, back into her world.

WHEN THE YOUNG MAN WITH the long, platinum hair and the quicksilver eyes had swaggered up to her at the autumn revel, Angyll Weaver had forgotten all about Christie Hart the jerk. She was currently ignoring her scowling little sister.

"He's bad."

"Yeah, he is—that's why I want him around." Angyll didn't look up from her iPhone. "He didn't give me a number though, or e-mail. That's weird. But interesting."

Anna lingered in the bedroom doorway. "Angyll . . ."

"You are *so* annoying." Angyll flounced up, gently shoved her sister back, and shut the door.

Caliban was a Fata. Angyll had kept a wary distance from Reiko Fata and her sexy brother and the others in that bizarro family she'd scornfully dismissed as wealthy inbreeds. But Caliban had taken an interest in her. He'd told her to meet him in Soldiers' Gate Cemetery, if she dared. She'd hesitated, sensibly, then shrugged and decided to send a text to a few of her friends, letting them know. That would cover the safety issue, and she had the pepper spray Kevin Gilchriste had given her.

She selected a coat, a silky silver dress, and heels that would match.

AT DUSK, ANGYLL WEAVER SLID through the iron bars and into Soldiers' Gate Cemetery. The thrill of doing something reckless made her feel brave as she threaded through the tombstones. A chilly wind sliced across her skin as she called his name.

"Here." Caliban Fata sat on the base of a headless statue. He leaped down and approached her. Angyll shivered as he clasped her hands in his. He wore a ring on every finger, and they looked like they'd belonged to kings.

"Look at you, all shiny and glittery." His smile was ferocious.

"You said you'd show me something amazing . . . and it better not be a sex thing."

He raised a finger to his lips. He turned and, still holding one of her hands, led her through the tombstones. She felt a little shiver of fear, but he looked back at her like some gorgeous, evil angel, and she decided they'd be perfect together.

He stopped in front of a mausoleum with a female sphinx on its roof and a stone door with the word *Luneht* carved on it.

"Luneht." Angyll moved up the steps, then twirled to face him. "You trying to scare me? I know the story—their son was led away into the woods and he came back different. He hung himself from an oak tree."

"Actually, it was an elder tree. Witches like elder trees."

"This isn't the amazing thing, is it?" She idly kicked the door.

"That's not it." He moved up the steps toward her. His voice was husky. "Brave girl."

She laughed, giddy.

Then he kissed her. His mouth was cold. His fingers were brutal as they twisted in her hair. She shuddered against him. He nipped at her ear and whispered something so low she couldn't understand. She said, "What?"

He leaned closer and spoke clearly, "You are such a boring, hollow, selfish thing."

She flinched. "What are you talking about?"

He spat in the grass. "I'll have to wash my hair now that you've had your fingers in it, and drink wine to get the taste of you out of my mouth."

She couldn't believe this was happening, couldn't imagine a more horrifying humiliation.

"You made me come here . . . for *this*?" She backed away. "They set me up, didn't they? Christie and his two *bitches* . . ."

"That's not why I brought you here." He walked to the door of the tomb and traced the name. "Thomas Luneht wasn't a witch. He was a fighter. He fought me when I strung him up. I didn't even have to lure him—he came right at me."

Angyll went very still.

Caliban turned and smiled at her. "He was one of my favorites—pretty and young and he thought he was clever."

Her eyes fixed on his face, Angyll backed down one step. "Stop it."

Caliban raised one hand, indicating the ring on his middle finger. "That was his." He lowered the hand and looked admiringly down at it. "I've got a ring for each of my favorite ones . . . if they didn't have rings, I had one made from something on their body. This was from a Greek shepherdess. This was from an Iroquois brave. I made him drink his own blood. This is my best—this girl loved me. For a whole year. I think I ate her. And this ruby is from a boy who thought I would save him from another of my kind. He was wrong."

Angyll shook her head and took another step down. "Stop. *Stop it.*"

"You want to see something amazing now?" He grinned.

She saw his shadow twisting and bleeding into a doglike form over the grass. She didn't look at him because she sensed what had happened—the lovely statue of Cal Fata had broken open to reveal something else.

She turned and ran for her life. As she hurtled among the tombstones, she felt something silvery and cold chasing her, becoming solid, massive, hungry. She didn't look back. She didn't dare.

She fumbled for the pepper spray in her purse, twisted around to use it—

A stone tilted beneath her foot. She screamed as she fell.

Her head struck granite, and blood splashed the face of a marble cherub perched on a grave.

THE DECAYING WEST WALL OF the Tirnagoth Hotel's ballroom was painted with a mural depicting a crowned man in armor holding a staff topped with a human skull. Wolves surrounded him, and in the shadows of a nearby forest, a woman in red watched, black hair veiling her face. Her bare arms were painted with inky spirals. In the mural's center was a boy in a green tunic and a wreath of flowers. He was crouched in the branches of a tree, his hair citrus-bright.

The Monarch, the Queen, the Fool.

Jack turned his back on the mural, striding down the hall. He passed beneath an arch shaped into an openmouthed gorgon's face, then stepped into an Emory-walled chamber where books were piled everywhere. The fragrance of old leather and aged paper was strong. Incense and candles flickered in lanterns of blue glass.

A girl was sprawled in a thronelike chair, one leg flung over an armrest, ivory hair spilling in plaits around her face. Tall and gawky, she wore hip-hugging jeans and a coat of pale fur. She was barefoot; tarnished rings decorated her toes.

She was the family librarian, the record keeper. She said, "Tell me why you've come, Jack, tell me true."

"I've a question, Norn. A family question."

"Your scent is odd. I don't like it."

"Does that mean you don't like me anymore?"

"Like is love's false sibling."

"Says one who has never loved nor liked."

She leaned forward, her face shadowy. "It is Seth Lot's lust and Reiko's greed that have placed all of us in peril."

"Yet they've got themselves a Teind." He tried not to feel rage when he thought about that.

"And so we escape from Death's cruel bind." She sat back, her hands, tattooed with silver spirals, resting on the arms of the chair. Because she was perverse, she said, "'I'll go to my queen and beg her Indian boy; and then I will her charmed eye release, from monster's view, all things shall be peace.'"

"You stole that from Shakespeare."

"Why not? He stole from us." She smiled. "Who is it that has you bleeding like a virgin girl from her bridal bed?"

"No one. I'm no different than I was. Norn . . . did you ever know a girl named Lily Rose? When you were in San Francisco? Because this girl named Lily Rose had an imaginary friend by the name of *Norn*. I find that odd. It's not a common name for an imaginary friend."

She shrugged. "I never remember the names of the ones I charm."

"I find names to be important. Lily Rose is dead now—suicide." He watched the girl carefully, but he saw nothing—the ice didn't crack.

"Jack." She leaned forward. "Do you think Reiko doesn't know you're bleeding? She's being indulgent."

"Why do you say Reiko's being indulgent?"

"Our beautiful boy Nathan, and the schoolgirl who made you bleed . . . they were meant to be. The girl could save him. Why do you think Reiko allows you to make eyes at her, Jack? To keep her from Nathan."

He ducked his head to conceal a flash of rage at the idea of Finn and Nathan, together.

"There." Norn sat back, remote again. "I've told you something you didn't know."

He stalked from the chamber to the first-floor conservatory, where his family lounged, playing games or instruments, surrounded by moonlit bromeliads and blackberry vines beneath a glass dome patterned with poisonous-looking art nouveau flowers. Nathan Clare sat in a lamp-lit corner, reading a book. When Jack approached, he looked up, apprehensive. He dropped his gaze, gripping the book.

Jack said quietly, "Look at me."

Nathan, starry-eyed with fear, obeyed. "What do you want, Jack?"

Jack slid into a crouch, hands clasped between his knees. He spoke gently, "Why did Finn invite you for croquet?"

"Because—we're friends. Nothing more. Look, I didn't know you were interested in her—Jack, please . . . just stay away from her. Just leave her be. She's—"

"Have you changed your mind? Or lost it? You've lasted this long without true love; don't bloody well start looking for it now."

Terror darkened Nathan's eyes and he whispered, "I know what I have to do, Jack, and I will do it—because I don't want to end up like *you*."

As Jack bared his teeth, Nathan flicked his gaze up and whispered, "*Jack* . . ."

Sensing something behind him, Jack rose to his feet.

A serpentine form bled from the shadows and Reiko Fata stepped forward, slender and gorgeous in a gown of black silk, her bare arms wound with bracelets. "Jack. Are you being cruel to Nathan?"

"We were having a conversation."

Reiko looked at Nathan, who glanced away, his mouth tight. She slid her gaze to Jack and sweetly said, "This conversation isn't about a girl named after a hero king, is it?"

Jack didn't give anything away. "Finn Sullivan's not interested in Nate. She's *my* trick."

"She is, Jack." Reiko leaned close, her lips against his. "And make certain she remains a trick."

CHAPTER EIGHT

See yonder Hallow'd Fane! The pious work
Of Names once fam'd, now dubious or forgot,
And buried 'midst the Wreck of Things which were:
There lie interr'd the more illustrious Dead.

　　　　　　　　　—THE GRAVE, ROBERT BLAIR

Once, a very young crow became lost from her tribe. She was their
storm gatherer, for the Rooks loved storms. One day, lonely, she took
human form. Dressed in black dewdrops and violets, she walked
into a gathering of the enemy. And a young man named Malcolm
Tirnagoth saw her . . .

　　　　　　　　　—FROM THE JOURNAL OF LILY ROSE

The morning brought common sense and sunlight as Finn wondered how she'd apologize to Jack. She'd let her imagination run wild last night. Jack and Reiko Fata, having lived in Fair Hollow all their lives, of course had ancestors who resembled them. She'd been crazy to think otherwise. And the crazy part was what worried her . . .

As the autumn sun burned away the chill in her room, she tucked Lily Rose's journal and the photocopies of Fair Hollow's past, with its old-fashioned, inky-eyed replicas of Jack and Reiko Fata, into Lily's trunk.

The sun was bright, and Finn savored it as she strode from her house to Christie's Mustang.

Christie was pale and shadowy-eyed behind the wheel. Worried, she halted. "Christie?"

"Angyll's in the hospital."

"Angyll Weaver?" She slowly slid into the car.

"They found her in Soldiers' Gate yesterday. She fell and hit her head against a stone. Who goes alone to a cemetery, at night?"

As the Mustang creaked forward, Finn murmured, "What was she doing in the cemetery?"

"She won't wake up so no one knows." He was clutching the wheel, his face bleak.

Finn hugged her backpack to her chest. Her stomach twisted with guilt, because a girl she'd hit in the face now lay broken in the hospital.

AT LUNCH, FINN LISTLESSLY TWIRLED spaghetti around her fork while gazing out the cafeteria window at Christie, who sat on the steps, his head down. Opposite her, Sylvie was slouched in her chair, gnawing at an apple. She said, "Let's go."

They dumped their food and went to sit next to him. He had an unlit cigarette between his lips. He said casually, "Kevin Gilchriste told me Angyll had a new fiend—I mean *friend*. Want to know who?"

Finn didn't like the bitter darkness in his voice as he flipped the cigarette in his fingers, pocketed it, and said, "He has pale hair and gray eyes. Sound familiar?"

Finn grimly remembered Angyll flirting with the pale-haired young man at the autumn revel. "The scary one we met at the Voodoo Lounge. The one who went at Sylv at the revel."

"All the Fatas are scary," Sylvie said, tugging on her dark braids. "They're like a bunch of mad aristocrats from the turn of the century."

"*Inbred* aristocrats," Christie gently corrected.

Finn wanted to tell them about LeafStruck and Colleen Olive, the eccentric and scary cousin Jack had introduced her to. She wanted to tell them about the antique photographs of Jack's and Reiko's ancestors. Instead, she said, "Nathan's not like them. Jack isn't either."

"Finn"—Christie's voice was quiet—"are you out of your mind?"

"Jack seems okay to me." Sylvie turned back to Finn, her eyes dark with concern. "And Nathan's adopted."

"I think Jack is, too. Where do the Fatas live? Don't either of you know?"

Christie opened his hands. "Some big estate out in a scary hollow?"

"Where, exactly? You and Sylvie have lived here all your lives and you don't know where the wealthiest, oddest family lives? Isn't that strange?"

"Yeah." Christie stared into space as Sylvie looked troubled and whispered, "Where *do* they live, Christie?"

AFTER CLASSES, FINN AND SYLVIE went to Hecate's Attic to see Angyll's sister.

Anna sat in a rocking chair near a display of painted toys. As Sylvie crouched before her and clasped her hands, Finn stood awkwardly nearby. Sylvie said, "Anna. Where are your parents?"

"The hospital. My aunt Penelope is here." Anna's hair was in her face. When she looked at Finn, one eye glittered behind the golden strands. "They are at war with us now."

Finn remembered Anna telling her she was going to die on Halloween and felt a helpless sadness for the younger girl. "I'm sorry about Angyll."

Anna sighed and shoved her hair from her face. "I didn't mean to tell you about Halloween. It's what the Fates showed me and sometimes they're tricky. I tried to find out more, but they won't show me."

"Anna . . . what happened to Angyll?" Finn chose to ignore Anna's schizy revelation about war and the Fates and her death on Halloween. She didn't believe it anyway. She didn't want to believe it.

Anna looked at the table, where three illustrated cards had been turned faceup. "The laughing moon got her."

"Anna—"

"You want to know where they live." Anna was gazing down at her hands. "That man, the rich one, gave his hotel to them in exchange for the dead bird bringing his children back."

"Malcolm Tirnagoth," Sylvie whispered. "The Tirnagoth Hotel."

"But you said it's a *ruin*." Finn didn't care to ask about the dead bird. "They *can't* live there."

"Only sometimes." Anna clenched her hands, fierce. "I hate them."

Finn scrutinized Anna's Tarot cards and saw the images of a curved moon dripping blood, a pale figure with a sword in its back, a black-haired female hooded in scarlet, holding a snake. The images made her skin crawl. She said with quiet determination, "Tirnagoth."

Sylvie groaned. "Oh no."

"Should we ask Christie to come with us?"

Sylvie sat back on her heels. "I wish you wouldn't—but he'll do it." She met Finn's puzzled look with a dark gaze. "For you. So, Anna, will the Fates let you come with us and get hot fudge sundaes at Max's?"

IN THE LATE AFTERNOON, CHRISTIE drove Finn and Sylvie to the warehouse district, into the parking lot of a grubby apartment building that vented loud music and the pungent aroma of something that probably wasn't incense.

"It's safe here." He tapped the rusty hood of his Mustang. "My friend Micah lives in the building—that's his Chevy. Tirnagoth is over there."

As he pointed to a woodsy road across the street, Finn strode forward, palming the flashlight she'd brought. They each had one. "Let's go."

"Obsessed, Finn?" Sylvie followed with a swagger.

"Curious."

"Is that why you brought the camera?"

Finn said defensively, "I need interesting photos for Basic Photography. It's just reconnaissance."

"This is about Jack," Christie informed Sylvie, "the Byronic and fashionable loner who's probably secretly wed to his sister."

Finn flashed her light on him. "Reiko's not his real sister."

"My bad." Christie's smile was wolfish. "Can you put a good word in for me with Reiko? Like give her my phone number—ow! Sylv, hands aren't for *hitting*."

They trudged through bushes and weeds until a pair of swirling metal gates loomed before them, beneath massive trees. The peaked roof of the hotel rose above the branches of a small forest.

"The gates are locked." Sylvie turned to Finn.

Finn gazed at the art nouveau metal swirled into the form of a moth . . .

She reached into her pocket for the moth key she'd found in a toadstool ring beneath her window. She scarcely believed it when it fit into the lock and there was a click. The gates opened with only a faint rustling of disturbed shrubbery.

"Where did you get that?" Christie stared at the key.

Finn shrugged. "It was a gift."

"From him?"

"Maybe." Finn moved forward.

Christie looked at Sylvie. "She's so enigmatic. Like Batman."

"More like Catwoman."

"Is Catwoman really enigmatic? I think she's pretty straightforward."

As they approached the hotel, it loomed before them, its trinity of briar-tangled buildings surrounding a courtyard fronted with more gates of wrought metal. The rooftops had greened with lichen. Gargoyles with the upper bodies of beautiful women crouched on the stairs leading to the entrance. The first- and second-floor windows were covered with plywood. It must have been gorgeous at one time, an architectural masterpiece of organic art nouveau and Gothic spikiness.

Sylvie whistled softly. Christie looked at Finn. "No one lives here. Unless the Fatas are ghosts."

Finn thought of ghostly girls, of the Fatas' pale skin, of Jack's abandoned movie theater. She had *tried* rational explanations . . .

"I want to see." She moved forward, ignoring the sudden tilt of vertigo.

Christie murmured, "Of course you do."

As they pushed through the thick undergrowth, Finn flinched as a pale face emerged from the wall of leaves, then sighed when she saw that it was only the statue of an armless girl. Beneath its eyes were water stains like black tears.

Christie peered up at the nearest window, a Gothic arch framed by a riot of briars. "It smells like a graveyard."

"That's just wet stone." Sylvie gripped the gate as she peered into the cave of the courtyard. The pool in the center was a pit of exotic plants twisting around rusty garden furniture and broken statues. "It smells green."

Finn raised her Nikon and took a picture. "We're going in."

They pulled open the courtyard gates, which produced a wince-inducing shrill. Insects fluttered as vines slid away to reveal the entrance, a swirling art nouveau staircase guarded by stone sphinxes with the heads of angelic boys. Bits of glass, leaves, and feathers littered the threshold. A padlock chain was looped through the door handles, and rust had bled in spatters over the wood. Finn again took out the moth key someone (Jack?) had left beneath her window and looked at the arch above the door, at the words of another language carved into the stone. "What do you think it says?"

"'*Abandon all hope, ye who—*'"

"Never mind." Finn slid the key into the padlock. The mechanism clicked, fell away. As the door creaked open, Sylvie looked concerned.

"Finn, seriously, where did you get that key?"

"Someone left it under my window."

"*Hell.*" Christie stared at her.

A moaning wind, accompanied by the tomb chill of solitary places, drifted outward. They lingered on the threshold.

Finn stepped forward and flicked the beam of her flashlight at a giant chandelier of red and green crystal, aiming it at the massive stairway branching before them, its posts two mahogany statues of gowned nymphs holding shattered lamps. The furniture was patched with mold and verdigris, the chessboard-marble floor littered with dead insects and leaves. A tree had clawed through the window and, like a grotesque concierge, now draped the lobby desk.

Finn moved farther inward, gripping her Nikon.

"This," Sylvie whispered, turning in a circle, "is *amazing.*"

"So I guess Anna was wrong." Christie directed his light over the mural of a stylized forest, where white hounds raced before a black horse and its rider, a knight in green armor. The knight's face was wrong—slanted, wild-eyed, inhuman. "No one's moved in. No Fatas."

Something stirred the leaves piled in a dark corner. Finn spun, flicking a beam of light at it. A tattered, old-fashioned baby carriage creaked in the drafts that had entered with them, swirling leaves up the stair.

"That's *classic.*" Christie moved toward the carriage draped in charcoal shadow. "I wonder if there's a dead baby in it. Nope. Not even a doll head. *That's* disappointing."

Sylvie was standing before a stained-glass window. Sunlight pushed through the plywood outside, illuminating the image of a youth in green armor, his red curls wreathed with roses. "This place must have been spectacular, once."

"Have you noticed something?" Finn murmured, stabbing her light all over the walls. "No graffiti. And there was none outside either."

"I heard music." Christie aimed his flashlight at the second-floor landing as Sylvie moved past him. Her purple Converses stirred dust and leaves as she loped up the stairs.

"Sylvie!" As Sylvie disappeared from view, Finn rushed up the stairs after, Christie beside her. Finn found the serpentine curl of the mahogany banister beneath her hand unsettling. Above them, lamps like flowers blossomed from pewter tendrils.

The second floor was eerily tangled with thick vines twining through the broken windows. Most of the doors, ornately carved with malevolent-looking plant life, were closed. Searching for Sylvie, Finn stepped into the first room. Its walls were stained, but a large bed and a divan of red velvet remained. Fading twilight slid through the window and glistened on dust, but it didn't touch the sepia shadows that stained the corner where the divan sat, facing the wall.

"I think she's down this way." Christie's voice sounded distant.

Finn turned to find herself alone. "Christie! Syl—"

The door slammed shut.

She ran to it, grabbed the knob. It was stuck. She couldn't even hear her friends on the other side. *It was just the wind. Just the—*

Something moved in the shadows near the divan—she saw it out of the corner of one eye. Reluctantly, she turned, gripping her flashlight.

She didn't believe the pale, mottled arm that slowly folded over the back of the divan.

Finn inhaled and couldn't exhale again as the light in the room changed, dimming slightly, so that, at first, she thought something was wrong with her vision. Then the air began to buzz as if swarming with hundreds of invisible flies. On the divan, a girl with a porcelain face and shoulder-length black hair peered over the bruised arm. The late-afternoon sunlight didn't touch her as she slid into a kneeling position, turning her head to gaze at whatever sat beside her. Finn heard a faint, jangling sound, as if a music box had fallen.

She closed her eyes. *She's just a homeless person. Maybe she's one of Jack's vagabond friends.*

But the cold in the room was that of cellars and icy night roads, and it hurt to breathe and there was that buzzing in her ears, as if something was trying to speak to her and her brain wasn't adjusting—

She opened her eyes. "*Stop it!*"

The divan had turned to face her. A second black-haired porcelain girl sat beside her twin, her ivory smock splotched with blood.

Finn reeled back and hit the door, fumbling frantically with the handle.

"She's bleeding." The first girl's voice was fragmented. "*Why did she die?*"

Finn put her hands over her face and wished the haunts away.

When she looked again, the divan was empty and facing the wall again. A broken music box glittered on the floor.

She yanked open the door and ran.

SYLVIE HAD WANDERED AWAY FROM Finn and Christie, following the faint sounds of music to a sun-streaked chamber where a harp loomed in one corner and a tall wardrobe painted with peacock images dominated the center. It was extremely cold in the room—gravestone cold. She rubbed her nose. She couldn't hear the music now, only a faint buzzing, like bees. "Christie! Finn . . ."

Something scratched at the inside of the wardrobe.

Because Sylvie had been raised with her Laplander father's tribal beliefs and her Japanese mother's Shinto spirituality, curiosity smashed fear. She didn't make another sound, but waited breathlessly. She *wanted* to see something.

A shadow stood before the wardrobe, a piece of darkness in a tasseled dress and a headband with a rosette . . . as if someone had made a 1920s flapper out of black matter—or as if Sylvie's mind had blanked out its true form to protect her sanity.

She swallowed sour fear and pulled out her cell phone, which had a camera. But the phone was as dead as what stood before her.

The figure glided backward and faded into the wardrobe.

Sylvie fled the room and screamed as she crashed into someone.

"Sylvie," Finn said, breathing fast. "*Where's Christie?*"

WHILE FINN PEERED INTO ONE room, and Sylvie explored another, Christie had tracked the murmur of voices to a glass door. He heard only the sound of dripping water from behind it. He pushed at the door and peered into a grimy, black-and-white bathroom with a rusting porcelain tub. He glanced up at a skylight clotted with leaves and dead insects. "Grim."

He looked down to find a boy sitting in the tub. And terror paralyzed him.

The boy wore a crimson Renaissance jacket, jeans, and boots. Red ribbons draped his wrists resting on the tub's edges. Bright hair framed an innocent, pale face with dark eyes, but shadows seemed to snake around him, and the cold in the air was rank. Christie's breath misted.

The boy, whose breath, if he had any, didn't mist, said, "You shouldn't be here."

Between one blink and the next, the tub was empty, the rust along its sides resembling old blood—

Christie slammed shut the door.

"Christie!" Finn grabbed him. Sylvie was breathless beside her.

Fighting the urge to be violently sick, he said, "This place is *very bad*. Someone died here."

"Christie"—Finn's voice was steady—"a *lot* of someones died here."

FINN WANTED TO SEE MORE, but fear of the unknown—and common sense—told her to get out. Christie and Sylvie, who had also seen things, were pale and shaky. As they hurried down Tirnagoth's sun-streaked upper hall, she thought she could hear sighs and giggles from the second floor, and, below, a deep voice muttering.

Rushing down the stairs, the three dashed toward the front doors. Sylvie and Christie raced out.

As Finn's foot touched the threshold, she felt something come to life behind her.

She twisted around to find the hotel lobby as it must have looked in the 1920s, a Polaroid negative swimming in sepia. Shadows moved but didn't take form. A familiar voice said, "Finn?"

Breathless, she grabbed the Nikon on the strap over her shoulder.

Then she was yanked out. Her breath hitching in her throat, she glanced back into the lobby, but she saw nothing except darkness and rot. The last of the sunlight vanished from the sky, and a cold, violet murk seemed to descend.

"Finn." Sylvie shook her from her daze.

"I think I'm going crazy," Finn whispered.

"No." Christie looked sick. "That *place* is crazy."

When they had fled a safe distance, they turned to look back at the hotel, sinister and barbed against the evening sky.

"It's haunted," Christie said with grim assurance. "There was a dead boy in the tub."

"Is that what you saw? I saw a shadow girl from the Roaring Twenties." Sylvie was backing away. She sounded awed. "It really *is* haunted."

As they began trudging down the gravel path, Finn told them about the two girls on the divan, shivering when she recalled their doll-like appearance, the stillness of the air around them. She didn't tell them about hearing Jack's voice back there. She continued, "I don't know what this has to do with the Fatas . . ."

Sylvie tugged at one of her own pigtails. "We should come back with film cameras—"

"I'm done." Christie's voice, so uncharacteristically flat, startled Finn. He turned and faced them, and he looked fierce. "I'm not curious anymore. I'm scared shitless. I won't sleep tonight. I doubt I'll sleep for a week—that bathroom smelled like blood . . . I think that boy killed himself in there."

Finn tried not to think of the ghoulish girls on the divan and knew she'd be thinking about them while *she* attempted to sleep.

Sylvie said, "Black mold causes hallucinations. I bet that place is filled with mold."

It was a lame excuse, and none of them believed it.

"It went bad." Christie stuck the ever-unlit cigarette between his lips. His hand shook. "The hotel closed after Malcolm Tirnagoth was killed. In Asia, don't they have this thing called feng shui . . ."

"Architects build to keep out bad fortune and direct good luck through the rooms—are you saying that Tirnagoth was built bad?" Finn resisted the urge to look over her shoulder at the menacing bulk of the hotel.

"I read that some mojo guy said the hotel was built to *attract* bad." Sylvie looked thoughtful.

Finn considered this as she continued up the gnarly road, her friends following. She was trying to figure some things out—so when they stopped talking, she barely noticed.

She *did* notice when a chill brushed across the back of her neck. She halted. "Christie? Sylv . . ."

Looking around, she found herself alone. Finn's courage plunged into an icy pool of panic as she yelled, *"Christie! Sylvie!"*

It was dark now. The leaves rustled as the wind whipped her hair into her face, and the gates creaked. She twisted back around—

A girl stood a few feet from her, black hair veiling her face, her skin white. She wore a black dress and stood too still.

Finn whispered, "What are you?"

The girl raised her head, revealing the face of someone her age, a pretty face, somewhat familiar, with dark eyes. "I'm Eve."

"Eve." Finn didn't know if she was talking to a real girl or a spirit, so she decided to be practical despite the clammy fear twisting through her. "Where are my friends, Eve?"

"Tricked away." The girl turned and walked, and Finn, bewildered, followed her down the Tirnagoth drive. The girl halted near a birch tree so white it looked unreal. "This is where I tried to be brave."

"How—" Finn broke off as the girl knelt beside the birch . . . but she didn't look at the girl—she stared at the letters carved into the tree in the middle of a heart: E+J.

"Here." The girl pointed at something in the roots of the tree. "This is where I dropped it."

Finn, still wondering about those initials, looked down at the cross-shaped hilt of an ornate dagger.

"It's pure silver," the girl solemnly told her, "made for the Templars to fight . . . what they fought. My sister gave it to me . . . I couldn't use it . . . not against him."

"Who are you?"

Light glimmered silver across the girl's eyes. Then she whispered, *"Why did she die?"*

"What did you say?"

The girl turned and ran into the woods.

Finn stared at the dagger. Then she bent down to pull it free. The hilt was cold, as if a human hand had never touched it. *Why did she die?* Those were the words that had haunted her since Lily's suicide.

The gates creaked again. She rose quickly to her feet, stepping on the dagger. "Chris—"

It wasn't Christie who stood between the open gates.

"Whatever are you doing here, little *coineanach?*" Platinum-haired Caliban Fata smiled, his dark coat billowing, glittering as if it were made of scales.

Finn's voice knotted in her throat. "Where are Christie and Sylvie?"

His silver gaze slid to her. "Don't know."

He was trying to scare her. But after being terrorized by Tirnagoth, Finn's brain had adjusted to the sinister. *"Where are they?"*

"Do you want to know who the girl was? *Ask Jack.*"

Aware of the knife beneath her foot, Finn didn't take her gaze from Caliban as he stepped toward her. He growled, "Tell me your name. All of it."

"Serafina Sullivan." She wanted to run, but he would catch her . . .

"Serafina Sullivan. But you left out your middle name." He reached toward her, and silver glanced across his eyes. "What is your true name? *Tell me.*"

"Don't touch me." Finn stumbled back. The dagger spun from beneath her foot. She absolutely believed, now, that he had hurt Angyll Weaver.

"Don't touch—what is that? Did Eve give that to you?" Caliban's eyes flickered to the dagger. "Such a fine, brave gir—"

Something loped from the shadows, catching him off guard, and slammed him against a tree—Finn stared at Christie, who yelled, *"Run!"*

Caliban grabbed Christie, smashing him against another tree. He struck it, face-first. Finn yelled.

Sylvie ran from the tangled trees toward Christie, but Caliban stepped in her way, grinning. She swung her flashlight at him. He knocked her down.

"Stop," Finn whispered. *"Stop.* What are you *doing?"*

Caliban picked up the dagger, smiled, and flung it at her feet. "See if you can get me with that before I reach the pretty boy or the crow girl."

He strode toward Christie, who was struggling to stand. Sylvie was on her feet, too, looking feral and angry and reaching for a piece of broken blacktop. When she lunged forward, Caliban laughed and casually shoved her away.

Finn grabbed the dagger, straightened—

Suddenly Jack stood before her, so close she could see the black-rimmed pupils of his eyes. Softly, he said, "Go."

He glided toward Caliban as Christie, still unsteady, backed away with Sylvie. Caliban bared his teeth. "*Sluagh*. I am *sick* of you."

"Jack!" Finn darted forward, but Sylvie grabbed her hand and Christie yanked at her other. They dragged her away until she finally ran with them.

When they reached the parking lot of the noisy apartment building and Christie fumbled with his keys, Finn, realizing she still had the dagger, slid it into her coat pocket. They ducked into the Mustang and Christie gripped the wheel. "Shit. Shit. Sh . . ."

"Where *were* you?" Finn whispered.

"I got lost." Sylvie was pale. "Alone."

"Me, too," Christie said. "Things just got . . . like I couldn't think my way through those trees. Like temporary brain damage."

"Caliban Fata . . ." Finn pushed her hands across her face.

"He was messing with us." Christie wiped at his bloody mouth, and Finn felt a snarling fury when she remembered how Caliban had struck him.

"Are you okay?" She pressed her shaking hands into her lap. She didn't want to think about what was happening between Jack and Caliban now.

"Should we call the police?" Sylvie sounded dazed. Finn saw that she still clutched the piece of blacktop she'd been about to brain Caliban with.

"No police—what the hell would we tell them?" Christie looked at Finn. "Don't let him near you."

Finn didn't know whether he meant Jack or Caliban. She pushed her hands through her hair. She hated that she was shaking. "We have to go back and help Jack—"

"No. That look in his eyes, Finn—it's like he doesn't care about anything, whether he lives or dies. Even that psycho Caliban or whatever he calls himself has something like goals. Evil goals, yeah, but still . . ."

"You're talking about Jack."

Christie started the car. "So ends our tour of the Tirnagoth Hotel. '*That thing all blood and mire, that beast-torn wreck, half-turned and fixed a glazing eye on mine.*'"

"Goddamn it, Christie." Sylvie's voice was sharp. "Stop quoting Yeats."

AS SOON AS CHRISTIE DROPPED her off, Finn thought of calling the police. She sat on the floor of her room, gripping her cell phone, as something within her whispered, *Don't.*

When someone tapped on the glass doors, her heart wrenched beneath her rib cage. She looked up and saw the silhouette on her terrace. *Jack.*

She slid to her feet and unlocked the doors. It was raining. He leaned against the stone railing, his head down and his hair hanging around his face. Beneath the coat, his black shirt and pin-striped trousers were splotched with dirt. His voice was blurry. "That was bad."

She lurched forward and took him by the wrists, pulled him in, and seated him in the red plush chair. He kept his head bowed, his booted feet braced, hands loose between his knees. She said as calmly as she could, "Did he hurt you?"

"A bit."

"You're so *cold.*" She was still clasping his wrists.

"That's not unusual."

His hair dripped into his eyes, and she felt that jarring sense of familiarity that had pricked her when she'd first met him. He was soaked and shivering, his eyelashes shimmering with raindrops. "You're bleeding. I'll be right back."

In the hall bathroom, she rummaged for supplies. She returned to examine the cut on his brow, the bloody scrapes on his knuckles. As he held a washcloth to his face, she poured alcohol onto cotton. "I only have pink Band-Aids. Like, neon pink."

He smiled. "No, thank you."

She sat back and gazed at him. The bruises and cuts made him seem vulnerable, and she didn't know why that suddenly scared her more than the Tirnagoth Hotel's spooks.

"He's seen me bleed," Jack quietly told her.

"You mean Caliban. So he knows you're vulnerable, so what?"

"That's not what I mean." His smile wasn't vulnerable at all. It reminded her that he might not be all that sane.

"Jack . . ."

"*Why were you there?*"

"I was curious."

"Curious?" He rose, astonished. "You wandered through a condemned building because you were *curious*?"

She scrambled up to face him. "I wanted to know where your family lived. All that you showed me was that crazy owl girl."

"She's part of the family you're so *fascinated* by."

His scorn made her temper flare. "Why were *you* there? Why was *Caliban* there? I saw the hotel lobby when the sun set . . . it was all new . . . I *heard* you say my name."

"Finn. You're getting hysterical."

"Tirnagoth can't be where your family lives. We saw things—"

"I'm leaving." He rose, and the shadows in the room seemed to ribbon around him.

She was losing him. She hated the panic in her voice. "I won't ask anymore. Just stay."

He stood at the glass doors, his back turned to her. He didn't look at her as he said, "Don't go to Tirnagoth again. Promise me. Please."

She wanted so badly to know about Tirnagoth and its ghosts, but she didn't dare ask now. "Okay. Sit down. You're hurt."

He laughed, gazing into the rain-swept night. "Not for long."

She walked to him, twined her fingers around his wrist, and led him back to the chair. As he sat, she knelt beside him to dab at the blood on his mouth. She had to brace herself against him to do so. She felt his heartbeat, strong and quick, beneath her hand. She breathed in his scent of fire and wild roses. "That bastard made you bleed."

"Finn"—his voice was soft with anguish—"it's you. *You* made me bleed."

"I'm sorry." She sat back on her heels. "You're right. It's my fault you got in that fight. You're all patched up now."

He reached to touch her face, his eyes dark. "Finn—"

She leaned toward him.

Something clattered to the floor behind her. She twisted around and stared at the silver knife that had fallen from the coat she'd draped on the bed.

"Where," Jack whispered, "did you get *that*?"

She began tentatively, "There was a girl named Eve—"

His eyes seemed to reflect the light, silvering, widening . . . as if *she'd* wounded him.

He whipped up and was gone in a flurry of shadows and raindrops. The glass doors clattered shut.

Finn was stunned. She curled up, her knees beneath her chin, and watched rain pelt the glass. She whispered, "That wasn't even a question."

JACK RETURNED TO HIS APARTMENT, weary and battered, wishing he'd ripped Caliban's spine out instead of leaving him on the ground and going after Finn. Without removing his coat, he sprawled across his bed. His eyelashes flickered, and his body, always coiled for movement, relaxed. As Black-Jack Slade curled beside him, he closed his eyes. *But I don't sle—*

The dream was of a street splashed with neon green, its shop windows marked with bloody handprints. Behind one window, violins glistened, mournful as coffins.

The window shattered. The sable beasts that had been disguised as violins came at him, ivory teeth bared. The flying glass bit into his hands—

Jack woke in moonlight and found that blood now flecked the sheets because the cut on his brow had opened. The fight with Caliban had exhausted him, and it shouldn't have.

I fell asleep. At night. And I dreamed. I bleed. What is happening to me?

He crawled from the bed and switched on the lights because he liked their normalcy—despite the theater's neglected state, the Fatas owned the building and still paid the electric and water. He gazed at the starry dark outside. It was three o'clock in the morning.

Caliban, he thought, and almost snarled.

He clawed one of the cinema posters from the wall on his way out of the apartment.

He prowled past the condemned building where the body of a murderer was buried. He strode down a railroad track, through a mobile home park where two monsters lived. Warehouses loomed on the riverside path he chose.

As Jack arrived at Tirnagoth, his boot heels crushing broken glass and withered leaves, he thought of Finn and knew he should not.

While crossing the courtyard, he noticed a girl in green gingham crouched on a gargoyle. She was reading a book of poetry by Baudelaire. She looked up as he passed. "Careful, Jack, *he's* here."

Jack had seen the tawny roadster outside of the gates. He knew what had come to Tirnagoth.

"I know." He heard familiar voices. "I suppose he's here for his girl."

He followed the voices up a spiral stair, his soldier's coat sweeping outward.

A slim boy stood in the hallway—Nathan Clare—and Caliban was circling him, speaking in a voice that was all mock and threat. "Are you having one of your moments, darling? Do you think it's going to hurt? I think it will . . . almost like your first time. Too bad it's not with me."

"Ariel'Pan." Jack slid forward, dissecting Caliban from his prey. He grabbed Nathan's wrist, which was enviably warm and fragile, and resisted an urge to break the bones.

"Go." He released the boy who had once been his friend.

The boy backed away, turned, and pushed through a set of doors.

Caliban laughed softly. "You should be more careful, Jack. Love can make you *bleed*. And it's not Nathan you love, is it?"

Jack remained silent as Caliban prowled forward and whispered, "Are those rubies decorating your hands, Jack? Because they look like scabs. It's disgusting. Has the schoolgirl infected you with their grue and gore?"

"What were you intending to do to Finn Sullivan and her friends?"

"Reiko's possessive of her things, Jack. You're one of her things. So is Tirnagoth. I was attempting to put the fear of *us* into them."

Jack leaned against a pillar. "Don't do anything like that again."

Caliban yawned. "Which one are you swooning over? The schoolgirl or the little crow girl? Or is it the pretty fox boy?"

"Ariel'Pan." Jack lifted a gaze that had gone black. "*Stay away from her.*"

"It *is* the schoolgirl. Do you remember when I was like your big brother?"

Jack bared his teeth. "You were *never*—"

"Who was the Jack who took you under his wing, the one who was a prince during the Renaissance . . . a long time for a *sluagh* to exist." Caliban smiled malevolently. "Ambrose . . . ah, *that* was his name."

"His name," Jack growled, "was Jack. All of us are Jack."

"He got sentimental, didn't he? *Jack.* And Seth Lot had to gut him, hyacinths and all, right in front of you. That schoolgirl of yours looks a lot like Ambrose . . . She a descendant of his? Was he watching over his family like some bloody ancestral spirit?" Caliban paused. "She is a lovely piece of flesh—do you remember what happened to the last girl you kissed?"

Jack didn't remember, and he didn't want to. He moved close to Caliban, threatening, and said through gritted teeth, "Why are you interested in her?"

"If I told you"—Caliban's smile curled as darkness bled into his eyes—"you'd kill me." He stepped back. "You've done something, *sluagh*. I'll find out what you're up to."

Jack lunged and grabbed Caliban by the throat. Sinuous and difficult to hold, Caliban slipped free, laughing, and swaggered away. He called back, "The last girl you kissed was named Eve. You killed her."

Jack slouched against the wall, his hands clenched, his head bowed. *Eve*, he thought, and almost remembered, before he banished it.

He'd been dead. Finn Sullivan had woken him. For that, he would never forgive her. And he might very well be the death of her.

He turned and Reiko appeared before him, sleek in a gown like fire and blood. "Jack. David Ryder wants to speak with you."

"No, thank you." He was aware of what waited in the rooms at the top of the stair. He could smell the visitor, a chill fragrance of forests, musk, and stone. It made his teeth clench. David Ryder was an arrogant bastard with pretensions of civility . . . like that ridiculous wake he'd insisted upon for the girl Caliban had brought him, the one now stuffed with flowers and stitched together. The Jill.

Reiko moved up the stairs. "I *insist*, Jack."

If he disobeyed, she'd begin to suspect what was happening to him. He began to climb the stairs.

He followed Reiko into a room with baroque furnishings and crimson lamps splashing light onto scarlet walls. Near the window, the shadows stirred. A man emerged, wearing a fur-lined coat over an expensive brown suit. His tawny hair was sleeked back from a handsome face.

David Ryder looked at Jack as if he were a derelict who had just stumbled into a fancy home. "I see you're still with us."

Jack leaned against the door frame. "I'm hard to get rid of."

David Ryder's coat brushed Jack as he moved past. "I want to speak to you, *sluagh*. If you'll please come with me."

David Ryder had been Reiko's lover, yet, somehow, his gentlemanly manners had remained intact. He was an exile from the English court, but Jack had never learned why—he suspected Reiko the outlaw had lured him away.

In Reiko's salon, Jack insolently selected the best chair. Ryder sat on the heart-shaped divan like a king. "You realize Seth Lot wants you gone."

Seth Lot. The Wolf—Madadh allaid. "Then why am I still here?"

David Ryder leaned forward, hands folded. "Because of Reiko. That is why you are still here."

"Shall I thank her?"

"You make her weak."

"I'm not the first. At least she hasn't grown a heart with *me*."

He had the pleasure of seeing David Ryder leash his fury with an effort. "That is a vile rumor. She was never infected with that."

"No?" Jack rested his arms on the back of the chair, stretched out his legs. "Her human lover, the Black Scissors, is just a fiction then?"

"Yes."

"A figment of our imaginations. Our bogeyman."

"You mock because you have *nothing*. You respect *nothing*. You are *nothing*."

"And who made me that way?"

"It makes you dangerous."

"Are we done?" Jack pushed to his feet.

"She's told me about your schoolgirl."

Jack froze.

"I do not harm innocents, *sluagh*. But if I need to use her to keep you from ruining this Teind, I will."

"Why"—Jack smiled as if his teeth were in Ryder's throat—"would I interfere with this Teind?"

"Because Nathan Clare used to be your friend."

"You said I cared about nothing. So there is no reason to threaten me. Because you are right. Go kiss your white serpent and pretend she loves you."

He strode out of the room, leaving David Ryder to simmer.

In the hall, Reiko confronted Jack, her sweet demeanor vanished. "Now *we* shall speak, Jack."

"Shall we?" He desperately didn't want her to see how exhausted he was.

She whispered, furious, "Those three children came *here*."

"Others have come."

"Others were turned away by fear. Your schoolgirl and her friends *entered* my domain. It took more than one trick to turn them away."

"They came before dusk. We weren't here, technically." Gently, he continued, "And we were nothing."

"She had a *key*, Jack."

"You think I would give it to her? Did you tell *him* about this?" Jack pointed back at the salon where David Ryder waited.

"If he knew about this, Serafina Sullivan and her companions would go the way of the Lily Girls."

"The who?"

"Oh, Jack." She cupped his face in her hands. "Selective memory, again?" Her eyes went black. "I could *make* you remember those three mistakes."

"No." His voice began to fray. He thought, *Eve.* "Why? Why are you letting me be with her? Just to keep her from falling for Nathan and rescuing him?"

"I told you. She is my gift to you."

He tried to pull back from her, but she wound her slim white arms around his neck and whispered into his ear, "'*And I shall purge thy mortal grossness so, that thou shalt like an airy spirit go.*' Jack, give me your heart."

He'd been a fool to think he could hide it from her, or resist her.

He opened his shirt to do as she asked.

CHAPTER NINE

The Monasty are solitary and have no alliances. They are nomads. They keep to themselves. They don't like to be bothered. They are the most unpredictable.

—FROM THE JOURNAL OF LILY ROSE

Lily Rose held Finn's hand as they raced across the field toward a huge house veiled by morning mist.

"Look. It wasn't here before." Lily Rose, lithe and fifteen, waved her hand as if performing a magic trick. Two wolves of pale marble curved along the house's stairway. It was a ruin, the house, its doors and windows gaping. Something nasty and dark and old seemed to seep from it, like rot.

Finn pulled back, but Lily Rose ran on, slowing when the mist across the field curled away from a man seated on the stairs. His hair had the sheen of autumn leaves. He wore a coat of black fur. He stood and began walking toward Lily Rose. His eyes were wolf blue—

Finn had encountered ghosts, and the striking boy named Jack was not at all like other people. Ordinary people didn't have fallen angels for enemies and elegant vagabonds for friends. They didn't act as if their families were to be feared.

They didn't hang out in abandoned places infested with spirits and bad mojo.

It was still raining and she felt frayed. She decided she wouldn't go to class today—there was only English Comp, math, and soccer, the phys ed requirement she'd reluctantly chosen. Her da, recognizing the signs, brought her tea and Irish oatmeal thick with cream and cinnamon. He placed her cell phone on the table near the sofa where she'd made her nest so that she could watch old movies.

Restless by afternoon, she dressed in jeans and a Mickey Mouse T-shirt and made coffee. She listened to her mother's music collection and checked her e-mail. She watched a Scooby-Doo marathon as she finally texted Christie and Sylvie.

Later on, she opened Lily's journal.

She was beginning to realize that, as children, she and Lily had probably seen things Finn had sensibly blocked out, or placed in the compartment called "Imagination," but Lily's illness hadn't allowed her to do that. And could Finn even really trust her own memories? She frowned down at the scrawls of black ink that described a perilous, secret world she'd only begun to discover. *Last night, in the park, he kissed my wrist. It left a scar. I know what he is now. He is a wolf.*

Some of the stories, she'd begun to realize with a faint unease, must be true. Whoever the children of nothing and night were, they had gotten to her sister first. And Finn knew she'd seen them as a child, but her mind had dismissed them. Even now, her common sense continued to fight what she'd seen, to push them into the realm of dream, myth, fairy tales, the world her father studied. And what had drawn him to *that*? she wondered. Her da had grown up in Fair Hollow, but obviously he hadn't a clue as to what was creeping through its quaint antiquity.

She looked down at a page of Lily's journal, saw the words *Mockingbird* and *malevolent*, and a sketch of a wicked face with wings. The image blurred. A memory trickled to her like sunlight through leaves—a boy's neon-green sneakers. She gripped her sister's journal and remembered Robbie Simmons, the small, quick boy who had lived next door in Vermont. She'd been nine, and winter hadn't yet taken her mother, when she and Robbie had found each other and spent the year making forts in trees, playing video games, and borrowing his parents' Dungeons and Dragons figurines to stage tiny battles.

Her fingernails dug into the pages of the journal. She didn't want to go any further. But she closed her eyes and the childhood images flickered through her brain as she and Robbie ran through the woods, wild kids, and the sun was setting, its descent tainting the air with an eerie glow—

—then she was standing before a boy who looked twelve, and there was another boy and girl with him, and they had hair so yellow it could have been gold. The tall boy had hold of Finn's wrist and he'd said he wasn't going to let go as his brother and sister stared at her with eyes as silver as his. Robbie had punched him in the shoulder—

She didn't remember anything else about that day. That was the summer Robbie had fallen from a tree and broken both legs. He hadn't been able to run as fast after that.

Finn looked down at her sister's handwriting: *The Mockingbirds are devious, a wealthy, clannish, rural family. Piss them off and they'll hurt you—*

She flung the journal against the wall and curled up with her hands over her head, eventually drifting into sleep.

WHEN FINN OPENED HER EYES, evening had fallen and Jack Fata sat in her father's armchair. At first, she didn't believe he was there. "Jack?"

"Do you want me to leave?" He wore a black coat sparkling with rain.

"*You* left *me*." She realized she wasn't worried that he'd gotten into her house—which should have worried her.

"I shouldn't have." His voice was soft, his hands locked together as he leaned forward. "I was angry."

"How did you get in? The doors are locked."

He unfolded from the chair and began walking around the parlor, his rings glinting dully as he touched objects. "The kitchen window wasn't."

A scent had filled the room, a fragrance of rain on rose petals, green and sweet. It smelled dangerous, like the air before a violent thunderstorm. "Jack."

"Finn." He caressed a doll. "Don't ever put anything outside your house with the word 'Welcome' on it."

He was crazy. He was crazy and lovely and leaving wet boot prints on the hardwood. When he halted before the photograph of Lily Rose sitting on the porch in San Francisco, he had his back to Finn.

"My sister." Finn moved to her feet. "Lily Rose."

He looked away. "The one who died."

He turned, discarding the coat. He wore old jeans and a long-sleeved black shirt. She scowled as he stooped down in front of the stereo and began riffling through her father's CDs. He said, "Do you have any Tom Waits? Paganini?"

"My da likes Tom Waits. Who's Paganini? I'm going to make some tea." She moved carefully toward the kitchen.

"Paganini was an Italian composer, a violinist, who made a pact with the devil. The devil seems to like violinists. Even Scooby-Doo could figure that out. Ah. Here it is."

Finn's hands were cold as she placed the kettle on the stovetop. When violin music soared through the house, heartbreaking, eerie, she shivered. She hated classical music . . . it was the last music her sister had listened to before ending her life.

But she didn't tell Jack to turn it off. She pushed her hands through her tangled hair and turned. She was going to ask him about Tirnagoth and its spirits . . .

He was leaning in the doorway. "Only it wasn't the devil they dealt with. It was a race of beings who've hidden themselves from mortal eyes for thousands of years."

She remembered Lily's journal—where had she thrown it? "That's interesting."

As he began to wander around the kitchen, touching things, she reached over and plucked one of her grandmother's china mice from his fingers. "Do you play the violin, Jack?"

"Sometimes. I've had time to learn."

"Have you? Did that red-haired fiddler teach you?"

"Stay away from him."

The kettle had begun to whistle. She grabbed it. "Why? Is he the devil?"

"He's *a* devil." His dark gaze suddenly fastened on something. She turned her head to see what had caught his attention and nearly dropped the kettle.

Lily Rose's journal hovered in midair, its ribbons twisting like tentacles, its pages fluttering as if someone they couldn't see was leafing through it. Finn set down the kettle and stepped back. "Jack."

"Finn," he whispered, "do you know you're not alone?"

The door that led to the garage opened, and her da stepped in, his head down as he struggled to get the key out of the lock.

The book fell to the floor. He looked up.

There was silence in the kitchen as Jack bent, picked up the journal, and set it on the counter. Finn was amazed by how normal her voice sounded, "Da. This is Jack."

"Hello, Jack." Her father looked too calm. He shut the door. He said, "Do you go to HallowHeart?"

"My family doesn't believe in higher education."

Finn winced as her father folded his arms across his chest. "And what family is that?"

"Da . . ."

Jack didn't drop his gaze from her father's. "The Fatas."

"Jack was on his way home." Finn moved into the parlor for Jack's raincoat, and Jack followed leisurely. Her da came after, frowning at the slender boy with the red-tipped hair and the ruby stud in his nose.

"I'll see you again," Jack promised as Finn pulled him toward the door.

She whispered, "Jack. What *was* that—"

His fingers wrapped around her wrist, and the touch of his bare skin against hers was a shock. He whispered, "Nothing to be afraid of. Get rid of that welcome mat."

"Jack—"

He was out the door, striding into the rain.

She shut the door and turned. Her da stood with arms crossed, an imposing, shaggy-haired Irishman. "And what was he doing here?"

"He brought me a book I wanted." Finn hated lying, hated even more how easily she did it. "He likes books."

"Surprising, since his family doesn't believe in higher education. You feel better then?" He definitely hadn't noticed the floating journal.

"Much. I'm getting rid of that old doormat outside, okay?" She hurried out of the kitchen.

As she opened the front door, she saw jack-o'-lanterns glowing throughout the neighborhood. She'd never longed for the ordinary as much as she did at that moment. As she picked up the Welcome mat, a paper fluttered toward her, swirling to her feet. She stared down at one of her printouts of the 1800s coachman who could have been Jack's twin.

She shut the door and ran up the stairs, bursting into her room.

Lily's trunk had been flung open. Scattered all over the floor were the prints of Jack's and Reiko's historical doubles.

Jack wouldn't have come up here to do this. She whispered to the air, "Who are you?"

No one answered.

"THIS IS INSANE, FINN."

"You didn't have to come, Christie."

"Sure, and you'd be here alone. We should've brought Sylvie as a lookout."

"You *followed* me."

"And I gave you a ride—"

Finn tensed. "Shh. I think I see him."

"I can't believe he lives here. This is probably his lair, Finn, where he brings girls and does unspeakable things to them—"

"*Shh.*" It was nearly midnight, and they were crouched in the weeds surrounding Jack Fata's abandoned theater, watching Jack leave by the fire escape.

Christie whispered, "*Why* do you want to go in there?"

She watched Jack vanish down the lane and wondered if he had a job—she couldn't even *attempt* to imagine him delivering pizza or working at Dunkin' Donuts. She said, "Because I need to know."

"Curiosity killed the cat."

"Cats have nine lives. You can leave. Or you can stay as lookout."

"Hell, that. I'm coming in there with you."

He followed her up the fire escape. She pushed open the window, which wasn't locked—*that* surprised her. As they slid over the sill, the smells of incense and candle smoke made her feel as if she were invading a sacred space, and guilt tweaked her. Christie bumped against a table as Finn switched on her flashlight. They didn't want to turn on the lamps because that would be a beacon to anything outside.

"What are we looking for?" He flicked his light over shelves crammed with books and oddities, something that looked like a wolf's skull. The black cat lounging in a chair closed its eyes against them.

"History." She opened the wardrobe and found Jack's clothes scented with mint and patchouli.

Christie was scanning the shelves. "Look at these. *Wind in the Willows. Alice in Wonderland. Peter Pan*—first editions. What the hell is a badass like Jack Fata doing with these?"

She crouched before a voyage trunk plastered with stickers and, feeling like Pandora about to let something terrible into the world, attempted to open it. There was a lock.

She yanked the moth key hanging from a ribbon around her neck, slid it into the lock, and smiled when it turned—so it definitely wasn't Jack who'd given her the key. Why would he? She lifted the trunk's lid. She saw a dusty Victorian hat of black silk, a collection of cuff links on brown velvet. Next to these were a serpent-headed walking stick and a wooden box carved with doglike images. Beneath the box was the film reel in red casing, the one Jack wouldn't let her watch. She couldn't believe her luck. She quickly grabbed it and tucked it into her backpack.

Her hands shook as she removed the wooden box. She opened it and peered down at old photographs, some in black-and-white, others sepia tinged with age. She spread the pictures on the floor and gazed at Jack in Victorian clothing, standing with his hands on the harness of a horse-drawn carriage. In another photograph, resembling one of those stars from silent films, he sat in a more modern suit and held a violin. In the next, he was dressed in a long leather coat, aviator's goggles pushed onto his hair as he crouched beside a 1940s motorcycle. In the final picture, he stood holding a fiddle, his hair crowned with lilies. He wore a stitched shirt and flared jeans straight out of the late '60s.

Caught between terror, disbelief, and awe, she rubbed at the photographs, tried to detect fakes, but the tinting and the quality were too authentic. Her stomach churning, she whispered, "So your family likes to play dress-up, Jack?"

"*Finn*," Christie whispered, and the panic in his voice made her head snap up.

Christie stood near the window, his face white, the beam of his flashlight aimed at whatever stood behind her, smelling of evergreens, smoke, and wild roses. She pushed back her hair, studying the photos of Jack in his different incarnations, and said, "Jack. Do you still play the violin?"

His voice, hoarse, sounded as if it had been torn from him, "You should not have come here."

Christie kept his flashlight beam on Jack as Finn rose quickly, lost her balance, and fell against the very thing she'd been trying to avoid.

Jack caught her. Her hand struck his chest and remained there, over his heart. Even through his thin shirt, she didn't feel a heartbeat. Her eyes widened. Her breath hitched. She pressed harder, using both hands. "*Jack . . . your heart . . .*"

Christie's light shook as Jack whispered, "I don't have one at the moment."

She didn't move away, breathing in his scent of wild roses and fire. She desperately twined her fingers around his wrist and gripped hard, her thumb pushing against the tendons, searching for a pulse. His skin was so *cold*. "What has *happened* to you?"

Jack's voice was almost gentle. "It happened a long time ago."

She stepped away, her shaking hands leaving him. He was white, bloodless but for the blood-red tips of his hair. His resemblance to the coachman in the photograph was even more apparent because of the black-and-white look of him now.

"No heart," she murmured as ice moved through her veins. "No pulse. *What are you?*"

His eyes silvered like a dead thing, and what little warmth remained in the room was vanquished by cold. "She keeps *her* heart in a box."

She stared at the young man who had betrayed her, unknown and alien.

Christie grabbed her hand, dragged her back. They whirled, scrambled out the window, and clambered down the fire escape. As a cold wind swept through the tattered weeds, they ran.

When they finally halted at Christie's Mustang and slumped against it, Finn was shaking so badly she thought she'd have seizures. Christie clutched at her hand. "*What happened back there?* First Tirnagoth, now this?"

She couldn't tell him because the words *He's dead* wouldn't form in her mouth.

SHE HAD THOUGHT SHE WOULD cry when she got home. But she was numb. A thousand different explanations ran through her head as to why

Jack didn't have a heartbeat or a pulse, medical miracles included.

Then she decided, firmly and simply, that she had been mistaken. Just because the woods seemed to be haunted by ghost girls and the Tirnagoth Hotel was a paranormal society's wet dream (Christie's words), it didn't mean Jack Fata and his kind were dead things that had learned to pretend to be people.

But a sick terror crawled through her when she remembered the hollow in Jack's chest, the photographs of him from different eras. As she sat on her bed and waited for the poisonous sleepiness to return—it didn't—she went over every encounter she'd had with Jack Fata and slowly realized her safe, dull reality had been shattered.

JACK USED HIS BODY AS a weapon against the air, moving across the rooftops of the warehouse district until he saw the woods and the silhouette of Tirnagoth. He descended and strode among the trees, bashing branches out of his way while briars scraped at his hands. This time, he didn't bleed.

Had he lost her?

He pushed through Tirnagoth's gates, then wove through the bonfires and dancing bodies. The music tonight was a heathen mess of drums and flutes and whining violins. Fortunately, their only close neighbors were the dead. He could smell candle smoke and blackberry wine. Harp music tinkled from a room above. Someone began to whisper a chant as he pushed through the heavy doors into the lobby. The hotel, once a resort to the rich and famous, was derelict now. Broken glass glittered instead of diamonds. The Gothic gate of the courtyard was knotted with briars instead of tiny lights, and statues were wreathed with dead vines and graffitied with obscure quotes. The rooms were lush with artifacts, tapestries, candles—all stolen from tombs or shipwrecks.

Jack ascended the stairs to the conservatory, where exotic flowers sucked at moonlight. Like these plants, he had been nurtured in an environment of spells and night.

A pale-haired young man holding a staff topped with the bleached, ribboned skull of a stag moved down the aisle of black trees. He wore white jeans and a kimono of ivory silk. His eyes were blue.

"Lazuli." Jack halted.

"Why aren't you in the black parlor, Jack?"

Ignoring that question, Jack asked his own. "Why would a book levitate in a mortal girl's house?"

Lazuli Gilfaethwy caressed a crocus and it seemed to swoon beneath his touch. Jack set one hand on the stag skull. "Answer me."

"What kind of book?"

"It looked like a journal. A girl's—" Jack was suddenly blindsided by a vision of a ballerina in black tulle, red tears streaking her face. He heard an echo of violins and a wolf howling.

"Jack, what did you see just now?"

Jack smiled, hard and bright. "Nothing."

Lazuli lowered his eyelashes and caressed the stag skull as if seeking divine protection. He avoided touching Jack's jeweled hand. "The answer to your question is a geist."

"A poltergeist?"

"A geist is a remnant of someone once loved. You had a vision just now. You recently had a heart and blood, Jack." Lazuli hesitated, then whispered, "You are becoming something unknown to us."

Jack gazed at him darkly. "You won't tell them, will you."

"No, Jack." Lazuli leaned against a tree, his head down. "I won't. Does she know? Your mortal girl? What you are?"

"She's not my girl. She doesn't belong to anyone." He turned and walked away, back into the shadows where he belonged.

Out of Lazuli's sight, his swagger vanished. He halted, stumbled. Something dark and glittering swirled through him. The unholy strength was returning.

He would use it against them.

CHAPTER TEN

When the soul has left the body, it is drawn away, sometimes by the fairies.
If a soul eludes the fairies, it may be snapped up by the evil spirits.
—*IRISH FAIRY AND FOLKTALES*, W. B. YEATS

Jack has no heart. As this thought spiraled in her head, Finn moved in a daze through her classes, bumping into things and flinching at every unexpected sound. In history, Professor Avaline fixed her with a clear, grave look before beginning a lecture on the War of the Roses, but all Finn could hear was the word *heart*.

Then Mr. Wyatt, whose dreadlocks and muscled body made him look like a pro athlete, not a metalworking instructor, summoned Finn to him in the hall outside Studio Photography.

"Miss Sullivan." His deep voice was gentle. "You know Nathan Clare."

"Sort of."

"And you have the enmity of Reiko Fata?"

Finn had never heard anyone use the word *enmity* in conversation before. "I barely know her." *What is* Reiko, she thought, *if Jack isn't right?*

"Leave the Fatas be, Miss Sullivan. And that includes Nathan Clare." He smiled as if he'd merely said *Have a nice day*, and he walked on.

"Mr. Wyatt," she called in the nearly empty corridor, "who *are* they?"

He halted and didn't turn. "You mean, *what* are they, Miss Sullivan. It's best for you if you don't find out."

As he strode away, Finn bemusedly wandered in the other direction and avoided speaking with anyone else. As she crossed the campus to Laurel Hall, she wondered about the connection between Wyatt and the Fatas. She didn't know what to tell Christie and Sylvie, who were the only ones who would believe her; she felt a terrifying isolation. The Fatas were uncanny and she'd been warned away from Nathan Clare a second time. And *Wyatt* knew about them.

She nearly ran into Angyll Weaver on the stair. They stopped, gazing warily at each other.

Angyll Weaver had had her own unpleasant encounter with a Fata, one that had put her in the hospital. When she stomped past Finn, Finn followed her down the corridor and called her name. Angyll twisted around. She was alone, perfectly put together in a little pink dress and heels. Her eyes were wide.

Finn approached carefully, said in a low voice, "What did Caliban do to you?"

The mask slid back into place and Angyll smiled brightly, but the stitches in her brow were still there, and one eye was shadowed with a bruise despite the concealer. "Who?"

Finn grimly forged onward. "The Fatas, Angyll. They're not like us, and I think you found that out in the cemetery."

"You're craz—"

"Don't say I'm crazy."

"You are." Angyll leaned forward, eyes narrowed. "Because you think Jack Fata is *different* from the rest of them."

Finn wanted to say, *Jack Fata doesn't have a pulse.* "Caliban Fata hurt you, didn't he?"

Angyll drew back and looked around, clutching her books as if they were a shield. When she returned her gaze to Finn, she whispered, "Annie knew. She tried to warn me. *He . . . turned . . . into . . .*"

Her pupils had dilated with terror. Finn stepped forward. "Angyll, it's all ri—"

"No, it's not." Her whisper was shrill. "Because I know now they're going to *kill me.*"

Finn heard Christie's voice behind her. "Can't you leave Finn alone? She doesn't need a queen bitch yapping—"

"Christie!" Finn whirled, shook her head in warning. Christie looked confused. She turned back. "Angyll—"

But Angyll Weaver had once again sheathed herself in ice and spite. She smiled. "They've noticed *you*. Don't think I'm the only one who needs to watch her back."

As she stalked away, Finn narrowed her eyes at Christie, who was gazing after Angyll, frowning. He said, "What was she saying to you?"

"She's scared. And I was going to find out if Caliban was in that cemetery with her, when you came along and sent her back into bitch mode."

"Ah. Really?" He slouched against a locker. "Maybe we could go to the Weavers' shop and apologize after work."

"She thinks the Fatas want to kill her."

"She's always been a little paranoid—"

"But she's not." Finn glanced up as the doors to the lecture hall across from them opened and students came pouring out. "We *will* go to the Weavers' tonight. I need to ask her about Caliban, Christie. Maybe you can use your charm."

He straightened. "Are you pimping me out?"

"Yes I am. I'm late for algebra." She gave him a quick wave good-bye. As she wove distractedly through the other students, he called after her, "Maybe you can borrow one of Jack's fur coats—you know, to complete your pimp image!"

"Later, Christie." And she tried not to think of all the stories she'd been raised with, about creatures who mimicked human beings and preyed upon the vulnerable.

LATER, BENEATH THEIR APPLE TREE, Christie presented Finn with a small box. "I made it . . . what's inside, not the box."

She opened the box and found a chunky bracelet of dark metal awkwardly formed into what seemed to be leaves. For the first time that day, she smiled.

"Wyatt had us working with iron today. I also made what appears to be a ring for Sylvie. I decided I'm not going to be an artist who works with fine metals, and engineering is out of the question."

She slid the bracelet onto her wrist, and the metal warmed to her skin. "I like it. So . . . you might want to know that Wyatt warned me about the Fatas. I find that to be extremely suspicious behavior on his part."

"Aren't they all suspicious, Finn? Miss Emory talks to her plants. Hobson is always reading books about alchemy—"

Sylvie dropped down beside them. "And Professor Fairchild writes poetry about beautiful young things."

"Wyatt works as a club bouncer at night. And Avaline and Perangelo are always trading recipes on bits of parchment. *Parchment.* Not paper. I think they're all aliases and part of some splinter pagan cult."

Sylvie pointed at the box in Christie's hand. "Is that for me?"

As Sylvie admired the clunky ring he'd made, Christie said to Finn, "Now tell Sylvie what you found when we investigated the dark heart of Jack Fata's den."

Heart. Finn's hands went numb. Then she told them, her voice steady, about Jack.

"No *heartbeat*?" Christie looked as if he wasn't sure he'd heard correctly.

"None. And I mean that in the anatomical sense. No heart. No pulse." Just talking about it made her feel less crazy.

As Sylvie rocked back on her heels and Christie rubbed his hands over his face, Finn knotted her fingers together so they wouldn't tremble. "I couldn't believe it either. I pretended it was a mistake . . . it wasn't. I had my hand on his chest for *two* minutes, at least. And he had no pulse."

"I can't believe it." Sylvie looked at Finn. "I can't believe you broke into his apartment without me."

"Sorry. Did you not hear the part where I said Jack had no heartbeat?"

"Maybe it's a trick. Like when those Indian fakirs stop their own hearts—want me to try and find Reiko's heartbeat? I will if you ask." Christie ducked from the withered apple Finn flung at him. It was actually comforting to her that they weren't taking this seriously. Maybe she *had* been mistaken.

She opened the binder where she'd placed the printouts of Jack's and Reiko's ancestral look-alikes. "Want to see something?"

"So I'm not crazy." Sylvie pulled the Kali lunchbox from her backpack and pushed up the lid to reveal a collection of old-fashioned photographs. "I get them from garage sales, friends . . . look at these."

She set aside three tattered photographs. First was a shot of a Victorian pub crowd gazing toward the camera; in the forefront was a girl in an elegant gown and hat, smiling—she had Phouka Fata's face. The second picture was of a group of young men in 1940s fedoras and suits, leaning against a roadster. One of them looked exactly like Caliban Fata. The last photograph was of a croquet party in the '30s, young men and women in sleek clothes holding mallets or lounging in wicker chairs. Sprawled in one chair, his head bowed, his face in profile, was Jack Fata.

Sylvie looked up, eyes wide. "I thought they were just, you know, strong resemblances . . ."

Finn touched the photograph with Jack in it. It hurt her, seeing him so far away, untouchable.

Sylvie lifted a sepia-tinted picture of three children in white clothing. The older boy had dark hair, and the other boy was blond. The girl's hair was black and blond. "These are Malcolm Tirnagoth's children, the ones who died from influenza. The Tirnagoths were one of Fair Hollow's first families. Their ancestors came from Ireland in the late 1700s."

"Are the Fatas one of those families?"

Sylvie shook her head. She flipped through the photos, pointed to family tintypes with script written beneath them. "Tudor. Kierney. Drake. Valentine. Luneht. Tredescant. Hester Kierney, Claudette Tredescant, and Ijio Valentine hang out with the Fatas. So do Nick and Victoria Tudor and Aubrey Drake. The Lunehts left Fair Hollow years ago, after their son killed himself. What I'm saying, Finn, is that the Fatas have always been here. And I don't have any photographs of *their* ancestors . . . so, maybe, in the pictures you have, *those* are their ancestors."

"Or maybe"—Christie's voice spiked—"maybe they don't have ancestors because they goddamn freakishly never age."

They were all quiet, gazing down at the photographs. Then Christie said, "Nah."

CHRISTIE CAME TO PICK UP Finn at the bookstore that night.

"I'm ready to charm Angyll Weaver." He took off his woolen hat and shook out his hair. He solemnly met her gaze. "How do I look?"

She studied him. "Could you at least take off the Parrot Games T-shirt?"

"I spilled coffee on the shirt underneath."

She sighed. "Let's go."

"So." As they walked from the bookstore, Christie shoved his hands in his pockets. "You think Angyll will clarify our impossible and insane theory? Or confound it?"

"You're talking like *them*." She had tried not to think about Jack all day, but he haunted her now. "I want to know what they are."

"I'm not sure I want to find out. Unless it was black mold hallucinations, we saw ghouls in the Tirnagoth, which the Fatas own—maybe they're witches?"

"No," Finn said, her voice low, "they're something *else*. They're a secret."

As they passed the Marlowe Theater, she saw the flicker of a scarlet gown in the matinee crowd, and a memory surfaced like a drowned thing, taking the form of the red carp in the pond near which Lily had used to meet the wolf-eyed man whose kiss had left a scar on her skin . . .

Finn had been fifteen and Lily Rose sixteen when their da had taken them to a performance of the San Francisco Ballet's *The Little Mermaid* at the War Memorial Opera House. It had been Lily Rose's birthday. Finn had glimpsed in the crowd a tall girl in a red gown, her black hair beaded with garnets. The beautiful girl had met Finn's gaze before turning away.

. . . another memory followed of San Francisco, and a banner that read "Scarborough Fair" fluttering between two striped poles. She'd been eating a caramel apple as Lily, in a dress of gauzy red cotton, moved toward a young man with wolf eyes and a scar across one cheekbone. She thought about the reel of film from Lily's boyfriend, Leander, and the shadowy man in the background. She stopped walking.

"Finn." Christie's nervous voice drew her gaze up. Only a few feet away, Reiko Fata was entering the theater on the arm of an elegantly dressed man whose face was shadowed.

Finn wondered if she'd really seen Reiko Fata in San Francisco when she'd been little. If she had, it meant Reiko had been there for a reason, to meet with the nameless, wolf-eyed man from Lily's journal and Finn's memories. Her stomach twisted as she began to suspect a very real and extremely horrifying connection.

"Finn, are you listening?" Christie was pointing at the poster of a male dancer dressed like a crimson Hamlet. "That poster's from the twenties. And that's the boy I saw in the bathtub at the Tirnagoth."

Since any clue to the Fatas was now crucial, Finn dragged Christie into the theater lobby, where they found the brochures with historical information.

They continued down the street as Finn scanned the pictures in the brochure, portraits of famous dancers who'd performed at the Marlowe. She found the

Hamlet as Christie read from his brochure, "Devon Valentine. Tragic suicide in 1926. Well, what a surprise."

They walked to Hecate's Attic, which had a Closed sign on the door, but the lights were on and Anna Weaver was dusting the shelves. When she saw them, she walked to the door, unlocked it, and beckoned them in. As faux Native American music fluted from the sound system, a woman peered from the stockroom and smiled at Christie. "Angyll's not here, Christopher."

Christie said, "'S'allright, Mrs. Weaver. I'm just here to talk to Anna. This is Finn."

"Hello, Finn. Anna, I'll be upstairs." Mrs. Weaver moved away, her heels clicking. She obviously didn't know Finn was the one who'd punched her eldest daughter.

"You came to see Angyll." Anna frowned. "To talk about the beast."

"Annie, you've *got* to stop that," Christie said as he looked around the shop. "I don't need to meet any more rejects from *The Shining* and you're acting like one of the creepy kids."

"I'll tell you what I know." As she sat them down at her table and touched the ivory box of Tarot cards, Finn grimly decided a fourteen-year-old girl in a Snow White T-shirt shouldn't be saying things like, as she did now looking at Finn, "They've noticed you."

Christie sat down at the table with Finn. His left leg began a nervous jitter. "*Who's* noticed her?"

"The serpents and the wolves. You need to be careful." Anna lifted something from around her neck and set it on the table: a tiny, Celtic cross. "The cross symbolizes two worlds which must, always, remain separate, yet intersect. The last divinity made the pact that keeps them from having any influence in our world, unless permission is granted from us. It is an ancient pact, but it's fading."

Finn actually pinched herself to make sure she'd heard correctly. Christie's eyes were wide. He said, "Can you tell us who they are?"

"They should never be named. But they are not nameless."

Christie knuckled a hand through his dark red hair. "Are they ghosts?"

"That realm crosses theirs."

Finn looked at Christie. She pictured Jack's sharp, shadowed face. "What about Jack?"

"That one"—Anna's gaze came to Finn—"that one is a jackal. Three are lost because of him."

"What does that mean?" Christie sounded worried. "That doesn't sound like a positive thing."

"What does that mean, Anna?"

Anna's eyes were wide. "He doesn't want to be in the dark anymore."

Finn bit her lip and shoved shaking hands into her coat pockets. She felt sick.

"You're not going to see him anymore, are you?" Christie wrapped one hand in a sleeve cuff. "He's literally *heartless*."

"There are a lot of Jacks." Anna began to chant, "Jack Daw. Jack in the Green. Jack Frost. Jack the Giant Killer."

"Jack the Ripper," Christie murmured.

The lights flickered, and shadows branched across the ceiling. A gust of wind smashed the shop door open, and a flurry of leaves and dead insects swept in. Finn rose, her hair whipping over her face. "Anna, how do you know all of this?"

"Absalom told me."

Christie, bewildered, said, "The orange-haired guy who sells pot?"

Outside, something laughed like a hyena and Finn's head snapped up . . . she remembered that sound from the night Christie had gotten a tooth shot into his ankle at the house called the Sphinx.

"No!" Anna rose. "By oak and ash and hawthorn too, I cast you out, into the yew!"

The wind was sucked back out. The door slammed shut, but the air stank like old ice.

When Christie raised his head, his eyes glinted silver.

Finn stepped back, shaking her head, denying it. It wasn't *Christie* gazing at her with hungry malice.

Anna pointed at him. "You are not allowed to do that! You're breaking the rules!"

"I always break the rules." The voice that issued from Christie's lips was mocking, male, furred with malice . . . and horrifyingly recognizable.

Finn looked down at the bracelet of iron flowers Christie had given her and wondered if her heart would burst. *This can't be happening. It can't. . .*

The thing inside of Christie ran fingers over Christie's face, his collarbones.

"He's a bit skinny, but he's got a sweet face. And he's innocent. Shall I trot him to a place where he can be *educated*?"

A ferocious anger overwhelmed Finn, breaking the fear-chill. "Caliban. *Get out!*"

The smile on Christie's face was malevolent.

"That is not the spirit's true name." Anna hadn't moved. "You must speak his true name to draw him out."

"That's right, darling." The thing inside Christie leaned toward Finn and the smile twisted. "Kiss me and I'll leave him. Promise."

Suddenly, the shop door banged open. A female voice spoke, commanding and calm, "Caliban Ariel'Pan. *Amach!*"

The silver vanished from Christie's eyes as the cold snapped from the air. Finn caught him as he slumped to the floor.

Standing in the doorway was a woman, her dark hair pulled into a coif, her stylish white coat and heels enhancing her Italian-model look. Her expression was fierce.

"Winter widow," Anna murmured as Finn, kneeling on the floor with Christie in her arms, stared at her history professor and whispered, "Professor Avaline?"

AS SOPHIA AVALINE, GRIMLY SILENT, drove them from Hecate's Attic, Finn felt the chilly night had become a threat. Christie was rubbing his hands over his face.

Professor Avaline met Finn's gaze in the rearview mirror, then circled her Cadillac around and cruised down a street of mostly closed shops and shabby row houses. She stopped the car near Max's Diner. "Out."

"What?" Christie sounded offended. "You're abandoning us *here*?"

She turned off the engine. "I'm coming with you. We need to talk."

Finn thought it felt amazingly good to get out of a luxury car and file obediently into a bright diner that smelled like french fries and coffee. And it was interesting how Italian-model Avaline ordered things off the menu as if this were the most familiar place in the world. When the waitress left, Avaline caught Finn's eye and tucked the plastic menu back behind the ketchup and mustard. "My father is the owner."

"You're kidding." Christie, fiddling with a fork, dropped it.

"After what just happened," Finn said to Christie as she retrieved the fork, "*that's* what astonishes you?"

"I'm pretending it didn't happen," he said, then to Avaline, "Do they have hard liquor here? I think I need some."

"That makes it worse." Sophia Avaline looked as if she was about to give bad news. "It's best to have a clear mind when dealing with them."

Christie winced and whispered to Finn, "She *knows*."

"She can hear you," Finn whispered back. She took a deep breath. She had to continue this conversation despite the quiet horror implicit in every word. "How do you know? About the Fatas? I mean, you're . . . older . . ."

Christie lightly kicked her ankle and Finn grimaced. "I mean—"

"You mean I'm not the target age of their usual prey?"

"*Prey?*"

"Most adults aren't aware of them. They are unable to affect—or are uninterested in—anyone past their midtwenties. But I am one of the gifted. And the ones who noticed you, Finn Sullivan and Christie Hart, are called many things . . . fallen angels, spirits, skinwalkers, djinn—"

"Fairies?" Finn spoke as the waitress arrived with their coffee and food and gave them a wary look before drifting to another table.

"I wouldn't use that term. 'Fatas' will do." Sophia Avaline sipped at her black coffee.

"But what," Christie said, as he gazed queasily down at his hamburger, "are they, really? Like if you were to explain them scientifically?"

"There is no science to describe them. They are spirit things who have found a way to mimic flesh and blood."

Finn ate a french fry and reached for her coffee with a shaking hand. "All of them?"

"All of them." Avaline didn't seem the least fazed by this. "And because they are, to most, an unknown element, they are dangerous."

"It isn't just you, is it?" Finn tried not to think of Jack as a ghost. "There are others at HallowHeart who are like you. Wyatt . . ."

"We found each other. We are the ones who have always known about them, when everyone else forgot."

"But you're not all from Fair Hollow."

"We've each had our own encounter with a Fata, in our youth. And in our youth, we met at HallowHeart. I was born here."

She looked away and it was the first time Finn had ever seen her cool composure crack. "Professor Avaline . . . who are the others that know?"

The remote dark gaze returned to her. "It isn't my place to tell you. We remained here, we became teachers here, because of Reiko Fata and her family."

"Let me ask you something." Christie glanced at her sidelong. "Does Reiko know that *you* know?"

"She does. There is a tentative settlement between us and them, for now. What the one who attacked you did"—Avaline looked at Christie—"would be considered, by Reiko's tribe, to be mischief, nothing more."

Christie's voice was tight. "Can any of them do it again?"

"Possession is a risky endeavor for them. Keep something of silver about you . . . a ring or a medallion, preferably with an image on it you feel is protective."

"You know a lot about them." Finn squinted at Avaline.

"Well." Avaline's mouth thinned. "We've had to. HallowHeart isn't just a place for *students* to learn."

"So *that's* what you're doing," Finn whispered. "You're teaching others about the Fatas."

"What little we know." Avaline sighed. "Then, of course, there are students like you, who create difficulties. We will try to keep you safe."

"So you're not some secret government organization?" Christie was peering out the window.

"Mr. Hart"—Professor Avaline frowned at him—"the two of you, and Sylvie Whitethorn, have come to the attention of malevolent creatures who manage to move unseen among us when they want to. I am advising you to end all associations with them, especially since you've been found vulnerable and were, just a few moments ago, influenced by one of the worst."

"Why can't *you* do anything about them?"

"We're an *informal* border patrol, Christie Hart. We're not organized. They have never, as far as we know, killed humans; they merely *influence*. They are territorial, and, sometimes, psychically parasitic, but I have no proof of murder. I'm afraid if we act against them . . . we'll only instigate a confrontation that would not end well for us."

"Can they"—Finn's voice was strained—"make someone *want* to die?"

Sophia Avaline's silence was an answer.

"Finn." Christie laid a hand on her shoulder. He looked at Avaline. "So they can't kill us, but they can make us crazy? What about those parties?"

Avaline was watching Finn, who sat with her head down, digging at the wooden table with her short fingernails.

"Those parties, their revels, are to recruit the vulnerable, Miss Sullivan. I can't tell you what to do—I and the others . . . we need to walk a fine line."

"You're neutral, is that what you're saying?" Christie pulled himself to his feet. "Let's go, Finn. We'll walk back; she's not on our side."

Finn rose. Although she still had a million questions, she couldn't ask them right now . . . she was too angry . . . and she didn't think Sophia Avaline would answer them.

Avaline's voice stopped them as they started toward the door. "Serafina. There have been disappearances, nothing proven. I am *not* on their side. Now let me drive the two of you home."

THAT NIGHT, FINN GOOGLED "FAIR Hollow disappearances."

There weren't many, but the four listed were disturbing enough. Each had occurred during a different time.

1925—Beatrice Amory, eighteen years old
1968—Abigail Cwyndyr, sixteen years old
1972—Thomas Luneht, seventeen years old (But he'd been found
in the woods, with no explanation as to how he'd come to be
there. Later, he'd killed himself.)
1997—Eve Avaline, seventeen years old

"*Avaline*," Finn whispered. The only commonality was the young ages; the times of the disappearances formed no pattern. The girls' bodies had never been found. She gazed at the pictures of the missing on her screen. She was sure that the ghostly girl she'd glimpsed at Drake's Chapel when she'd first arrived had been blond Abigail, and Eve had given her the silver dagger at Tirnagoth.

Finn covered her face with her hands, and a shudder ran through her. Christie, only a few hours ago, had gone darkside. Professor Avaline was a witch and a member of a secret society. Jack's family was as terrifying as things from a horror movie. And a ghost girl named Eve—probably related to Professor Avaline—had given Finn a silver knife.

She wanted to crawl into her closet and lock the door.

She drew Lily's journal from where she kept it beneath her pillow. She hadn't read all of it—it was scary and amazing and it was a part of her sister she'd only just discovered. Now she scanned it, searching the stories and scribbled references and sketches for something she dreaded finding.

There was no mention of a Jack, only one scrawled sentence beneath the drawing of a girl with a snake's body: *I saw her again, the girl in red. Her skin is so white. I know she is one of them.*

Reiko . . . ?

Finn knelt beside her backpack and drew out the silent film in its red casing, the film Jack hadn't wanted her to see.

She hurried down to her da's office, calling to him that she needed to use the projector. She could hear eggs frying and his voice on the phone.

As she pulled the projector out and spooled the reel, Finn felt grateful to Lily's boyfriend for showing her everything he had about photography and film. Then she turned the projector on.

The film began as it had before, in what she now recognized as the Tirnagoth lobby in black-and-white. The young man finished his turn toward the camera, his eyes inky, his dark hair sleeked back, his smile wicked. His black suit seemed to breed shadows as he beckoned. *Jack.* A pretty girl in a flapper dress appeared, a bandeau in bobbed hair that Finn imagined would be red. She was the third girl gone missing—Beatrice from 1925.

On the screen, the title card appeared, ornate script on midnight: *He is not a gentleman.*

The jittery film told the tale of the young man with the inky eyes seducing the girl to her ruin. At the end, she flung herself from Tirnagoth's roof in a dramatic bit of old-fashioned trickery that nevertheless made Finn feel as if it was mocking Lily's death.

The film snaked to a stop. Finn sat quietly. She didn't feel hysteria or a separation from reality. This *was* her reality, this world tainted with dread and darkness and old secrets.

She could not see Jack again.

JACK LEANED ON A BANISTER in the Tirnagoth Hotel and watched Nathan Clare moving through the lobby. In one corner, a skinny boy in jeans, a tattoo of raven wings on his back, was playing a harp while two young women in gossamer competed at jacks on the floor.

When Jack closed his eyes, he saw Finn, all long limbs and a searching gaze, a blossom mouth and tawny, tumbled hair. She had found out he was not a gentleman, and heartless as well. So he'd lost her. It was the best thing that could have happened to her. He . . . he would return to feeling nothing.

At the moment, he felt as if he were choking on iron nails.

"Jack." Phouka leaned back against the banister beside him, her elbows on the wood. She was splendid in a corset of white leather and hip-hugging jeans, her auburn hair threaded with raw pearls.

He said, "Do you ever think about what they took from you?"

"Old age? Disease? Big Macs?"

"We're like them now. The children of nothing and night."

"Get over it. You've had two hundred years to do so."

"They set me on Finn Sullivan to keep her from Nathan. She's just an innocent girl and I almost . . ."

Phouka sighed. "I was once an innocent girl. Serafina Sullivan's obviously not jonesing for our Nate. She won't be stopping the Teind. They'll leave her be."

"Nate." Jack pushed his hands through his hair. "Do you remember fine wine, Phouka? The kind that burns your throat? Or steak, charred and filled with red juice? Or Belgian chocolate? And love—"

"I remember those things." Phouka looked lush and mournful. "I liked you better when you were bleeding and brooding."

He smiled. He leaned toward her and whispered into her lavishly pierced ear, "Do you miss it?"

She stared at him. "I don't know what you're referring to."

"I think you do." He stepped back. In his rare moments of dreaming, he sometimes pictured another life, a life of mundane wishes, childish beliefs, and sunlight. "Do you remember when you became part of the family?"

"Why are we having this conversation on a stairway?" She paused. "I believe I became part of the *family* in 1967. Or was that just my favorite year?"

He rested his arms on the banister and examined the old rings on his fingers. "You're not as young as you seem, are you?"

"Are you calling me *old*?"

He clutched the wood of the banister, and it splintered beneath his fingers. He whispered, "I don't know how much more of this I can take."

"Jack." The lightness had left her voice. "You mustn't give in to it now."

"You come from England. Do they celebrate the Teind there?"

"Nathan made his choice."

"He was desperate, like I was. He was my friend, once."

"And Reiko sent him away for years because of that. Jack, she's already placed us in debt . . . with you. If *this* Teind isn't paid . . ."

"Then death will become us." He gazed down at the lobby and the creatures he'd come to think of as his family. "What is she planning?"

"She's planning an offensive."

"Is she?" His voice was as soft as a predator's paws on snow.

"A trick that might save our lives."

"It won't"—Jack unfolded from the banister and walked away—"save mine."

CHAPTER ELEVEN

*Those who have received their touch waste away from this
world, lending their strength to the invisible ones; for the
strength of a human body is needed by the shadows.*

—Visions and Beliefs in the West of Ireland, Lady
Gregory

*The water folk are the most dangerous. They feed on our blood to keep
their shapes. Mermaids, selkies, kelpies, the Afanc . . . their clan is called
Uisce, so beware of anyone with that name.*

—From the journal of Lily Rose

Finn hadn't slept, worrying about Christie. Her phone was tucked close to
her pillow so she could have instant contact with him. When he finally texted
her, it was to let her know that he wouldn't be going to classes until later on.
She'd wanted to hear his voice, just to make sure he was okay.

It was as she was setting down her phone that she remembered Lily Rose's
phone . . . a phone she'd just tossed in with her sister's stuff, a phone she'd never
checked. She scrambled from bed and hurried down the stairs into the dining
room, to the boxes holding Lily's things. She went through two of them before
she found the iPhone and its adapter. She'd have to wait before going through
any photos on it; Lily's laptop had died a year ago and she'd never looked at her

sister's files—she regretted that now. The world Lily had seen, the one Finn was only beginning to glimpse, might have been visible in more technological ways than Lily's journal.

As Finn drifted to the hall table and began thumbing through the mail, her heart jumped when she found the crimson envelope.

SHE TOLD SYLVIE WHAT HAD happened to Christie when they met in Origen's courtyard between classes.

"Christie was *possessed*?" Sylvie's shoulders convulsed in a shudder. "But that's not—"

"Don't say it's not possible, because, really, it is." Finn didn't want to talk about it anymore. She wore silver and iron for protection and knew that, last night, Christie hadn't worn his.

"And Professor Avaline knows—things?" Sylvie said, looking wary now.

"*Lots* of things."

"And Absalom the dealer is probably one of these . . . people, according to Annie Weaver? He's a Fata, too, and all the Fatas are . . . ?"

"Let's just call them Fatas. Oh, and I got this, this morning." Finn held up the crimson envelope. "It's—"

"I know what it is." Sylvie pulled an identical envelope from her backpack. "It's an invitation to another Fata party."

CHRISTIE HAD ALSO RECEIVED AN invitation.

Later, the three of them held a desperate, whispered conversation in HallowHeart's library. It was a gloomy afternoon, spitting rain, and the library's fluorescent lighting was giving Finn a headache.

"Did it really happen, Christie? A *possession*?" Sylvie was studying him with narrowed eyes.

Christie gazed out the window. He looked exhausted. "I don't know. It felt . . . bad. Like I got shoved into the back of my head while someone else did the steering."

Sylvie looked down at her wrists braceleted with charms. "How did Caliban do it, do you think?"

"I don't know, but we'll make sure it doesn't happen again," Finn said. She didn't know how they'd manage that, but they needed to protect themselves now. "I don't think he'll try it again."

"They're not *human*. How do we stop *anything* they do?" Christie shuddered. "This can't be real. It can't."

Sylvie sidetracked his meltdown with calm words. "What about what Avaline told you? There are *others who know about them*. And who gathered them *here*?"

"She didn't tell us."

Christie looked sick. "We're not going to that party, Finn."

She didn't say anything, because she planned to attend the Fatas' party without her friends. She would go for answers. She would go with defenses, because her sister had had none.

Christie was watching her. Sylvie was skimming through several books on folklore she'd pulled from the shelves.

"Can't you just forget him, Finn?" Christie sounded desperate.

Finn looked down at her hands and whispered, "You don't understand."

"I don't want to."

"I don't need you to."

"It's like"—he leaned forward—"you're in a dream, like you don't care what happens to you. You're not thinking you can actually get *hurt*. You're like an adrenaline junkie."

"And the Fatas are the drug? Thanks for the psychoanalysis."

"Don't snap at me."

"I did not snap at you."

"You did snap at him." Sylvie looked concerned.

Finn *did* snap then and pushed to her feet. "I'm leaving." And she stormed off, ignoring Sylvie's call and Christie's charming apology.

As she stalked across the lawn, Finn nearly ran into Nathan Clare, who said, "Finn? Are you coming to the party?"

She took a deep breath, knowing this meeting wasn't a coincidence. "Nathan. I *know*."

His smile vanished, and he looked weary and wounded. "It's an invitation. You'll be safe by our laws."

Our laws. She said, "Yes, I'm going."

He leaned toward her, and his voice was low and urgent. *"Be careful."*

"Nathan—"

"I can't talk now." He backed away. "I've got to go."

As he turned and strode away, she started after him. "Hey—"

"Finn Sullivan."

She turned and scowled, because Aubrey Drake was making his way toward her, black hair rippling around his fine-boned face. He wore a cashmere coat with careless elegance, a white shirt crisp against his cocoa-colored skin. "You're invited to Nate's party?"

"It's *his* . . ."

"Well, it's a Fata revel, so . . ." He shrugged and Finn realized the source of his charm—Aubrey Drake, captain of the Ravens football team, was one of *theirs*.

"They're not bad people," he said, "the Fatas. They just have their ways."

"And what have they given you in exchange for *your* soul?"

He was quiet a moment, gazing at her. Then he smiled again. "You're a firecracker. No wonder they're worried. Besides, it's not so fantastic—I could've gotten into Penn State and Hester was accepted at Columbia. But we're consigned to HallowHeart. Because that's the way it is."

Her pulse jumped—no more pretending.

Aubrey's eyes darkened as he said seriously, "Finn, you've got to be straight with them. No lies. Be respectful. You've heard that Rolling Stones song 'Sympathy for the Devil'? Well, some of those lyrics could apply to *them*. See you tonight—and don't forget to come to our last game, weekend after next—we're playing against the Riverwood Badgers."

He strode away, calling to a group of his friends gathered near the stairs.

Finn clutched her backpack's straps and gazed past the apple and oak trees, at HallowHeart, with its child-faced gargoyles and Emory-shrouded windows. She watched the students who wandered the grounds or sat on the steps. Two girls in dark coats ran across the grass, laughing, their braids crow-black. A young man with pale hair and a girl who looked like a Brontë heroine crouched on the stairs, passing a cigarette back and forth. Nearby, a group of students, their hair twined with flowers, sat beneath an oak with a pile of books between them.

Between, Finn thought. This was a between place, and nothing was as it seemed. The black-clad sisters' laughter sounded like crows calling. The students reading leather-bound books had spiral tattoos on the backs of their hands, and the eyes of the boy and girl sharing the cigarette glinted like rubies. Their teeth seemed sharp.

So there you have it. Finn backed away. *I'm either crazy . . . or this whole town is infested with the supernatural.*

FINN WAS CHOOSING SOMETHING TO wear for a party held by dangerous, otherworldly people, and listening to her mother's favorite Bee Gees song, "Spirit," when a tapping sounded on the glass doors. Her breath hitched. Jack.

He has no heart.

He stood outside, in a Victorian coat. He tapped again and his rings clicked against the glass. She walked slowly to the doors, opened them. The night swept in, riddled with tattered leaves and moth wings. He said, "You idiot. You're going, aren't you?"

"If you're going to be rude, you can leave." In her red Mickey Mouse T-shirt and old jeans, she was again underdressed against his elegance.

His gaze, upsettingly, was cold. "May I come in?"

She stepped back. "Can I stop you?"

He entered, bringing with him the perfume of burning wood and wild roses. As he sprawled in her rocking chair, she closed the doors and tried not to look at him. "Why are you here, Jack?"

"You've been invited to a family gathering." He curled his hands on the armrests.

"I've already been told the rules"—she leaned against the bookshelves—"by Aubrey Drake."

"Aubrey. Do you know who his famous relative was?"

"You're not going to say Queen Elizabeth's Francis Drake, are you?"

"Aubrey's family came from Jamaica. Long ago, Sir Francis Drake stopped in the islands and took a shine to one of Aubrey's female ancestors."

She stared at Jack, this striking young man from a secret mythology. She'd followed him that night at the lake concert because he'd seemed mysterious, cool, unbreakable and she'd sensed his danger, the darkness trailing him like black ribbons. He'd made her feel as if she were walking on a very high ledge while believing she had wings. Now that adrenaline rush was too close to fear. When he tilted his head, the tiny ruby piercing his nose shone like a drop of blood. She had woken him, quickened his dusty soul, *invited* him. She said in a small voice, "*Tell me why you came.*"

"I came to tell you how to behave *properly* at a Fata party. Aubrey Drake isn't a reliable source on manners. Don't drink any wine, and don't wear iron or silver—by our laws, we can't hurt you when you've been invited and such adornments would be a declaration of war. They'll be serving *ordinary* food, as an act of honor."

"Why am I—are we—invited?"

"They want to seduce you." His gaze was hot.

She felt her face flush, and it was hard to breathe, even with him all the way across the room. What had she been letting into her house? She'd read enough fairy tales to know that girls with demon lovers never came to a good end.

She was not one of those girls. "So . . . no iron or silver. How am I supposed to protect myself?"

"You know any poetry? Poetry spoken by someone like you has the power of prayer and, unlike prayer, won't make them angry. They can't create any poetry of their own—it's a sword they can admire, but not wield. When they speak it, it means nothing."

"Is it everyone, Jack?" She moved toward the drawer where she kept her sewing kit. "Is everyone here under the influence of Reiko Fata and her tribe?"

His voice sharpened. "What are you doing?"

She lifted a pin. "Can I prick you, Jack?"

The room's light seemed to darken, and the shadows of familiar things became crooked. The CD player had drifted into silence.

"Can I prick you back?" His teeth were showing as he gripped the arms of the chair.

"I want to *help* you. What did they *do to you?*" Finn said.

"Ask me what they did to Lily Rose."

It was worse than being threatened or smacked. She curled her hand around the pin and spoke as if she had broken glass in her throat. "Lily Rose is dead."

"And how do you know it wasn't *me* who tricked her?"

"It wasn't you."

"How do you know?" He rose and sauntered to the wall of books, where he delicately reached out to touch the photo of a little girl in a white ballet costume. "Is this her?"

"Yes. *Was* it you?" She watched him step back from the photo of Lily. "Was it you who gave me the moth key?"

"No. Finn . . . the moth key—did it open the way to Tirnagoth?"

She nodded. "And your voyage trunk." She turned and took the film reel in its red casing from behind a pillow on the window seat. She held it out to him as he raised inky eyes to hers and accepted it. "I sort of suspected. Jack, that journal you saw floating in midair . . ." Her voice caught. She composed herself. "It was Lily's. She wrote . . . things."

"Things?" He was looking at her now as if she would do him some terrible harm.

"Anna Weaver once talked about the children of nothing and night—and that same phrase is in Lily's journal. She knew about the Fatas. That's what they are, aren't they? The children of night and nothing." Finn walked to Jack as he stood with his head bowed. She reached for one of his hands and pricked his finger with the pin, then sighed when a bead of red appeared. "Let me help you. I *couldn't help her* . . ."

He clasped the back of her neck and pressed his brow against hers. "Do you know what you are doing?"

"I know. And I'm doing it."

"You are walking in the shadows, wading through a river of blood. They don't like things being taken from them. *Don't come tonight.*"

"You expect me to do nothing? Not going to happen, Jack." She slid her arms around him, pressed her face against his neck. She pictured him, in black-and-white, standing beside a horse and coach in another century. She felt his breath quicken as he kissed her beneath her ear. Her hands were splayed across his back; she could feel his muscles tense as his fingers, strong and slender, cupped her hip, the nape of her neck, then knotted in her hair. She whispered his name, even though she knew, in that sensible fragment of her brain, that a kiss from him could mean death.

She fiercely wrapped her arms around him. Maybe a kiss from her could mean life for *him*.

"Finn," he whispered as he raised his hands to her face, "listen to me. This is what I do. This is what I was made for, by her."

"I won't break into pieces. I promise."

"You will." His lips were so close, it was like a kiss. His voice was low, his muscles like steel cables beneath his skin—as if *he* would break. "They all do, eventually, the ones she sends me after."

"Let's pretend," she whispered, "that she didn't send you. That *I* came after *you*."

Jack closed his eyes as Finn kissed his temple, the slope of one cheekbone, the line of his jaw. Now she felt his heartbeat pulsing like a small animal beneath the hand she laid against his chest. When her mouth touched his, his lips parted with a breath.

He flung himself away, through the doors, which creaked with his passing.

Finn sank to a crouch, her head in her hands.

MERMAID HOUSE SWAM INTO VIEW from the violet haze of descending evening as Finn's cab slid up the drive. The time on the invitation had been very specific.

As the cab left her, she began to regret coming alone. But she had to *know*. She felt that, tonight, the Fatas would reveal themselves and she'd have some idea as to what she was battling. And they couldn't hurt her—she'd been *invited*.

After a second of hesitation, she walked quickly up the lane before the insane courage deserted her. She wore a dress of antique-green silk that had belonged to her sister and the Doc Martens she'd bought at a flea market. The hood of her red coat was flung over her hair, which she'd coiled with holly. The house suited its name. It looked old and uncared for, the fountain—a mer-boy of white stone clutching a fish—clogged with Emory. Two green marble mermaids curved over the entrance, above paint-peeling doors. The glass of the windows was blue beneath the grime—in the day, the interior must seem as though it was submerged beneath water. Beyond the house, she heard violin and flute music. It was another party held on the grounds of a dead house. *They must collect them*, she thought with a twist of fear, *places without hope*.

She was debating whether or not to ring the bell shaped like a cowrie shell, when the door opened and Absalom Askew, slim and elegant in a suit of tawny suede, smiled at her.

"Finn Sullivan." He had a daisy tucked behind one ear, and she wondered if his hair had been dyed that extraordinary orange. "We've been expecting you."

Looking past him, she saw a chandelier of blue glass, mirrored walls, and large furniture shrouded in plastic. He stepped out and closed the door. "Come on. Everyone's in the garden."

Finn followed him to the garden, where tiny lights twinkled in ornamental trees and a table was set with crystal goblets and platters of food. The guests were scattered in groups, drinking and talking while a trio of musicians played instruments beneath a canopy. The air was fragrant with the scents of smoke, wine, and flowers. Everyone was young. Everyone was glamorous.

Fighting skittish panic, Finn counted twelve guests as she followed Absalom across the lawn toward Reiko Fata, perfect in an empire gown of red gossamer. She was speaking to a white-haired young man with a delicate face and a silvery moth tattooed beneath his left ear.

"Lazuli," Reiko Fata said, as she turned to Finn, "this is Serafina Sullivan."

The white-haired young man nodded but didn't speak. When his eyes flashed silver, Finn forced herself not to shiver.

"Shall I wander elsewhere?" Absalom was watching a slender girl in a black gown. Finn glimpsed Nathan seated beneath a tree, speaking to the violinist vagabond with the long, red hair.

"Go on." Reiko moved forward. "Walk with me, Serafina." Trailing expensive perfume and a darker scent that reminded Finn of reptiles, Reiko led her across the lawn. "What do you think of Fair Hollow?"

With its revels and parties and odd residents, Fair Hollow wasn't like any other place Finn had ever been. And this girl who radiated menace—her black hair too sleek, her skin velvety white—made Finn's spine ice. She said, calmly, "I think my sister would have liked it here."

"Oh, Serafina, you are too young to hold grudges. Your sister chose to take her own life. I am sorry for that."

You're not sorry for anything, Finn thought savagely. *You are a monster pretending to be a girl.* "I remember seeing you in San Francisco."

"Serafina." Reiko stopped walking. "It's a coincidence that we were in San Francisco at the time of her death. Someone told her stories—nonsense things—and she believed them. It made her crazy."

Finn, studying that innocent face, found herself wanting to believe those words, because it would make everything so much easier.

Reiko said gently, "I want you to be comfortable with us. Whether you like it or not, you're connected to us now. You *know* us."

"I don't know what you *are*," Finn whispered.

"You don't need to. You like Jack. You like Nathan. Your friend likes Phouka." Reiko was looking past her.

Finn turned, and flinched, then breathed deeply and almost snarled. Christie had come, and he was talking with the girl chauffeur. And Sylvie, in striped stockings and a little black frock, was speaking with Nathan. They had figured her out. "Damn."

"They're ours, Serafina, only they don't know it yet."

"I don't believe you. I don't believe anything you say."

"Serafina. You don't want to be my enemy." Reiko still resembled a girl, but her eyes had become dark and her voice held a tone that flattened the air—and that was just the hidden part. Her mask was everything that made Finn feel inferior. She was the flawless model, the head cheerleader, the *other* girl who would always be more beautiful, more accomplished.

As Finn remained stubbornly silent, Reiko moved away. "Come. Everyone is being seated."

Finn reluctantly followed her to the table cluttered with a small feast Jack had called "ordinary." A dark-haired boy was tending to the grill, forking slabs of meat onto black plates. There were dark red apples, a crimson cake, mounds of strawberries, chicken and ribs drenched in barbecue sauce. *A murderers' feast.*

Everyone took a seat at the claw-footed table, Reiko choosing a chair at one end, Nathan at the other. Finn sat opposite Christie and Sylvie. Absalom, languid as a caterpillar, was flirting with a girl whose golden hair was coiled in braids. The tall youth in white—Lazuli—watched Finn as he peeled an apple. There were others at the table, and none of the faces were plain or uninteresting.

Then Jack swaggered into view, in black-striped trousers and a black shirt with buttoned cuffs, a strand of tiny rubies across his collarbones. He didn't look at Finn as he set one hand on Nathan's chair and leaned down to speak to him. When he looked up, past her, she apprehensively turned her head.

Caliban Ariel'Pan was moving across the lawn, platinum hair shimmering.

She gripped the table's edge and met the gazes of Christie and Sylvie, who seemed as scared as she felt. Reiko was a calculated danger; Caliban was a wild card.

As the wild card sprawled in the chair near Reiko, Jack took the chair next to Sylvie and smiled grimly at Finn over the crimson cake. Someone had poured wine into her black teacup. She ignored it and leaned toward Sylvie. "Why did you come?"

Solemnly, Sylvie murmured, "We're your friends."

"Where are the Rooks?" Reiko leaned gracefully forward to cut the cake with a butcher's knife. "I told them not to be late."

Jack gazed at Finn as he replied, "Maybe the Rooks are jealous this isn't their party. Happy birthday, Nathan."

"Thanks, Jack." Nathan was staring into his wineglass.

Finn slouched back in her chair and observed the Fatas, watching for anything supernatural. Music from the small orchestra soared over the conversations as the guests, revealing an ornamental affection for one another, began to eat and drink. Caliban and Jack acted like rival siblings. Phouka passed a plate of cake to Nathan while Lazuli, the young man in white, remained quiet. When Sylvie asked him about the apples, he smiled and handed her one.

"Finn." His plate piled with ribs and black rice sprinkled with red peppers, Christie leaned forward. "Eat something."

"No. And I wish you wouldn't."

He looked wistfully down at the tempting meal. "I know I shouldn't, but I'm *starving.*"

"That might not be your fault." Sylvie sniffed at her apple.

"Our hospitality doesn't involve poisoning the guests, does it, Lazuli?" Jack reached over, stabbed a small roast hen with a fork, and dropped it onto Finn's plate. He met her gaze. "It's safe. Eat. Don't drink the wine."

Then the Rooks arrived.

Trip, Hip Hop, and Bottle strolled across the lawn, the boys in black ruffles and red silk ties, Hip Hop dressed in a black corset and a skirt of red tulle. She carried a crimson parasol. Trip held a rectangular bat. Reiko gazed at them with cool displeasure. "You're late."

As they leaned against one another in a pose that struck Finn as familiar, Trip spoke, his eyes dark and sly: "We were at a game of cricket."

"You know how we love cricket." Hip Hop tilted her head. Beside her, blond Bottle didn't say anything.

Finn suddenly recognized that pose, those sly faces and almond eyes. The world tilted. She felt that uncanny shiver in the air, a sting in her sinuses, as if her frontal lobe was being pinched. *No. They can't be.*

Caliban spoke courteously to Finn. "Want to know about the Rooks' names? Bottle looks like the angels in Botticelli's paintings. Hip Hop is what a rabbit does, and this bunny can lead anyone to a good time. And Trip? He's good at making accidents happen."

"Caliban." Reiko's voice sliced the smile from his face.

Finn had straightened in her chair. The three Rooks in their Victorian-punk clothing held the same pose as Malcolm Tirnagoth's three children in their photograph from the 1920s, the one Sylvie had shown her. And Sylvie, the collector of old photographs, was staring at the Rooks as if she, too, had realized they were dead things from another century.

The Fatas had almost fooled her tonight, with their false affection and their attempts at family eccentricity. Although they mimicked humans, they were *not*. Finn and her friends were seated here with white-skinned, silver-eyed beings and the living dead, the children of nothing and night.

Finn's stomach churned. She looked at Jack, who was eating a piece of cake with his fingers, picking it neatly apart. The nightmarish reality of the other-world suddenly blindsided her, and she felt that enchanted sleep prowling closer. "Jack . . ."

"Jack." Reiko's voice slid across the table, chimed against the crystal goblets. "I want to dance."

Jack looked at Finn. He rose and sauntered toward the musicians and Reiko followed. As the band began another song, a delicate, Renaissance harmony— "Greensleeves"—Reiko slid her arms around Jack and they began to dance as if they had been together since the beginning of the world.

Finn made a small sound, feeling an almost physical pain.

The conversations at the table continued as the Rooks approached and rudely began picking delicacies from the platters. As Bottle stuffed a red-frosted cupcake into his mouth, Christie pushed his food away.

Finn glanced away from Jack and Reiko, to Sylvie and Christie, who watched her with solemn expressions.

"I think the Rooks are . . ." Finn couldn't finish.

Sylvie nodded, while Christie looked wary. "*What?*"

"They're Malcolm Tirnagoth's children," Sylvie said. She resembled one of the present company with her tilty blue eyes, the black hair rippling around her face.

The lights flickered, and the violins changed to a gypsy reel as the three friends stared at the Rooks. Nathan had begun to dance with a girl in a white gown, her pale hair like a dandelion puff. As others waltzed with delicate precision around them, Finn wondered if that was the someone Nathan hadn't wanted his family to know about. What had changed?

Christie said quietly, "Did you notice how they keep Nathan watched, like he's some kind of good luck charm? And he's the adopted one."

So is Jack, Finn wanted to tell them, but he wasn't, really, because the Fatas weren't a family . . . they were a *tribe*.

Phouka Fata was walking toward them, her hair wound with pearls and her body sleek in a kimono-dress of mauve silk; she wore sandals that laced to her knees. When Phouka smiled at Christie, Finn saw the enchantment begin, even saw him resist at first when Phouka held out a hand.

"Christie," Phouka said and, as her voice drew his gaze up, Finn reached out to grab him, but he was out of her grasp and letting the Fata girl lead him away.

Finn turned to find Sylvie had also gone. "Damn it." She remembered what Reiko had said. *They're ours. Only they don't know it yet.*

Jack was suddenly seated beside her. "Did you drink the wine?"

Finn looked startled as she realized she had. "Yes. I forgot—"

"Idiot. That was blackberry wine. Don't look at me. Find your friends. I need to keep Reiko distracted."

"What? Jack—"

But he was already walking back toward Reiko.

Finn blinked, rubbed at her eyes, and wondered why the air had begun to shimmer.

CHRISTIE WASN'T USED TO BEING nervous around girls. Phouka, walking beside him, made him nervous.

"You're not afraid of my family, are you?" She sounded as if she knew he was.

"I'm very afraid of your family. Your tribe."

They paused beneath a window of Mermaid House, where interior light illuminated the blue face of a girl drowning in the stained glass. Christie looked down at his new Timberlands and frowned. He pictured Phouka in sunlight, her hair sweeping around her face. When he spoke, his voice was low. "What's your real name?"

"It doesn't matter."

"It does." He thought of happy girls lured away from ordinary lives, into a world where sunlight never warmed their skin. "It does matter. I bet it mattered to your family."

"You went to Tirnagoth." Phouka idly walked around him. "You saw some things."

"Tell me you don't live there. Or in any of these house wrecks."

"You're asking me a question," Phouka said, smiling slyly, "that you already know the answer to."

He felt as if he was walking through the woods, naked, on a winter night. He refused to let her see how scared he was. Her eyes, in the Harlequin shadows and light, glinted an inhuman silver. Christie had never believed in anything he couldn't see, not in any of the spooks that supposedly roamed Fair Hollow. But now he stood before one of the causes of that supernatural activity, and his brain had seized up like his car had in front of the Luneht house.

"What are you?" He wanted to run, but her silver eyes pinned him.

"Again, Christie: Question? Answer: You like learning things, don't you? Would you like to know things?"

"No."

She stepped toward him, quick and graceful, not at all like a spook. But he knew better. She whispered, "Say something pretty to me. Something of yours."

He looked down at his boots again. "She was a spirit, once wild and free. She became Other, wild, not free. I looked for her, but cold was she. I said to her, 'I would bleed for thee.' That pale, lost, and wild beauty."

She leaned toward him and kissed him, and her mouth was warm and sweet and not at all cold.

SYLVIE HAD ONLY LEFT FINN'S side for a second, to try to catch Nathan Clare's attention—he seemed the most normal of the Fatas—when she heard someone call her name. She walked toward a figure standing near the house and felt apprehension when the figure seemed to be nothing more than a clot of shadows.

Sylvie, something whispered.

A black rabbit darted past her feet. As it loped away, she found herself on a path that led to a greenhouse lit from within by old-fashioned lamps.

When she saw what waited for her in the doorway, she whispered a curse. Hip Hop smiled sweetly. "She wants to speak to you. She knows you can see the dead."

Sylvie didn't move until Hip Hop had swaggered away. Then she walked slowly toward the greenhouse, because she had to *know*.

Reiko stood in the center aisle, clipping leaves from a spiky plant, the red gossamer of her gown smoking against the dark leaves. Her looped hair was threaded with medallions. She didn't look at Sylvie as she spoke. "What do you think of this garden? It has been neglected."

Sylvie, on the threshold, asked with false casualness, "What do you grow?"

"What you'd expect: monkshood, wolfsbane, nightshade, thornapple. Mandrake. Other things."

Sylvie knew she should be afraid, but the drowsy buzz from the apple wine—she'd avoided the blackberry—made her bold. "Are you a witch?"

Reiko Fata set down the shears and brought a handful of leaves to her nose, then inhaled. "All girls your age are witches. You keep the power hidden, use it for the ordinary. But you . . . *you're* something different."

Sylvie shivered.

Reiko moved down the aisle, caressing the plants. "There's no need to be ordinary, Sylvie Whitethorn. Come to us and see things you've never dreamed of."

Sylvie stepped back.

"I know you see them sometimes, the *sluagh*." Reiko walked around a table of bromeliads. "Would you like to meet Thomas Luneht?"

"He's dead." Sylvie felt all the romance of her fascination with the dead and their histories sinking into a swamp of fear. The young woman standing before her knew all the secrets that Sylvie had, idiotically, wanted to learn. At that instant, Sylvie became aware of something moving in a dark corner of the greenhouse; she heard a breath like a young man's sigh. Lifting her gaze to look past Reiko, she felt a wrenching nausea.

"He's fond of you. They're drawn to the ones who show interest in them." Reiko, whose green eyes were now a shimmering silver, smiled at Sylvie. "Poor boy made the wrong kind of friends. You can be a pawn in this game, Sylvie Whitethorn, or a player. Thomas was a pawn."

"*Game?* What kind of *game*—"

"The one"—Reiko smiled as the shadow in the corner began to move forward—"between our kind and yours. Join us, Sylvie, and be so much more than you are."

Sylvie stumbled back into a table as Thomas Luneht, who had committed suicide nearly forty years ago, stepped forward, looking as warmly alive as she was. He met Sylvie's gaze and said, "Don't liste—"

Reiko quickly waved a hand and he became a shadow that vanished in ribbons of darkness.

"No." Sylvie began to back away. Dazed by the eerie night, the splendid Victorian greenhouse, the tall, electric-eyed queen offering her another world, she couldn't think. So this was how it happened, how they lured people to them. She thought of being Other, of losing all that she was. "I *can't.*"

She turned and walked swiftly from the greenhouse, hugging herself against the solitary cold of being human.

THE GARDEN PARTY HAD BECOME less quaint and more wild as the torches and candles blazed and the musicians slashed their instruments in a frenzy of familiar melodies gone mad. The Fatas in their punk-romantic clothes seemed to have increased in number, and the three Rooks were crouched on the empty chairs, picking at the feast. They didn't resemble Malcolm Tirnagoth's children anymore. They reminded Finn of monstrous birds. As she turned away from them, she thought she heard feathers rustling.

She stalked past a boy who seemed to have antlers growing from his brow and avoided a girl in a golden gown, her hair like flames. When the dancing crowd parted for an instant, she saw Caliban Fata speaking with the white-haired Fata named Lazuli and her vision blurred again—Caliban's face became a hideous mask of jagged teeth and yellow, glowing eyes. Lazuli turned his head and his face was a deer skull.

Finn cursed softly and didn't raise her head again. Her gaze fixed on the ground, she wove through the Fatas; she thought she glimpsed hooves beneath one gown, a clawed hand holding a goblet. She needed to get away before she looked at Jack and *saw* him. The blackberry wine was doing something terrible to her brain—it was showing *them* unfettered by whatever glamour made them seem human.

"Serafina."

The breath left her, because it was Reiko's voice, but whatever stood behind her—Finn didn't dare look—no longer wore the shape of a girl. She closed her eyes as tentacles of cold shadow streaked with old blood and fire whispered around her.

"Do you think Jack is interested in you?" Reiko continued. "I told him to charm you, to keep you from another. This will be your last night with him, mayfly. He's waiting for you in Mermaid House."

Wishing she hadn't come, Finn headed toward the house, which was probably not really a house, but a trap. She halted, hoping Jack would come out. She didn't want to go in there—but she'd been promised she wouldn't be harmed, because she'd been *invited* and, maybe, to the Fatas, that quaint notion was to be honored.

The door was unlocked. Finn stumbled into a hall lit by lamps of blue glass with a trail of water glistening on turquoise tiles. Following the water to a bathroom with copper fixtures, she found a tub filled with a rank sludge that reeked of dead fish. She twisted away and desperately called out Jack's name.

The watery trail became wet footprints, which she followed to the doorway of a parlor with a fireplace shaped into a huge, black shell. A chandelier like frozen water glittered from the ceiling, and a dark, salty fragrance tainted the air. She heard the voices before she saw the speakers.

". . . don't like it here."

"It's too hot."

"Do you smell that?"

Three strangers sat in chairs of twisted wood. The girl's hair was coral red, her lips mermaid blue. She wore strands of pearls and a gown of pale blue gossamer. A boy with wet hair sprawled in the chair beside; he was dressed in a kilt, and his eyes were as black as those of a seal. The third figure had its back to her, its hair silvery, its shoulders broad. This one spoke in a deep voice. "I smell it, too, selkie boy. Virgin blood."

He turned his head, revealing a horselike profile and a claw-fingered hand that held a red cup.

Finn flinched as the figure became an older man in jeans, his eyes bright with malice. The girl turned and looked directly at Finn, her eyes glinting silver. "I see her, kelpie. And she sees *us*."

Keeping her gaze on the trio, Finn backed away.

Someone grabbed her hand and whispered, *"Run!"*

As the silver-haired man rose, Finn whirled and ran with the girl in the white gown, the one Nathan had been dancing with. They burst from the house, running toward candlelight and laughter.

"Wait." Finn leaned against a tree to catch her breath and the girl turned. As Finn sank down, arms on her drawn-up knees, the girl crouched beside her, her expression wary. There was glitter in her dandelion-puff hair and she had freckles.

"They're the *Uisce*," she said. "You shouldn't have gone in there."

Finn felt as if she'd nearly drowned. "Who are they?"

"Guests come for All Hallows."

Finn slumped against the tree. *You will die on All Hallows' Eve*, Anna Weaver had told her. She whispered, "What happens on All Hallows?"

The girl didn't seem any more human than the eerie trinity in Mermaid House. "That's when we pay the Teind."

The word made Finn flinch. She knew what that word meant. If she felt she had been drowning before, now she could see no way to the surface—

"My name is Booke." The girl's voice, like a lamp, brought Finn out of the dark. "Mary Booke."

She held out a hand and Finn shook it. "I'm Finn."

The girl grinned. "I know. Nathan likes you. It's difficult for him to make friends."

"Well," Finn said, thinking of the three people in Mermaid House, "his old friends are kind of intimidating."

"Yes." Mary Booke looked down at her hands, folded on her knees. "They are all the things you should fear."

Finn couldn't tell if the girl's eyes silvered or not. She said softly, "Are you and Nath—"

"No." Mary Booke looked up, and her eyes were only gray. "We don't love, Finn Sullivan. Love for us means death."

She was gone in a swirl of gauzy fabric.

A shadow fell over Finn, who flinched as a voice said, "What have I told you about entering these houses?"

She squinted up at Jack. When he didn't blur into something else, she realized with relief the blackberry wine had worn off. "You told me not to enter Satyr-Night."

"Well, they're all the bloody same."

"Don't talk to me like that." She rose to face him. "Reiko told me you were in there."

He looked away, his profile regal against the dark. "I was. I had to speak with one of Reiko's . . . friends."

"Would the friend be one of the three wet weirdos who said they could smell my blood?"

His mouth tightened. He didn't reply.

"What is the Teind, Jack? Or should I say, *who*?"

Softly, he said, "And why would you want to know that?"

There was a bench behind her. She sat on it and stared defiantly up at him. "I know what it means. What does it mean to the Fatas? What aren't you telling me?"

"What are you doing?" He reached out and brushed his curled fingers against her brow. "What are you doing, Finn? You are mucking about with *demons*—"

"I don't need a lecture from *you*. Don't tell me you didn't suspect what she was when you first met her."

"Even knowing they existed, I was still fooled. And how charmed has *your* life been since meeting me?" He sat beside her.

"I've got to find Christie and Sylvie—"

"Your friends are safe—they're smart." His hand folded over one of hers and tightened, but he didn't look at her, watching the Fatas. "Don't leave me." His voice, hoarse and broken, made her throat hurt. There were rose petals in his tangled hair. His profile was cameo pale. She thought, *What have they done to you*—

The vision that struck stopped her breath . . . Jack, younger seeming than he was now, huddled in a stone room. Around him were roses, red as Valentine's

Day hearts. A wreath of them crowned his hair. He wore only dark trousers, and there were no rings on his fingers. Finn was there, like a ghost, kneeling before him, speaking without a voice. The fragrance of the roses was overwhelming, mingling with the heavy aroma of the blood that congealed on the floor and streaked his bare feet. He pushed his hands through his hair, and she saw the raw, red wound on his chest, a Frankenstein surgery bound with scarlet thread. She cried out and reached for him—

—and stared into the present-day Jack's wide, dark eyes. Her voice sounded crumbled. "What did they do to you?"

"It's done, Finn. What they did happened a long time ago."

They had butchered him. She reached out and parted his shirt, gazed at the jagged white scar across the smoothly muscled planes of his chest. She pressed one hand over a new wound, raw and red, and stitched with scarlet. She laid her head against his chest and listened to the steady, faint beat of his heart. She whispered, "Is that mine?"

"The second one," he murmured into her hair. "I didn't want you to see that. How did you see that?"

She lifted her head and gravely met his gaze as his own eyes silvered.

He kissed her as if he were drinking her, dragging her against him until she was in his lap and stars exploded in her brain. His cool skin warmed beneath her hands as he tangled his fingers in her hair while his other arm curved around her back. She kept one hand curled over his pounding heart.

"Finn . . ." His mouth slid from hers so that she could breathe. He pressed her back against the marble bench, his body sliding over hers with predatory grace. "Stop."

She pulled him against her, closing her eyes as his fingertips slid over her thigh and his narrow hips pinned hers. She curled her hands beneath his coat, against the muscled warmth of his back. His mouth brushed beneath her ear and he whispered, "Finn Sullivan, *remember what I am.*"

She refused to picture his gory second birth as his mouth opened over hers again, taking her breath, and her own heartbeat began to fill her ears. She moved her hands to his hips beneath the shirt, felt more scars, and, with every kiss, fiercely knew that she was breaking a link in the chain that bound him to Reiko Fata. Finn scarcely noticed when the heat between them began to cool and her skin iced and her heart stuttered and her own breath became as faint as her thoughts—

She realized he was killing her. She began clawing at him, struggling.

He tore back, sliding to his feet, away from her.

"Jack . . ." She scrambled up.

He raised his head, his face shadowed, eyes dark. "You see now?"

She reached up and laid her hand against his chest. "But your heart—Jack—it's beating again—"

"I should never have smiled at you." Then he was gone.

Cold and dazed, she lay back on the bench that was like tombstone marble, her arms over her face. Why had this happened to her?

She had to find Christie and Sylvie. She slid to her feet and ran swiftly down the garden path, back toward the party.

She halted when she saw a slight figure with blond hair in the shadows near a fountain—Bottle. Seated on the rim, the Rook was swinging his feet and singing softly, "He kissed the girls and stole their breath, kissed them 'til there was nothing left . . ."

Finn tried the name she suspected he'd been born with, that of the youngest of the Tirnagoth children, "Eammon."

He looked up like an abused child, his eyes smudged with black.

A shadow scythed from the night and gripped his shoulder as it bent and whispered to the boy. Light glistened on silvery hair and a barrow king's ransom of rings.

Bottle rose, watching Finn. Then he loped away.

Caliban turned to face Finn, who wore no iron, no silver against him. He smiled, his teeth very white. "Why it's Greensleeves, alone in the garden. I don't smell any iron on you, darling. And I don't see any silver."

"Jack—"

"He's with Reiko. They're planning a celebration of their own. I'm sure they won't mind if you join them, though Reiko thinks of you more like a sister."

She didn't believe him. A cold knot formed in her stomach. Jack *wouldn't* . . .

He began to move toward her, his boots crunching frost-laced leaves. "Ah, don't weep. I'll comfort you."

If she ran, he would catch her. As he drew closer, she smelled frost and old metal. His eyes flickered ghostly silver as his fingers curled around her wrist, the tarnished rings he wore biting into her skin. "Come. Dance with me."

"No, thank you." Her voice had a ragged edge.

"You don't have a choice, darling."

There was a brief struggle, until she relented, her mouth tight, her eyes downcast. He began to glide with her as if they were at a prom. He said, "A dance like this. There's only one way it can end."

"I was *invited*."

"I'm not one of Reiko's. I'm from a different *family*. Haven't I told you? The rules don't apply to me. I am *sluagh* and you will never see me in sunlight."

She tried to pull free, but he was horribly strong. As he backed her up against a tree, panic sheared through her.

Poetry is a weapon against them, Jack had once told her. So she recited the only poem she knew by heart, "*Beware the Jabberwock, my son! The jaws that bite, the claws that catch! Beware—*"

He tore back from her, releasing her as if he'd just touched iron. He snarled, "What are you spitting at me? You think pretending to be crazy is going to save you—"

She reached for the only weapon she had, more words. "Who were you before they got you?"

He stepped back from her, his eyes wide.

"Caliban."

The voice that came from the woods was deep, masculine, a voice that ruled blood-fed oaks, bones beneath roots, nights before electricity tried to keep away the dark.

"*Damh Ridire*." Caliban bowed his head. Then he turned quickly and strode away. The tall shadow in the dark, which looked as if it had antlers, also vanished, taking with it the otherworldly chill.

Finn slid down against the tree, her arms over her head, dead leaves crackling around her.

She heard whispers in the nest of trees nearby and looked up, squinting into the dark. She spied Nathan's bronze hair glinting and his shadowy profile as he bent his head to kiss a slim shadow with dandelion-puff hair. She watched as Nathan and his girl kissed and felt a wistful, anxious sadness.

Christie and Sylvie, looking as if they'd fought battles of their own, eventually found her.

IT WAS CALIBAN WHO CAUGHT Nathan and Mary Booke together. It was Jack who was ordered to watch Nathan Clare in Tirnagoth's ballroom, and who now sat with legs apart, arms on the back of the divan as he tried not to think of Finn and what Reiko had attempted with her and her friends.

Nathan, who sat huddled in a chair, looked up, his eyes red. "Jack, you know how I feel . . . I can't live like a *dead thing*."

"And what am I supposed to do about that, Nate?" Jack kept any thoughts of Finn from his eyes.

"I *love* her." Nathan's voice broke. "Reiko told me it was all right. Because Booke's a changeling—"

"Reiko tricked you." Jack unfolded himself from the divan and leaned forward. "Do you realize what you've done? Aside from endangering your girl? Their bloody *Teind*—"

Nathan rubbed his hands across his face. "Booke is different. She isn't going to interfere—"

Remembering how the Fatas had converged on Nathan and the girl called Booke, Jack settled back on the divan, shoving his hands over his face.

"Jack. *Please* help her."

A sudden flare of anger made Jack lean forward again. "And how do I do that, Nate?"

Caliban entered as a swift, icy shadow, hauled Nathan up, and slammed him against a pillar. Nathan choked, but he didn't fight back.

"If you've mucked us with that pale girl, pretty boy, I'll claw your guts out and make *her* eat them—"

Jack said, "Leave him alone."

Caliban whispered into Nathan's ear, then released him and strolled from the room. Nathan, sliding down against the pillar, his hands over his face, didn't see Reiko enter, her crimson kimono dripping against the black and white tiles.

She moved to him and crouched before him, holding his face in her hands. "Sweet Nathan. Haven't we made you a prince? Don't you still love us?"

He closed his eyes. "Just don't hurt her and I'll do what you want."

"Of course you will, Nathan. You will die for us."

Jack rose and stalked from the room.

He found Caliban seated on a windowsill in the hall. The bastard smiled. "How are you, jackal?"

"Fine. And you, hyena?"

Caliban stretched lithely. "I've had a talk with Nate's girl. You know she's one of us? I've never noticed her. Her name is Mary Booke."

Jack's hand slid to his breastbone, to the painful growth there—the heart.

"You know, your schoolgirl has caught Seth Lot's eye. He likes 'em skinny and virginal and he can't have leggy Nathan." Those silver eyes flashed, malevolent.

"Go near her again and I'll pull your teeth."

Caliban bared those teeth, because he didn't like to be reminded of what he'd been before becoming a Jack. Jack smiled as if his teeth were in Caliban's throat and sauntered down the hall as the sun began to rise, revealing the ugly decay around him.

Chapter Twelve

At ordinary times they do not see us or know we are near, but
when we speak to them, we are in danger of their deceits.
—*Visions and Beliefs in the West of Ireland*, Lady
Gregory

Her name was Annie Briar and she was sixteen and she was a
hedgewitch. She had learned her craft from an elegant young man who
called himself Lacroix. Then she met a boy beneath the hawthorn tree.
And Lacroix, who was not, after all, young, or a man, became jealous . . .
—From the journal of Lily Rose

Finn didn't see Jack all weekend, and the separation was like an amputation, because he'd left her as if he never intended to return. It wasn't as if she could call or text him . . . and she was too afraid of what he'd say to her if she went to his apartment.

She felt as abandoned as she had after Lily had left her.

PROFESSOR JANE EMORY'S BOTANY EXPEDITION was scheduled for early Monday morning, so Sylvie spent the night. Finn discovered her friend wasn't a six-in-the-morning sort of person and had to be supplied with coffee and pancakes before she could even open her eyes all the way. Seated at the kitchen table with her black hair in her face and a plaid shawl wrapped around her shoulders, Sylvie looked like a waif. "Everything feels upside down."

"That's because it is."

"That garden party—Nathan's birthday?—was so bizarre." Sylvie shuddered and Finn frowned at her, because it seemed like Sylvie wanted to tell her something. Sylvie murmured, "*What* are they?"

Finn didn't want to talk about *them* in the sensible world of daylight. "Not like us."

AS THE REST OF THE class trudged ahead with Jane Emory leading, Sylvie pulled Finn along the sunlit path. Nathan Clare, who seemed to be genuinely interested in botany, was with them, his bronze curls tucked beneath a newsboy's cap—he looked pale. There was a bruise on his cheekbone.

As Jane Emory—who preferred to be called Jane or Miss Emory—pointed out a ring of red toadstools speckled white—"Fly agaric. Pretty but poisonous."—Finn stared at the toadstools and thought of Reiko Fata in her crimson dress.

Sylvie murmured, "I once read a book that gave a mushroom recipe for a wine that would allow you to see spirits. I think one of the mushrooms was poisonous though."

"What kind of mushroom keeps spirits *away*?" Finn watched Nathan Clare moving among the trees.

"None. Fairies like mushrooms."

"Please don't say the 'f' word. Do you suppose *Jane Emory* knows about them?" She watched their botany instructor clamber over a fallen tree and felt a whirly panic at the idea of her secret world being known to an older generation.

Sylvie trudged beside her, in silence for a while, then said, "Let's not talk about them anymore, okay? I don't want to think about it."

Jane Emory's short, yellow curls glowed as she halted in a beam of sunlight. "Watch out for the hawthorn. It's infamous."

Finn glanced at the tree, a hawthorn like the Queen's tree Christie had shown her, only this one was bare of ornaments. It had tiny thorns and small, reddish-orange fruit.

"It's the resting place of two lovers." Jane Emory shifted her basket to her other arm. "He hung himself from the branches, and she poisoned herself beneath it. Love," she continued, her gaze passing over Finn, "causes all sorts of problems."

Finn scowled as someone—she thought it might have been Aubrey Drake—said, "That's not a very nice life lesson, Miss Emory."

"Look at *those*." Sylvie moved toward a ring of pale green toadstools.

"Sylv—never mind." Finn, leaving the hawthorn, picked her way to Nathan's side. When no one was paying attention to them, she said, "Tell me about the Teind."

"It has nothing to do with—"

"Tell me."

He rubbed at the bruise on his face and looked at her with such a bleak expression, she wanted to shake the truth from him. She whispered, "I saw what they did to Jack."

He nodded. "Follow me."

Nathan walked away from the noisy, distracted group, and Finn moved after, through trees sheathed in emerald moss, with crimson leaves falling silently around them. As they clambered over roots and rocks, she soon couldn't hear birds or insects, only an eerie hush. Then he was leading her into a cavern of green shadow.

A mammoth oak towered before them, a prehistoric thing, its gnarled branches so heavy with leaves the air beneath had become subterranean. Its immense roots snaked into the forest on one side, through a pool of dark water on the other. The trunk was a tower carved with strange symbols, some of which had been overgrown by bark. The resulting atmosphere around the oak was one of stillness and immense age.

Finn moved toward it and reached to touch the bark as ridged as an ancient warrior's skin, gazing into the branches, a cathedral-ceiling pattern of red and gold and green leaves. Something inhuman and millennial, an *awareness* breathed over her—hostile, secretive, and alien.

She stepped back, awed. *"What is it?"*

Nathan said, "They see it as a symbol of their family, a reservoir of their power—an old god. It's dying." He looked at her. "The Teind will renew it—and their pact with what lies beyond it."

"And what lies beyond it?"

He seemed wary as he said, "The tree, the god, is a guardian . . . to the land of the dead."

Finn regarded the tree as if it were an enemy. There was stillness around them, as if something was listening. She began to back away. "How old are you, Nathan?"

"Seventeen." He kept his lashes lowered.

She turned on him. "What are they going to do on Halloween?"

"There'll be a sacrifice. To save something so old, there's always a sacrifice." He turned and trudged away.

She whispered after him, "What kind of sacrifice, Nathan?"

He didn't reply, and Finn, looking over her shoulder at the oak as she strode after him, began to suspect a terrible answer.

THAT EVENING, COMPLETING AN ENGLISH Comp assignment on her laptop, she typed "Teind" into the search engine. The results, at first, were benign. The definition she was familiar with: *an offering; an exchange of Celtic origin.* The searches became darker, the illustrations sinister . . . "*A price paid*" captioned the picture of a hanging man; "*An offering*" titled the illustration of a girl, drowning; "*Sacrifice*" labeled the painting of a burning figure.

As she gazed at the last horrific illustration, she got a panicked text from Sylvie: Someone's here to see you. Get to the shop.

A THUNDERSTORM GLOWERED ABOVE THE Blackbird Mountains as Finn hurried the three blocks to Whiskey and Pearls, the salvage shop owned by Sylvie's dad. When the mermaid figurehead in the shop window appeared through a sudden torrent of rain, Finn ran toward it and pushed through the door.

Sylvie, in a black dress with ribboned sleeves, sat beneath a wooden angel. Draped against the mermaid figurehead, his wrists laced with pearls, was a slender youth in a tangerine raincoat and striped trousers. His black T-shirt was scrawled with the letters WYSIWYG in Gothic crimson. His hair was like sunset.

"Absalom Askew." Finn sank down onto a voyage trunk. Since she knew what he was, she took the advice from her sister's journal and spoke politely. "I'll listen to what you have to say."

"Good. Miss Whitethorn and I have just been having a bit of a talk, haven't we?"

Finn glanced frantically at Sylvie. "Are you okay?"

"Peachy." Sylvie raised her eyebrows.

Absalom looked at Sylvie. "Miss Whitethorn, might Miss Sullivan and I have some privacy?"

"I'll be close by." Sylvie walked toward the back, glancing over one shoulder.

Absalom sat on the mermaid's curved tail. "Our Jack is suffering because of you. You have been hurt because of him. So, on his behalf, I ask that you pretend you never met him. Can you do that?"

"No. How are you his friend?"

"That"—he lifted an index finger and pointed it at her—"is a very good question and a long story with which I won't bore you. Jack doesn't remember anyway . . . A century or so will do that to you."

Finn clenched her hands and breathed deeply so that she wouldn't scream at him. This wasn't a human boy sitting with her, and if she thought about it too long, she'd be too petrified to play pretend. She said, "I'm not forgetting Jack. I will never forget him. I'll leave myself notes to remind myself of him if something happens. *Are* you his friend?"

"Yes. And I also happen to dislike bullies."

She pictured Reiko Fata's arrogant assurance. "And by bullies, you mean the Fatas?"

He sighed as if his heart was breaking. "I am a neutral party, Finn Sullivan. Well, for now. I sort of root for the underdog. Now, if the situation was reversed and *they* were in danger, well"—he winked—"then you wouldn't like me."

"And Jack?"

"Jack." Absalom looked at her with ancient eyes in a boy's face. "He died some time ago. But you already knew that."

The tips of Finn's fingers and toes went numb, and her eyes felt hot. Her vision blurred. Absalom gently said, "Even now, you won't admit to yourself what they are—*don't fall asleep*. You mustn't do that anymore."

Her voice was ragged. "What do I do?"

He leaned toward her. "You can walk away. And she'll forget you—she *does* forget, you know. And they'll call off Caliban. You'll never hear from us again . . . We'll be strangers to you, nothing more."

Forget Jack. She thought of Caliban, who was something that could kill her. "His name really is Caliban. Like Shakespeare's monster."

"It's the name he chose—let's give him credit for being somewhat literary. *I* can help you forget." There was something like kindness in his gaze.

She didn't doubt he *could* make her forget . . . what else was enchantment, bewitchment, but a sort of mind control? "Has Jack done something to me—"

"Bewitched you? That's his purpose. He *is* a Jack. But it isn't glamour, unfortunately, that has you all knotted in thorns, *leanabh*."

She pictured Jack, his head bowed, ragged hair brushing his neck as the drowsy look in his eyes was replaced with anguish. "He isn't one of you."

"He is now. If you refuse my offer to make you forget, you should remember this—Fair Hollow is a between place. If it ever gets to the point where you need to fight back, confront Reiko in territory that is not solely hers—the Dead Kings, for instance, *not* Tirnagoth—and she'll have no choice but to answer your questions. Those are the rules. You'll be allowed a limited number of questions— make them relevant. And don't bring any weapons."

"Was it you who left that key beneath my window? The key shaped into a moth?"

Absalom said darkly, "Moths are treacherous creatures."

"They're bugs."

"But they begin as larvae, they incinerate themselves for no reason, and they generally serve no purpose."

She wondered irritably how old Absalom really was and if his kind could become senile. "Never mind."

"Are we done then?"

"The Teind, Absalom. And *you* called *me* here."

"I will not speak of the Teind. That's a question you'll need to save for Reiko." He rose and sauntered toward the door. As it swayed shut behind him, she heard him say, "And if you want to keep Jack, follow the rules—rules are what keep us in shape."

When he'd gone, Sylvie stomped defiantly from the back. "Are you okay?"

Finn gazed out at the rain. "I need to get into the Dead Kings."

Sylvie panicked and called Christie, who arrived fifteen minutes later.

IT HAD STOPPED RAINING BY then, so they sat on the courtyard fountain behind the salvage shop. Like the building, the courtyard was old, tangled with crabapple trees and blackberry bushes and twisty little trees in stone urns that had cracked with age. Surrounded by buildings, with a church in the back, it was a good place for a secret huddle.

Sylvie still couldn't believe what Finn wanted to do. "Absalom said to *confront* Reiko?"

Christie scrubbed a hand through his hair. "That is *such* a bad idea . . ."

Finn looked around as a wind tainted with the scents of rust and candle smoke drifted over them. She said, "Absalom said if we confront Reiko in a place that isn't just hers, we can ask questions. About Jack, and Nathan."

Christie looked exasperated. "Finn, one of those . . . whatever they are . . . got *inside* of me. I still puke whenever I think about it. And you want to walk into their lair? After that party? For *him*? A thing without a heart?"

"They did something to Jack," she said, keeping her voice level. "They tricked him a long time ago. They did . . . terrible things. And, because of them, *my sister is dead*."

"*What?*"

"I saw Reiko Fata in San Francisco when I was thirteen. I think my sister knew about them. I found a journal of hers—and it's filled with stories about them."

Christie wore silver and iron and a sprig of mistletoe behind one ear—he was admired at HallowHeart and could get away with it—and he looked primitive when he said, "What exactly happened to your sister?"

She spoke as if there were razors in her throat. "Lily broke up with her boyfriend. She left for the ballet studio. It was on the third floor of a building downtown. She was wearing her dancing shoes when she threw herself through a window—it was an old building. The glass wasn't shatterproof. She lived for a week after, but she never woke up."

She felt as if something sharp had been taken out of her. Then, Christie said quietly, "We'll go to the Dead Kings tonight."

FINN PREPARED FOR BATTLE IN her room. She'd selected a dress of fig-brown silk that had belonged to Lily Rose and borrowed a pair of Sylvie's platform sandals because they had ribbons of brown satin. She lined her eyes with black kohl. She armed herself only with silver. She didn't want to look afraid or ordinary.

Christie arrived with Sylvie and looked too vulnerable in an Oxford shirt, black trousers, sneakers, and a red plaid tie. Silver rings banded his fingers. He'd laced Emory through his tousled hair. Finn said, "Nice touch."

"Thanks. So . . . no weapons? 'Cause Sylve has—"

"*No* weapons."

Like Finn, Sylvie had dressed for war. Her plaid kilt and black T-shirt with a silver spider glittering on the front were fierce. The knee-high boots, the silver hoops in her ears, and her expression announced her intentions. They all wore silver, no iron, because they wanted to be protected, but subtle. Symbols had power, after all.

"Ready?"

The evening smelled of cedarwood and cold as they walked to the nightclub. Finn remembered a line from Lily's journal. *They are bloodless and heartless. They are powerless without us.*

They reached the building of gargoyles and shuttered windows and found the street already lined with parked cars. Finn knocked on the metal door, which opened to reveal Mr. Wyatt, glitter dusting his ebony skin and his lion's mane of dreads. He narrowed his eyes. "No."

Sylvie whispered to Christie, "Don't say anything about his secret life. Don't say—"

Christie smiled. "Mr. Wyatt. How goes border patrol in the land of the weird?"

Finn sighed and Sylvie glared at Christie. Mr. Wyatt merely said, "If I were doing my job properly, I wouldn't let you in. Do you have your IDs?"

Christie held out their IDs.

Mr. Wyatt didn't even glance at the cards. He waved them inside. "Don't drink or eat anything. You haven't been invited."

They walked down a crimson corridor where fake candles flickered in metal sconces, and portraits of stern, spooky people hung on the walls. A pair of doors was painted with the image of a black-haired knight in green armor, a blood drop gleaming beneath his left eye. Music pulsed from behind him.

"I don't want to go in there," Christie said grimly. "This'll be like Friday's mad tea party, only in an enclosed space where no one can hear us scream."

The doors opened, splitting the pretty knight in two, and a hurricane of savage music, dancers, and colored lights washed over them as they stepped forward. The stage was a crimson grotto, where a singer's eerie wailing was accompanied by the beat of drums and a symphony of violins. The fragrances of incense, cinnamon, leaf mold, smoke, and wine tainted the air.

"Keep close," Christie murmured as they wove among the dancers. "We're in fairy land now."

"Don't use the 'f' word." Sylvie nudged him as they passed a bare-chested boy with ivory antlers tied on his brow, standing before an altar of green candles. Three young women, their white hair in serpentine loops, drifted around a young man whose arms were spiraled with tribal tattoos as he danced with an Asian girl in a school uniform. Scarlet wings were strapped to her back. Her silvery gaze followed Christie with hungry fascination.

"What are we looking for?" Sylvie said into Finn's ear.

"This is terrifying!" Christie yelled, standing among the heathens with his hair in his eyes and his red plaid tie undone. "I'm afraid for my virtue—"

"Hello." A black-haired girl in a yellow sundress appeared at Christie's side, smiling. She grabbed his hand, his fingers that glinted with *silver* rings.

When she screamed as if burned, Finn felt the nape of her neck prickle.

"Shit." Christie snatched his hand from the girl, who sank against a pillar. Sylvie clutched one of Finn's wrists as, around them, people stopped dancing. Faces turned toward them—haughty faces, masked faces, faces sprinkled with glitter or tattooed like Maori warriors. The music faded in a discordant jangle. Finn, flanked by her friends, watched a dark figure glide from the still bodies.

Jack Fata, dressed in Victorian-punk black, gazed at her with calm fury.

"Sylvie"—Finn couldn't look away from that face that stopped her breath—"do it. Now."

Sylvie spoke the words Christie had written, her voice made eerie by the acoustics in the club, "We, as Three, invoke the law of hospitality, which guards our safety and our sanity."

"You," Jack spoke idly to Finn, "are an idiot."

Finn refused to be hurt by his words. "Where is she, Jack?"

He stepped close. Scented with fire and cold, he murmured, "You couldn't have chosen to do this somewhere else?"

"Somewhere else wouldn't have been safe."

His attention slid to Sylvie and Christie, both of whom looked warily back at him. His gaze returned to Finn. "So your little witch has been reading the proper books, and you've found yourself a mortal knight."

"Jack," a young woman said. "Leave them be."

His eyes dark, Jack stepped away.

Reiko Fata, ravishing in a dress of red silk, was walking toward them, the candle flames glittering in her green eyes. "Finn Sullivan."

Finn met those green eyes and flinched . . .

. . . she saw the corpse of a drowned boy in old-fashioned clothes . . . a skeletal hand knotted in the roots of an oak . . . crimson butterflies fluttering across a girl's blood-streaked leg—and she realized that Reiko Fata was made of those deaths, those last breaths, the final glimmering of those souls.

Wide-eyed, Christie whispered, "*'Her teeth are red with rust, her breast is green with gall, her tongue suffused with poison, and she never laughs except when watching pain.'*"

Reiko laughed in delight. "Ovid. An interesting choice for a boy your age." She didn't sound like a girl when she said, "Do not think, Serafina Sullivan, that I will forget this."

"Lily Rose." Finn clenched one hand at her side. Her voice shook.

Reiko turned and scathed the Dead Kings' inhabitants. "All of you—leave."

Shadows fell, light expanded, and tiny orbs swept through the air like hundreds of fireflies. Whatever doubts Finn had had about the Fatas' *otherness* vanished in a moment of terror followed by calm shock. She heard Christie swear brokenly, but Sylvie was silent.

Finn mightily regretted involving them.

Then the Dead Kings was empty but for Finn, her friends, and those she'd come to challenge, Reiko Fata, Jack, and Caliban, who leaned against a pillar, watching.

Wyatt silently entered the empty club and stood there, arms folded. Reiko frowned at him, but his presence gave Finn the conviction she needed.

"Lily Rose," she said again, refusing to be distracted by the vanishing of the Dead Kings' inhabitants.

Reiko spoke with soft malice. "Why are you asking me about a dead girl?"

Finn stepped forward. "I invoke the guest law, that no lies are spoken, no promises broken."

Reiko didn't move, but Caliban stepped forward.

"Caliban," Reiko said, smiling sweetly, "is not of my family. He is not bound by our laws or your invocation. I charge *him* to answer your questions."

And so, neatly, Finn was defeated.

"Finn," Sylvie whispered, "ask him questions with yes or no answers."

"There are seven of us here." Reiko gestured as her chauffeur, Phouka, emerged from the shadows. "So. *Seven* questions."

Finn didn't look directly at Caliban, but her voice was steady, "Did Reiko Fata know my sis—"

Sylvie gripped her hand, hard. Finn changed her wording. "Did Reiko Fata know Lily Rose Sullivan?"

Caliban regarded her from beneath snow-white lashes. "I don't know."

Finn calmed her ragged breathing. "Has any girl in Fair Hollow died because of Reiko Fata?"

Caliban narrowed his silver eyes. "Yes."

"Careful, Serafina Sullivan." Reiko's gaze silvered also. The air began to buzz. "There are some things you might not wish to know."

Finn recklessly continued, "Who is the wolf-eyed man in San Francisco?"

Jack inhaled sharply, and Caliban smiled. "Got a better description? There are many of us with wolf eyes."

"Only four more," Christie murmured. Finn flinched when she saw blood trickling from one of his nostrils, but he didn't take his gaze from Caliban.

She looked back at Reiko and whispered, "How can I free Jack and Nathan from Reiko Fata?"

There was a chilly silence.

Caliban shrugged, the gesture so graceful, it was as if he'd been doing it for ages. "Jack and Nate aren't prisoners, so your definition of 'free' is spotty."

"Finn." Although Jack's voice distracted her, she didn't dare look at him. She whispered, "Are you human, Caliban, you and the Fatas?"

"We are what you see and that question, lambkin, is open to interpretation. Shall I give the poetic answer? We are the children of nothing and night." His beauty, unlike Jack's, was disturbing, the beauty of something that shouldn't be walking and talking, a thing that dressed itself in skin, leather, and velvet and didn't care whether its alien nature was known.

"How do my friends and I keep ourselves safe from your kind?"

Caliban stared at her. Finn could smell burning things and roses as Jack drew closer. Reiko seemed to become a shadow with luminous eyes, whispering, *"Answer her."*

Caliban moved one step forward so that only an inch of air separated him from Finn. His hair was like strands of silk. Faint freckles silvered his flawless skin, and he smelled of frost and rust. He whispered something, an old, dark word.

Then Jack slid between them, and Finn was scarcely aware of being gently pushed back as Caliban blithely answered, "Iron and salt. Poetry. Silver. Running water. Church bells. Incense. Mirrors. Blessed ribbons. Rowan wood. Parsley. Various other botanical varieties. These are your defenses."

"Last question." Reiko was no longer smiling.

Finn said, softly, "What will happen at the oak tree on Halloween?"

The Fatas went still. Their eyes glistened like moonlight on ice. Caliban said, "A celebration."

"There now." Reiko was a girl again, but her smile curved in a promise of ruin and her eyes were electric. "We've answered your questions, Serafina. Caliban and Phouka shall escort you over the threshold."

Finn didn't like how Reiko had phrased *that* last statement. She searched for a trick. She looked over her shoulder at Jack, who said clearly, "Phouka. Make sure they move *safely* over the threshold of this *building* and into *Fair Hollow.*"

"I'll go with them," Wyatt said, gesturing. "Come along, children."

The glee on Caliban's face was replaced by a sullen scowl. He looked at Reiko. "Do we really need to be policed by—"

Reiko's voice belonged to a terrible thing. *"Caliban."*

He bowed his head.

Outside, autumn smoldered. The night was rich with cedar smoke and the chocolate smell of damp soil.

"We didn't come in a car." Finn refused to look at the two creatures on either side of them. They were, she thought, bloody nightmares. Wyatt was a steady and reassuring presence behind them.

"Shall we walk you home?" As Caliban pretended concern, Finn felt an insane desire to hit him. Phouka was watching them, the brim of her chauffeur's cap shadowing her face as her lips curved. Her gaze fastened on Christie as he touched his bloody nose, frowning.

Finn said, "We can find our own way home."

"We do know it." Sylvie smiled, but her eyes were angry, and she looked pale.

Wyatt placed himself between Finn and her friends and Caliban.

"Come, Caliban." Phouka sauntered back toward the Dead Kings. "We're not wanted."

Caliban followed, swaggering.

Wyatt looked at them. "Now you know. Go home."

Hopelessness bled through Finn as she walked quickly down the street with Christie and Sylvie. "We shouldn't have done this."

"We learned some things," Sylvie said, sliding her arm through Finn's, "that we wish we hadn't."

"They just vanished." Christie hunched into his coat. "Like they hadn't been alive. Like *ghosts*." He breathed out.

Finn said quietly, "I think Reiko killed my sister."

LATE INTO THE NIGHT, FINN read Lily Rose's journal while candlelight flickered over the symbolic things laid beside her—the moth key, the locket Jack had given her of the Renaissance prince, a red leather book of Grimms' fairy tales. It was a weirdly humid night for autumn in the north, and she'd opened her glass doors. The CD she'd clicked into the stereo played an anguished version of "Greensleeves" by a young singer.

When the CD stopped, she heard creaking beneath the gentle patter of the rain.

The swing set.

She rose and pushed onto the terrace.

A slender figure stood on one of the swings, swaying back and forth, head bowed, dark hair brushing his throat. Old rings gleamed on fingers wrapped around the chains. As Jack looked up, starlight stroked one sloping cheekbone.

Finn still wore her jeans and T-shirt. She tugged on her sneakers and hurried down into the yard. As she walked toward him, she saw fresh scratches on his skin, as if he'd torn his way through briars to get to her. She halted, the light rain kissing her skin. "Jack."

"I'm bleeding again. And soon she'll know my heart is growing back. Just the thought of you now does it." He held out a hand to her. She wrapped her fingers around his and said, "It'll break."

"My heart?" He pulled her up onto the swing with him, and she balanced her feet between his.

"I meant the swing." The forest-smoke scent of him was dazzling. She gripped the chains above his hands and closed her eyes. "Jack . . . did Reiko kill Lily Rose?"

"No. Someone was feeding her information about our family."

She whispered in his ear, "You know who the wolf-eyed man is."

"The journal . . . may I see it?"

She drew back and gazed into his eyes. There was no silver taint to them now. One was blue. One was gray. "She was *eighteen*. His mouth left a *scar* on her wrist . . . What kind of monster did Reiko send after my sister?"

His body was cool and taut against hers as he lowered his eyelashes. She wanted to wrap her arms around him and hold him until the world ended. She didn't want him to return to Reiko.

"That's not how she works." He didn't look up. "Reiko poisons you with whispers and doubts until you don't know your own mind anymore . . . and, Finn, that's the *least* of what she does."

She pressed her brow against his, and her voice broke as she said, "You aren't like her."

"There were three girls before you." His voice was dull. "I kissed them. I shouldn't have kissed you."

A cold wind swept her hair across her face. She gasped, inhaled rain, clawed the hair away, and found herself alone on the swing. She couldn't believe he'd done it to her again. She shouted into the dark, "Jack! Come back to me or I'll come looking for you!"

PICTURING FINN'S TAWNY GAZE AND sweet mouth as he stalked down a hall in Tirnagoth, Jack was able to ignore the flashes of decay around him. He shoved open a rusting door and found Reiko crouched in the center of her red room, a kimono of crimson satin pooling around her. He could see the curve of one breast beneath the long chains of jewels glittering around her neck. She held a pink music box in both hands, and her eyes shimmered as she looked at him.

"Jack." Her voice sent a shiver down his spine. "Do you still love me?"

"Always," he lied.

She opened the music box, and the tiny ballerina inside began to spin as a delicate melody tinkled through the air.

He was blindsided by the vision of a dark-haired girl whose blue eyes were lined with Egyptian kohl, a ballerina who dressed in T-shirts and jeans. Her name burned his throat like smoke. *Lily Rose.* Had he seen her *before*?

Reiko touched the tiny ballerina. "Look, there, on the table beside you."

He saw a book, its cover depicting a mysterious face surrounded by thorns and flowers. The title was *Between*. He opened it to find paintings of grotesque, beautiful, whimsical creatures. And the author . . .

Jack looked up at Reiko as he said, "It's by Daisy Sullivan. *Finn's mother.*"

"It was never published. The oldest girl inherited the mother's ability to see us. They knew too much. Someone told the girl . . . things. Secrets."

He recalled Finn talking about her sister's journal and the hollow place inside of him, still raw, began to ache. "You killed her mother and her sister."

Reiko said calmly, "Their ugly world killed her mother. And the oldest girl made her own decision."

His hands ached to twist those necklaces tight around Reiko's throat. "Did Seth Lot help Lily Rose Sullivan with that decision?"

"Jack"—she shut the music box—"ask me about Serafina Sullivan."

"I am done with her."

"You are not done with her. She has offended me. You will continue to court her, and you will bring her to us."

"You say you love me." He wondered why he had not grown weary of her beauty, why it still moved him as if she were the innocent yet worldly young woman she pretended to be. "But you don't. Not really."

"Jack." She rose and her eyes were wide and dark. In that moment, she *did* seem to be a mortal girl. "You are all that I want."

She drew close to him, and he stood very still as she kissed him.

By the time he realized the shadowy venom from her mouth was entering him, it was too late.

CHRISTIE FOUND FINN HUDDLED ON her terrace in the cold morning.

"Your mascara is running," he said gently. "Has *he* been here?"

She only looked at him, unable to conceal her misery as he crouched beside her. He muttered, "If I put a stake through his black heart—"

"He doesn't have a heart."

"I suppose asking you not to have anything to do with him is pointless?"

"You don't understand." Her voice was raw. "I think they're going to kill Nathan."

He sat on the steps. "*Why?*"

She breathed the apple-chill air. "The oak tree he showed me, the Teind they keep talking about—it means 'sacrifice.'"

Christie muttered under his breath and yanked off his hat.

"Don't swear. My da already thinks you're a shady influence."

"*Me?* Has he met the dark prince?" He looked down at his bare hands. "I don't know what to do, Finn. I want to help you. And I will. But just think about what you're doing."

They sat quietly together as the morning sun blazed, and Finn decided that, because the Fatas had taken Lily, she would take something from *them*—and keep an innocent boy from dying.

CHAPTER THIRTEEN

*Why is the Night-crow in the next place? Not hard. This is the month
when we refrain from carnal pleasures because of terror, which in Irish
is uath, and the Night-crow brings terrible. Terrible is its color.*
— THE WHITE GODDESS, ROBERT GRAVES

*A girl fell in love with a statue that stood in the garden of a house
known to be one of Theirs. She passed the statue—a marble boy with
an angel's face—every morning on her way to school. One day, she put
a ring on its finger. She kissed its lips. It came to her that night and
crushed her while seeking another kiss.*
— FROM THE JOURNAL OF LILY ROSE

This is the last time you'll see me.

Finn curled up in her bed and didn't want to get up. Rain had descended like
a curse on Fair Hollow—it made the thought of rising, dressing, eating, and
pretending her life wasn't wrecked seem impossible. She opened her eyes and
tracked her gaze around the room. She, Christie, and Sylvie had gone on a trea-
sure hunt for protective charms the day before. Her walls were now scattered
with ornate little mirrors, wreaths of rowan, Buddhist bells, and three Celtic
crosses made of old stone. Sage and patchouli incense from Hecate's Attic per-
fumed the air.

She grudgingly got out of bed and looked at herself in the mirror crowded with old postcards and photos. Her face was white, her lips red, her eyes dark. She looked like one of *them*.

She thought about Halloween and the Teind no one would talk about.

RAIN CONTINUED TO SMASH AGAINST the roof as Finn, hurrying down the stairs, heard her da speaking with someone on the porch. As a draft fragrant with green things and earth swirled through the house, she halted. Her father was speaking with Jane Emory. The botany professor had tucked a marigold into her yellow hair, and, beneath her jacket, she wore a T-shirt printed with the words I HUG TREES.

Finn stood still as her da ducked his head like a kid. When he turned and saw her, he looked defiant, as if she'd caught him at something. "Finn. D'you want to come out with Jane and me for coffee?"

Finn stared at Jane Emory, who looked innocently at her. *Jane?*

"You left something on the field trip bus." Jane Emory held out the iron bracelet Christie had made. "It looks valuable."

Finn came forward and took it, murmuring, "Thanks." She glanced at her father. "Sylvie's coming over, so, no thanks."

She tried not to stomp back up the stairs.

"JANE EMORY." SYLVIE LOOKED THOUGHTFUL. "And your dad. Hey, at least it's not *Avaline*."

Finn sipped at her chai, her new favorite drink. They had taken a cab to Winter Street, where cafés and antique shops cluttered two blocks, and the pavements rippled with the roots of maples. Blood-red leaves swirled, brightening the autumn gloom. Done with an afternoon of shopping, they sat in a tiny café with ravens painted on the walls.

"How do you feel about it?"

"He's been so unhappy."

"You know, Finn, when I first saw you, *you* looked so unhappy—you reminded me of one of those silent movie actresses with the big eyes. I just wanted to hug you. Christie"—Sylvie's mouth curled—"wanted to kiss you, but then, that's his solution for brightening *any* girl's day."

Finn smiled and pulled at a thread on her blue peasant blouse embroidered with yellow daisies. She'd put on her bracelets, the iron and the silver. Sylvie's defenses were Christie's iron ring and the silver hoops in her earlobes. Finn pointed to the iron ring. "Did you know Mr. Wyatt had his class make those?"

"Metalworking." Sylvie caught the connection. "He's obviously one of Professor Avaline's." As she stirred her crimson lemonade, she continued, "I think Christie's gone to see Phouka Fata."

Finn felt a shiver of fear for Christie and looked around at the people in the café, envying them their ignorance of the Fatas' existence. "What can we say to stop him, Sylv? Especially me."

"Must I take a shine to scary Caliban? Or that orange-haired boy with a girl's face?"

"Absalom Askew. And he's not a boy. He's older than Moses. Don't even *think* about Caliban."

"Maybe Christie's under a spell."

"No. Not Phouka. She's charm, not glamour."

Sylvie reached out to grip Finn's hand, and the iron ring Christie had given her clinked against Finn's iron bracelet. "We can pretend, right, but it won't make things go back. *They* know *we* know."

"Sylv, I've been here a *month*. I've gotten nothing but average marks in my classes. and I've read *one* book. I haven't even finished unpacking . . . and now I need to find out what horrible thing the Fatas are planning on Halloween. 'Celebration,' Caliban said."

"What exactly did Nathan tell you?"

"He showed me a gigantic oak and said the Fatas thought of it as a god to the land of the dead. It's dying. Then he started talking about sacrifice. I really don't like that word."

"Why is he with the Fatas, if he's human and they're . . ."

"I don't know."

"You know what they are, don't you?" She looked at Finn, eyes wide. "All of those things that ward us against them . . . silver. Iron. Salt."

In the daylight, it was hard to imagine the Fatas as a tribe of rogue spirits that preyed on humans like the malign forces from a Grimms' fairy tale. Finn's voice shook a little. "I know what they are."

"It scares me."

"It terrifies me. And that damn oak gave me the crawls."

"I've never heard of that oak, but there's a yew tree in Soldiers' Gate where Malcolm Tirnagoth called on the supernatural to bring back his dead family. Absalom and I were talking about Tirnagoth before you came. Finn . . . you could *summon* Jack. He'd have to follow the rules, then."

The rules, Absalom Askew had said, *keep us in shape*. Rules kept them *in* their shapes. "So, exactly, what was Absalom telling you, Sylvie?"

Sylvie fidgeted. "Stuff."

"Stuff? Like how to summon people at yew trees?"

"He said it would make Jack less likely to go off the rails."

"Why? Why would he tell you these things?"

Sylvie explained to her what Reiko had offered her in the conservatory of Mermaid House and Finn's breath hitched. "*Why didn't you tell me before?*"

"I walked away—deal with the devil and all that."

Finn shuddered and tucked her hair behind her ears. "Have you always lived in Fair Hollow?"

"Always."

"And you never noticed . . . them?"

"Well, there are lots of theater and film people from New York City. And every town has something spooky in its history. But the Fatas . . . they are are mad, bad, and perilous to know."

Finn looked out at the rain. "I don't want to spend my life protecting myself with iron and sea salt, Sylvie."

"Maybe it doesn't matter." Sylvie's gaze was dark. "Maybe Jack and Nathan and Phouka once tried those things, too. And look where it got them."

AT EIGHT IN THE EVENING, the doorbell rang and Finn found Christie on her porch, his face grim. "I need you to come with me."

He was acting dodgy. When she noticed the rings he wore, old and twisted, she drew back. "When did you begin decorating yourself with *those*?"

"With what?"

"The rings, Christie."

"Are you coming with me or not? It's Phouka Fata. She wants to talk to you."

"Why would she want to see *me*?"

"I think you should ask her yourself."

THE FRAGRANCES OF WOOD SMOKE and pine mingled with the gasoline smell of Christie's Mustang as Finn watched familiar streets become Route 95, with its strip malls, Morrisey's Auto, a McDonald's, and a billiards hall. Then they were driving up a tree-lined road into the mountains. She hadn't asked Christie how he'd ended up as Phouka's messenger boy because she didn't want her faith in him compromised.

He steered the Mustang into a parking lot in front of a building that resembled a Buddhist temple-turned-roadhouse. Red lanterns hung from the roof, and a bronze deity sat in a fountain near the door, a lotus lamp cupped in its hands. The sign above the door read LOTUS AND LUNA.

They entered a dim interior, where a pink neon lotus glowed behind a bar crowded with university students. The air smelled like aftershave, alcohol, and deep-fried appetizers as Christie led Finn to a corner booth, where Phouka sat, passing for normal in a black Beatles T-shirt and rock star jeans. Her auburn hair was threaded with tiny braids, and her hoop earrings were gold. There were two others at the table with her—Aubrey Drake and a sleek girl wearing a Dolce and Gabbana dress of green silk, her black hair cut short.

"Finn Sullivan." Aubrey smiled and gestured to the girl, who also smiled, her gaze warm. "Hester Kierney." He looked at Phouka. "Well?"

"Are they going to sit?" Phouka was lazily stirring a drink, which was probably there for show. As Finn and Christie sat, she said, "The road outside was where Ichabod Crane fled the Headless Horseman. But the Horseman had a head. And antlers. He's a hunter who transports souls to the land of the dead. You know who else takes souls on trips? Chauffeurs. Coachmen."

"Phouka." Hester Kierney looked concerned.

Phouka continued, "Jack became a coachman, like his dad. In some places, long ago, coachmen were shamans, medicine men. They had a second business, most of them—driving out evil spirits. They were exorcists."

Finn softly said, "That's why you took him. Why am I here? Why are *they* here?" She pointed to Aubrey and Hester.

The girl chauffeur's eyes were absolute silver now. "An outlaw King and Queen of the Faeries have made their home in a little town in upstate New York and you've gotten their attention. These two are Blessed"—she indicated Aubrey and Hester—"which means their families have been rewarded for outstanding service, and you're here, Finn Sullivan, to be warned."

Aubrey said, "Ignorance is bliss. Now that you know about this, you need allies. With us or against us."

"So Malcolm Tirnagoth isn't the only one who made a deal with the devil," Christie said contemptuously. "You lot did the same. No wonder you're all rich."

"Christie," Hester chided. "It's not like that."

Aubrey leaned forward. "And since when have you found religion, Hart? Anyway, our *ancestors* made a deal with devils—hell, my parents don't even remember them. We're just getting the benefits. Good looks. Good health—"

"—and a future as one of the living dead?" Christie said helpfully.

"I won't," Finn said in a low voice, "be *with* you. I might be *against* you."

Christie whispered to her, "You probably shouldn't have said that last part out loud."

"Serafina," Hester Kierney gently said, "please think about it. They're not evil—"

"Is this what you wanted me here for?" Finn was mildly astonished.

"Finn," Aubrey said, leaning toward her, "Hester's dad is the dean of Saint John's U. He got *your* dad the job there. The Fatas *brought* you here, in a roundabout sort of way."

Finn felt her pulse jump as she met Phouka's silver gaze. Her sense of reality began to teeter dangerously. "No. I don't believe it."

"Christie"—Phouka looked at him—"you've lived here all your life. *Convince* her."

"I won't convince her of anything. Come on, Finn."

Hester's voice, pleading, followed them as they walked away, "Then you're alone."

As Finn stalked into the parking lot with Christie, who was clenching and unclenching his hands, he said, "Finn. I'm sorry—"

She spun to face him. "You *know* what Phouka is."

"And you know what Jack is. She said she could help—"

Finn gestured to the rings Christie wore and her voice broke, "What did you do? Let her give you pretty things? You heard her—chauffeur? Transports *souls*?"

"I didn't give her my *soul*, Finn." The bitterness in his voice and eyes had replaced the lightheartedness she missed. "But I *am* trying to save ours, while you risk all of us for someone who died a long time ago."

She stepped back as if his words had been a slap. She whispered, "He's *eighteen*. And he's frozen, forever, until someone helps him."

"Then you'd better make a choice." Christie headed toward his Mustang. "Because you can't save everyone. And, for the record, all these goddamn thrift-store rings are silver or iron. I bought them."

She closed her eyes and felt as if the starlight were bits of glass on her skin.

JACK WAS ON THE ROOF of his theater, playing the violin with a savagery that was scarcely human, when he heard Finn's voice say, "Jack."

The bow swerved from the strings. He rose to look down at the girl standing below, and was furious that she would come here after all he had done to frighten her away. "What are you doing here?"

Her face was pale. There was a bicycle on the ground near her, its wheels still spinning. "I spoke with Phouka. And Nathan."

He stepped forward, dropped, and landed in a crouch before her. He straightened and took a swaggering step closer. Finn's eyes were sooty with silver liner, her tawny hair knotted with thin braids. He could smell the pomegranate gloss on her lips as he said, "Is that parsley in your hair?"

"Yes."

His gaze dropped to the dark bracelet around her wrist. Iron. "I'll ask again, *What are you doing here?*"

"Who is going to die on Halloween, Jack?"

He took a deep breath. "No one."

"Who are the Fatas, Jack?"

"You're wearing a salad in your hair and an iron bracelet. You know what they are."

"And you?" Her eyes were huge, the pupils drowning the whites. "What are you? I know you're not like this because you want to be. You're not one of *them*."

His coat swirled in a wind that swept their hair across their faces. "I am a dead man, Finn."

False breath burned through him, nudging at the seedling in his chest. The poisonous reek of the iron made him dizzy. He stepped back from her, this girl with her princess face and ferocious innocence. In jeans and a red coat, she was armed—he could smell silver too—and her voice went into him like a thorn as she said, "I think they killed my sister because she knew about them. I think they're going to kill Nathan."

He felt Reiko's venom stirring within him and took another step back, whispering, "She's poisoned me against you. *Leave.*"

"No."

"*Go!*" He put his hands over his face before she could see the blackness fill his eyes. He stood very still, not daring to move as the venom whispered to him, urging him at her, the fragile creature willing to die for him. *Finn. You're a smart girl. You're a clever girl. Run away from me . . .*

When the savage darkness had withdrawn, he dropped his hands from his face.

He was alone in the lot scattered with ragged leaves. This time, it was *she* who had abandoned *him.*

FINN HAD RELUCTANTLY BICYCLED AWAY from Jack, leaving him in darkness . . . because she'd realized there was only one way to help him. Back home, she texted Sylvie and Christie, and they came. As she sat with Christie on the swings, it was Sylvie who explained to them what Absalom Askew had said must be done to bind Jack Fata. "The yew stands in the territory of something the Iroquois called Dead Bird, a spirit the Irish immigrants named *Marbh ean.*"

"Marvin?"

"That's right, Christie. Just keep making smart remarks." Sylvie scowled at him.

Christie looked skeptical. "So we call on something called Dead Bird and we're trusting a pot-dealing fairy boy with orange hair?"

Finn pictured the despair in Jack's eyes and thought of innocent Nathan. "This won't hurt Jack? It'll only keep him from doing what Reiko says?"

"It'll bind him to you."

Christie's swing swayed back and forth. He said, "But first we've got to ask permission from Marvin. And what do you think *he'll* want in exchange?"

Finn stood. "Let's try it."

Christie looked from Finn, to Sylvie, and swore.

NEAR MIDNIGHT, CHRISTIE DROVE THEM to the blackberry field near Soldiers' Gate Cemetery. When they got out of the car, he carried the wooden chair that Sylvie and Finn had painted red. As Finn stood before the swirling art nouveau gates, watching leaves drift around the tombstones as if something invisible was playing among them, she thought that the cemetery was an eerie, wild place, the stone figures that sorrowed over its graves seeming to wait for humans to pass before moving in secret. "Okay."

Christie pushed at the gate, which clanged and didn't open. He stepped back. "They actually lock it now? Oh, well. I guess we can't talk to Marvin. Let's go."

Finn touched the moth key she wore around her neck and walked forward. She fitted the key into the gate's lock. *Click.* The gates fell open. This time, Christie and Sylvie didn't ask about the key, but Finn caught them exchanging a glance as they followed her down the path. As she and Sylvie held up their electric lanterns, Finn grimaced at the fragrances of dark loam and mildewed stone. "Where's the summoning tree?"

"Did you hear that?" Christie scanned the monuments, the scraggly trees, the tricky darkness that might reveal, at any moment, something they didn't want to see.

"That was an owl."

"No, it wasn't, Sylv."

Finn hushed them. Her skin was crawling, and her hands were cold.

As they walked forward, the yew rose from mist and weeds, looming behind a black mausoleum carved with images of skeletons. A hooded figure of black marble stood near the mausoleum doors, its face hidden, hands clasping a rose. Christie's light flicked over the name carved above the doorway. He whistled.

"Tirnagoth," Finn breathed.

The yew was impressively spooky, with its twisting trunk and branches clawing at the sky. Christie muttered, "Are yews supposed to be this big? No? I didn't think so."

They set candles from Hecate's Attic around the tree. Sylvie, using a wand she'd carved herself—with specifications from Absalom, Finn grimly suspected—drew the pentacle. She rose, brushing leaves from her stockings. "Christie?"

Christie crouched nearby, leaves fluttering in his dark red hair. Softly, he spoke.

"*Gaze no more in the bitter glass, the demons, with their subtle guile, lift up before us when they pass.*"

Sylvie stomped her foot. "Why are you quoting Yeats?"

"Should it be Poe? Something from 'The Raven'? We *are* trying to summon a dead bird named Marvin."

Sylvie pointed at him. "Your cynicism and lack of respect are going to *ruin* this."

"We no longer worship the sublime," Finn murmured, lighting the first candle with a butane wand. Her hand trembled slightly. "Like Professor Fairchild says."

"Damn, I can't believe I didn't get into that class." Christie sighed.

A wind scented with smoke and mist swirled tattered leaves across the red chair that had once sat so innocently in Finn's kitchen. Finn rose, saying, "Go on, Christie."

Christie said, "How about this? '*Where got I that truth? Out of a medium's mouth, out of nothing it came, out of the forest loam, out of dark night where lay the crowns of Nineveh.*' That's more Yeats—"

A howling wind tore the breath from them. The candle flames burned blue, igniting a flurry of leaves, turning them into smoldering skeletons. Finn gripped Sylvie's hand as Christie folded his fingers around her other. Starlight glittered behind the birches, and cold descended over the field as the wind stilled. Shadows from the trees crawled across the chair and crows cawed above, as if warning them. Finn thought she heard drumbeats, then realized it was her own heart.

Sylvie whispered, "*Marbh ean. Gabh I le!*"

Finn closed her eyes. The world shifted. An electric current sizzled through the cables above the road, and the air became heavy with the smell of rain. Unable to bear it any longer, she opened her eyes.

What she saw in the chair, at first, confused her. Someone had placed a dead crow on the seat. A shadow slanted over it. She blinked; the crow vanished.

A black figure sat there now, reality tugging at its ragged edges. Finn wondered if terror could really kill a person. Shaking with cold and the urge to run like hell, she stared at the shadow in the chair and said with steady determination, "*Marbh ean.* I've come to ask a favor."

The voice that replied was like none she'd ever heard—mocking, male . . . ice sliding across velvet. "Shall I grant it?"

Candlelight swerved and lit the figure.

Sprawled in the chair was a young man of indeterminate Asian descent, his body lean and lithe in an ivory T-shirt and white suede trousers stitched at the sides. Bleached feathers and totems were knotted in his black hair. A diamond stud glinted in the side of his nose, and his dark eyes held a silvery light. He was as fanciful as a '70s rock star. He was as old as the stars in the sky. Finn resisted the urge to fall to her knees and bow her head as terror and sweet desire overwhelmed her. *The uncanny valley effect,* she thought.

The young-man-who-was-not smiled, and his voice seemed to echo, "You'd best tell me why I'm here before I get angry. Or bored."

Christie tightened his grip on Finn's hand. "Tell us what you want in exchange. Sir."

As his black gaze settled on Christie, the young man—and Finn couldn't bear to think of him as anything else—drawled, "Pretty boy. What do we ever ask in exchange for anything?" There was nothing human in his gaze as he continued, "Blood."

Christie whispered, "Yeah. I figured."

Finn, whose mind had decided to pretend that this was a dream because her common sense wouldn't have anything to do with the situation, asked, "How much?"

"That depends on how many favors you want."

Finn's body shuddered from the tomb chill in the air. "One. I want to . . . bring someone to me."

His eyes narrowed. "*Someone.*"

She nodded.

"Ten drops for *someone,*" he said, and Finn winced as he extended a goblet of dented metal. The age-tainted rings on his fingers reminded her of Jack's. He smiled at her, and his gaze flickered with ghosts. He said, "Use that silver spike the *ban leannan* gave you and give me my due. Then, I shall answer."

As Finn took from her coat the small silver knife with the cross-shaped hilt, the one given her by a girl named Eve, Dead Bird averted his gaze.

"Why are you afraid of the cross?" Sylvie's curiosity had apparently overcome her fear.

Dead Bird's voice was cold. "Would you like to give your blood for the answer?"

"Never mind. Sir." She had gone white.

Finn stepped forward and accepted the tin goblet with numb hands.

"Here." Christie took the knife while Sylvie held the cup. Sylvie whispered, "Are you sure—"

"Just do it." Finn held her hand over the goblet and felt the knife prick her finger. Dismissing her nausea at how disgusting this was, she squeezed out precisely ten drops, wincing at the brightness of her blood. She took the cup in her other hand and walked to the *Marbh ean*, who accepted it with an inclination of his head. She didn't want to watch as he drank, but she couldn't turn away. When he tossed aside the cup, what fell to the ground was a crushed beer can.

He spoke dreamily, "*I saw a staring virgin stand, where holy Dionysus died, and tear the heart out of his side, and lay the heart upon her hand, and bear that beating heart away.*"

"Why is *he* quoting Yeats?" Christie sounded strangled.

Sylvie said, "Because that's how you summoned him."

Quietly, the *Marbh ean* continued, "*And though it loved in misery, close and cling so tight, there's not a bird of day that dare extinguish that delight.*"

"Is it *all* going to be Yeats?" Sylvie stared at the *Marbh ean*. The silver designs beneath her eyes glinted. Christie's hand, painted with the same designs, tightened around Finn's as Finn, listening carefully, felt the air tremble.

Dead Bird said, voluptuously, "*The bride is carried to the bridegroom's chamber through torchlight and tumultuous song. I celebrate the silent kiss that ends short life or long.*"

Sylvie whispered, "It *is* all going to be Yeats."

The *Marbh ean* rose and his voice, wild and strong and inhuman, cemented the summoning. "*That there are still some living, that do my limbs unclothe, but that the flesh my flesh has gripped, I both adore and loathe.*"

Shadows tracked across his face and he was gone.

In the circle, the candles flickered out. Leaves rustled like the gowns of long-dead ladies. They waited. Nothing happened. A sense of disappointment lingered.

"Tengu," Sylvie whispered. "That's what he was."

"A Japanese trickster spirit," Finn informed Christie. "And I'll bet she's right. The bird thing . . ."

"Can we trust him?" Sylvie looked worried.

"I'm not in the mythology club you two seem to have started, but I'm scared stupid. Here." Christie took from his coat a piece of paper and shoved it at Finn. "Read this. It's a Christina Rossetti poem. I thought we might need it, for extra impact. Anyway, it's very appropriate."

Finn carefully recited the words, "*Yet come to me in dreams, that I may live my very life again though cold in death: Come back to me in dreams, that I may give pulse for pulse, breath for breath—*"

The wind howled again, and the rustling of the leaves became frantic. Finn spoke before panic took her voice, "*Speak low, lean low, as long ago, my love, how long ago—*"

The leaves stopped moving. The wind fell away. The world became a film that abruptly halted.

Then the circle of candles flared to life, burning blue.

Jack walked from the darkness clotted near the yew and remained within the circle of candles. In his long soldier's coat, he looked like a ghost, his eyes rimmed with designs of red kohl that heightened his otherworldly appearance.

"*What have you done?*" He set his hands on the back of the red chair. His voice, so soft, bit at Finn, who let the paper fall as she reached across the candles and said, "I summon thee, Jack Fata, to my hand."

His eyes glinted as she took from her red coat the ring she'd bought with carefully hoarded money. It was made of bronze, the shape of two lions clasping a heart. She stepped forward. One candle fell, was extinguished. The circle broke—

—and Jack reached out and grasped her wrist, dragging her toward him.

"Let her go!" Christie lunged.

Jack yanked Finn into the circle, released her, and whirled on Christie like a striking snake. He grabbed Christie by the collar. When Sylvie flew forward and clutched at Jack's arm, he caught her by the wrist.

Finn recovered as Jack effortlessly held her struggling friends and turned his head to smile at her. His eyes were black. "They broke the circle, Finn."

She whispered, "It was *I* who summoned you. Come get *me*."

Jack set Sylvie aside and shoved Christie away, watching as Finn backed up against the tree. Never taking his gaze from hers, he crouched and set the fallen candle into place. He rose and stepped close to her, bracing both arms against the tree on either side of her. He leaned toward her and whispered, "So. What now? How will you appease a vengeful spirit?"

She could feel the coolness breathing from his skin, see the unholy silver glow in his eyes. All she wanted to do was kiss him and bring him back into the world of sunlight and sorrow. "Stop it. You're not—"

Sylvie ran toward them, then fell back as if she'd hit an invisible wall. She yelled, but Finn couldn't hear her voice.

"Jack." Finn didn't drop her gaze from his. "*I bind thee—*"

"Use that knife"—his hand dove into her coat and pulled out the cross-hilted dagger—"against me. Or, Finn, I promise, I'll *ruin* you."

He pressed her fingers around the hilt.

"Jack." She kept her voice steady. "I'm not—"

He gripped her hand. She winced as he made her slice his palm with the blade. The skin parted, but there was no blood. She looked into his eyes. "*I'm not afraid of you.*"

"But," his voice was raw, "you should be."

"*Should* be? I won't be. So you can stop *this.*"

Outside the circle of candles, Christie looked terrified as he struck at the transparent barrier, pushing at the air like a mime. Sylvie was hunkered on the ground, staring intently at the candles she couldn't touch.

Jack told Finn, "They can't get into the circle. Circles will only hold two souls—summoner and summoned."

"Then you *do* have a soul, Jack." She grabbed his hand and shoved the bronze ring onto his only naked finger. "With this ring, dark spirit, I bind thee."

His voice broke as his eyes flooded with anguish. "*Finn.*"

He vanished into the dark. The candle flames flared, then were extinguished. Christie and Sylvie fell into the circle. As they scrambled up, Finn sagged against the tree and whispered, "Let's go home."

BACK IN HER ROOM, FINN picked up Lily's phone from where she'd set it on the floor near the outlet. She began to scroll through the images: the ones of her and Lily at the beach, in Shakespeare's Garden, on the carousel at Fishermen's Wharf. There were a lot of her sister and Leander, looking perfect for each other.

Then she came to Muir Woods.

The Muir Woods was a nature preserve of giant redwoods in California, mysterious and ancient, and a hike their da had insisted on at least once a year. The photographs had been taken just before sunset, before the park closed . . . images of trees and shadows and willowy strands of light. Some of the shadows looked like figures . . .

Finn peered closely at one image that looked as if a large, dark animal was slinking between the trees. She shuddered and set down the phone. She remembered Dead Bird drinking her blood and the shadows bleeding into Jack's eyes.

I am going to end up in a mental hospital. I just know it.

She lifted the phone again and returned to the Muir Woods pictures.

Another photo came up, startling her, because it was black-and-white. In it, her sister stood facing the lens, her skin luminous, her sleeveless black gown swirling like gauze, her eyes black as ink. She had become a phantom, caught forever between the world of the dark and the world of the light.

Like Jack.

Finn set down the phone and opened Lily Rose's journal. These were not fairy tales, Lily's stories. Reading them made Finn hurt, because, although they were disguised in fantasy, she knew they were truth. *Their names are Dandelion, Wormwood . . .*

He is the Black Scissors, the Dubh Deamhais, *and he is a faery doctor, a force of nature, neither good nor bad . . .*

The girl who had been born without arms was a friend to owls because she had been one . . .

She riffled to the beginning. *They call us things with teeth because they don't have true forms, no real biology . . .*

In the beginning was nothing. From nothing emerged night. Then came the children of nothing and night . . .

Lily Rose, her sensible sister, had known about them. And they had tricked her. And she had died.

Finn flinched as branches rattled against the window. Had the Fatas always been here, in Fair Hollow? And why had Reiko Fata been in San Francisco? And the wolf-eyed man flickering at the edge of her childhood recollections . . . what was he?

When a book fell from the shelf, she froze.

Another book slid to the floor. She couldn't move, couldn't breathe.

Four more books swept from the shelves.

The Tempest had fallen open to one of Caliban's speeches. *Wuthering Heights* lay nearby, displaying a description of Heathcliff. A volume of stories by Edgar Allan Poe revealed the first page of "The Fall of the House of Usher." A book of Hans Christian Andersen's stories had been flung beneath the window and Rackham's Snow Queen glittered cruelly on the page.

From downstairs, her father yelled. She ran.

He stood in the parlor, rubbing his head, a slim book in one hand. He looked bewildered. "The bloody book *flew* off the shelf . . ."

"What book is it?" She tried to sound casual, not panicked.

He looked at it. "Scottish poems."

She took the book from him and dropped it on the floor. As he stared, the pages fell open. She said, "*Tam Lin*. I don't remember *Tam Lin*."

He strode toward the shelves and began checking them, intent on finding a fault. "It's a ballad about a young woman who rescues her beloved from the Queen of the Faeries. There must be something wrong with this bloody shelf. It must be coming undone."

Finn stared down at the book and felt that *she* was coming undone.

SOMETHING WAS TRYING TO WARN her. And it was in the house.

Finn lay on the floor of her bedroom, in a pool of lamplight, surrounded by the books that had fallen from her shelves, and she thought of Jack. *Please come to me.*

She folded one arm across her face, but sleep was impossible. A strange longing and despair had begun to gnaw at her. Her fists clenched as she curled up on her side. In binding Jack to her, what had she done to herself?

A breeze threaded through the room, warm and summery, scented with Nag

Champa incense and tangerines, fragrances that reminded her of San Francisco and—

She sat up, her breath leaving her in a gasp. *"Lily?"*

JACK WALKED IN THE NIGHT, not daring to return to Tirnagoth yet, not with the binding spell just placed on him by a reckless girl. He paused once, to gaze down at the ring she'd bound him with, the two lions holding a heart between them. *Lionheart,* he thought, and almost smiled.

He changed direction and pushed through the woods, toward the park. He came to the street with LeafStruck Mansion rising at its end and was drawn toward a flickering dot of light on the stairs.

The light came from a cigarette, and the cigarette was held by Nathan Clare, who slouched on the steps midway to LeafStruck. Jack sprawled beside him. "You look like a delinquent."

"I'm entitled." Nathan glanced at him, frowned. He breathed out, *"Jack . . .* what happened to you?"

"It's that obvious? You think she'll notice?"

"It's like a beacon." Nathan's gaze fell to Jack's hands. The ivory scars were clearer now that he'd gotten rid of the ancient rings—all but for that one. "Was it Finn Sullivan? How could she possibly know a binding—"

"Someone"—Jack said savagely—"told her how to do it. One of her friends has witch blood."

Nathan regarded his cigarette. His voice was almost a whisper. "Do you understand now?"

"Why are you *here?*"

Nathan's gaze lifted to a second-floor window that glowed with lamplight. "You don't remember things very well, do you? Well, I do. I remember when we lived here, when we were happy."

"Nate, I was a different person then."

Nathan bowed his head. His cigarette was burning to a nub, but he barely noticed it. "I'm sorry, Jack."

When Jack thought of Nathan and All Hallows' Eve, he didn't like the heavy, twisting sensation in his chest. "What are you going to do?"

"Only be with Booke . . . until then."

"And what does Booke think of that?" Jack, also using the girl's Fata name, gazed into the night.

"She understands."

Jack thought of Finn and laughed softly. "You can't possibly believe that."

"I'll do what needs to be done, Jack, don't worry."

Jack looked at him. "That's not what I'm worried about."

The lit end of Nathan's cigarette reflected pinpoints of red in his eyes. "Is it so terrible? The . . . final moments?"

"More than you can imagine. And when you've lived so long, it gets harder to die."

CHAPTER FOURTEEN

*A man or woman or child will suddenly take to the bed, and from then
on, perhaps for a few weeks, perhaps for a lifetime, will be at times
unconscious . . . these persons are, during these times, with the faeries.*

—VISIONS AND BELIEFS IN THE WEST OF IRELAND, LADY
GREGORY

*The Redcap prince named Heartsblood has neither a heart, nor blood.
Though red-haired, he isn't one of the Dragon clan. He is cruel, a love-
talker. He was the first ganconer, the creator of the Red Thorn spell,
which turns people into green things.*

—FROM THE JOURNAL OF LILY ROSE

After Mr. Wyatt's appearance at the Dead Kings and Professor Avaline's
rescue of Christie from a possession, Finn had come to the conclusion that most
of HallowHeart's professors were more than they seemed. Professor Fairchild
always wore cuff links with images of stags on them, and Miss Perangelo, the
art teacher, had an amulet engraved with the same animal. Hobson, Finn's math
professor, with his red hair and beard, was grim and stocky, and always talking
about the mysticism of arithmetic.

When Jane Emory caught Finn looking at her bracelet with its charms of
crows, she smiled. "Do you like it? It was my granna's."

"What does the crow mean?"

Jane Emory's short hair, haloed by the afternoon sun, shone golden. "It means life after—" She hesitated. "Finn. I'm sorry . . . about your mother and your sister."

Finn felt a flash of anger toward her father as she realized he had told this woman about their personal family business. She wanted to ask about the Fatas, just to see her expression.

"Why? You had nothing to do with their deaths." She strode away before Jane Emory could reply.

AS NIGHT FELL, FINN SAT on her back porch reading the book of Scottish poetry that had been flung at her father by an invisible hand. Troubled by the lyrical menace of *Tam Lin*, she set the book aside and looked at the tin box Sylvie had let her borrow. A geisha was painted on the lid, and inside were tiny tiles inked with words like *Forbidden Door, Lavish Menace, Ivory Tongue*. She didn't know what they meant, and neither did Sylvie, who suspected the tiles were either a fortune-telling device or a compilation of erotic acts.

Finn shook the tin. Opening the lid, she chose seven tiles and set them down.

"Don't look at them." Suddenly Jack was on the steps beside her. In jeans and a black shirt with dragon cuff links, he didn't seem to notice the cold.

"You shouldn't have spoken to me that night at the concert."

"No. I shouldn't have. I'm apologizing. I can't keep away from you, it seems. You've tamed me."

"You're not mad at me?"

"I'm not mad at you."

She turned up a tile. *Bestial Prince*. "How can I pretend you're ordinary?"

"What are you reading?"

She slid the *Tam Lin* book beneath the tin box. "Poetry. The sort your kind likes. Or is afraid of—I forgot which."

"That wouldn't happen to be a poem about a girl who challenges a fairy queen, would it?"

"Are they going to kill Nathan?"

He looked away, and that was her answer.

"How can . . . you can't let it *happen*—"

"I can't stop it . . . only Nathan's true love can do that."

"Does he have a true—"

"She's hidden away. I don't want to discuss this, Finn."

The silence was chilly. She decided they would have to pretend tonight. "What are your favorite movies?"

"I liked them when they first came out. Especially the ones with Mary Pickford."

"We were going to pretend you're ordinary. So why did you come to me?" She poked at another tile. *Bitten Kiss.* "Aren't I supposed to magically summon you?"

"I'm inviting you for a walk."

"It's raining."

"It's just rain."

"Let me tell my da. And I'll change."

WHEN SHE STEPPED BACK OUT, the expression on Jack's face made her look down at her red raincoat and boots and the yellow dress she'd been saving for her birthday on Halloween. Maybe he didn't like primary colors.

He smiled and held out a hand bare of rings but for the one with which she'd bound him. "Come on then."

They walked to Rose Tree Street, which had bistros and kitschy shops that sold everything from old records to homemade candles and retro lunchboxes. They wandered into a record store, where Jack bought a Robert Johnson vinyl and gazed admiringly at it as they walked out. "He was a blues singer—he also made a deal with the devil."

"Speaking of the devil, you play the violin. Who taught you?"

"My mother. She was an actress, but she'd learned to play as a child—most gypsies then had a talent for entertaining."

"And your dad?"

"A coachman, and someone who helped people with a particular problem."

"Spirit problems."

He leaned forward and said, his voice low, "Do you know why I'm answering these questions? Because, Finn Sullivan, you bound me to you."

"I didn't know what else to do after you left me."

"How did you do it? That concerns me, as in 'I'm concerned that you made a big mistake.'"

"Absalom Askew," she said, "told Sylvie how to do it."

"Why Sylvie?"

"Reiko told Sylvie she was a witch."

"So. Absalom told Sylvie about Tirnagoth's yew. I believe that particular place has a guardian."

"Yes, Jack. There was a guardian and his name was Dead Bird."

"He's dangerous. He's more elemental than Fata. *And* an outlaw."

"Look, it's done. Can we talk about other things?"

"What shall we talk about?"

"Normal things. Like . . . what was your first toy?"

He raised his eyebrows and she muttered, "No. Never mind. What were your parents like?"

"Finn," he gently reminded, "they've been dead for a long time."

She attempted several more questions, but became frustrated as each innocent inquiry was thwarted by his impossible existence of two hundred years. There would be no normal or ordinary between them, not even with words.

"Let me try. What was your favorite thing to do as a kid?"

"Taking circus classes because I wanted to be an acrobat." This was much better.

"I can picture you, flipping around."

"Can you? Lily and I took karate . . . she was better than I was. I've got no balance."

"And where was your first home?"

"Vermont," she said wistfully. "It was pretty there. Especially at Christmas. Do you celebrate the holidays?"

"Christmas? Well, I get a tree, and I decorate it. I watch old movies and then I put on holiday music."

She wondered if he was making fun of her, but when he lifted his gaze, she saw a desolate sorrow there. She reached out, clasped his hand, and felt the ring she'd given him warm between their twined fingers.

"Well, we tried, didn't we?" He spoke ruefully. "Being ordinary isn't as easy as it looks."

When he bought her coffee, she wondered if his money would turn to leaves, like the fairy currency in stories. As they continued walking, they kept the conversation to music and books, which seemed safe. She found herself gazing at his mouth, noting the way his lashes made shadows beneath his eyes. "So, Jack. What now?"

"This way." He led her down a street where office buildings and department stores had closed for the evening and become as silent as pyramids. On the corner was a brick warehouse with a neon sign flickering "Arcade."

"It looks closed." She drew back.

"It is." He rapped at the door. After a few minutes, an irritated man wrapped in a plaid robe answered, squinting at Jack while raking a hand through a mane of graying hair. "Hell, it's you." His voice had a strong Scottish burr. "Did you get the elephant?"

"I did not get the elephant, Murray. May we come in?"

"It's closed, Jack. Come back during business hours—"

Jack held up what looked like a one-hundred-dollar bill. "I'm trying to impress a girl."

The older man quickly accepted it and jerked his head. "Go 'round the back, you and—?"

"Finn." Finn smiled.

"Murray." He nodded once and shut the door.

As Finn followed Jack into the alley, she whispered, "Was that real money?"

"Of course it was."

"Does he *know*?"

Jack turned as they came to another door of streaky metal. "He knows enough. But he's way past the age for being able to see my . . . family."

"What was that about an elephant?"

"You'll see."

The door opened and Murray beckoned them into the arcade, which glittered and glowed as if he'd just flung on a power switch. The clamor of the electronic games, accompanied by a melody from a giant carousel in the center, was extraordinary.

"It's all yours." Murray beckoned proudly. "That carousel is one of a kind, Finn. Knock when you're done. I'll be in my apartment."

"Thanks, Murray."

"One hour," Murray said and shut the door.

"You have tokens?" Finn headed for the carousel, and Jack sauntered after.

"I don't need tokens."

The carousel animals were unusual, among them a reindeer, an ostrich, and a unicorn. Each was obviously an antique, lovingly restored with new paint. Finn swung up onto a tiger as Jack walked among the animals, checking them. She knew he was trying to distract her, to keep her from asking about his terrible family and what they planned. She would, she decided, get it out of him somehow.

"It needs a bear." He leaned against Finn's tiger. "Maybe I can find him a bear instead of an elephant."

"*You* found all of these for him?"

"Each one, from a different place."

"Have you been to many different places?"

"Many."

She slid from the tiger and into his arms. He held her carefully, before stepping from the carousel. He reached up and swung her down.

"*No* fortune-teller, thank you." She strolled past the creepy automaton in its booth painted with Zodiac symbols. "Pac-Man. I bet you're an expert at Pac-Man."

"Now I feel old."

"Pinball?" She turned to face him with a mischievous smile, walking backward. "How about pinball?"

The hour went too quickly, and it was probably the best sixty minutes of her new life. When Murray eventually returned, he allowed Finn to choose a prize from the gift shop before pointing to the exit.

AS THEY STROLLED TOWARD THE park, Jack said, "I thought you'd pick one of the stuffed animals."

She twisted the ornate, fake sword she'd chosen in the gift shop. "Why? Look, the hilt is shaped into a dragon. Maybe you could collect a dragon for Murray's carousel."

"He does pay me well to collect things for him."

"Does he?" She saw a rise in the pavement between the trees, a glitter of water—a bridge. She halted. "Is there some other way?"

He turned to her and looked wary. "Why?"

"I don't like bridges."

"I'll walk over it with you."

She drew in a deep breath, as if she were already struggling in the water, and her heart began to slam against her rib cage. "Okay."

They moved forward, toward the little bridge and the night-blackened pond, which seemed all sloping earth and choking weeds. As she set one foot on the bridge, she felt his hand slip from hers. She turned. "Jack?"

He was staring at her as if he'd just recognized her. Softly, he said, "Why did you choose that dress? That coat? Those colors?"

She frowned, gripping the sword, its point on the ground. "What are you *talk*—"

"I know why you don't like bridges." His voice was filled with a wondering fear—he was remembering something. "You were walking over one when you first saw Reiko. When she first saw *you*."

She forgot about the bridge behind her.

"It was just after your mother's funeral. You were walking on a—"

—bridge that arched over the cemetery pond. She'd been straggling after her grieving da and her sister and her grandparents while trying to open her umbrella against the rain. She'd looked up to see a beautiful girl in boots and a coat of scarlet fur crossing the bridge with three companions. And Finn, a little girl in a yellow sundress and a ladybug-red raincoat, had been in their way. Angry, stubborn, and hurting, she'd said to the tall girl, "You're not a real person."

Reiko Fata in her scarlet fur had crouched down, her black hair swirling, her voice as viciously sweet as her smile. "And you'll never become one, little mayfly."

In the present, Finn whispered, "Jack . . ."

Ten-year-old Finn had stood very still as the tall, unreal girl and her elegant companions had breezed past. A blast of wind had tugged the umbrella from her hand, into the water . . . her favorite umbrella, the one with the mermaids on it, the one her mother had given her. She'd flung herself down and, reaching between the railings of the little bridge, had tried to grasp the handle of the umbrella twirling like an upside-down sunflower in the water. She'd reached too far—

—and lost her balance in an instant of horror and dismay that became a desperate struggle against icy water and weeds, until strong hands banded with rings had caught hold of her and lifted her to the surface. She'd opened her eyes to see a young man's face veiled by wet, dark hair . . .

The world spun away. Back from the memory she'd been made to forget, she sank to her knees, gripping the sword. "*It was you.*"

He hunkered down beside her. "I didn't remember any of that until now. I almost did, earlier, when I saw you in the yellow and red. The bridge . . . it just triggered something."

She gazed at him and her throat ached. "You were there, in Vermont, and you never remembered me. And I never recognized *you* . . ."

"I'm sure Reiko did something to make us forget. And, Finn, I think something in us *did* remember." He clasped one of her hands. "I think we recognized each other at the lake concert."

"It was you." She wanted to cry and laugh. "Why were you in *Vermont?*"

"Do you remember that locket I gave you?"

She lifted it from where it hung around her neck. He reached out, clicked the locket open, gazed at the portrait of the Renaissance boy. "His name was Ambrose, and he was a friend of mine. His last name was Cassandro."

She breathed out, "That's my mother's maiden name."

"People your age married young, way back when. Before the Fatas took him, Ambrose had a bride and kids—which led to descendants. He kept track. When someone in his family died, he would try to pay his respects. Secretly."

Finn gripped his hand, the same hand that had pulled her ten-year-old self from the water eight years ago.

"Ambrose went to your mother's funeral. Reiko went with him because he was her Jack at the time. And I went with Reiko." He looked at her. "To Vermont."

She pushed a hand against her mouth as the memory of another young man's face emerged. "Ambrose was there . . . after you pulled me out. You were on your knees, talking to me. I was crying. He lifted me up and handed me to my da."

Jack was solemn. "That was him."

She leaned toward him. "Do you think *Reiko* remembers *me?*"

"I don't know, Finn . . . but I'm thinking yes, because it's too much of a coincidence that you're here in Fair Hollow."

"She was in San Francisco. I saw her, Jack. And Aubrey Drake—he told me

Hester Kierney's dad got my dad the job here . . . the Kierneys and the Drakes are connected to the Fatas."

Jack was very still, a symptom of what she now recognized as worry. He said, faintly, "So she brought you here. Full circle."

"She *does* remember me." Finn clutched the fake sword and wished it was a real one. "What happened to Ambrose?"

"He's gone." He rubbed his hands over his face. "I don't like this. There are too many knots."

Finn rose. Dragging the sword, she faced the bridge—Reiko had placed that fear in her. She stalked forward.

"Finn!"

In the middle, she halted and looked over one shoulder at him. "I bound you to me. Do you have to do as I say?"

"No."

"If I get up on the railing of this bridge and walk the rest of the way, I want you to kiss me."

He straightened and started toward her, but she'd already climbed up and was balanced on the bridge's wide railing. She tried not to look at the black water below.

"Finn . . . don't be an idiot."

"I'm not. I'm showing you that a kiss is not going to be dangerous and that I won't let Reiko make me afraid. Besides"—she held the fake sword horizontally with both hands, like a balancing device—"you'll save me."

"A minute ago, you wouldn't even *walk* over this bridge." He strode toward her. "And now you're being reckless. You were right—you shouldn't cross without me."

She was exhilarated by the fact that he'd always been with her. "Were you with her in San Francisco, Jack?"

"Yes," he said quietly, "but I don't remember seeing you there."

"Let's get Nathan away from her."

"If you don't come down, I'm *dragging* you down."

"But I might fall the other way, so don't try it."

"Finn"—his voice was soft—"don't you remember, when you fell, what was *in* the water?"

She halted. He wasn't looking at her, but at something beneath her, between the railings of the bridge. When she'd been a child, struggling in that water, had something grabbed her ankle? "Jack. I don't want to remember any more."

He still had his gaze fixed on the railings beneath her feet. She watched as he crouched down and began speaking in a language she didn't understand. She didn't dare move. She heard a ruffling hiss, the scrape of something against stone, a splash in the water.

As Jack rose, she slid down into his arms, against him, and whispered, "Did you just save me again?"

The fake sword clattered to the stone as his mouth fiercely and hotly set on hers. Her lips were chapped, so there was a sting to the kiss, but it was sweet. She clung to him and he lifted her, clutching her so tightly the breath left her and went into him. Tangling her fingers in Jack's hair, Finn didn't let him pull back this time.

He took his mouth away and whispered, "I'm stealing you from your *life*—"

"No." She tightened her arms around his neck. "I'm stealing *you* from *yours*."

"It's past midnight," he murmured in her ear.

"Da will never let me out of the house again." She reluctantly stepped away. She snatched up the sword. "Take me home."

"This way." He clasped her hand. "Lionheart."

As they walked from the bridge, she whispered, "What was it that you were speaking to? The thing in the water?"

"He doesn't live in the water," Jack said without breaking his stride. "He lives under the bridge."

Wide-eyed, she looked over her shoulder and saw a shadowy figure in a hat and coat crouched on the bridge, watching them. She closed her eyes and muttered, "I am never going over that bridge again."

"Even if I'm with you?" he teased.

"Even if you're with me." She paused. "You don't think he looked up my dress, do you?"

THE RAIN HAD BEGUN AGAIN as she hurried alone up the path to her house. She halted when she saw her father on the porch, holding a jack-o'-lantern and speaking with a dark-haired woman in a skirt and blazer.

Professor Avaline turned as Finn approached. "I'm glad we had the chance to speak, Sean. Serafina."

As the woman lifted a black umbrella and clicked toward her sporty Cadillac, Finn frowned at her da. "What did she tell you? You can't trust her, Da—"

"Come inside and we'll talk—"

"I'm staying here until you tell me what she said."

He faced her as the rain sleeked her hair to her head and stung her eyes. "Jack Fata's involved in some things. He's—"

"And you *believed* her?"

"She's concerned for you, Finn—by the way, you *forgot to call.*"

"Why would she know these things about Jack?"

"*Will* you come out of that rain?"

As she moved grudgingly up the steps, he said, "Why don't you invite Jack to dinner?"

"Why don't you invite Jane Emory?" She stalked into the house and slammed the door.

CHRISTIE HAD DECIDED TO STAY home on family fun night so he could comb through every mythology and folklore book he'd been able to find in the library. Just for the comfort of noise, he'd turned on the upstairs television and the widescreen in the family room. He found the Food Network comforting. Lately, he felt as if his spirit had nettles in it. He often found himself thinking of Phouka—of her curvy lips and rippling hair, her fragrance of cinnamon and patchouli. It was like craving something he knew would eventually kill him, but he couldn't help it.

When water dripped onto his nose, he looked up, saw the stain on the ceiling, and swore.

He pelted up the stairs, groaned when he saw water trickling over the floor from the bathroom. The door was shut, but he heard splashing inside. It was one of his brothers, probably Conal, playing a trick. He pushed at the door. "Con—"

The door gave way. He fell in—

—and scrambled back, accidentally slamming the door shut behind him.

The tub was overflowing with black water. A beetle skittered across the toilet as an unearthly chill made mist of his breath. When something moved in the tub, he wanted to close his eyes and wish it away. "Stop . . ."

What emerged from the water was the head of a nightmare horse. Black and rotting, its eyes sulfurous, dead, it made no sound as its head was followed by shoulders, a torso, arms, a miasma of decay.

Even sliding into shock, Christie found the words he needed. *"You weren't invited."*

Baring yellow teeth, the thing said in a clotted voice, "Water is my domain. And this house stands above my well."

I'm dreaming. Christie pushed back against the door with a whimper, his legs useless. He was wet with sweat and shivering in the chill vapor. *Please let me be dreaming. Please . . .*

The thing with the head of a horse clutched at the tub's rim, its claws leaving scratches on the porcelain as it heaved its black, glistening body up—

Christie yanked the door open and pelted down the stairs, flinging himself outside—

He tumbled down the steps. As he landed heavily in the weeds, his teeth went through his bottom lip. Spitting blood, he staggered to his feet with a sobbing breath.

A large shape appeared in the doorway, its head misshapen, its fingers long with claws. Through a film of tears, he watched it slope down the steps.

A voice cut through his shock. "Christie."

He turned to find Reiko Fata smiling at him. Sleek in a crimson coat and boots, dark hair writhing from beneath the coat's hood, she was corruption in the form of a girl as she extended one hand, her eyes silvering. "I'll send it away. From you. From your family . . . if you come with me."

He heard the horse-headed thing grunting as it followed his scent.

Blood in his mouth and tears in his eyes, he held out a trembling hand to her. As his fingers touched hers, her breath sliced across his skin and flayed it away.

ON THE ENCLOSED BACK PORCH of her parents' apartment, Sylvie went through her collection of photographs; she touched the image of Thomas Luneht, the boy who had killed himself in the 1970s. With his dark hair and fierce blue eyes, he seemed her kindred spirit—and he still existed in some eerie, Fata fashion. She knew Caliban was afraid of him, but why? What happened to those who accepted Fata promises? Although Reiko Fata's offer had frightened Sylvie, those who dealt with the Fatas—the Drakes, the Valentines, the Kierneys—seemed to prosper. But what about those who'd fallen out of favor . . . like the Lunehts?

"Sylvie." Her stepmom came to the door and leaned against it. The lamp Sylvie had brought onto the porch made her blond ponytail shine golden. She was the absolute opposite of Sylvie's mother, the velvet-haired beauty from Tokyo. She was nice enough, but she had no pathos. "I've made tea."

"Did you put it in the green porcelain again?" Sylvie closed the lid of the Kali lunchbox filled with antique photos. "I don't need a tea ceremony every time I drink tea."

"I thought you liked it in the porcelain." Kim, eyes downcast, turned and moved away.

SYLVIE HAD TO GET OUT of the apartment after that.

As her bike whirred past the Emory-covered wall surrounding the old church, she heard fiddle music and halted, peering into the churchyard. A young man sat on the steps, his hair long, darkly copper, his face that of an Egyptian pharaoh. He wore black jeans and nothing else. When he stopped playing the fiddle and looked at her, his eyes flashed silver. "Sylvie Whitethorn. May I speak with you?"

He knew her name—it didn't matter. She wore Christie's iron ring and an ivory netsuke charm. The hoops in her earlobes were made of pure silver. She slid from the bike and wheeled it toward him because she was curious, and Reiko Fata had not threatened her.

"How do you know my name?" she asked.

"She told me." He raised his fiddle and played a few quick notes. "She needs an apprentice. A snakeling. She wants you."

Aware that she must be extremely courteous in dealing with his kind, Sylvie said, "No, thank you."

"You did very well with Dead Bird."

She flinched.

He rose, looked down at her, and began to whisper, "Take those things from your body that hold me from you, *aillidh, aingidh faodalach.*"

She unclipped the silver earrings and let them fall. She slid Christie's ring from her finger. Gazing into the man's quicksilver eyes, she began to unknot the netsuke charm from around her throat as he reached into her coat and carefully drew out the steel dagger she'd bought at a Renaissance fair. With an amused smile, he tossed it away.

The ringtone from her phone woke her.

She stared in disbelief at her discarded armor, whirling to run—

Cold fingers knotted in her hair and tore the netsuke from around her neck as, tenderly, he said, "I am the ganconer. No girl or boy has ever refused me."

As she tried to claw his fingers from her hair, he whispered into her ear and she slumped against him.

AS THE COPPER-HAIRED FIDDLER CALLED Farouche closed the churchyard gate behind him and walked away, wheeling Sylvie's bike, he began to whistle.

WHEN FINN WOKE, SHE BANGED her head against glass and winced—she'd fallen asleep on the window seat in her room, with Lily Rose's journal in her lap, opened to the story of a prince who had fallen in love with a creature made of lilies. *His name was Black Apple*, Dubh ubha, *and he was the only son of the queen of witches* . . . Black Apple, she recalled uneasily, was the name of one of Jack's vagabond friends.

Her da knocked at her door. She called out for him to come in. When the door opened and she saw his face, she gripped the journal. Carefully, he said, "Finn . . . there's been an accident . . . Sylvie . . ."

Dread coiled through her as the journal slid from her nerveless hands.

SYLVIE, WHILE BICYCLING, HAD SOMEHOW fallen and hit her head against a tree. Now she lay, unable to wake, in the stillness of a hospital room.

Finn ran down the path to the Hart house and felt wild relief when she saw lights in every window. As she loped onto the porch and rang the bell, her vision blurred. Sylvie . . . she couldn't lose another. She couldn't bear it.

Christie's brother Liam answered the door, his eyes red. "Finn. Christie's not here . . ."

A terrible apprehension knifed through her. "Where is he?"

Liam sagged against the door. "They took him to emergency. I don't know what's wrong . . . he had an attack or something. They'll make him better. I mean, that's their job . . ."

She couldn't answer. Her lashes fluttered as she fiercely fought the urge to fall down. She turned and trudged away, ignoring Liam's call. As she moved through the trees that separated her house from Christie's, she thought, *He's only had a seizure, epilepsy, a brain injury, a psychotic episode.* But she knew it wasn't any of those.

Sylvie and Christie had been *attacked.*

Finn leaned against a tree so that she could be sick. Cold air washed over her face. She twisted around in the silver and black light and realized she had strayed from the path. She was alone. *They* had made it so.

"Reiko Fata," she whispered, as the leaves rustled and icy air pulled the breath from her. She wanted to run to her house and tell her father everything.

Then something dark and snarling untangled within her, and she knew that whatever direction she took, it would lead to the enemy and an answer. So she began to walk.

The house that appeared through a scrim of branches turned out to be Sun-Stone. With smiling suns carved above its round windows and its glass doors painted with images of solar radiance, it seemed deceptively innocent. As Finn followed a path of yellow tiles, she saw no signs of life. Gripping the balustrade carved into twisting lines of mice, she stomped up to the doors and took the moth key from her coat, fitting it into the lock. She hesitated, her spirit crackling with rage and anguish and fear, before shoving the doors open, revealing golden shadows and ghostly silence.

She stepped in. She wore the iron and silver, and Eve Avaline's cross-dagger was in her coat pocket. As moonlight slid through windows that resembled topaz suns, the air was suddenly lit with an eerie glow that mimicked morning. Gilded furniture was wrapped in plastic, and a wooden floor was covered with dust. A fireplace shaped into a rayed sun gaped beneath an odd painting of two mice in fancy clothes. She remembered that Apollo, the Greek sun divinity, had once been a god of mice and plagues.

Something whispered from deep within the house, *Come*. Finn thought of Sylvie and Christie and gripped the hilt of Eve's dagger as she stepped into a room scattered with figures wrapped in plastic—manikins, naked and lifeless. In the middle of the floor was a red corset.

Fear had left her and been replaced with an exhausting anger. She walked slowly toward the corset, then wrinkled her nose at the reek of meat. When she realized what caused the smell, she stumbled to a halt and couldn't believe what she saw—the corset was soaked with blood, congealing, streaking the floor beneath . . .

Her courage broke. She whirled to run.

Then a shadow moved beneath a window, and the yellow light silvered a feral eye, long teeth—

Finn bolted, racing back through the house, out the doors, into the woods.

When she tripped over a root and hit the ground, she swallowed a cry of pain. As she lifted her head, she saw a light in the woods flickering orange. Struggling up, she glanced over one shoulder, wincing at the sharp pain in her knee, and lurched forward.

It emerged from the shadows between the trees—a low, sloping form, white as bone, with long teeth in a banded muzzle.

She scrambled away from it and plummeted toward the orange light and the voices. The hyena followed with a cackling cry.

As she broke through the brambles, the people around the campfire fell silent, firelight glinting in their eyes. A young man with long red hair lowered a fiddle and lavished her with his gaze. "It's Jack's sweetheart."

"She's skinny," said a blond girl in a gown of green gauze.

A black-haired boy, his hands poised over a drum, frowned. A blue flower was tucked behind one of his ears. "Yes, Aurora Sae, but she's brave. What do you think she's running from, Atheno?"

The man in torn jeans and a necklace of charms smiled. His silver hair, streaked with black, fell to his hips—Finn recognized him as the snake magician. "She's running from the *crom cu*."

Finn pressed back against a tree as the firelight caused tattered shadows to dance around the vagabonds.

A tall girl, her bald head painted with designs, sniffed the air. She wore a black corset and jeans embroidered with red wasps. "I smell him near. He's slinking."

"Darling Emory's right. He's here. I won't cross the crooked dog." A brown-skinned boy with rippling hair rose, his elegance enhanced by a suit of shabby velvet and a necklace of pearls gleaming against his chest.

"Hush, Dogrose." A silhouette moved forward, firelight glinting from the ruby stud in his nose. "The crooked dog is gone."

"Jack." Finn turned on him and almost collapsed. With a mighty effort, she didn't, remaining stone still as he walked to her. He shrugged off his fur-lined coat and held it out to her, but she backed away even though she couldn't stop shivering. "Did you know what she would *do to them*?"

He tossed the coat over a tree stump, his face turned away. "What did she do?"

"She *hurt* Christie and Sylvie. Were you supposed to *distract* me while she did it? Jack?"

The young man with the red hair sighed. "I only did my duty, Jack."

Jack turned on him. "*What did you do, Farouche?*"

The young man stepped back. "You know what I am."

As Finn listened, her hands curling into fists, Jack gently asked, "And the boy who likes poetry?"

"Fox-struck, is all. Reiko did that also." The bald girl rose. She was pretty, but her eyes glowed, feral. "This girl will bring us all to grief, Jack."

Finn wanted to kill them, but Jack said to her, quietly, "These are my friends, Finn. It is Reiko striking at those you love. Where is your father?"

"Da . . ." Finn whispered.

FINN AND JACK RAN FROM the woods, onto her porch, and Finn fought a wavy of dizzy fear as the door fell open, revealing a dark hall with wet leaves scattered across the floor. The feathers of the fake raven on the bureau rustled. The eerie wallpaper seemed to form faces that spat vines and leaves. Shadows were oddly cast, as if the light had gone sour. "Da!"

"Finn." Her father appeared in the parlor doorway with Jane Emory. "Jane's come. She heard about Sylvie."

Jack remained on the porch.

"Jack." Her da looked grim. "Hello."

"Mr. Sullivan. Miss Emory." Jack looked at Finn, his gaze shadowy. "I'll speak to Reiko, Finn."

"Jack, wait—"

But he was already gone into the dark.

Finn turned back and met Jane Emory's gaze and *knew* that she was one of Professor Avaline's.

IN THE MIDDLE OF THE night, Finn opened her glass doors, stepped onto the terrace, and let the chill and the starlight calm her. In her desperation, she'd thought of going to Professor Avaline, but Avaline had betrayed her. *Don't think. Don't think. Just breathe.* She whispered, "Jack. I know you're here."

He moved from the night and sat on the railing opposite her. "I spoke to her."

She nodded, waiting, her stomach in knots.

"To save them, you must agree to whatever she says."

Her throat closed. She wrapped her sweater-coat close around her. "She took them because I bound you to me. And because I know about Nathan."

"Yes, Finn. You can't trick her. Others have tried."

"Jack"—his name sounded like it was being scraped out of her—"help me."

"I *am* helping you." His eyes were dark with soul damage. "Just *do as she says.*"

But she knew what Reiko would demand in exchange for Christie and Sylvie. She felt it might kill her. "I can't."

He looked away from her. In a low voice, he said, "When I first saw you, when she told me to speak to you, you were a game. Then I actually spoke to you and I was intrigued—why did Reiko choose you? Then I wondered if you could be used against her. Then I came alive." He closed his eyes, whispered, "Without you, I will die again."

"Jack." Her throat closed up. "I won't—"

He looked up and smiled coldly. "I'm already dead. So is Nathan. Your pretty friend and the fox poet aren't. Now, listen."

She sat on the railing beside him and listened and all the while felt as if her heart was being devoured, piece by piece. When he was done, she whispered, "What it if doesn't work . . ."

His smile was quick and bitter. "You haven't got a choice. It's either me or them. And you're a good girl, Finn, not a selfish one. You won't desert them."

"I won't forget you."

He smiled again and rose before she could touch him. "If you do, you'll only bring good to the world. Farewell, Finn Sullivan."

He vaulted over the railing, abandoning her again. Fiercely, she repeated, "*I won't forget you.*"

CHAPTER FIFTEEN

I saw pale kings and princes too,
Pale warriors, death-pale were they all;
They cried—"La Belle Dame Sans Merci
Hath thee in thrall!"

—LA BELLE DAME SANS MERCI, JOHN KEATS

They had been named Rue and Ruin, and they were lovely, sinister,
as soulless as barracudas. There is a rumor among the tribes and the
courts that the two brothers are the children of divinities, of a king of
graves and a queen of battles.

—FROM THE JOURNAL OF LILY ROSE

Ordinary life had been infected by an otherworldly menace that had struck down Finn's friends with terrifying ruthlessness and left Finn alone.

Alone, she planned a rescue.

She met Anna at the Weavers' shop and gave the girl the mysterious moth key along with Lily Rose's journal. "I need you to keep these safe."

Anna touched the lid of the lockbox that contained the key and the journal. "I will. Would you like your fortune told?"

"No, Anna. I know how this will end."

FINN DIDN'T WEAR IRON OR silver because they wouldn't allow her to see Reiko if she did and she knew she must follow Jack's instructions with the precision of an agent entering enemy territory. She put her hair up with the dragonfly pin her mother had given her. She dressed in Lily Rose's favorite black T-shirt, the one with an image of a punk fairy holding a skull. The jeans with the rhinestones on the sides and the red Converses had been gifts from her da. Her last ornament was a tiny medallion of the White Rabbit from Alice in Wonderland, given to her by Gran Rose. *Arm yourself with things from loved ones*, Jack had said. *No weapons . . . that gives them an excuse for violence against you.* He would deliver her message. He'd told her she would receive an answer at sunset.

She waited on the front porch, gazing at the jack-o'-lanterns on the lawn across the street and listening to Lily's music through her iPod earphones. At five, exactly, a red Mercedes glided into the driveway and Phouka slid out, dressed in white leather, auburn hair tucked beneath a chauffeur's cap. She winked at Finn as she held open the door. "Reiko got your message."

Finn slid into the front seat as Phouka tucked herself behind the wheel. Unsettled by the other girl's surreal loveliness, Finn looked away from her. "When did they take you?"

Phouka effortlessly backed the car out of the driveway. "That's not polite, Serafina. Don't ask such questions."

Finn hadn't slept, and she was wired from too much espresso and sick to her stomach. "Where are we going? Can I ask that question?"

"Tirnagoth, and don't be sassy. Why did you take up with him? You could have stayed a *happy* girl."

Finn, glimpsing people's lives in lamp-lit windows and watching kids playing on lawns as the sun began its descent below the horizon, murmured, "But I wasn't happy. What did she do to my friends?"

"They've been taken." Phouka looked grim.

"Taken *where*? What are those . . . things in the hospital that look like them?"

"Bits of Fata trickery—fetches. As for where your friends have been taken . . . I can't tell you, Finn. My advice—just do as you're told."

She hit the car's CD button and a gorgeous violin reel accompanied by drums pulsed through the car. Finn recognized it as the music that had been playing the night she'd first met Jack and said, "Tell me why she took Jack."

Phouka looked at her, one hand on the wheel. "Because his dad was an exorcist in Hungary. His mom was a gypsy witch in Ireland. They pissed off a lot of . . . people. He's a Jack, Finn. A Jack of Thorns. A *sluagh*. You don't grasp the concept, but you should not be feeling for him what you do."

"What, exactly, is a Jack?"

"A Jack or a Jill is a harnessed spirit, one who has come to the attention of a powerful Fata."

"How are they . . . made?"

"You don't need to know the gruesome details." For a while, they drove in silence, and Finn wondered if she was being driven to her murder. Then Phouka said, "Here we are."

The Mercedes slid up the scarcely there road, to Tirnagoth's gates, which opened gracefully despite a veil of creepers. In the early evening, the hotel looked beautiful, its pale stones kissed with rose and silver, its ruinous mass surrounded by blood-red roses and apple trees that sharply scented the air. It was a between place now. Waiting.

This is their world. Finn shivered.

Phouka halted the Mercedes and waited for her to get out. "You're on your own from here. Good luck, Serafina Sullivan."

Finn walked alone toward the metal gates shaped into a face framed by swirling hair. She told herself she wasn't being tricked into an abandoned building where she would be murdered. They were subtler than that—they worked at their victims' psyches. She didn't have the moth key, but the gate opened at her touch. She remembered a phrase from Lily Rose's journal: *Without us, they can't do anything in the physical world. They are shadows whose kings are Rue and Ruin.*

But they were more than that.

As she stepped forward, the last of the sunlight vanished and the veil of ruin was swept away in one golden, swooning moment scented with clover and smolder as the weedy courtyard and clogged pool became as neat as new, and red lamps made the water blush. The windows glowed with an illumination that brushed the faces of the graceful statues, which looked newly sculpted. The garden glimmered with tiny lights.

Finn remembered to breathe. She straightened her coat and strode toward the entrance, and it was fury that drove her up the stairs, through the doors, into the deserted lobby, where the chessboard floor glistened beneath a chandelier of red glass and, at the top of the stairway, a black window depicting a white serpent glowed malevolently, like something out of an otherworldly church. She called into the silence, "Hello?"

"She knows you're here." Caliban Ariel'Pan leaned against a pillar. He still seemed alien, even in a black T-shirt and jeans. He straightened and ambled toward her, and something about the way he moved made Finn flinch. She knew he wanted to kill her—the desire to do so glinted in his eyes. He held out a hand. "May I take your coat, madam?"

She removed her coat and handed it to him. He took it, smiled, gestured her up the stairs. The rings he wore gleamed dully. "Go on, if you want to save your friends. Take a left."

Reluctantly turning her back on him, Finn moved slowly up the stairs, past portraits of gorgeous people in glittering costumes, until she reached a corridor of red-patterned wallpaper, where she heard music, old-fashioned and crackling, a sound that reminded her of where she was and what she was dealing with. Dread snaked through her.

Two figures in an archway parted to watch her. Both had red hair and eyes so black it was as if the pupils had bled to drown the whites. The girl was sleek in a tasseled flapper's dress. The boy wore a black suit and a crimson tie. She could feel the cold drifting from their snow-white skin, their *otherness*. They weren't attempting to conceal what they were.

There was a scarlet door at the hall's end. She moved past them toward it and pushed through, into a scarlet room, where her reflection gazed at her from night-darkened windows, and light from crimson lamps stained the wall painting of a naked boy leaping over a bull. A statue of a goddess in a skirt, snakes twined around her arms, stood on a table between censers burning myrrh. It felt like a temple.

"Serafina." Reiko Fata moved forward, her body draped in a slip dress of green silk. She looked unnervingly like a teenage girl as she smiled sweetly. "Would you like something to eat? Drink?"

Finn had come without armor and only Jack's words and her wits as weapons. She whispered, "What did you do to Christie and Sylvie?"

"Remember your manners." Reiko's eyes went black.

Finn continued, her voice stronger now, "What did you do to them? If you're so afraid of me, why don't you kill *me*?"

Reiko's eyes narrowed. "You live because I *don't* fear you, Serafina Sullivan. By law, I cannot harm *thee*, but I can bring harm to those around thee."

"I won't let you."

"Won't *let* . . ." Reiko breathed. Then she smiled. "I see. Reckless girl. Have you really stopped caring what happens to you?"

"You tried to *hurt* me when I was little. *I remember you.*"

"Do you, Serafina Sullivan?" The room became a ruin, its walls streaked with mold, broken windows bleeding moonlight, shards of glass littering the floor. There was an odor of wet stone and earth, a graveyard fragrance. The air had become shatteringly cold. "*And I remember* you."

Reiko vanished into a ribboned shadow streaked with blood red.

Finn stumbled back and choked on a scream.

It was over in an instant. The elegant apartment returned, and Reiko was sauntering toward her, her platform shoes like cloven hooves, her eyes green again. "You are alone, Serafina Sullivan. Avaline and her lot won't help you. No one will. You'll say farewell to Jack. I'll take away your memory of him. Every friend and family member who comes near you will also forget him. Only then will Sylvie Whitethorn and Christie Hart return to what they were."

Jack. Despite her fear, Finn thought of his delicately scarred hands and darkened eyes, the pain he disguised with careless remarks. He had warned her about what she would need to do, and the pleading words that came from her hurt her stomach. "I'll do what you want. Just give them back."

Reiko didn't smile. "Go up those stairs."

Finn turned and walked toward a staircase of spiraling metal, which creaked as she ascended. When she came to a black door with a dirty pink window in it, she hesitated. She didn't know what waited for her on the other side, some unnamed horror . . .

She shoved it open and stepped into a candlelit chamber.

Jack sat beneath a painting of a pterodactyl flying with a lady's white evening glove in its beak and that image made Finn shiver—it reminded her of the Fatas, with their reptilian desire to exist beneath illusions of elegance and politeness. Jack's black velvet shirt was unlaced to reveal the serpent tattoo over his heart, and his sleeves fluttered with ribbons like funeral banners. When he looked at her, his eyes bled dark. She wanted to be angry at him—he had led her into this, knowing what his family was, knowing what they were capable of. She said, "I'm here to say good-bye."

He glanced away from her as if he couldn't care less, but his body was taut. "You're only a schoolgirl. I was playing with you, you know."

"Stop it."

He smoothly stood up and closed the distance between them before she could speak again. As he gently took her hands in his, she saw that he still wore her ring, the lions clasping a heart. He whispered, "Forget me and be safe."

As he stepped back, the dead look returned to his eyes. Refusing to just let him go, she stepped forward, pressed a hand over his heart, felt the faint beat of what Reiko would take from him—and she saw how it would happen: Jack cutting out his own beating heart and handing it to a smiling Reiko.

As she spoke, she felt as if something were being torn out of her, "Will you be—"

"It doesn't matter. Save them, Finn, before they become lost. Let me worry about Nathan. *Forget us.*"

"*I can't.*" She hated the wretched sob in her voice.

"Go." He gently removed her hand from him. "You're in the house of your enemy."

She turned and stumbled blindly down the stairs.

Reiko Fata stood in the center of her chamber, holding a basket. In it were clothes and a wooden box. She spoke with no smile in her voice. "Listen carefully, Serafina Sullivan, and I will tell you how to bring Christie and Sylvie back."

FIFTEEN MINUTES LATER, FINN STOOD outside Tirnagoth's gates. Phouka and the Mercedes had gone; the Fatas had left her to find her own way back. She clutched Reiko's basket against her and lifted her gaze to Tirnagoth's windows. The hotel had returned to its illusion of abandonment, its shattered windows dark, drafts rattling through its moldering insides.

She might never see Jack again, but *they* were in there, unseen spirits who could manifest into flesh and blood, pretend to be people. She wanted to scream at the ruin. She wanted to claw Reiko Fata's heart out.

She sank down against a tree and huddled there, feeling as helpless as a child.

When something whispered in the shifting shadows, her head jerked up. She thought she saw a girl's face behind a screen of brambles.

Go. Now, the voice whispered.

She rose and stumbled away in a scattering of autumn leaves.

After an hour of walking, she reached the Elder Street Church, which was an eerie sight with its crooked roof and tiny graveyard. When she opened the gate, she saw the tree Reiko had told her to look for; Finn shuddered, because its graceful trunk reminded her of a girl's body, and its leaves glistened like tear-filled eyes. She refused to think further as something close to madness fluttered around her brain. She moved forward, placing the charm Reiko had given her on the tree. With calm terror, she crouched down and spoke Reiko's word.

There was a rustling in the bushes knotted around the old tombstones, and a red fox slinked out and sat nearby, its eyes familiar, madness skittering in them. The nightmarish, unreal beauty of the moment made Finn cold. She was in a between place.

She tossed the second charm over the fox's ear and spoke the chant Reiko had scrawled on a piece of parchment. The words stung her throat.

And the world went black, because her mind was unable to accept what happened next.

"FINN. FINN."

Someone was shaking her. She opened her eyes, saw the night sky twinkling with stars, and smelled loamy earth. She blinked and said hoarsely, "Sylv?"

Sylvie was huddled beside her, naked and shivering, her eyes shadowy. Christie lay in the leaves nearby, unconscious and also naked.

Finn scrambled back, her hands over her mouth.

Sylvie whispered, "Where are we?"

Finn drew the basket toward her. With shaking hands, she pulled out a gown of black silk and handed it to Sylvie, who slid it over her head. "We're at the old church on Elder Street."

"How?"

Finn was mightily fighting the urge to be sick. She wanted to throw herself on the two of them and hug them to make sure they were solid, and not a tree and a fox. "You don't remember?"

Sylvie looked around and shivered. "No."

Christie moaned, sat up, looked down at himself. "Oh, sh—"

When he saw Finn and Sylvie, he blushed. They politely looked away as Finn handed him the basket and he took out the jeans Reiko had given her and slid into them. He said, "Will someone please tell me what happened? Did I black out?"

"The Fatas happened." Finn pushed her hair from her face as she rose, her legs like jelly. "Once we walk through the gate, we'll forget. We'll be safe."

Christie looked around, his face white. "Why do I smell like an animal?"

Sylvie looked at Finn, her eyes wide, pleading: *Don't tell us.* Then she whispered, "What about Jack?"

"Jack belongs to her." Finn tugged up the hood of her red coat, refusing to let them see her anguish. "Let's go. I want it done with."

Christie and Sylvie clasped Finn's hands and, flanking her, they walked with her through the gate.

Jack's memory slid from them like a shadow.

FINN DIDN'T REMEMBER HOW SHE came to be walking down a street with two barefoot friends on either side. She had an awful headache, and she felt hollow and sick.

"Sylvie? Christie?" She let go of their hands. "What happened?"

They looked as bewildered as she was.

HER DA CALLED SYLVIE'S FATHER and Christie's parents, and their parlor became the scene of a confused reunion. There'd been no explanations, because Sylvie's father didn't ask any questions, just looked carefully at his daughter before breathing a sigh and hugging her and whispering, "*En ym-marra.*" Her stepmom stood back, looking troubled and relieved. Christie tried to field his parents' inquiries, but he looked confused and exhausted.

Christie, Sylvie, and Finn could only remember falling asleep—Christie in the psych ward, Sylvie in her hospital bed, Finn in her room—before waking up in the churchyard.

When everyone had gone and the house was silent, her da made tea and brought it to Finn where she huddled on the sofa, wrapped in the butterfly quilt from her bed. He sat beside her and pushed his hands through his hair. He looked more rumpled than ever. "Will you tell me what happened?"

"I can't, Da." She raised a pleading gaze. "Because I don't remember."

He looked away, and it seemed as if he wanted to ask her something else, but didn't. He nodded once. "Well. We'll find out."

AFTER SEVERAL DAYS, FINN INSISTED on returning to her classes because she wanted things normal again and she had a paper due in her Women in Surrealism class. Christie and Sylvie wouldn't be returning until next Monday, as they were enduring a series of doctors' visits. Finn's da had taken her to the emergency room to have her checked for a head injury, but none had been found. But there were holes in her memory. Certain sights would trigger an irrational fear: a student's hand glimmering with rings; a deep shadow; leaves rustling in a sudden wind.

As Finn sat alone at the picnic table in Origen's courtyard, numb to the apple-biting chill and wondering again what had happened, she saw Angyll Weaver stalking toward her. She was shocked—Angyll was pale, gaunt, her blond hair tangled, her lips chapped.

"I see you're not hanging with the Fatas anymore." Angyll leaned over the table. "Did you find out they're *monsters*?"

"Pardon?" Finn, afraid the other girl might be mental, drew back.

Angyll bared her teeth, clutching a small, silver cross on a chain around her neck. "You and your friends? The Fatas are *playing* you."

Finn's stomach was twisting. "I don't know what you're talking about, Angyll. Who are the Fatas?"

Angyll went white. She backed up a step.

She twisted around and ran.

WHEN SYLVIE CAME TO VISIT Finn, they conspired in the yellow parlor Finn had hung with family photographs. Looking fragile with a bruise along one side of her face, Sylvie curled around a pillow as Finn told her about Angyll's freak-out. ". . . and she said something about the Fatas."

"The Fatas? They don't even attend HallowHeart. They're rich kids from a weird family."

"Why would she call them monsters?"

"Angyll Weaver is a moron."

"Christie used to see something in her."

"Christie sees something in nearly every girl he meets. The Fatas don't mingle with anyone except at festivals. Christie thinks we were abducted by aliens—or roofied."

"We were *not* abducted by aliens. And who would drug us all together? And I'm glad our parents didn't think that or we'd be talking to the police."

"Finn. I fell off my bike and bashed my head. Christie had a mental break-down. We were in the *hospital* and we woke up, without anything wrong with us, in a *churchyard*, with *you*. We can't remember whole spots in our recent lives—ever since the day we met *you*."

Finn felt defensive and wanted to say she felt like Fair Hollow was destroying her sanity because she was constantly apprehensive and anxious and never had been before. She was also forgetting things. She felt the same way she had after Lily's suicide, when she would come home or wake up and expect her sister to be there . . . but there had only been a void, and the strangling grief.

"It was something bad," Sylvie whispered, "that happened to us, wasn't it? The hospital staff never even saw me and Christie leave."

"Maybe we shouldn't try to remember, Sylv. There must be a reason we don't."

"You don't believe that. You know what else? I don't dream anymore. I asked Christie—he doesn't either. Do you?"

I don't sleep *anymore.* Finn folded her hands in her lap. "No. Let's talk about regular stuff. So, I hate soccer. What other phys ed course can I switch to?"

Sylvie stayed the night, and they watched a movie about a teenage Red Riding Hood and eighteenth-century werewolves until Sylvie fell asleep on the sofa. Finn looked up as her father peered in and whispered, "It's midnight."

"I'll sleep here."

"How is she?" He glanced at Sylvie.

"Not catatonic. Da . . . I'm sorry I had an attitude about you and Jane Emory."

He looked as if he'd say something, then murmured, "G'night," before vanishing from the doorway.

Finn shut off the TV and sat in the dark room, careful not to disturb Sylvie, who was snoring softly. She gazed at a photo on the wall, of her mom, with her dark hair and its one blond streak, sitting in their Vermont garden and looking so young and happy.

Then she looked out the window, into the yard, and saw the figure on the swing.

Its hands, glittering with rings, clutched the chains. Something tapped at her brain, like fingers against a window.

She slid from the parlor, walked through the kitchen, and pushed out the back door, emerging into the yard.

The swing, abandoned, creaked back and forth. She moved across the frosty grass and touched the chains. The metal was still warm.

SYLVIE EVENTUALLY WHEEDLED HER FATHER and step-mother into letting her return to school. As she and Finn arrived, striding toward Armitrage Hall wreathed with granite fairies and leafy masks spitting Emory, she noticed that the faces of some of the students were grim and pale. On the stairs, one girl was crying softly into her hands.

In the corridor, they met a shadowy-eyed Professor Fairchild, who said, "Miss Sullivan. Miss Whitethorn. You knew her. I'm sorry."

ANGYLL WEAVER HAD RAZORED HER wrists to the bone. She had bled out at the feet of an angel statue in Soldiers' Gate Cemetery.

CHAPTER SIXTEEN

Perhaps a fairy's most potent power derives from human fear of what might ensue if we don't obey fairy rules. Rather than the showy three wishes, incantations, or magic hats, human imagination and anticipation is the essence of their power over us.

—THE ULTIMATE FAIRIES HANDBOOK, SUSANNAH MARRIOTT

There are Lily Girls and Jills. The Lily Girls, the ghosts of murdered girls, are usually harmless. The Jills are female versions of the Jacks, cold bodies stuffed with flowers, without hearts, without blood. And, like the Jacks, they are the Fatas' assassins.

—FROM THE JOURNAL OF LILY ROSE

When Christie returned from Angyll Weaver's funeral, Sylvie and Finn were waiting for him on his front porch. He let his bike fall into the leaves and, somber in a black suit, a black wool hat pulled down on his hair, walked toward them. They folded their arms around him and stood silently for a while in the sunlight, mourning a girl only Christie had truly known.

Finn thought about Anna Weaver, who, like her, had lost a sister.

The wind gusted. When she raised her head, she saw a lily-white Rolls-Royce parked across the street. Beside it stood a girl in a pale coat, auburn hair rippling around her face.

"Phouka Fata," Sylvie murmured. "What's *she* doing here?"

Christie looked over one shoulder, frowning. "She was at the funeral. Some of the Fatas were."

Finn gazed at Phouka Fata and remembered what Angyll Weaver had said about the Fatas being monsters.

A LITTLE PAST SUNSET, FINN walked home from Sylvie's, cutting across the park as it began to rain. The unpleasant day had grown worse, and she wanted nothing more than sweet hot tea and a bubble bath.

When she glimpsed something fluttering against the darkness beneath the trees, she halted.

A whisper so cold, so otherworldly it made her skin crawl, came from the girl standing there. Gently silvered by the moonlight misting through the clouds, her feet bare, her blond hair woven with thorny vines, she was statue still, her sleeveless gown of black silk rippling like liquid night.

Finn's backpack slid from her shoulder and fell to her feet. She wanted to believe she'd fallen asleep, that this malevolent apparition of Angyll Weaver was only a nightmare. But she was awake and the world had become a stranger.

Angyll's lips moved. Finn clearly heard her words, as if just tuning into a certain frequency, "*. . . what . . . they have done to me.*"

Finn backed away and felt gut-wrenching terror.

"*. . . want to know what he did, the crooked dog? He sliced my wrists with his teeth. They call us things with teeth, but he had so many . . .*"

Finn whispered, "Go away. Go away. I can't help you. Please—"

The dead girl screamed.

Finn put her arms over her head and almost screamed herself.

"Angyll." A calm, girlish voice drew her gaze to a small figure in a white coat, sheltered by an umbrella as she moved toward the dead girl, one hand outstretched. "Come to me."

Angyll clasped her little sister's hand. There was a soft sigh.

Then Finn and Anna Weaver were alone. Finn whispered, "Were you *looking for her?*"

Anna wiped the back of one hand across her face, which glistened with more than rain. "I've got something to give back to you. Come with me?"

"Anna . . ." Finn grabbed her backpack and followed her through the park, across a bridge that arched over a pond clogged with dead leaves. She felt her world going completely off its axis. "Anna . . . stop . . . *tell* me where we're going . . . and your *sister* . . ." She pushed a cluster of branches out of her way as Anna slid past a broken gate of black metal. Hurrying after the girl, down a path through someone's neglected garden, Finn saw a house rising at the end, an old place tangled with oak trees and elms. She halted. "LeafStruck."

"Come on." Anna walked back to her and took her hand. "This is where I hid it. The owl lady doesn't mind."

"The owl lady . . ." Something struggled in Finn's mind.

Anna led her up the stairs to the door and pushed into a gloomy interior scattered with leaves and insects and graffiti. Spiderwebs glistened on the cracked glass of the windows. Anna moved toward a cavernous fireplace.

Finn slumped against the wall and tried not to think of a luminous, dead, and malicious Angyll Weaver.

She spotted a rusting metal box beneath a pile of leaves and pushed at it with her foot. The lid fell off, revealing a dusty picture. She crouched down and peered at the photograph of a man and woman in old-fashioned clothes. She didn't recognize them, but the boy who stood between them looked like someone she knew at HallowHeart—Nathan Clare. She turned the picture over. Scrawled on the back were the words *Home, 1907.* Finn thought of Angyll Weaver's ghost, shivered, and dropped the picture. What was happening to her?

Anna returned and handed her a small lockbox. "The crooked dog took my sister, and the serpent doesn't want you to remember. You gave these to me, because you told me they were taking something from you."

Thinking of the story of Pandora, Finn slowly opened the metal box; she saw a journal of black velvet bound with silver ribbons, a key of tarnished pewter shaped into a moth. And a letter.

"So," Anna said, calmly, "remember."

Finn unfolded the letter with unsteady hands. It was her handwriting, and it told her which file to open on her laptop. She had the laptop with her. She pulled it from her backpack, flipped open the lid covered with peace stickers, and tapped the file labeled *Moth.*

REIKO FATA. CALIBAN. PHOUKA. DEAD Bird. Absalom Askew. A tall, shadowy man with a crown of antlers.

And Jack, Jack, *Jack*.

"Jack." Finn remembered all of it, as if her brain had just switched on. It actually hurt. She felt her nose bleeding a little.

"See?" Huddled beside Finn, Anna looked at her intently. She seemed almost awed. "*You* tricked *them*."

"What are you doing here?" The new voice made them twist around.

Nathan Clare stood in the doorway, and he looked angry. It was strange, seeing him that way, with his angelic face and curls. Finn couldn't think of anything to say as her gaze fell to the picture of his family. Her memories were beginning to settle, but she still felt strange, as if she were in someone else's body.

She remembered what the Fatas were planning for him on Halloween.

"I said what are you doing here?" He wore a shirt and tie and gray trousers and looked as if he'd just stepped from *The Great Gatsby*.

Finn lifted the old photograph. "When did they take *you*, Nathan?"

"I don't know what you mean. That's not me."

"It's not your fault," Anna told him. "They tricked you. Like they tricked Tom Luneht and my sister and those girls."

"Girls?" Finn repeated as Nathan sagged against the door frame and crouched down, hands loose between his knees.

He whispered, "I was sick. They promised me one hundred years. My parents died in a hotel fire in Paris and I was the only child. I was seven and all this"—he waved, meaning LeafStruck and its grounds—"was mine. My governess, Colleen Olive, she saw an opportunity."

"What do you mean?"

His hands knotted together. "She was a Fata. We were one of the oldest families, and all this property? *They* wanted it. Someone came to rent our carriage house, someone who was working for a family called the Fatas."

"Jack," Finn whispered.

"One hundred years, Finn." He circled his arms around his bent knees. "They gave me that."

"And after one hundred years?"

He said, dreamily, "Every one hundred years, there must be an offering—a mortal, because we are real, flesh and blood, a payment to the king of the dead in exchange for not harvesting among the Fatas. The sacrifice must always be willing."

Finn's voice shook as she said, "You can't *let* them."

"Can't let them?" His voice was raw. "I can't stop them."

"What will they do to you?"

"Does it matter? It will be done. And I've lived one hundred years like a king."

"They murdered Angyll Weaver. I saw her *ghost* . . ."

"Caliban did that." Nathan rose, brushing leaves from his expensive trousers. He looked sad as he said, "Go home. Both of you. I'm sorry, Anna."

Finn watched helplessly as he walked from the house. Then she looked at Anna.

It was Lily's journal that had told her *Even the dark ones won't harm young children, who are more spirit than flesh.* But they had harmed a child's sister . . . and perhaps her own as well. And now they were going to murder a boy they had deceived into dying for them.

Something woke inside of her, ferocious and roaring. She lifted her head. "Anna. Thank you. Now let's go home."

AS FINN STEPPED ONTO HER terrace, she whispered into the night that was his dawn. "Jack."

Silence.

She knew he was there, that her forgetting hadn't made him cease to exist. *"Jack!"*

Leaves rustled like immense wings. She pictured his eyes darkening with the desperation to be human again, remembered his strength, how he had protected her at such great cost to himself . . .

There was a whisper of fabric behind her. She turned and remained very still, scarcely believing he was here, solid and dashing and . . . menacing.

Jack was crouched on the terrace railing. He didn't look human doing it. His ragged hair was threaded with leaves and Emory, and moonlight painted his cheekbones, glinting in one dark eye and across the rings on his fingers. His coat billowed. He'd gone feral again. "You've been a busy girl." The hateful mockery had returned to his voice.

She wanted to throw herself against him. She whispered, *"How long have I forgotten you?"*

"Oh, it's been ages."

"It hasn't. It's been a week since I made that computer file, and don't talk like that. I hate it when you talk like that, as if you don't care . . ."

He slid down and took a swaggering step toward her. "You think you tricked her, the Queen of the bloody Faeries—I didn't even suspect your conspiracy with little Anna Weaver—but you can be sure *Reiko* did, and Angyll Weaver's death was the result." His voice tore. *"I told you to forget about me."*

She backed into her room and was almost sick at the thought of having caused Angyll Weaver's death. She said brokenly, "I saw . . . Angyll . . ."

"I'm sorry I said it that way." He looked away from her. "It wasn't your fault. Angyll Weaver knew things and couldn't handle them. She killed herself."

He is lying, Finn thought, watching as he straightened and pulled an antique board game from the shelf. Snakes and Ladders. He shook the game. "I remember this."

"I saw her *ghost*, Jack. Angyll's—"

"Ghosts get confused." He looked directly at her. "They can be as malicious in death as in life. And she was certainly malicious toward you when she was alive." He shook the game again and pieces rattled. "Where did you get this?"

"You said it was my fault."

"I shouldn't have. I was angry."

"Could *you* make me forget you . . . if you wanted to?"

He looked at her and something like anguish flickered in his eyes, but it was quickly vanquished by the dark lie of coldness. "I could."

She pointed to the game. "It was my gran's. She also gave me a rocking rabbit."

"A rocking rabbit." He sat on the floor in the pool of his black velvet coat and unfolded the board, traced its patterns.

"Like a rocking horse, only it was a rabbit. I named it Surreal." She sat opposite him. He wore all those damn rings again, but hers was among them.

He gazed at her as he shook the game pieces from the pouch. "What an interesting child you must have been."

"Didn't I just tell you not to speak to me like that?"

"Like what?" He sorted out the pieces and twirled the dice between his fingers.

"Like you're from another century."

He looked at her. "I am. You know, all that iron and silver you're wearing makes me want to sneeze. Shall I toss first?"

"Go on." She watched him and tried not to think of Angyll dying, alone and bleeding, in a cemetery, or of Nathan walking away, knowing that Halloween was his last night on earth.

Jack flung the dice, moved. "Rabbits aren't a reliable totem animal. They're tricksters and shape-shifters."

"I know that, Jack. I've seen Bugs Bunny cartoons. You need to tell me, exactly, what Reiko is. And try speaking in a straight line, please." She wanted to touch his hair, which glistened with rain and leaves. Reiko had taken him away from her, only for a few days, but it was a terrifying display of her power. "Is Anna Weaver in danger?"

"No." He slid the dice toward her and sat back, drawing his knees to his chin, gazing down at the board. "Anna Weaver is protected. Shall I tell you a story?"

"Is it about you?"

"It is."

HE'D BEEN BORN IN IRELAND, his mother, a gypsy; his father, a coachman. When Jack was sixteen, his mother had died because they couldn't afford a doctor. Angry at his father, he had left. As a coachman's son, he'd known how to handle horses and the unwieldy vehicles they pulled. He'd found employment at the house of a wealthy man named Seth Lot. "Your sister's wolf-eyed man," he gently told her. "A Fata."

He had thought the beautiful girl in red silk, her black hair in loops and braids, had been Seth Lot's bride. *Reiko Fata.*

"I didn't know what they were." His eyes closed briefly and Finn hurt for him. "If I'd known. If I'd listened to my father . . ."

"Jack . . . when was this?"

"The 1800s."

She rolled the dice and moved to disguise a shudder.

"Seth Lot and his family were nomads. They'd made their home in Dublin because they'd been driven from country to country by others of their kind. They were criminals—breaking every Fata law they could."

Finn looked down at the snakes on the board. Jack traced one of them. There were remnants of black around his fingernails, as if he'd wiped dark polish from them. "Reiko's name back then was Vouivre. In French, that's a half serpent, half woman. She was . . . and then she kissed me . . ."

Finn grimly knew it had been more than a kiss. "Do you love her?"

"Once . . . I used to be able to see what she had been. Just a girl."

Finn felt grubby and graceless and doubted Reiko had ever been "just a girl." Jack's words made her wonder, though, what the Fatas really were . . . fairies, the offspring of angels, the ancient dead . . .

He looked at her and said, "It was like loving a stone. Or a python. She doesn't have a heart. She cut it out and hid it somewhere." He leaned forward, desperation in his voice. "*Why* did you remember, Finn? You were *safe*."

"I wasn't safe. Why do you think she took my memory of you away?"

"I don't know." He was very still. "Why did she? And she was so easily tricked."

"Hey!"

His mouth curled. "And Angyll Weaver is dead. It doesn't make sense."

"Jack . . . do you think she loves you?" *Even though she's a monster*, Finn thought sadly, *does she love you?*

His hand tightened on one of the game pieces. "She loves nothing." He blinked, then looked up at Finn distractedly as he said, "There is a legend." He sat back, looking thoughtful, tossing the dice and the pieces in an amazing bit of juggling he didn't seem aware of.

She curled up with her arms around her legs, chin on her knees, and watched him. "Tell me."

"In the seventeenth century, in Virginia, before she settled in Dublin, or Fair Hollow—while she was a nomad, or, more likely, a bloody pirate—she tricked her way into a family called the Tiamats. She was to wed their son."

"Were they Fatas?"

"The Tiamats were the worst sort of Fatas—clannish, powerful, with roots in a human community. The Tiamat son was killed with cold iron—something went sour there, I've no doubt, between him and Reiko—and a young tailor was accused. He'd been Reiko's lover. He became lawless, that human fool, a highwayman. I suspect Reiko tricked him into murdering the Tiamat."

"How romantic," Finn said wryly, trying not to analyze how he'd said "human."

"Not really. I believe he began killing people for money. One night, the Tiamats, the children of the dragon, laid a trap for him. And cursed him."

"How?"

He shrugged. "I don't know."

She leaned forward. "What happened to the tailor-highwayman?"

"He became an outcast, walking between two worlds, an outlaw sorcerer, neither human nor Fata. The *Dubh Deamhais*. He wasn't like the Jacks and Jills . . . He just . . . changed. Naturally, Reiko later found this irresistible when he tracked her down. They were an item for a while."

"So . . . what happened?"

He dropped the dice and met her gaze. "While with him the second time, she grew a heart."

"I thought her kind couldn't—"

"They can't. After the highwayman left her"—Jack smiled—"she cut it out of herself and hid it somewhere, because it had the power to make her vulnerable."

"That's grotesque. How could she even . . ."

He lowered his head and raised one hand to his chest and she remembered what Reiko had done to *him*. She slid forward, cupped his face in her hands, and looked directly into his eyes. "When I first met you, I *felt* your heart. Then, later, you didn't have one. Jack, what did she do to you?" She pressed her brow against his. "Please tell me she didn't make you cut it out."

He whispered, "Before you, I was nothing."

"Before you," she breathed, "I was disappearing."

They looked down at the dice. Snake eyes. She thought of snakes, serpents, Reiko. Jack's head snapped up and he stood quickly. "I'm leaving."

She slid to her feet. "Reiko promised she'd leave us alone, but they killed Angyll Weaver."

"I told you it wasn't your fault—"

"She murdered *you* somehow. She murdered my sister. They're not supposed to kill—"

"Who told you that? And how do you think you can help me? Or Nathan?" His face was white. "Is it because of your sister? Revenge? Because you can't save anyone if revenge is your motive. This isn't a goddamn fairy tale."

"*Tell* me what I can do to get you away from her!"

He looked at her, disbelieving. Then, he shed his coat. He sauntered to her bed, where he sprawled and stretched out a hand, his smile devastating. "Come here and I'll show you what you can do."

The air in the room twisted up in her throat. She didn't move.

"Finn, it's going to take a lot more than a kiss to bring me back." His gaze didn't leave hers as he kept his hand outstretched. "Come on."

She wanted to throw something at him and fling herself at him all at the same time. She stood her ground, silent, accusing, yearning. "That's not true. If it were that simple, you'd have found someone for that a long time ago."

Jack moved to his feet and walked toward her, through the light and shadows. And he became another thing, its gaze burning, its skin white. He metamorphosed into Finn's double, a white-skinned corpse with tumbling brunette hair and black eyes—

Finn closed her own eyes. Calmly, she said, "If you think you're scaring me, you're not. *Stop it.* It's just tricks . . ."

She opened her eyes, and Jack stood before her again. He stepped close and she could feel the peril practically materializing in the room as his eyes silvered and he whispered to her, "Do you know what a trick is, to us, Finn-named-after-a-king?"

Smoldering and mutinous, she glared at him.

"It's the worst sort of fate for any mortal. It means we've seduced, corrupted, charmed, deceived you, usually to your death."

"Stop saying *we* and stop saying *you*." Her words sounded cracked.

"And it's so easy." He gently gripped her jaw in one hand as the fingers of his other touched her throat, pausing above the locket he'd given her, the one containing the picture of his friend. "You young ones, with all your damage, your soft skin, your spirits burning for so much more than this world can give you . . ." His lips brushed the line of her jaw as he pressed one hand against her midriff beneath her T-shirt. She felt the coldness of those ancient rings down to her insides. She put her hands between them, against his heart.

"I don't want to kiss you right now," she lied.

"This isn't," he whispered in her ear, "about a kiss."

He stepped back. She let him take her by the hand and lead her toward the bed. She felt drowsy and safe as she reached out to touch the nape of his neck beneath the dark silk of his hair. Her fingertips brushed the black, thorny Celtic cross tattooed there, and the sight of it woke a faint horror within her.

She pulled back. He let her hand slip from his as he turned to face her, his eyes human again, flickering with despair.

"No," she said, taking a step back. "Not when you're like this."

"Like what?" Contempt curled his mouth, but she knew it wasn't meant for her. "Someone who'd seduce a chi—"

"If you call me a child, I'm going to hit you."

"The things I've *done* and you are here, speaking with me as if I'm a schoolmate and not a killer. I've ruined girls like you. I've been her weapon against your kind since she made me one of hers."

When a lamp bulb shattered, she flinched. His eyes were completely black now. She tried to believe he wouldn't hurt her. "You're not like Caliban."

"He's older than me. Most Jacks don't last as long as he has." He smiled, wild and dangerous. "But I'm younger and faster."

She hated the way he spoke so casually of his life—his unlife. He continued fiercely, "She *knows* you've gotten your memory back, Finn. She hasn't spoken to me or acted against you. That worries me."

"Angyll Weaver was murdered. *That* was her strike against me. And she might also be distracted by her plans to sacrifice Nathan. They kill an innocent person to keep their precious long lives. Is that what they tried to do to you? Is that why you're the way you are?"

"I'm not going to be able to talk you out of this, am I?"

She clutched his cold hands, careful not to let her iron bracelet touch him. "There's got to be some way to save Nathan."

He looked at her and the darkness left him as he said, "Only his true love can save him. And she's in hiding."

"Then let's find her and help her."

TOGETHER, THEY WENT IN SEARCH of true love.

Jack led Finn down a street where scraggly trees clawed at run-down brownstones and dogs barked while music thumped from several bars. They were in the warehouse district, which seemed a little too close to Tirnagoth, and it was as if the energy of the neighborhood had been drained by the Fatas, leaving it muted and cold. Jack said, "Nathan told me that there was an angel above her door."

Finn stepped over a rusted bicycle, her boots leaving deep prints in the mud of someone's yard. She scanned the doorways. "You don't know where, exactly? You people need to get phones."

Jack stopped walking and turned to her. "Why are you doing this, Finn? For a boy you barely know?"

She looked at him and frowned. "Why wouldn't I?"

"I see." His voice was soft.

"I mean, they're going to kill him, right?"

"We're not going to find Mary Booke on our own." He clambered onto the hood of an abandoned car—she hoped it was abandoned—and began to speak quietly in another language.

"What are you doing?" She was trying not to look at the shadows.

"You'll see. Mortal eyes see patterns they expect. Look into the negative spaces, Finn. Look between."

She didn't want to do that, but she stared at the street before them. Half the lamps had blown out, and rusty shadows dirtied the yellow light, which seemed to haze for a moment. She heard footsteps.

A wiry figure emerged from the air and darkness.

Jack slid down to face a boy in ripped jeans, his torso bare but for a bronze pocket watch on a ribbon around his neck. He was all bones and bruises, his eyes the color of rotting wood.

"Jack." His teeth gleamed metallic. "He seemed made from the neighborhood's decay. "Fancy meeting you here." He turned to Finn, who pretended not to notice the beetle that skittered across his chest. "Hey."

"This is Finn." Jack acted as if vagrant Frankenstein boys with spooky eyes were common. "Finn, this is Wormwood. Wormwood, we need to find a girl named Mary Booke. She lives in your neighborhood."

"I'll tell you." Wormwood smiled metal again. "If your girl gives me a kiss."

Jack's smile glinted like a razor. "How about if *I* give you a kiss?"

"I'm not scared of you." Wormwood circled them, his bare feet scarcely touching the cement. He smelled like old metal and gasoline. "I'm older than you. I'll settle for a trinket. Finn, you got anything pretty for me?"

Finn took a quick inventory, unclasped the white rabbit medallion from around her neck. She held it out and tried not to stare at him. Her hand shook.

Jack seized the medallion before Wormwood could. "*No* exchanges, Wormwood. Do you remember that kelpie in 1970? He made me very angry."

The Fata boy sighed. "I've no desire to end up in pieces."

He closed his eyes, curled one hand into a fist, and opened it. A large, rust-colored moth glided from his palm, down the street. The boy turned and smiled at Finn as he said, "Follow that, pretty girl. And you'd be wise to lose the Jack— you can't ever trust them."

Jack grabbed Finn's hand before she could answer back, and they ran after the moth, down an alley that seemed to twist more than it should. When the insect fluttered up into a window of a building with a clock tower, Jack and Finn halted. Above the building's door was the face of a sinister angel with wings for hair and stains beneath its eyes. As the moth landed on the hand of the broken clock, Finn moved forward, but Jack slipped past her, up the stairs, and knocked on the door.

A moment later, a boy with black hair and blue eyes opened it. Finn recognized him as one of Jack's vagabond friends. He said, "*Jack?*"

"Hey." Finn hurried up the stairs and smiled, trying to lessen the effect of Jack's . . . Jackness. "I'm a friend of Mary Booke's. Is she here?"

"Yes, Black Apple, is she here?" Jack lounged malevolently against the door frame.

The boy blinked. There was a lotus on his black T-shirt, and his jeans were spattered with paint. "Her apartment's upstairs. Jack, don't tell Reik—"

"I won't." Jack surged forward, and the boy skittered back.

Finn followed Jack up another flight of stairs, into a hall that smelled like incense and mice. The door to Mary Booke's apartment was painted fairy-tale blue and opened at his touch.

They stepped into a tiny apartment with paintings hung on red walls. A lamp glowed against the night-darkened windows. An old-fashioned sofa stood before a wall of shelves crammed with books. Finn said, "You people do like to read."

"We've enough time." The floorboards creaked beneath Jack's boots as he investigated the galley kitchen, the bathroom. Finn wandered to a vanity near the sofa and gazed at a half-eaten apple, a handful of glossy red leaves, a shabby doll with half its face missing. She touched an empty perfume bottle. From the apartment below, she heard opera music. Her attention returned to the half-eaten apple as Jack sauntered toward her and said, "She's not here."

Finn glanced at the nightstand near the bed and saw something that didn't seem to belong in a Fata place. She walked over, crouched down, and pulled a battered laptop from beneath the bed. She opened it.

The screen flickered onto a poem: *The Black Scissors came to me, and a cold dark man was he. My soul he stole and swallowed whole, and took a faery doctor's fee.* Beneath that were the words *Gazebo 1029. Dusk. Her Enemy. Her Enemy. Her Ene—*

The computer blinked off as Jack's shadow fell over her—Fatas had that effect on batteries. He frowned at the laptop. "That's an unusual thing to find here."

"Mary Booke isn't a Fata." Finn rose, walked to the table, and lifted the bitten apple. "She eats."

He said quietly, "She's a changeling."

"Are changelings what I think they are?"

"Humans stolen as infants and replaced with a dead child."

"That's what I thought. Then"—she pushed her hands into her coat pockets—"how can she save Nathan?"

"If she is his true love, she can sever his promise to the Fatas. She can claim him—that has power. She is a changeling, and mortal, so it would trump *their* claim on him. No wonder they went ballistic when they found out about Nate and her." He sat on the windowsill, his lovely scent of Emory and roses drifting toward her. "You've read *Tam Lin*."

"And it can only be done on Halloween?"

"The victim would have all the elements in his favor."

The glass doors to the balcony creaked, and a gauzy scarf snaked across the floor. Finn stared at the doors, her insides twisting. "Jack . . ."

He moved past her and pulled the doors wide. Finn saw what lay on the small terrace before he crouched beside the figure, obscuring it.

They had found Mary Booke.

JACK LED HER BACK TO his car. They didn't speak until the warehouse district had vanished behind them. He kept his eyes on the road as he said, "I'm getting you home. I should never have brought you."

"She's dead. She wasn't one of you." Finn covered her face with her hands and felt a nightmarish despair. "She was someone they stole away. And now she's dead, like Angyll Weaver. They're *murdering* people—Jack, pull over."

He swerved the sedan to the side of the road. She opened the door and was burningly sick in the grass. As he slid to her, touching a cool hand to her face, she closed her eyes and relaxed against him. He gently said, "Angyll Weaver was killed to warn Anna, who can see us, and who may know things she shouldn't. Reiko seems intrigued by her. And Booke—Booke could have taken their Teind from them."

"You said Anna's protected. By who?" She pushed away images of Angyll Weaver's ghost and what she had seen of Mary Booke, the curled hand streaked with blood.

Shadows crossed his face. "I honestly don't know. But I can sense it."

"Do you think Anna really knows what they are?"

"I hope not."

"Did you ever love Reiko?"

"Once."

"Was she ever kind to you? Did it ever seem like she might change for you? Grow a heart like she did for the tailor-highwayman?"

He turned his head and his eyes were filled with anguish. "You believe I might change for you?"

She looked away from him, out the window. "Yes."

"I'm a selfish, dark thing without a heart."

"No. You're not. Now, please drive me home."

JACK HAD TWISTED UP HIS life for a fragile, warm thing, a girl with cinnamon hair, a crooked smile, and haunted eyes. It pricked at him that Reiko's gambit to strike him from Finn's memory had so easily failed—it was like a chess move Reiko had made to distract, to keep an opponent's attention on the other pieces while she went after the queen.

As he pulled into the parking lot of his abandoned theater, he saw the red Mercedes parked in front, with Phouka leaning against it. When he got out and walked toward her, she said, "There's been an incident—we no longer have a Teind."

NATHAN CLARE HAD ATTEMPTED TO kill himself with a goblet of nightshade wine. He was recovering only because of Lazuli's druidic abilities.

Jack, hunched on a divan in Reiko's parlor with Phouka beside him, could hear Reiko and David Ryder arguing in the next room. How had Nathan known his girl was dead?

"You know what this means." Phouka's body was taut. "Suicide is attempted murder of oneself, an act of cowardice. We're done for. The sacrifice isn't pure."

Nathan had lived for one hundred years, carefully guarded, taught to believe his life would mean one hundred years of immortality for his foster family, and it had all gone to ruin when he'd fallen in love with a girl named Mary Booke. "Were there other candidates?"

"Seven, as tradition warrants."

"Let me guess—the other six are no longer candidates."

"Well, David Ryder's girl offed herself and is now a Jill—she was Reiko's second choice."

"And what struck the others down?"

"What do you think? They were all human, Jack. They all had hearts. And you. You might act badass, but you've got a noble wolf complex when it comes to little lost lambs. You saw your schoolgirl, all wounded and solitary, and that was the beginning of the end for you."

He was about to rudely reply when the doors crashed open and Nathan Clare was flung across the floor. He struck a wall and curled there, arms over his head.

Jack rose as Caliban entered, his silver eyes glinting, his coat streaked with blood. He placed himself in Caliban's path. "Leave him alone."

Caliban gently said, "They gave him to me."

Phouka glanced at Nathan, who remained kneeling.

Jack didn't look away from the *crom cu*. He knew what Caliban had been and was now. Once a youth in a Celtic tribe, a warrior in a kilt and whorls of blue paint, Caliban had traveled to a faraway land where he had tried to save a girl. And far from the Emerald Isle, in a desert place, Caliban had been turned into the crooked dog. Jack stepped close, murmured one word, and Caliban's eyes went wide and black.

Then the red doors opened and David Ryder emerged, his gaze cutting across all of them. Dressed in a tawny suit, his hair knotted back, he still looked savage.

As Caliban slid to one knee, head bowed, and Phouka curtsied gracefully, Jack did nothing.

David Ryder walked past Nathan, out of the room.

Then Reiko called Jack's name. Jack said, "Phouka."

Phouka placed her slender body between Nathan and Caliban as Jack sauntered into the other parlor, where Reiko was seated, barefoot in a red velvet babydoll dress. It was the first time he'd seen her since she'd made the bargain with Finn and Finn had broken it.

She gazed at him and didn't bother to conceal the ancient thing that moved behind her eyes like a shark in a swimming pool. She never changed. She still smelled of apples and young skin and acted as if she loved him. He had used to wonder if she truly *did* feel love. He had learned, over the battlefield of years, that it was an alien love, webbed with blood and shadows and the dust of stars. Gently, she said, "We are not ruined."

"We're not? Nathan is."

She moved to her feet and walked to him, cupped his face in her hands. She kissed him and he didn't flinch when her teeth sank into his bottom lip. As she stepped back, she smiled. "Does she know, Jack, what you are? A husk? A revenant?"

His body tensed as if every muscle had been strung on the bones. "No."

"Selfish Jack. Selfish as a kelpie. With her, you are not a dead man. You are flesh and blood. Brave. Self-sacrificing." She slid one hand into his shirt. "I can feel your heart, Jack. Would you die for her?"

He had only one answer. "Yes."

CHAPTER SEVENTEEN

The seers and faith-healers who combat their malign influence do so by being, in some sense, in league with them, and able to steal their charms.
—*VISIONS AND BELIEFS IN THE WEST OF IRELAND*, LADY GREGORY

The Black Scissors came to the house on a stallion the color of lung blood, and a cold, dark man was he. He knew their ways, for he'd been taken by the children of the dragon.
—FROM THE JOURNAL OF LILY ROSE

Finn woke to the sound of Jefferson Airplane's "White Rabbit" thrumming on the stereo downstairs and raised her head to drowsily regard the rainy morning. "White Rabbit" had been one of her mother's favorite songs. It made Finn feel an aching sense of loss. Then she remembered Mary Booke the changeling and buried her face in the pillow, pushing a fist against her stomach. There would be no mother to mourn Nathan's true love, who had been stolen away and murdered. What would they do with her body—

Don't think about it. Don't think—

She curled up and thought of the Fatas, how they wore masks over their true forms of darkness and desire, how Halloween was only two days away, and how, in two days, Nathan Clare was going to die.

Eventually, Finn dragged herself from bed, because putting a pillow over her head and remaining in a nautilus position all day wasn't going to accomplish anything.

In the hallway hung with some of her mother's watercolors, she paused. The haunting subject matter of those paintings had been so familiar to her growing up she'd scarcely noticed the surreal patterns of boys with peacock wings arching from their brows and mermaid girls in powdered wigs. Each figure seemed to be accompanied by a shadow anchoring and sharpening its softness.

Lily might not have been the only one to have known about them. How would her mom have explained the Fatas? She'd been a genetic biologist. Daisy Sullivan would not have been fascinated by them—she would have been horrified—and finding out about the Fatas might make someone with a set worldview question her sanity.

When Finn entered the kitchen, her da was making strawberry waffles and he eyed her as she slouched to the refrigerator to take out a carton of orange juice. In the bright kitchen, where the strangeness of Jack's world didn't seem possible, she carefully approached the subject of her mother. "Was Mom's accident really an accident?"

He looked startled. "What would make you ask—"

"Well, I was just looking at her paintings and they got me thinking . . . She saw things, didn't she?" Finn remembered her mom's smile, her hands smudged with paint, the sunlight in her hair, how she'd been as moody as Lily. After leaving her career in genetics to paint whimsical, eerie images, Daisy had spent hours in her painting studio, sometimes neglecting her daughters. "Why did she give up her career?"

"People change, Finn."

"Then Lily Rose began to act the same."

"Finn . . . it won't *happen* to you. You're not—"

"Was it here? When she came here, to go to college—did you notice it? Mom acting funny?"

He frowned as if he'd never considered it. "I don't remember . . ."

"Do you remember anything weird? From when you were a kid?"

"This *conversation* is weird." He shoved a hand through his hair. "I'm getting old, Finn. My kid memories are full of holes."

"You're not old." Her stomach sank into a cold pit. At any time in his life here, those creatures could have spoken to her father, manipulated him, made him forget. And what had they done to Daisy Sullivan, to make her want to leave Fair Hollow for Vermont and eventually die on a winter road?

"They've always been here," Finn whispered to herself, "and everywhere else."

The smell of burning filled the kitchen, and her father swore, flipping open the wafflemaker. "Ah, you're right. This thing is defective." He looked sharply at her. "Why all these questions about your mom?"

"I just needed to know some things." She wanted to tell him that her mother and her sister had seen another world, but he wouldn't believe her, would think she was falling victim to whatever had possessed her mother and her sister.

Lily had been led to her death. Were the Fatas doing the same to her, while she relied on Jack to keep her safe? And he might be the biggest trick of all . . .

Something thumped in the living room. Her da looked up. "What—"

"I'll see." She hurried out of the kitchen.

A book had fallen from one of the shelves. She walked slowly toward it, then crouched down to look at it. It was a picture book of *Snow White*, opened to an illustration of the wicked stepmother pointing to the huntsman. The caption read "*Bring me her heart.*"

A shudder rattled through her. She thought of Mary Booke, a corpse now, and closed her eyes, but that only made the dizzy spell worse. She opened her eyes and whispered, "Lily, what are you trying to tell me?"

Bring me her heart.

Heart.

Jack had lost *his* heart, horrifyingly and literally—Reiko had taken it. Finn flinched when she remembered that vision of the living organ being taken from him, the pain and the anguish and the blood of it . . .

She rose with the book. Jack had grown a heart because of *her*. And he'd told her Reiko had managed to form a heart, which had made her vulnerable, with a mortal man, a tailor who had become a highwayman—

"A tailor . . ." She remembered the poem on Mary Booke's computer . . . *The Black Scissors . . . a cold, dark man was he . . . Her Enemy.*

She dashed up the stairs, into her room, and grabbed Lily's journal, tore through it until she found the entry: *The Black Scissors . . . highwayman . . . wanderer . . . her true love . . . Dubh Deamhais . . .*

She sank down onto the window seat and thought of a hidden heart and vulnerability. She closed her eyes and pictured the words on Booke's laptop. What had followed the poem? *Gazebo 1029 Dusk.* The numbers, she realized, were a date. "October twenty-ninth."

She breathed out. She'd only seen one gazebo in town, and that was in the park. Could Mary Booke have somehow arranged a meeting with Reiko's infamous tailor-turned-highwayman? And why?

FINN WAS SCHEDULED AT THE bookstore that night, but not until seven. She had time.

She didn't call Sylvie or Christie—this was *her* fight now; besides, they still hadn't remembered all the things that had happened; she hadn't explained to them, either, about her recent contact with Jack. She geared up in her red coat with the hood, and iron and silver charms. She didn't know if the iron and silver would be any kind of defense against a person who was an anomaly even to the Fatas, but she had to take the chance. She had to keep Booke's appointment with the Black Scissors, Reiko's enemy, the one who had made her grow a heart, the one she had led into a curse.

Finn crossed the deserted park and approached the gazebo in its cluster of sad-looking trees. The roof had half caved in from the weight of fallen leaves. Someone had wreathed tiny lights around the gables, but they were rusted and broken.

She hugged herself and trudged up the steps. The floor of the gazebo beneath the debris was made of wood. Finn stomped on it, lifting her gaze to the treetops and the final pumpkin smolder of the sun. She could smell wood smoke and damp earth, and those fragrances made her feel alive and real.

As she waited, she paced. She checked the time on her cell phone. When the screen went blank as if the battery had just gone dead, she jerked her head up.

Nothing moved in the park. A car drove past, its headlights swerving comfortingly past her. She said, to the shadows, "Mary Booke wanted to help someone named Nathan Clare. You were human once, before *she* took you. Reiko's going to murder Nathan and send his soul to whatever they've made a deal with. I need to stop it."

Instantly, everything in the park went still. Even the rain stopped. Out of the corner of one eye, Finn saw something dark and swift moving across the grass. She stared, stepped back, and inhaled as a cloud of black moths swept over the gazebo, one of them fluttering on the railing near her so that she could see the skull pattern on its body.

She slowly turned her head.

Beneath a birch a few feet away stood a figure in a sweeping coat and wide-brimmed hat. The upper half of the face was in shadow. A voice, young, masculine, velvety with power, drifted toward her. "Serafina Sullivan. You'd best name me, for your own safety—I am still theirs."

He knew her name, the *Dubh Deamhais*, the Black Scissors who walked between but wasn't one of *them*. With a calm that frightened her because it meant she was accepting all of this like an insane person, she said, "*Dubh Deamhais*."

An icy shiver slid across the back of her neck.

When she turned, the Black Scissors stood before her. He smiled gently. "I did not expect *you*, *alainn cailin*."

Despite the archaic greatcoat with its ribboned sleeves, he wore jeans, a T-shirt, and biker boots. Beneath the hat, his face was young, a Slavic mask of slanting bones with an ivory scar crossing his brow, golden hair streaked with black spilling to his shoulders. His eyes, an otherworldly green, were rimmed with blue designs.

"But you know my name." She looked at a moth fluttering nearby. "You. *You* left that moth key under my window."

"You came to ask me a question. Would that be it?"

"No. How do I"—she hesitated—"destroy Reiko Fata?"

"There is a price for such a precious secret." He unfolded one hand and he didn't look young as he did it. "A kiss."

"*Oh* no. I read that poem about you." She stepped back and wondered why these people always wanted a kiss. Or blood.

"It's only to get a bit of warmth," he murmured. "And that poem was written by another ex-lover. I don't steal souls. I steal hearts."

She couldn't believe she was standing here, with someone even the *Fatas* didn't trust. *Deal with it*, she told herself. "Okay." She closed her eyes, every muscle pulling taut as she felt him come close, his scent like old stone and fires. She steeled herself as his mouth touched hers.

The kiss was as cool as a minor medical procedure. She felt something drawn out of her, a bit of warmth that left her slightly colder than she had been. When he stepped away, she opened her eyes, grimacing at the metallic taste in her mouth.

The *Dubh Deamhais* stood now in a slant of shadow. He bowed, golden hair swaying, the moths whirling around him. "For the kiss, Finn Sullivan named for angels and an Irish hero—a key."

Disappointment made her voice faint. "Another key?"

"The key to her heart." She realized how young he must have been when his life had been frozen by Fata malice. He watched her, his unnerving eyes almost luminous. "Finn Sullivan, it is the world of the dead you have been dealing with. If I didn't have such a selfish motive, my advice to you would be: 'Have nothing more to do with them.'"

"You hate her . . . Reiko."

"More," he said with deadly tenderness, "than you can ever imagine."

"So why don't *you* do something?"

"They can sense me a mile away. Keeping hidden from them *now* is costing me."

"They have, like, a magical restraining order against you?"

"Exactly. The key I'll give you is to the spell box that contains her heart, the heart that should never have grown, because of me."

"I'm sorry about—what happened to you." Gazing at his otherworldliness that was more like a beautiful mutation than a blessing, she meant it. "The key . . ."

"It must be made from the bone of the one who caused that heart to grow. That's her twisted magic, to open the box containing her heart. It took me a long time to figure *that* out."

"*Bone . . . ?*"

He raised one hand to display a missing pinkie finger. Finn couldn't say anything to that.

"She'll give the heart to your Jack, if you're clever enough. You must destroy it on All Hallows' Eve." His eyes glinted, and she thought she glimpsed a flicker of malice

"How? How will Jack get the heart from her?"

"I'll leave that up to you. Good evening, Finn Sullivan." He turned and began walking away, the moths trailing after him.

"But you didn't give me the k—"

He called back, "I did," and vanished into the night.

She choked as air solidified in her throat. She hunched over and spat out an object that had materialized from the bitter taste in her mouth. Trembling, she stared down at what had come from her mouth like gruesome ectoplasm—an ivory key carved into a serpent. She remembered the Black Scissors' missing finger and sank to her knees, staring at the key that would undo Reiko, not wanting to touch it.

CALIBAN ARIEL'PAN'S ASSIGNMENT HAD BEEN to watch over Nathan Clare, to make certain he remained with his heart intact, that it was not given away in love, or broken by it. Somehow, the cloistered boy had managed to make Caliban look like a fool. But Caliban couldn't rip him apart, because that would upset Reiko's precious Jack, who had a bit of a history with the pretty idiot. So Jack naturally became the focus of Caliban's frustrated malevolence. And Jack had a weakness.

As Caliban strolled to BrambleBerry Books, he grinned at the welcome sign over the door. He stepped in, freezing the annoying bells every shop in Fair Hollow seemed to have over the door.

When Finn Sullivan saw him, she dropped the book she'd been reading and watched, wide-eyed, as he moved idly to a shelf of books and placed one finger on the spine of a book titled *Sacred Lovemaking*.

She said, "Get out."

He admired her courage, shaky as it was, and looked at her, aware of the effect of the fluorescents on his white skin and silver eyes. "Make me."

She wore a black T-shirt, a tartan skirt with black tights and clunky shoes—she wouldn't be able to run fast in those. She had bracelets, one of silver and one of iron—his nostrils flared at the poisonous reek of both metals. A draft stirred the tawny hair that tumbled around her Renaissance-prince face. Dark-rimmed eyes and a sweet mouth . . . he could see what Jack found enticing. He imagined her in nothing but her tawny skin and a necklace of pearls and let his thoughts show in his eyes.

She bolted for the door.

He reached it before her. She struck out, the iron bracelet searing across his face. He yowled in pain and recoiled. Finn dashed back through the shop.

The door chime rang. As the pretty crow girl stepped in, Caliban grabbed her by one of her braids.

"Sylvie Whitethorn," he whispered. She had a tiny silver skull piercing one earlobe. He kept his lips away from it. The burn across his nose made him clench his teeth. "Let's talk."

Something slammed into him, crashing him against the door. He snarled and turned on the fox poet, who backed away as Caliban stalked toward him. "*Christie.* Let's see what your insides look like."

As both girls fled onto a street scattered with witnesses, the Christie boy followed.

Caliban laughed as he sank to a crouch and touched the wound across his face.

AS SYLVIE TAPPED 911 ON her cell, Christie sat with Finn on the bench a block away from the shop. Finn, thrumming with antagonism and fear, pushed her hands through her hair as she hunched over. Christie said wryly, "Bad night?"

She looked up at him through a tangle of hair. "You have no idea."

"Who *was* that psycho?"

They still hadn't remembered because of Reiko's spell. Finn took a deep breath and spent the next fifteen minutes telling her friends about her recovered memories and recent escapades. It was as if a light went on inside of each of them, as if her words had triggered *their* memories—they looked stunned, scared, and, then, horrified.

After Finn finished, Sylvie sat quietly. She was pale, her braids almost unraveled. Finally she said, "I remember now. Damn it."

"The Fatas. How could we . . . ?" Christie, looking uncertain and confused, was trying to make sense of what Finn had just told them; he clenched his hands as the police cars pulled up to the book shop. "I just slammed into Caliban-the-psycho a second time. Should I go for a third? I've always wondered what my spine looks like and I'm sure he'll show it to me. What if the cops can't see him?"

"Oh, they won't."

THE POLICE HADN'T CAUGHT CALIBAN—HOW could they? And Mrs. Browning had closed the bookstore for the night.

When Finn returned home, she found a note from her father—he had gone to poker night with Sylvie's dad. She was alone in the big, old house.

She locked all the doors and windows, checked them a second time, then sprinkled the sills with sea salt. She went to her bathroom, closed the door, and sank against the antique tub, her face in her hands. Curled in the dark, she thought of Angyll and Anna, of Mary Booke and Nathan. And of her sister, who hadn't been able to tell anyone about the things she knew, and so had been all alone.

She couldn't do this anymore. She couldn't let Jack's world devour her. And, as she finally realized she couldn't save him without sacrificing everything else she loved, the darkness collapsed over her.

She knew what she had to do.

ARMED WITH IRON JEWELRY AND silver, with mistletoe and vervain in their hair, Finn, Christie, and Sylvie walked through the rainy woods on a mission. Christie, as usual when dealing with Fata things, was grouchy. "Why, Finn, did you tell the prince of darkness you'd meet him at Drake's Chapel?"

"I didn't tell him. I had to call a friend of his—the guy who owns the arcade . . . Jack doesn't have a phone."

Christie muttered something about dead people not needing phones because they could just possess people and tell them stuff. She ignored him.

"Christie. Quiet. Finn needs us."

"Yeah. Well . . . I do not approve of this. Why did you say I'd like this?"

"Trust me," Finn told him. She hadn't told them everything; she hadn't mentioned the Black Scissors or the bone key or Reiko's heart. They didn't need to know the sordid stuff.

They continued forging through the trees until Drake's Chapel appeared in the moonlight. Inside, dozens of candles flickered on the altar, illuminating glittering graffiti on the wall: *The Children of Dragons have red hair.*

Jack was seated on the altar steps. Behind him, the altar was now cluttered with small tombstone statues, old wine bottles, ornaments, broken clocks, and figures made of twigs. Finn, wondering who was leaving such items in a chapel supposedly built by Queen Elizabeth's dragonish buccaneer, Francis Drake, moved forward. "Hey."

"Murray gave me your message." Jack looked at Christie and Sylvie. "They smell like they're afraid."

"Maybe if you didn't say things like 'They smell like they're afraid,' they wouldn't be. And we were attacked by Caliban tonight."

Jack cursed, and Christie and Sylvie drew back. Finn moved to the altar to crouch beside him. She couldn't let anyone guess what she was doing. "Jack—"

He said, his head bowed, "Nathan tried to kill himself."

She whispered, "*No.*"

"He's fine. I've got him stashed somewhere. He argued with me, got hysterical, and I had to shut him up—I think there was a kiss in there somewhere—"

"Stop trying to distract me. It doesn't work." She was aware of Christie and Sylvie taking positions nearby. "Is he okay?"

"He's no longer a candidate for All Hallows' Eve."

Sylvie gazed warily at Finn. "What is he talking about?"

"They were going to sacrifice Nathan on Halloween . . . right?" Christie guessed. "So, what are they going to do now, your *family*, to pay the devil?"

"They've got alternatives—and it's not the devil they pay."

"And what are the alternatives, Jack?" Finn watched him.

"Ghost man," Sylvie's face, shadowed by two braids, resembled a spooky doll's as she leaned forward, "if something happens to Finn because you've dragged her into this, I'll—"

"You'll what, pretty girl?"

"I'll stomp you."

Jack's smile was dazzling, and Finn heard Sylvie's breath catch. Then he turned his attention to Christie. "And you, fox boy? What'll you do?"

Christie's voice was ragged. "I'll see you buried if anything happens to Finn or Sylvie."

"Don't make threats you can't carry out."

"Finn." Christie turned to her, his eyes wide. "He's not a real person. He's a horror movie."

Jack straightened. "Let's set aside our delicate feelings and remember who knows what will keep all of you alive. Now, listen, children—"

"Remember, there are two of us here who don't trust you," Christie reminded him.

"Look at them, Finn." Jack's eyes silvered. "A witch and a knight, untrained. These are your allies. And she, *she* has an entire *tribe* of carnivores and ghouls."

"Tell me what's going to happen on Halloween, Jack."

"They are going to choose another willing victim."

"They can't use Nathan. How will they find someone willing to die for them?"

"Shakespeare's plays are based on the Fatas' histories. He was a favorite of theirs—*Titus Andronicus, The Tempest, A Midsummer Night's Dream* . . . all of their wars and tragedies, played out before a mortal audience. They are ancient, Finn. Don't you think they planned for this potential setback? They'll find another. The one hundred years of coddling isn't always required; that's just a bribe. They only need someone willing."

"He's trying to scare us," Sylvie murmured as the candlelight cast crooked shadows across the walls.

"I can't scare you"—Jack gazed at Finn, his eyes dark—"can I? Fearless girl."

She had never understood why the word *fearless* was used with fairy-tale heroes. There was always fear, especially when one was being systematically terrorized. But she *did* understand how that fear could become an insane form of anger, so she leaned close to whisper, "If I prick you, will you bleed?"

"Yes." And he looked at her as if he had lost everything.

"None of them will ever be safe, will they?" The Black Scissors' serpent key, his finger bone, hung on a silver chain between her collarbones, burning against her skin. "Not my friends. Not Anna Weaver. Not my da. *She'll* find a way to wreck them."

"Yes."

Her fingers unsteady, Finn unhooked the thin chains holding the Renaissance prince's locket and the moth key from around her neck. She pushed them into his hands and felt cold as she let them go. "I can't do this. I can't. I'm sorry. I'm so sorry."

He stared at her with such naked despair, she almost broke. Then his lashes flickered down, his eyes became silver, and, softly, he said, "What a shame."

Sylvie whispered, "*Finn,*" and Christie stared at her as if she'd lost her mind.

She continued, backing away, "Don't come to me anymore. I should have forgotten you, because this isn't a fairy tale. People can really get hurt. People have been *killed.*"

His face was white, as if all the blood had drained from him. "Go, then."

"Sylv, Christie . . . can you leave us for a second?" She knew that she sounded bad, but they did as she asked, stepping out of the chapel. When they had gone, she turned back to Jack, who remained as still as a corpse. It hurt to see him like that, as if he were dying before her eyes. She wanted him to be free. She wanted him to live without the desperation and anguish revealed in the way he hunched his shoulders, lowered his eyelashes, rubbed at his chest where there was either a heart or a hollow. She wanted him to smile without shadows and feel sunlight again. She leaned down to him and whispered fiercely, "If you want me to be safe, find her heart and bring it to me."

Jack looked at her as if she'd stabbed him. His voice scraped out, "Finn . . ."

She backed away, toward the exit. She turned and ran.

JACK DIDN'T REMEMBER LEAVING DRAKE'S Chapel, because the tawny warmth of Finn's gaze deserting him was all he could think of. She'd made a choice, the only choice that would save her. Already, he felt the heart shrinking inside of him, the blood fading.

As he moved swiftly through the woods, he smiled despite the anguish twisting through him like barbed wire. When he was no longer flesh and blood, Finn would have robbed the Fatas of their Teind.

When he slid over the sill into Reiko's Tirnagoth apartment, she was waiting for him. He collapsed then, arms over his head, because this was all that he had now, this terrible slavery.

"What has she done?" Reiko walked toward him, her voice urgent. "*Jack?*"

He lifted his head. "She's gotten her common sense back. She told me to go away. Unless . . ."

"Unless what?" Reiko knelt beside him, her black gown slithering, her dark perfume like poison.

He looked at her and whispered, "If you want me to die for you, I need proof that she'll be safe from you. I need your heart."

Reiko's eyes narrowed and menace breathed from her, harmful as a snake's venom. She smiled charmingly. "And how did she learn about my heart? My little vulnerability?"

"I told her."

"Of course you did." She bared her teeth. "I need you to be flesh and blood— already it's fading from you. You need this girl's love. She needs yours." She rose and left the room for a moment.

When she returned to kneel beside him, she folded his hands over a glass box etched with symbols. He stared at it and saw within it a fist of glossy red stone shaped like an anatomical heart. His hands tightened on the glass.

She smiled. "The heart that grew inside of me—a *sidhe* heart. You'll never be able to open that box or break it or do me harm. She may keep it and believe I can be defeated. You'll remain mortal and die for us, while the girl you love will be safe from us forever. And you do love her, don't you, Jack?"

"How do I know you won't take this back from her once I'm gone?"

"Jack." She folded herself around him. "I've nothing to fear from her once the Teind is done. You'll willingly die for us, won't you? For her?"

He felt breath and blood returning and didn't know whether it was despair or relief that shook him.

JACK WAS SITTING AT REIKO'S feet when David Ryder arrived with Caliban Ariel'Pan and a pretty Jill who didn't look frightened. A savage Victorian figure in brown velvet, with spurs on his boots and one jeweled hand gripping a stag-headed swagger-stick, the *Damh Ridire* sat in a carved chair and ignored Jack, who removed one of his knives and began trimming his nails.

Ryder said, "Are we having difficulties, Reiko?"

Reiko had dressed for her consort in a crimson gown and red platform heels. Red cochineal was painted in designs around her eyes. Phouka, the subtlest of bodyguards in a black frock, a spiky umbrella folded against her legs, stood to her right. Behind Reiko's chair were the three Rooks, their slender bodies sheathed in mourning costumes and malice.

Reiko's smile matched the glitter of Jack's knife. "How is your little Jill?"

"All other women pale in comparison to you, my love." His true aspect flickered in his brown eyes.

Jack looked at Ryder's new Jill, who sat on the window seat, her head down. She looked exactly like her picture from the wake. Her gown was of green gossamer, her daffodil hair wound with turquoise beads, and there were scars on her wrists from when she'd killed herself. She was only another of the walking wounded the Fatas had charmed to their death.

Reiko smoothed out her red dress. "We have had a candidate among us."

The *Damh Ridire*'s expression was feral. "Tell me."

"It will be a trick, like the old days, a marvelous trick."

"The sacrifice must be willing."

"Oh. This one bleeds and breathes and shall be extremely willing. We will not lose all that we have."

"And we have *so much*," David Ryder said contemptuously. "The Terror, the Glamourie, riding the shadow—we would have had more, if it had not been for the previous failure." His gaze settled on Jack.

"Jack?" Reiko gestured.

Jack slid his blade across the palm of his hand. As blood beaded, Reiko smiled at David Ryder. "He's mortal again, thanks to a schoolgirl."

David Ryder ripped up from his chair. "Are you *insane*? Sacrifice a *sluagh* to the—"

"A flesh-and-blood *mortal*. It will be a great trick. It will fetch us more than one hundred years. No more living in the dark. No more ruins. For the Luck."

"For the Luck." David Ryder spoke ritually, gazing at Jack with inhuman despair. He turned and stalked from the room, accompanied by his daffodil girl. Before Caliban followed, he glanced at Jack, his eyes glinting death-silver.

Phouka and the Rooks left the room when Reiko gestured at them.

When they were alone, Jack, even with heart and blood and breath, made himself feel nothing as Reiko walked to him. She said, "Tonight, you will give her the heart. Tomorrow, you will die. And, from then on, I will forget Finn Sullivan exists."

He raised his head to the queen of nothing and night, and said, "And I'll finally be free of you."

Her eyes went black. He thought she would strike him, but she drew away, raising one hand over her face. Veiled by her hair, she whispered, "*Get out.*"

He did what she asked and left her.

FINN DIDN'T KNOW IF JACK would understand what she had done. She felt as if she truly *had* lost him, as she sat in her room, attempting to read Lily's journal and hoping, *hoping*, that he would do what could free them all.

When she heard the tapping on her doors, she unfolded from the window seat and saw him. She walked slowly to the doors and opened them. She couldn't say his name as he raised his head, revealing eyes smudged with shadows.

Jack held out a small box wrapped in black paper with silver stars. "I've gotten you a present."

She realized what it was as she took it from him and breathed out as an almost electric shock ran through her when her fingers brushed his. The "present" seemed to attract darkness. "Come in."

He did, reluctantly, as if he were a stranger. He looked so ordinary dressed in a dark T-shirt and jeans beneath his coat. His hair fell into his eyes—she wanted to brush it away. She sank down onto the pink velvet chaise near the TV and tore the wrapping paper away from his present to reveal a glass box etched with runes. Beneath the runes, she glimpsed something red and glistening. Although she'd expected it, she almost dropped the box.

Finn set the box carefully onto the floor and wiped her hands on her jeans. She felt sick and triumphant. "Her heart."

Jack crouched before her and said, "Finn. You're safe from her now."

She lifted her gaze from the heart to his face, the face of someone whose life had been thieved away by what she was now resentfully beginning to see as a race of soul-sucking parasites. "What do I do with it?"

He laid one hand on her knee. "You can't open the box. It's a hallowhex box. It can only be opened with a finger bone of the beloved, in her presence, on All Hallows' Eve." He jerked his chin at the box. "But she promised me . . . you keep that and she'll stay away."

"And you'll die. They've chosen *you* for the Teind, haven't they? Because of me. Because I made you human."

"Finn . . . I died a long time ago—"

She lifted the bone key shaped like a serpent. He sat back on his heels and looked absolutely devastated. He whispered, "That . . . is that what I think it is?"

"Reiko's made a lot of enemies. Mary Booke was going to meet the Black Scissors. I kept the appointment. He gave this to me."

He rose, his face white. "I've done this to you. Now you're dealing with dark spirits and demon highwaymen—"

"*What* have you done to me?" She stood to face him, and fury cracked her voice. "Saved me when I was a kid? Saved me when I was drowning in other ways? As bad as things have gotten, I wouldn't change any of it—I mean, the parts where people haven't died . . ."

He drew close without touching her and said, desperately, "You can't do this. She'll kill you. *Caliban* will kill you."

"I'm doing it. I've got a silver knife. Is that what it'll take? I open the box in front of her and stab the heart? The Black Scissors said it had to be on Halloween. Can't I do it now?" She turned to push the bone key into the lock, hesitated.

He placed a hand over hers. "Please. Please don't do this."

"I'm going to do it."

He looked as if she were being killed before his eyes. "Fata spells are very particular. The box will only open on Halloween. You can only destroy the heart before her. And she must be present for it to have an effect. Now you're going to murder for me."

As he sank down, she sat beside him and gazed down at the heart in its box between their feet. "It's not murder—I think of it as more of a dragon-slaying thing, because she's a monster."

"Thinking about it is not the same as actually doing it." He watched her, his gaze serious.

"I can do it. Now, you need to tell me exactly what's going to happen on Halloween." She clenched her hands on her knees. She'd put the finger bone key back into her pocket because she didn't like holding it. "Where are they going to . . . murder you?"

"The oak."

"I figured."

"It'll be at midnight. They'll meet there. I'll be given something to keep calm."

"How are they planning to do it?"

"You don't need to know." Which meant it was going to be awful. Finn fiercely wished she could open that box now and cut that heart to pieces. She said softly, "It's my fault—"

"Now *you're* doing it. I'm *alive* because of you. Even if I die tomorrow, it'll still be one of the best days of my damn life."

"Idiot." She let her head drop to his shoulder and closed her eyes.

"You've read *Tam Lin*. This is the reality. This is what you need to do." And he told her, and she didn't want to believe him. She murmured, "Jack . . . can't you just run away?"

"I've got nowhere to go." He whispered in her ear, " '*Thou art mine and I am thine. 'Til the sinking of the world, I am thine and thou art mine.'* "

The poetry was from Percy Bysshe Shelley. She remembered the poem—it hadn't been romantic; a demon had spoken those words to a mortal warrior. "Hey, that's—"

He kissed her and it was an otherworldly kiss, desperate and shimmering, stealing her breath but causing something to prowl to life inside of her. When his mouth left hers, he whispered in her ear, "Don't trust me unless I bleed."

Morning tinted the sky behind him, and as dawn touched him, Jack vanished like a moth's wings unfolding in flame and she was left holding nothing.

CHAPTER EIGHTEEN

But had I wished, before I kissed,
That love had been so ill to win,
I had lock'd my heart in a case of gold
And pinn'd it with a silver pin.

—*WALY, WALY,* OLD BALLAD

There once was a girl who tried to save a Jack. She was just an
*ordinary girl, but he was no ordinary Jack. He belonged to the **ban***
***nathair.** And when the girl failed to win her lover at the Teind, the*
***white serpent** made a cake of her blood and furniture from her bones.*

—FROM THE JOURNAL OF LILY ROSE

Sylvie and Christie arrived in the morning. Finn took them into the sunlit yard where they could discuss strategy on the swing set. Finn's strategy was to tell them as little as possible about what she planned to do, which was to somehow destroy Reiko's heart before they could murder Jack.

"I don't know if there'll be a sacrifice now." She sat on a swing and tried to look as if she wasn't lying. "Maybe Sophia Avaline and her people will stop it, maybe not . . . I doubt they even know about it . . . they think Fair Hollow is a no-kill zone."

"They killed Angyll," Christie said, raising his head, "even though Avaline said they've never murdered anyone."

"Should we go to Professor Avaline and tell her about tonight?" Sylvie was knotting a finger in her hair.

"No." Finn gripped the swing's chains. "We can't trust anyone."

"The sacrifice was supposed to be at the oak Nathan showed you," Sylvie murmured. "And that's near Drake's Chapel, where the party's taking place."

Christie watched Finn. "What do you think the dark prince will be doing during all of this?"

She raised her head and stared at them. They *knew*. They knew she hadn't meant that breakup with Jack. "Dammit."

"It's Jack," Sylvie said, "isn't it? He's the one they're going to kill. He's the perfect choice . . . brave, beautiful—"

"So what are you going to do, Finn?" Christie leaned toward her. "Because we're not letting you out of our sight. We're gonna be on you like black on a crow."

"I don't want you involved." She hunched over and wearily pushed her hands through her hair. "I've got a plan. I just need you both to stay safe—and out of my way."

"Tell us the plan."

"Just trust me."

Christie looked desperate. "*Finn.*"

Sylvie gazed at Finn. "That's the plan—just trust her."

"No, because you know what? It's not *her* we're trusting. It's the goddamn dead guy who's got her so messed up, she's willing to die for him." He stood up. "I'm going to Professor Avaline."

"Christie, you *can't*. We can't trust her."

"But we can trust Jack Fata?" He stalked away.

Sylvie jumped up. She looked at Finn, the wind slashing her black hair across her face. "I'll talk to him. We'll see you tonight, Finn. And *I* trust you."

Finn bowed her head. She continued to sway back and forth on the swing. She hadn't told them it was her birthday today.

AN HOUR BEFORE THE HALLOWEEN party, Finn sat on her window seat and watched the sun set and felt calm. She knew that she couldn't abandon Jack, pretend she hadn't met him, let him die, while Reiko and her tribe resumed their secretive reign of terror. She didn't want to save Jack because she thought he was hers, or because she couldn't live without him. She wanted to save him to set things *right*.

She curled up, her arms around her knees. She'd celebrated a quiet birthday with her da, an early dinner out, a pretty cake, and presents. She'd wanted to tell him everything but, for his safety, had not. She'd faked her way through the day. It was her first birthday without Lily.

"Lily." She pressed her forehead against the window. "I'm scared."

There was no answer. Whatever haunted her house had become silent.

"DA. LEAVE IT." SHE WATCHED as her father painstakingly sewed a button back onto her red coat. He said, "It's almost done."

She sat in an ivory tulle gown that had belonged to her sister. Her hair was powdered and pinned up with gauzy butterflies. She wore lip gloss the color of apples, and her eyes were shadowed with the smoky liner Sylvie had given her. Circling one wrist was a silver bracelet, while the other was banded by Christie's iron flowers. Her feet tapped nervously in the red Converses she wore for practicality.

Her da looked up. "You look like Marie Antoinette on her way to the guillotine."

"The theme's Victorian steampunk."

"Why is this dance in the bloody woods, in a ruin?"

"It's *Halloween*. And the chapel belongs to Aubrey Drake's family." She put her arms on the kitchen table, her chin on her hands, and watched him finish her coat. She wanted to tell him how much she loved him, but then her throat closed up. After a while, all she could say was, "Nice job."

A car horn beeped outside. She slid to her feet. As her da handed her the coat, she impulsively hugged him. "I love you."

He looked puzzled. "I suppose this is a grand way to celebrate your birthday."

She smiled and wondered how she'd learned to lie so easily, "Yeah. It is. See you later."

"Twelve o'clock. Midnight. Like Cinderella."

She moved slowly to the door. "Good-bye, Da."

She spun around and hugged him again.

CHRISTIE PARKED HIS MUSTANG ON the grass with the other cars. As he, Finn, and Sylvie moved up the path toward Drake's Chapel, now surrounded by lights and music, Finn studied her friends with a mix of worry and admiration. Christie had old-fashioned aviator's goggles pushed into his russet hair and wore a black pin-striped suit with a waistcoat and tie. Sylvie had come in an Empire gown of black gossamer and looked like one of Dracula's brides. Her ornaments were a necklace of little skulls and a black parasol.

"You didn't tell Professor Avaline?" Finn didn't look at Christie as she asked the question. They were all gazing at the party glittering and glowing around Drake's Chapel.

"I didn't tell Avaline. Sylvie threatened to hurt me. Didn't you, Sylv?"

"That I did."

They began walking. Mr. Wyatt, his dreads tucked into a top hat, stood farther up the lane, greeting the students making their way toward the chapel. As two girls in scarlet gowns sauntered past, holding red parasols over their heads, their jewelry made of gears and bits of metal, the light reflecting silver from their eyes. Sylvie whispered, "*They're* here . . ."

Christie said, "We don't separate. Ever. Got it?"

"We'll be fine." Finn reached for their hands and led them toward Mr. Wyatt, who tipped his hat and waved them on. Conscious of Reiko's heart in her small leather backpack, Finn smiled at him. He didn't look at her and seemed tense and watchful.

They know, Finn thought with dread. Professor Avaline and her people knew about the sacrifice.

The music, gorgeous and sinister, crashed over them as they approached the chapel, where Professor Fairchild leaned against a tree, reading a book, his brown curls shimmering beneath a bowler hat. Beyond him was the chapel entrance, its doors open to reveal red candles, a crimson cake, a feast of scarlet things. On a stage built in front of the stained-glass window, a girl with raccoon eyes and rosebud lips was playing a fiddle as her band of Mad Hatters attacked their instruments.

Finn recognized HallowHeart students, but not others who had come as guests or from St. John's U. Most of the girls wore gowns with corsets and ribbons, top hats, or pretty masks. The boys strutted like rock stars in punk Victorian gear and stovepipe hats decorated with clockwork.

"Hello." Miss Perangelo, the art instructor, appeared, slinky in a gown of emerald silk, her short red hair wreathed with marigolds. Accompanying her, holding a toad as if it was a pet, was a Gothic-eyed girl wearing green tulle.

"Miss Perangelo." Sylvie acknowledged her, warily eyeing Miss Perangelo's companion.

"Do you like the music?" The band had begun playing an ancient reel with drumbeats, the vocalist's voice operatic and eerie. "They're called the Lazy Gentlemen."

"I like it. Are the Fatas here yet?" Sylvie smiled innocently.

Miss Perangelo's gaze shimmered. The cameo around her neck was an ivory stag's head on a black background. "They're here. Somewhere. Come, Maeve."

As Miss Perangelo and her companion glided away, Christie whispered, "Her friend's a Fata—Finn . . . Avaline *lied*—they're in with the Fatas."

Finn murmured, "You're only just noticing?"

"Just for the record . . . snark is *my* thing. It's not an attractive quality in a young lady."

Sylvie rolled her eyes.

Aubrey Drake appeared at the chapel door. The captain of the HallowHeart Ravens football team looked dashing in jeans, a waistcoat, and a shirt of scarlet ruffles, his black hair clubbed back. He was speaking with Victoria Tudor, whose gown was made of flame-orange silk. An ivory mask covered the back of her head.

"They're all here." Christie looked around. "The children of the damned. I see Hester Kierney. The one in pink is Claudette Tredescant. And that's Ijio Valentine in the goggles."

"Doesn't anyone here have normal names?"

"The normal ones do."

Finn wondered how the parents of those privileged kids, the Blessed, had continued their pact with the Fatas when they'd forgotten it with age. Were their children now the ones who dealt with the otherworld? The idea was vaguely horrifying.

"What's the plan again?" Sylvie looked as if she were about to start pacing like a caged thing.

"Just stay safe. And trust me." Finn leveled her gaze on Christie, who looked away.

"There's Hester," he said. "I'm going to talk to her for a sec."

Another performer had taken the stage, a girl in white gossamer, who wrapped her stockinged legs around a crimson cello and began to play a sweet, mournful tune—"November Rain" by Guns N' Roses. Finn went cold all over. That song, the one she'd heard after Lily's wake, was Reiko's first strike against her.

"Finn." Aubrey Drake approached. "You're here."

She kept Sylvie and Christie in view as they spoke with Hester Kierney. She was desperately trying not to think about the sacrifice, the cadaverous oak, and the Fatas' potential revenge. "I'm here."

"Don't be that way." He was watching her. "I like your hair clips. My girl-friend's into moths and butterflies."

She touched one of her hair clips. The bone key she'd gotten from the Black Scissors was secured into her hair, a serpent among the butterflies. "Aubrey—"

"Aubrey!" a blond girl called, interrupting Finn.

He backed away. "Coming, Claude! Finn, later, we need to talk—"

A storm of music drowned his words. People began dancing again. Turning, Finn realized her friends were gone.

Aubrey called to her as she pushed through the punk Victorian girls and kohl-eyed boys in bowler hats; Finn sensed menace like an icy blade across the nape of her neck. She saw, moving among the dancers, a figure in a skull mask, his pale greatcoat billowing in a wind that simmered with ashes and the wings of moths. She could smell things burning . . . incense, firewood. She didn't say Caliban's name out loud, but she thought it, and that skull face turned toward her.

She moved in the other direction, realizing Reiko's second strike against her might be aimed at her friends.

CHRISTIE FOUND HIMSELF ALONE IN a confusing crowd of schoolmates and potential enemies. When a girl in a black suit stepped up to him, a top hat wreathed with flowers tilted over her brow, he thought the pretty face and the orange hair looked familiar. She said, "Looking for someone?"

"My friends."

Her cherry lips curved. "Kiss me and I'll tell you a secret."

Light slid across her eyes, which were golden, not silver. And she was so luscious. He stepped close, touched his mouth to hers, tasted sweetness. The girl whispered in his ear, "The mirror is a third eye."

He blinked, then watched her glide away through the dancers. Had she just felt him up? He reached into his back pocket and pulled out a pewter compact mirror, an antique engraved with a Greek hero holding a decapitated head, its hair a mane of snakes. Why had she stuck the thing in his pocket? He started after her. "Hey—"

Someone caught his sleeve. For a moment, he didn't recognize Phouka. The Fatas' girl-chauffeur had gone glamorous in a sleeveless gown of silver satin, her arms and throat gleaming with jewelry shaped into leaves, her auburn hair piled onto her head and tangled with little white flowers. She slid an arm through Christie's and began walking with him. She smelled like apples, and her eyes were rimmed with silver, details that magnified her exoticism. Idly, she said, "I saw your friends."

"Sylvie? Finn?"

"I'll take you to them." She led him toward a line of trees. He could smell burning wood as leaves swirled and crackled. The sky was velvet black, the stars cold. The birches were ghostly in the light from the hurricane lamps. Christie wondered if he should ask Phouka if she knew about the sacrifice. Then she said, "You shouldn't have kissed the Fool, Christie."

Christie grinned. "Are you jeal—"

Caliban Ariel'Pan swaggered from the trees, followed by a red-haired Fata and the blond—and dead—dancer, Devon Valentine.

Her eyes otherworldly silver, Phouka let go of Christie's hand.

SYLVIE HAD LOST CHRISTIE AND Finn. She kept calm as she threaded through the crowds, feeling naked beneath the gown of black gossamer and silk she'd chosen to wear because she felt she was becoming what those others kept calling her—*witch*. The weird coma, Reiko's promises . . . they had changed her.

Tonight, she didn't feel like a witch. Whenever she thought of someone—Jack—being murdered for Reiko's lot, she wanted to cut someone's head off.

Then Sylvie saw a boy who looked hauntingly familiar and her pulse jumped. *This is the night the dead walk.* She began to follow him as he moved through the masked students, into the trees.

"Thomas?" She halted when she stepped among the shadows and thought, *What the hell am I doing?* The music from the revel had grown faint. She stood alone in a scrimshaw of rustling shadows with the Queen's tree looming before her.

When the tiny dolls and ornaments hung in its branches began to twirl, Sylvie backed away. The air, tainted with fire and clover, had chilled. Someone stood beneath the tree, black hair framing his face, honey-brown skin radiant against a suit of sapphire velvet.

Thomas Luneht, who had committed suicide in the '70s, moved from the shadows. Black wings seemed to sweep from his shoulders. His eyes were a burning blue. He didn't speak, but a sound seemed to vibrate from him as he held out a hand—

She stumbled back and whirled—

—only to find her way blocked by the three Rooks. Trip, Hip Hop, and Bottle smiled at her, their pose exactly that of Malcolm Tirnagoth's three children from the antique photograph.

She heard a warning cry from behind her before the Rooks' shadows, swooping and tattered, fell over her.

"TRUFFLES?"

Finn jumped as an orange-haired girl in a top hat and black suit offered a tray of chocolates.

"No, thank you."

"I suggest this one. It's Mayan chocolate." In her other hand, the girl held an ivory wand shaped into some sort of long-stemmed toadstool. Her angelic face, mischief in the golden eyes, seemed familiar.

Finn knew she was a Fata. "Do you have a brother named Absalom?"

"My name's Salome, and no." Salome pointed to a truffle. "You should take a chocolate. They'll help you see things as they really are. Tonight, you'll need to do that."

Finn whispered, "Who are you?"

"Salome." The golden eyes shone. "Take one."

Finn leaned forward. *"Absalom?"*

Salome winked, and Finn selected a chocolate and bit into it, tasting only chocolate.

"Pssh." Salome's mouth curved. "You shouldn't have done that. You're not supposed to eat our food."

Finn choked and swallowed the bittersweet truffle as Salome glided away. When the dancing figures began to blur and shadows swirled over Drake's Chapel, she leaned against a tree as the fiddle music reeled through her and her body ached, *ached* to dance. Why had she eaten the damn truffle? Because she'd trusted someone who resembled trickster Absalom?

As a violin solo razored the air, the music suddenly slid into a threatening pulse of drums. The masked crowd parted, forming an aisle.

Two figures moved from Drake's Chapel.

Reiko Fata was raptor elegant in a ball gown of scarlet leather and red silk, its sleeves billowing, its ruffled collar framing her face, her corset revealing a fortune in rubies strewn across her collarbones. Her inky hair emphasized her inhuman green eyes, lined now with scarlet designs. Beside her, a savage bridegroom in ivory, Caliban Ariel'Pan carried a cane topped with a small skull. Platinum hair swept across his corpse-silver eyes.

A hand grasped Finn's and dragged her against a lithe body.

Jack, in a black fur coat and pin-striped trousers, smiled at her, his dark hair falling raggedly from beneath a top hat. The skin around his eyes was painted with black glyphs. She could see, on his chest, the inky curl of the serpent-biting-its-tail tattoo. He looked as wicked as Caliban and twice as deadly. The music slid into a slow reel as she said, "Are you high now?"

"Most likely." The wavering light chiseled his face. *"Dance with me."*

As a girl began a mournful song accompanied by gentle violins and drums, Jack placed one hand on Finn's hip. Still holding her other hand, he glided with her across the emerald moss. She ducked her head and braced herself against the feline muscularity of this young man who had come into her world like the hero in a Gothic romance or a spaghetti western. She closed her eyes and wished that this dark myth who bled for her would kiss her. She whispered, "I've figured it out, Jack. She took you in the 1800s. That gave you one hundred years with them, to live like a prince. And, at the end, you were sacrificed, but it didn't work and you lived another one hundred years as a Jack. What went wrong?"

The drowsy, dead look had returned to his eyes. "She stopped it."

"She . . ." Finn stepped back. "*Reiko?*"

"Don't do it, Finn," he whispered, and slid away. "Let me go."

"*Jack!*" She pushed after him, desperate not to lose sight of him.

Phouka stepped in her way. "Your friends are looking for you."

Finn halted and felt a sharp fear. "Where are they?"

Phouka pointed to Drake's Chapel, veiled in flickering firelight and shadows, its crimson interior glowing. "In there."

CHRISTIE BARELY STRUGGLED AS HE was hauled through the woods between the Fata with long red hair and the blond dead boy in scarlet. He'd fallen because Phouka, treacherous girl, had whispered in his ear until he'd had no will. He couldn't hear anything now except the sinister clatter of branches and the faint whistling of the wind in the dark. He'd attempted screaming, but the red-haired man had placed a finger against his lips and sealed them shut.

When they reached a looming gate of rusted metal, the red-haired man opened it and he and his companion dragged Christie toward the silhouette of the Tir-nagoth Hotel, its windows lit as if for guests. Christie's hopelessness vanished, and he began to fight, but the two creatures on either side of him held him with preternatural strength. When he hunched over and threw up, the blond boy stepped disdainfully back. "This doesn't seem fair, Farouche."

"Hush, Devon."

Christie shuddered when he looked at the blond boy. The dancer who had slit his wrists in a bathtub decades ago gazed soberly back at him, his eyes silver. As for the other man . . . Christie saw the glint of gold hoops in ears that seemed to curve beneath the red hair.

This isn't real. This isn't . . .

They yanked him into the hotel courtyard, and Christie stared at the glamorous, manicured place that had been in ruins only a few days ago. His gut clenched again as he was pulled through art nouveau doors into a salon shining with lamps and polished mahogany.

This isn't happening . . .

He was dragged down a hall toward a pair of mahogany doors.

"No!" He could yell now. He tried to brake with his feet, but they lifted and hauled him.

The doors opened to reveal a swamp of decay that had once been a ballroom. The only light came from a lamp of red glass set on the floor. Velvet wallpaper peeled in swaths from scabbed walls. A broken chandelier glittered against the mold-stained ceiling. They hadn't bothered to disguise a killing place. He couldn't tell if there was anything in the shadows, which were heavy and unnatural.

Then his eyes adjusted to the gloom and he saw the girl seated in a chair.

"Sylvie!" He tried to break free, but Farouche and the dead boy held him tight.

Sylvie flashed him a brave, bruised smile as the three Rooks standing around her stirred. Inky-haired Trip, leaning against the chair, slid one black-nailed finger down her cheek. "Fox boy. You come to save the little crow girl from a fate worse than death?"

Christie tore from his captors and ran at the Rook. Neither Farouche nor Devon Valentine tried to stop him.

The Rooks moved forward, their antique finery rustling. Christie lunged—

Farouche strode forward then and grabbed him by one arm, murmuring to him as he twisted to fight, "Don't, boy. You can't win against this."

"You." Sylvie, who looked as though she'd been crying, pointed at Farouche. "You're the one who bewitched me in the churchyard that night."

"A *nice* young lady wouldn't have been in the churchyard at night." Hip Hop primly tucked her hair behind her ears.

Christie tried to free himself from Farouche's grip. "*Monsters.*"

Farouche flung him at Sylvie, spun on his heel, and strode out with Devon. The Rooks swept past, laughing, and the doors slammed shut behind them.

Sylvie rushed forward and pulled Christie up. "Christie . . . did they hurt you?"

"I'm fine. Are my hands shaking? *Who hit you?*"

"Stop roaring." She whispered in his ear, "*Something's in here with us.*"

Averting his eyes from the breathing shadows, he pulled her to the doors. The scarred wood wouldn't give. When he heard a click from behind them, the sound made him shudder. Sylvie gripped his hand.

From the darkness came a rustling of fabric followed by a delicate, sinister hiss.

Sylvie and Christie, turning, kept their backs to the doors.

The things that evolved from the dark as Christie's and Sylvie's eyes adjusted to the gloom might have been human-size dolls or people in masks. The one veiled in gossamer stood very still. Crouched near her was a male, a pair of raven wings at his shoulders. A third figure, in a long coat, its face ominously hidden by blood-red hair, was the closest.

The terror/run/scream instinct paralyzed Christie, because the veiled bride doll—without his actually seeing it do so—had moved.

He blinked again and the black-winged doll was also now posed differently, head tilted, one arm outstretched.

"Sylvie," Christie whispered, fumbling for the door handle. "Are they *moving*?"

He blinked again—the doll veiled in scarlet hair was now posed in a slinking crouch.

"*How come I don't see them moving?*" Christie whisper-shrieked.

Sylvie murmured, "*Between.* Christie, I saw something like this on *Doctor Who*—don't take your eyes off them."

"*What?* Are you *kidding? Doctor*—"

"The Fatas inhabit between places, right? So those things—they must move between—no! I've got sweat in my eyes . . . *Christie* . . ."

The bride doll was alarmingly close now, head down, red lips parted to reveal delicate fangs.

Christie had heard about people dying from terror. He'd never believed it possible until the Fatas had erupted into his life like a bad infection. "Can we smash their heads in with someth—"

"Shh! They can hear you. They're playing with us. Just don't look away—"

Christie shouted as he found the black-winged doll gripping Sylvie's wrist. As she frantically tried to pull herself free, he struck at the doll, hitting a surface like porcelain.

Sweat stung *his* eyes as the creeping doll-thing in black rose before him, its clawed hand an inch from his face. One eye, its pupil like a goat's, glared from beneath the veil of red hair, and he felt his desperate courage dying. The doll-things smelled like blood, as if they *gorged* on it. Christie backed up against the door—and felt the mirror in his back pocket. What had that girl said? *The mirror is a third eye . . .*

"Sylvie." He pulled the compact mirror out, flipped it open. "You got one of these?"

The black-winged doll made a noise, a horrible, creaking hiss, and froze in place, releasing Sylvie, who fumbled in her little backpack and triumphantly raised a small mirror. A dot of reflected light slid over the faces of the bride and the angel. Sylvie stepped back—

She tripped, stumbled, and dropped the mirror. Christie lunged toward her, glimpsed the bride doll moving—

Behind him, the doors fell open. A strong hand yanked him back. Christie grabbed Sylvie from the bride doll's grasp and they tumbled backward. The doors slammed shut over the furious face of the bride doll as its jaw unhinged to reveal a cage of teeth.

Christie scrambled up and felt Sylvie breathless and fierce beside him. He said, "What . . . *what*—"

Phouka put a finger to her lips and pushed open a metal door with the word Exit in black scripted across the top. Sylvie sobbed once and swore. Christie grabbed Sylvie's hand as he shouted at Phouka, "Whose side are you *on*?"

The chauffeur carried a walking stick, its handle shaped like a fox's head. "If you'll stop bellowing, I'll tell you. Not all of us agree with her. Some of us can be good." She moved away. "When we're not being bad."

"Like goddamn Tinker Bell," Sylvie whispered as she and Christie moved with Phouka among brambles and twisted, dark trees. "Your hearts are too small to hold both good and bad, but only one at a time. So now you're good?"

"I don't have a heart. And Ariel'Pan and I only lure away the *unhappy* children." Phouka raised two masks of metal. "Wear these. Maybe you can blend in a little."

As Christie and Sylvie accepted the masks, Christie looked back at the hotel. He didn't want to ask about the doll-things—they would return in his nightmares.

Phouka saw him looking. She said, "They're called Grindylow. Now come along. Things are about to get ver . . . ry exciting." Phouka began walking through the dark, her gown slithering. She spoke in a singsong voice, "'*And we fairies, that do run, by the triple Hecate's team, from the presence of the sun, following darkness like a dream . . .*'"

"Shakespeare," Christie muttered as he and Sylvie trudged after her. "Do all of you steal from him?"

"Why not? He stole from us."

FINN ENTERED DRAKE'S CHAPEL, WHICH had been decorated like a Gothic theater with fake birds, red candles, skulls, a statue with bat wings, and various ephemera from some crazy antique shop. She didn't see Christie or Sylvie, but Aubrey Drake stood near a table weighed down by a feast of crimson things. He was laughing with a boy in a black frock coat and a white-as-snow girl whose eyes flashed silver when she looked at Finn. With them was Sophia Avaline, gorgeous in a gown of black satin, feeding a truffle to a willowy young man.

Traitor, Finn thought. She didn't see Christie or Sylvie, so she backed out of the chapel, turned, and moved through the small fires that had sprung up in stone bowls. The taint of wine and smoke made her eyes sting. She felt a prowling apprehension for her friends.

Reiko *must* know she was planning to save Jack.

The girl onstage began to sing "Scarborough Fair" as if her heart were breaking. Finn lifted her gaze and felt as if an old wound had opened up inside of her.

Reiko Fata, a creature of flame and blood, moved across the lawn toward Jack, who held out one hand gleaming with rings. Finn watched them dance like two figures from a hellish realm, perfect together because they had known each other for two hundred years. And Reiko had an advantage Finn did not.

Reiko was immortal.

As Jack tilted his head and whispered in Reiko's ear, Finn pushed a fist against her stomach and turned away. *Don't be an idiot.* When she raised her head, she saw a line of masked figures heading into the woods—none of the other revelers seemed to notice.

Wide-eyed, she looked back at the party.

Jack and Reiko were gone.

Finn ran after the masked figures, and the trees instantly closed around her. It was moonlit and quiet. Through a filigree of branches and briars, she saw lights moving and raced after them.

And lost them again. In the moonlit dark, she twisted around, hopeless.

She saw a little altar in the hollow of a tree, where a miniature angel reigned over the skulls of small animals and keys strung on dirty ribbons. She approached it, puzzled.

"Don't touch it."

She jerked around and met the gaze of a tall girl in a gown of cobweb gray, her bare arms glinting with bronze bracelets, her hair a mane of white gold strung with glass crescent moons.

"It belongs to the Lily Girls. They worship something around here." Her voice was as quicksilver as her gaze. She didn't even attempt to disguise herself with human warmth or movement and seemed as cold as a Viking's sword.

"The Lily Girls?" Finn didn't like that name.

"The dead girls. I am Norn, by the way. Since I know your name, Finn Sullivan, it is only right that you know mine."

"Norn," Finn whispered as the world tilted.

Norn's face was solemn. "I remember Lily Rose. She was little, but clever."

An earthy wind kissed Finn's lips and swept leaves caressingly across her skin. Lily's imaginary friend stood before her. "She didn't *make you up* . . ."

"She didn't make anything up." Norn bowed her head. "I was all alone back then. And I saw her, a little ballerina, pretending to fight something with a toy sword. I began to talk to her."

Finn shivered as she imagined this cold angel of a girl materializing from the dusk and walking toward her nine-year-old sister. "*You* told her those things, the things in her journal?"

"Stories," Norn said, lifting her head until her face was in shadow, "to a child."

"And now she is dead."

The Fata girl turned, and her voice was faint as she strode away. "You are *among* the dead, Finn Sullivan. Come with me and remember that nothing is as it seems."

Finn looked back over her shoulder, once. Then she hurried after the Fata called Norn.

AS CHRISTIE AND SYLVIE MOVED among the revelers, the party became wilder. Although they'd masked their faces and Phouka had told them what to do, they were still nervous. Sylvie was trying not to jump at every noise that distinguished itself from the music. She was scared for Finn, who had lost so much, who had come to Fair Hollow to begin a new life, only to fall in love with someone who had died over one hundred years ago. "Do you really think they're going to kill some—"

Someone snatched the mask from Sylvie's face.

Caliban Ariel'Pan smiled at her as he tossed the mask away.

Christie pushed his metal face up and stepped between Sylvie and the beast. "You can't kill us in front of witnesses."

"You could drop dead of a stroke. The crow girl could have an epileptic fit, swallow her tongue." Caliban's gaze slid across them. "Fox boy."

"Get away." Christie didn't move, again ready to fling his whole body at the monster smiling sweetly at them.

Caliban stepped back with a velvety laugh. "Doesn't matter. You're both more fun alive. Let's see how long you stay that way."

He swaggered across the lawn and vanished among the dancers.

There was a glint of lantern light on silk—a line of masked figures was moving up the path, into the woods.

"*Where is she?*" Christie frantically scanned the crowds.

"Come on." Sylvie tugged him toward the path. She had retrieved the mask Caliban had taken from her. "We need to follow those people."

CHAPTER NINETEEN

Out then spoke the Queen of fairies
And an angry woman was she:
"Shame betide her ill-faired face,
And an ill death may she die,
For she's taken away the bonniest knight
In all my company."

— TAM LIN, OLD BALLAD

Finn had lost Norn. The Fata girl had been gliding through the woods as if she'd been born there and had suddenly vanished—but Finn had again seen the lights flickering in the dark and now followed them. They had, at first, seemed like dancing orbs, but, as she'd gotten closer, she could see they were small lanterns carried by masked figures moving as silently as spirits.

The Fatas were going to the oak. And the sacrifice. And Jack's second death.

Finn began to run. Twigs and leaves ripped at her gown, scratched at her face, pulled her hair. Her breath seared through her lungs as she raced toward the lights blinking through the trees. She expected obstacles, attacks, but nothing came at her.

She pushed through a lattice of blackthorns.

Hundreds of lit candles reflected from the metal masks of a gathering that was silent but for primitive music from flutes, drums, and the mournful *screeing* of a violin. There seemed to be others in the shadows, seeming not quite substantial and wrongly shaped. Her gaze skewed away from them and wouldn't focus.

The oak, the god, loomed over the gathering, its roots webbing beneath all the woods, its branches, spreading impossibly far, laced with the sharp, shiny leaves and white berries of mistletoe. There was a cavern in the side of its trunk, a black hollow she hadn't seen before. The fragrances that swept from this hollow were of wet earth, burning stars, glacial hours. The oak, dark with age and sickness, scarred by graffiti, was dying.

Finn tore her gaze from the monstrous tree to the thing set before it: a scarecrow of bones, thorny vines, Emory, and wildflowers woven into the shape of a man, fluttering with black ribbons. The human skull crowning it wore a wreath of mistletoe, like some gruesome, Druidic Day-of-the-Dead sculpture. It was a primitive, horrifying thing, a symbol of blood power and ancient bargains.

A procession came from the night, its leaders a tawny-haired man in a coat of brown fur, and Reiko Fata, trailing scarlet. Jack came after, wearing only his jeans, pendants gleaming against his bare chest. His dark brown hair was wound with a crown of red leaves and tiny apples. He was barefoot.

The trinity moved down the aisle of silent figures masked by the metal faces of cruel gods. Jewels and eyes glittered like tooth and claw. Reiko and her consort separated as they approached the oak. Jack stood alone before the scarecrow of thorns and Emory, his head down, his hands at his sides.

Now, someone whispered in Finn's ear, and she whirled, seeing nothing but flickering shadows behind her.

She drew in a breath and stepped forward, yanking the backpack from her shoulder.

They turned toward her, the Fatas, firelight glistening in their eyes, across those beautiful masks. She tugged out the glass box and nearly dropped it because she was shaking so badly. "I have Reiko's heart."

Reiko turned on her, her gown swirling like flames. She seemed impatient, not angry, and that worried Finn. "What are you doing, fool? You can't open that without the ke—"

Finn raised the Black Scissors' bone key and steeled herself against the cold murder in Reiko's gaze. "Free Jack. Or I open this, with the Black Scissors' blessing."

No one spoke. Some of the masked figures at the edges of the gathering stirred. Finn didn't think they were Fatas or anything that had ever resembled humans.

"Serafina Sullivan." As Reiko spoke, a wind fluttering with leaves cast itself across Finn, whipping her hair into her eyes. "Give me that or we will take it from you."

"No." Finn looked at Jack, who still had his head down, his hands clenched at his sides. "You won't."

And she pushed the bone key at the lock.

It didn't fit.

She tried again, frantically. She sank to a crouch, jamming the key into a lock that wasn't made for it. A nightmarish sensation of impending death stunned her.

Finn Sullivan, Anna Weaver had said, *you will die on Halloween.*

A shadow swept over her. She slowly raised her head to see a terrible thing— Reiko, smiling. The queen of nothing and night began to circle her, her voice scornful. "Do you think, little mayfly, that I didn't know he was here? My enemy, my *Dubh Deamhais*? The heart I grew for him withered long ago. It's *dust*."

Finn felt as if she were all hollow bones filled with ice. Her ears began to buzz, and her old enemy, the enchanted sleep, began to creep over her. The glass box and the bone key fell from her hands. Unsteadily, she pulled herself up.

Reiko continued with gentle malice: "That is a new-grown heart and no key exists that will open *that* box. You've failed, girl. You've risked yourself for a ruined boy who only loved you out of desperation and fear."

Finn heard Jack, in his drugged daze, speak her name, and her heart twisted fiercely. She whispered, "Even though you made him bow his head to you, treated him as if he were a beaten dog, pretended to love him, made him kill for you, you never . . . you *never* broke him."

Reiko smiled. "I broke your sister."

Finn lunged and slammed a hand across Reiko's face.

Caliban, snarling, was at Reiko's side in an instant, but she held him back with one arm, her green gaze fixed on Finn while Finn stared, uncomprehending, at the blood that smeared the Fata queen's mouth.

"Back, Caliban," Reiko said.

Glaring at Finn, the *crom cu* grudgingly moved away.

Reiko and Finn locked gazes for a moment. Reiko slowly raised one hand to wipe away the telltale blood before anyone else saw it.

"That heart," Finn whispered, "it's not from the Black Scissors . . . it's from *Jack*. You *love* him. Why—"

"It is the ultimate sacrifice."

Finn was still shaking. She had failed. The Fatas' eyes glinted malevolently behind their masks. She was alone, without friends or weapons. So she said what the girl in *Tam Lin* had said when saving her love from the fairy folk: "I claim him."

The masked people murmured. Someone swore. David Ryder, the consort, looked furious and said, "Where did you find this nettlesome girl, Reiko?"

"This nettlesome girl"—Reiko turned—"is challenging us. We must honor that challenge, David." Reiko looked back over her shoulder at Finn, and her smile was beautiful and frightening. "Go on, mayfly. Try me."

Finn felt the sleep spell fade and, with it, her fear. It was as if she were suddenly filled with a clear, bright light, like sunlight on a steel blade. She stepped over the glass box with Reiko's heart in it and moved toward Jack, who raised his head to stare at her, his gaze dark, desolate. *That* drew her on as the masked figures parted for her, torchlight rippling crimson across metal faces, reflecting gold from the rustling, cathedral ceiling of leaves.

"Jack." She reached out and clasped his hands, feeling how cold they were despite the pulse thrumming beneath her fingers. She said, " *'Thou art mine and I am thine. 'Til the sinking of the world.'* "

The dark left his eyes. *"Finn . . . don't . . ."*

She slid her arms around him and held him close as she pressed her ear to the strong pulse of his heart. His body felt as familiar against her as if they'd grown up together. She heard Reiko's voice, succulent with satisfaction. "If she can keep hold of him, she can have him."

"Jack," Finn whispered, "what does she—"

Jack said, in her ear, "Close your eyes."

She closed her eyes.

It began as all Fata tricks began, with a disturbing buzz in the air like thousands of flies, a pinching in her sinuses. Finn felt blood trickle from one nostril.

She wound her arms tighter around Jack, knotted her fingers in his hair, and fiercely whispered, "*They won't have you.*"

When she felt his body diminish in her embrace, she made the mistake of opening her eyes and saw his skin unravel to reveal a burning, blue light. Her terror slid into cool shock as the ribbons of what had once been Jack took the form of something vicious and winged in her arms, a feathered monster that slashed at her face, her arms. She cried out, struggling, but she didn't let go as the eagle shrieked, its powerful wing beats making it impossible to hold—

It's a trick, she thought while another part of her brain begged her to run. Jack had said it. Norn and Absalom Askew had warned her. *Nothing is as it seems.*

Despite panic and the feeling of her skin being slashed to ribbons, she closed her eyes again and held tight to the predator in her arms. As its beak slashed across her brow, she remembered her mother rescuing a small bird that had injured itself and gently setting that tiny creature into Finn's hands. She tasted blood in her mouth as the powerful shape shrank into a fluttering softness. When she opened her eyes, she gasped, because a sparrow, warm and tough, nestled in her hands.

The tiny shape caught fire and burst outward and Finn screamed as flames swept over her clothes, into her hair, bit into her lungs. Her flesh blistered. Her arms surrounded a small inferno that ate into her body, and the agony almost broke her—

Nothing is as it seems.

Sobbing in pain, she cupped her shriveling hands and fiercely imagined what *she* wanted. She pictured the summer she and Lily Rose had caught fireflies in jars . . . the fire vanished and cool, crisp air filled her lungs, soothing her skin as a lightning bug flickered between her cupped hands.

Someone shouted.

The insect suddenly curled outward and grew into a limbless, muscular form that thrashed around her and hissed into her face, baring fangs like fishing hooks. She choked and doubled over as it coiled around her, constricting, its odor of reptile making her gasp before its body tightened like a scaled corset around her. Something broke inside of her. She nearly fainted.

I can't. I can't do this, Jack. I'm sorry . . .

As the python continued to strangle her, she thought of the grass snakes she used to chase in the Vermont garden. Blood burst into her mouth as something else ruptured—

The pressure was suddenly gone. She could breathe again, and she brokenly gasped air into her lungs, lifting one arm to gaze at the grass snake twined around her wrist. She touched it carefully, her breath coming in hiccups.

The snake exploded into a fountain of water and she was holding a wet, shivering young man. She didn't cry when he whispered, "*It doesn't hurt . . .*" But she knew it did, because he wouldn't look at her and there were bruises all over his arms and chest.

He cascaded into the shape of water, which she caught in a silver cup frantically imagined into existence. From the water flew a silvery moth, which she lunged for, and fell to her knees with it fluttering in the cage of her fingers. As she gazed at it, the moth became a shadow, like smoke. She firmly told the shadow it was a ribbon, and it solidified into silk, twining around her wrist, sliding away, swirling into a darkness that became a mass in her arms—

—a black jackal lunged at her throat, its cage of teeth glistening, its claws tearing at her shoulders. She cried out and staggered, but she held on, burying her face in black fur that smelled like wild roses, remembering the dog she'd wanted as a little girl in Vermont. "*Jack.*"

The big, muscular shape relaxed against her, still snarling, laying its wicked head on her shoulder. One blink later, she was holding a sleek black Labrador that whimpered, its paws heavy against her.

David Ryder's voice slid through the silence. "Well played, girl."

Finn lifted her head and defiantly met Reiko's poison-green gaze as the warm dog shape in her arms became human and cold. She smelled corruption, rot, and closed her eyes, shivering as icy water dripped onto her face. It wasn't over.

"Open your eyes, girl."

She did as she was told. In her arms was a naked young man, his white skin streaked with blue, wet dark hair falling into eyes that were a gelid green laced with the silver of death. He was burning cold. From the corner of his left eye, a drop of blood appeared and became a rose petal. Another rose petal slid from one nostril and drifted against her lips. He didn't move or speak. Finn felt sickness burning in her throat. She no longer held a living boy; she held Death.

"This is the truth of what you love." Reiko spoke tenderly, flicking her gaze over the decaying body. "A corpse stuffed with roses."

The origin of Jack's faint fragrance of roses was horrifyingly clear now.

Finn cried out, staggered back . . . let go . . .

. . . and fell into the embrace of the black-ribboned scarecrow.

Shadows and light blurred. It was not a corpse, but Jack, gazing at her, stricken.

"Jack!" Finn tried to lunge toward him, but she couldn't move.

"And so the trick is done." Reiko smiled. "Serafina Sullivan, you have no power here. And your life is forfeit."

Jack stared at Finn until two masked Fatas grabbed him and began dragging him away. He howled her name. Finn felt the helplessness of starring in a nightmare.

The Rooks, the three dead children of Malcolm Tirnagoth, removed their masks to reveal solemn faces. Phouka stood nearby, her head bowed. They were all taking off their masks now. She saw strange faces and glamorous ones, disturbing beauty and grotesque—the Fatas, the fairies, the children of nothing and night. Aubrey Drake stood among them, looking shocked. Beside him, Hester Kierney had her hands over her mouth. Professor Fairchild and Sophia Avaline had emerged from the shadows, their expressions grim. As a wind heavy with the scents of rotting leaves and burning swept through the gathering, and Professor Hobson, Miss Perangelo, and Mr. Wyatt came forward, Sophia Avaline said, "Reiko Fata, this *wasn't what was agreed upon.*"

Reiko ignored her, her scarlet gown slithering as she moved toward Finn, who could still hear Jack's raging cries as he was dragged farther away. He couldn't fight them; he was human. And Finn had done that to him, made him vulnerable. Reiko spoke as if they were having a conversation over fries and soda. "I remembered you, too, little mayfly, from the bridge. The moment my Jack dragged you from the water, I decided to make you into something deserving of his regard."

"Reiko"—David Ryder sounded impatient—"don't taunt her. There is no honor in it."

"This," Reiko said, gesturing to Finn as she addressed the gathering, "is our true Teind, the one we've sought for so long, our braveheart . . . a girl who sacrificed love for her friends, who risked her life for a fool like Nathan Clare, who was willing to die for another. We've watched over her for years—and now she is ours."

It was a death sentence. The urge to run made Finn instinctively scan the gathering for escape, for a way out . . . but no help would be coming. The teachers looked defeated, and Aubrey Drake and his friends were useless. The inevitability of death closed over her like a wolf's teeth, and she put her hands over her mouth and blinked away tears. She was shaking so badly, she felt as if her bones had become icicles. Her gaze, seeking an ally among the crowd, met Sophia Avaline's.

Avaline, almost imperceptibly, shook her head and looked at a bright figure in the shadows.

Reiko's voice and gaze were gentle. "You came to us, Serafina Sullivan, just as we needed you. Your path to us has been a serpent biting its own tail."

Finn, watching the orange-haired figure in the darkness, felt the breathless shimmer of hope.

Someone shouted, "No!"

It was Christie, breaking through the ranks.

Mr. Wyatt hauled him back, saying something that froze him in place. As Christie stared at Finn, his eyes wide and dark, Sylvie darted forward.

She nearly reached Reiko with the silver dagger in hand, the one she'd taken from Finn's abandoned backpack, before she was surrounded by the Rooks, who pushed her back. Hip Hop shook a finger at her. "Naughty girl."

Reiko turned her back on them and faced Finn. "Be honored. Your death will give us one hundred years."

Christie's anguished yell was echoed by a cry from one of those gathered beneath the tree—Aubrey Drake stepped forward, his eyes wide with disbelief. With him were Hester Kierney, Ijio Valentine, and the four other descendants of the families who had made a pact with the Fatas. Aubrey said, "No. Absolutely not. Not her."

"Boy. Mind yourself." Caliban showed his teeth.

"Professor Avaline." Hester Kierney turned toward Avaline and the other professors —Jane Emory was not among them. "*Please . . .*"

Sophia Avaline closed her eyes, opened them, met Finn's gaze again. "Only one. Every one hundred years. If that is the price we must pay to keep the peace here . . ."

"*Peace?*" Christie turned and pointed at Caliban. "He *murdered* Angyll Weaver!"

"And Mary Booke," someone in the masked crowd called out softly. Finn recognized the voice as belonging to one of Jack's vagabonds, the bald girl with the cat's eyes. Darling Emory.

Mr. Wyatt frowned and looked at Caliban as Professor Avaline carefully addressed Reiko. "Lady. Is this true?"

Reiko was silent, and her chin lifted. David Ryder looked at her. He whispered, "*Answer her.* Did your dog *murder* a mortal?"

"He is not my dog, and whoever killed those girls is not of my court. An outlaw is responsible. I will find the murderer and punish him—"

"He's standing right *next to you!*" Christie shouted, as he was pulled back by Aubrey and a grim Professor Hobson.

Caliban cast them all a disgusted look. He stepped back and bowed to Reiko. "Lady, it is almost time. Can we do this?"

Finn felt rage and strength and hope fading. When she staggered and almost fell, a hand beneath her elbow gently steadied her. She looked up at handsome David Ryder, who inclined his head to her like a knight acknowledging a queen.

She looked at his true queen, and something ferocious rose within her again. "Reiko Fata. If I . . . die for you, will my friends be set free, unharmed forever?"

"Of course."

"And you'll let Jack go?"

"He shall live the life your sister never did." Reiko moved closer, and her expression was almost tender. She reached out and tucked the hair back from Finn's face. "You are my little sister now. Soon, you'll be like us."

As Reiko moved back, Finn thought despairingly of the thing that had taken her mother and sister and now waited for her, its form bound with black ribbons, its patience monstrous. *Death.* She met Reiko's gaze and said steadily, "I want to say good-bye to my da."

Reiko moved aside. "Of course. *Amadan.*"

Absalom Askew emerged from the night. He wore a black suit with a ruffled collar and ribbons and Finn thought she glimpsed tiny horns in his orange hair, the glint of dying stars in his golden eyes. He stretched out a hand, and the wind scattered crimson leaves around them as Finn twined her fingers with his. She felt a shiver of air like invisible bees passing over her skin. The candles and the Fatas and the dying oak slid away into darkness as she and Absalom walked toward a stone arch glistening with Emory.

"Go on, braveheart," he said. "Through there."

She hesitated. Her da was there. She couldn't tell him the truth . . . but she could say good-bye.

She stepped through—

—into the book-cluttered parlor with the sun-yellow walls and the photographs of her family. She heard laughter and closed her eyes, wondered if she could escape—

Reiko and her Fatas would take revenge on all that she loved.

She opened her eyes and walked into the kitchen, found her da at the stove, his shaggy blond head bowed over a pot. He was speaking to Jane Emory, who was pouring wine into two glasses. In the background, the stereo was softly playing "Darkness, Darkness."

Finn's heart broke as she realized her da would be fine without her. When he looked up, concern and alarm flashing across his face, she could barely speak, "Da . . ."

"Finn? When did you get home? Dinner's almost done." He took a step toward her where she stood in the dark.

"I can't." She drew back into the unlit hall. This was no longer reality, this place she'd taken for granted. She was a thing of the shadows now. The warm light of home blurred.

Looking confused and afraid, her father took another step forward, held out a hand. "Finn—"

"Good-bye."

"Good night, you mean." Jane Emory, her eyes luminous, had not moved. "Only good night. We'll see you in the morning, Finn."

No. You won't. Finn turned and walked away down the hall, toward her death.

"Finn!"

Darkness swallowed her . . .

. . . and she was back in the firelight, among the shadowy figures of the inhuman creatures gathered there to watch her die. Reiko, a goddess in glistening red, smiled and raised one hand.

The ribbons on the scarecrow lashed around Finn's wrists, dragging her back against its thorny shape. This time, she screamed.

NATHAN CLARE WAS LOST.
He'd come late to the event that was supposed to end his one hundred years. Dressed in Victorian black, an aviator's cap with goggles concealing his face, he moved through the Halloween party, among the laughing, mortal children whom he could no longer pretend to be one of.

His girl, who had always wanted to be called Booke, was dead. They had killed her. Nathan wanted to die. He waited and watched and, near the end, followed the *others* up the wooded path.

Somehow, he lost the winking lights in the dark and the cold and the rustling leaves. He twisted around and stumbled as a pale figure emerged from the trees.

"Lazuli! Help me."

"You were a prince," the Fata Druid said, pointing the stag-skull staff at him, "for one hundred years. And you betrayed us."

Nathan felt tears clot his throat. "I'm not one of them anymore! I'm *one of you*."

Lazuli spoke gently. "No, Nathan Clare. You are nothing."

AS NATHAN RAN AWAY, LAZULI Gilfaethwy, who had lived much longer than his young face would have others believe, stood in the sacred grove and raised a hand over his eyes. He wanted his room in Tirnagoth, the rosewood guitar, and the white dog that kept him company.

When he lifted his head and saw a dark figure standing beneath one of the birches, he flinched. The white face and dark eyes of the figure terrified him. He was not used to fear. Or love. If he'd had a heart, it would have jumped into his throat.

Jack's voice was low. "You will tell me how to save her, Lazuli."

As the other walked toward him, Lazuli closed his eyes, unable to defend himself from what he loved.

CALIBAN ARIEL'PAN HAD BEEN SENT to fetch Lazuli Gilfaethwy, one of the few who could safely call Death's ambassadors to the Teind: after the schoolgirl was offered, despite her promise, Reiko would have Jack executed. He grinned when he thought of Jack's anguish, his useless blood-and-breath life, which Caliban planned to end as soon as possible.

As for the schoolgirl . . . Serafina Sullivan was all the things that even a one-hundred-year-old, willing candidate couldn't bring to the Teind: pure of heart, all courage and innocence. Reiko had always planned to bring Finn Sullivan to them, parading her darling Jack at the lakefront concert so that the girl would follow his false chivalry to Reiko's doorstep. That Finn Sullivan had been lured to them by the wicked thing that had come to love her was all the more delightful. It had been a marvelous trick.

"Ain't love grand, Lazuli?" Caliban said as he approached the white-clad figure of the Druid seated in the sacred grove.

Lazuli did not respond.

An unfamiliar wariness pricked Caliban. His boots crushed frost-glittering leaves as he loped to the Druid and knotted one hand in the pale hair, raising the head to gaze down at a face set in an expression of frozen sleep. There was a line of blood across his throat. Lazuli the bloodless had bled to death.

Caliban followed a trail of red to a human heart cradled in the hands of a kneeling statue. He began to swear in a language that hadn't been heard in centuries.

Jack, the lunatic, had cut out his own seedling heart. He wasn't human anymore. He wasn't vulnerable.

FINN CLOSED HER EYES AND whispered a child's poem as the ribbons tightened around her wrists, binding her to the thorn-and-bone scarecrow behind her. Drums beat a sinister rhythm as a flute breathed its strange melody into the autumn air. A girl was singing, her voice high and wild and inhuman. Someone was crying. Someone else was yelling. Finn wondered if she should even try to fight the sleep attempting to drag her down.

"Serafina Sullivan." As Reiko Fata spoke, Finn opened her eyes. Reiko was walking around the scarecrow, the train of her red gown swirling in air electric with smoke and cold. "Orfeo. Persephone. A girl named Isis. A boy named Izanagi . . . like them, you will be death's companion for one hundred years."

"The hell with this." On the borders, Aubrey Drake flung down his mask and stalked away. His friends followed, dragging Hester Kierney with them. Finn looked at Christie and Sylvie, who, encircled by HallowHeart's professors and instructors, watched helplessly. She was so sorry she'd brought them into this.

A wind reeking of old stone and frost sheared over her as she thought of Jack, who had seen death when they had brought it to him. He had once stood where she was now. *He'll feel the sun again. Fall in love. Grow old. Without me.*

If Reiko kept her word. And how likely was that?

Finn realized she did not want to die.

CALIBAN ARIEL'PAN LOPED TOWARD THE grove of yews where the Fatas had dragged what they had believed to be a helpless, *human* Jack. He slowed and swore when he saw the two lifeless bodies of the guards. A low, animal sound escaped him. Moonlight slid over his pale form, and it was the crooked dog that leaped toward the glimmering lights of the Teind.

THEY BROUGHT FINN BLACK WINE in a cup. Phouka handed it to her. "Drink it, Serafina. It will be easier." But her eyes held a warning, and Finn turned her head away. Terror had long ago left her so that only a stony exhaustion remained.

"We can't begin without Lazuli." David Ryder wouldn't look at Finn.

"Oh, yes, we can." And Reiko began to speak in a language that bit at the air, slithered across the ground, and crawled across Finn's skin. The leaves of the dying oak tree rustled above her as if whispering. Firelight and shadows writhed over the assembly as the dark powers descended.

Finn's eyes widened as antlers seemed to unfurl from David Ryder's brow. Reiko's gown clung close as a serpent's skin and horns appeared to curl from the night of her hair. Things buzzed and hummed beyond Finn's peripheral vision, marionette-like creatures with burning eyes and bat wings, lurching in the darkness that swirled like a graveyard wind through the oak grove. Her terror felt distant, as if her spirit was already leaving her.

Reiko circled her. She didn't look like a girl anymore, but some hell-thing that fed on blood and hearts. Finn remembered Sylvie's Balinese mask of Rangda, a creature of darkness and death. Reiko had murdered. She was a spirit that had killed flesh and blood—she would not keep her word.

"It will not be knives," the thing with a girl's face hissed, continuing to walk around Finn and the oak. "It will be *fire*."

Anger glimmered through Finn and began to catch at synapses and muscles and a fading hope. She looked around. She and the oak were circled by a border of blue light and toadstools the color of Absalom Askew's hair. It was a circle Reiko had enchanted into existence, but hadn't yet stepped into.

Finn spoke the summoning, " '*Thou art mine and I am thine. 'Til the sinking of the world.*' "

A shadow stepped into the circle. A scent of wild roses and evergreen shielded Finn from the darkness writhing around her as cool hands cupped her face and a mouth blossomed over hers in a lovely, biting kiss that drew out all the fear even as it warmed her iced body. She could taste the salt of her tears on Jack's lips.

He drew away. The moth key and the locket he'd given her gleamed against his blood-streaked chest. There were rose petals in his hair. One hand was wrapped in strips of blood-soaked cloth; the other held the glass box she'd discarded, the one encasing the heart *he* had caused Reiko to grow.

"Jack." The black ribbons of the thorn and bone scarecrow snaked loose from around Finn's wrists. "What have you done?"

"No." Behind him, Reiko Fata was in her human glamour again, her gown a blossom of fire and blood. She stepped forward and struck an invisible barrier, shrieking, "*No!*"

"Only two souls in the circle, Reiko—the summoner and the summoned." Jack didn't drop his gaze from Finn's as he held out the glass box. He smiled. His hands were shaking. "I brought you a present."

"It's the same present," Finn whispered. "Jack, it won't—"

"Jack"—Reiko's voice held a note of panic—"Jack, what are you doing?"

"My lady, like most old things, you are a creature of habit. Same box. Same spell." Without dropping his gaze from Finn's, Jack raised one hand. Between two fingers, he held a bone roughly carved into the shape of a key. "Different key."

Finn, dizzy and sick, looked at his hand wrapped in bloody cloth and a small, hurt sound escaped her. Jack had caused the birth of Reiko's new heart. Jack's finger bone would be needed to make that key. "What did you *do*?"

"I'd rather not go into detail," he whispered in her ear, pressing the grotesque key into her hand, "but I believe I've come to your rescue."

Reiko spoke in a voice close to shattering. "*Serafina.* Do you want this world of absolutes and accidents? Of hopelessness and ugly deaths? If *we* die, there will be no hope, nothing but what you see."

"Wysiwyg." Her heart slamming, Finn gently took the glass box from Jack. "What you see is what you get."

Reiko stepped forward. No one else moved. "Serafina. *Listen.* You will grow middle-aged, ugly, thick. Your hair will gray. You'll be a crone while Jack remains as he is. Serafina, I can make you *immortal.*"

Finn pushed Jack's finger bone into the lock. There was a click and, at the moment, it was the most wonderful sound she'd ever heard in her life.

Reiko whispered, "*I can bring back your sister.*"

Finn's fingers froze on the lid.

Jack spoke gently. "You can't bring back the dead."

Reiko turned on him, her alien glamour veiled by a schoolgirl's anguish. "You choose *her* over *me*?"

Jack looked at her. "It was never a choice."

Finn lifted the lid of the glass box. Nestled within black velvet was the knot of shiny red coral shaped like an anatomical heart. No one came at them. No one spoke. The branches of the corrupted oak clattered softly. The candles sparked with falling leaves that became webs of golden soot drifting over the gathering.

Reiko lifted her head, inky hair falling away from her face, her wide, green eyes. She took another step forward, and desperation broke the beauty of her voice. "Serafina Sullivan. Give me the heart and I will give you the *world.*"

Finn carefully lifted the heart from the box and met Reiko's gaze as she held the thing over a bowl of fire. Her voice was raw. "I'm eighteen—I already have the world."

She dropped the heart into the flames. The border of blue light around the oak flared and vanished. Tiny fires began in the foliage. Reiko screamed and lunged at Finn. Jack grabbed her.

A pale figure swept forward and snatched the heart from the bowl of flames. Straightening, Caliban grinned at Finn. "You're dead, girl."

A body struck the *crom cu*, tackling him into the leaves. When Caliban twisted away, he no longer held Reiko's heart. He held a knife, and Christie was curled on the ground. Caliban snarled, *"You? Again?"*

"No!" Finn ran toward him.

Caliban went for her. She reeled back from the shine of his knife.

Then Jack was there, yanking Caliban back and flinging him against a tree.

As the Fatas and their guests drew away from the fight—David Ryder had turned to them and was speaking—Finn dropped to her knees beside Christie. Sylvie was already crouched beside him as he clutched at his side. Blood stained his hand. *"Christie . . ."*

"I'm good." He tore open his shirt, revealing a shallow cut. He grinned and handed her Eve Avaline's silver knife. "Break the bitch's heart."

Finn took the knife and slid to her feet. She glimpsed Wyatt and Hobson pushing through the Fatas toward her. Jack and Caliban were still fighting. Reiko crouched near the scarecrow, her hair in her face, the heart glistening in her hands. She raised her head to glare at Finn and her voice slithered through the air. *"Girl. I will make you crawl for a thousand years."*

Gripping the knife, Finn moved forward.

David Ryder appeared behind Reiko, who rose to face him. He grimly took the heart from her hands. They began to argue. Finn turned away from them. The Fatas and their allies continued slipping into the night, discarding their masks, their faith.

"Serafina!" Sophia Avaline was also trying to reach her and was being held back by the crowd of retreating Fatas.

Jack and Caliban had slammed against one of the lanterns, which broke against the scarecrow. The scarecrow became an instant inferno, fire leaping into the branches of the oak, shadows swooping as mayhem erupted. The remaining Fatas shouted, avoiding the smoke and snaking flames.

When Finn felt someone grab her by the hair, she yelped, her hands scrabbling against a relentless grip. The knife was ripped from her hands. She fell, and someone started to drag her through leaves and cinders.

"Reiko!" David Ryder shouted. "What are you *doing*?"

"Saving us, my love." Reiko looked down at Finn, and her smile was pure malice. Her eyes were green and wide and filled with horror.

David Ryder shouted, "Reiko—let her go!"

Finn was released. She twisted around and up, avoiding the black blade Reiko slashed toward her. Reiko whispered, "Not fire. It *will* be knives."

"Reiko!"

Finn cried out as the blade slammed into the tree beside her. Reiko pulled it out, her teeth bared. Finn shoved her away and realized no one could help her in the chaos.

David Ryder dragged Reiko back. She whirled, and Finn saw David Ryder's eyes widen.

Still gripping the knife, Reiko stepped back.

David Ryder slid to his knees. His hands dropped to his sides. Blood, impossible for his kind unless they loved, began to stain his shirt.

Finn backed away.

"*David . . .*" Reiko dropped the knife.

He coughed, smiled. It was a terrible, bloodstained smile. "Do you see now, Reiko? What we are?"

He collapsed into the leaves.

Reiko turned on Finn. Her face was white, her green eyes electric with rage. "I *knew* it when I saw you two together that night, that bloody innocence between you like armor. You think you have won? That you've taken *everything away from me?*"

Finn felt an invisible force slam her back against a tree. She cried out and slid to the ground as bits of burning leaves fell over her like butterflies made of flames. Reiko's fingers knotted in her hair and yanked, and Finn felt as if her scalp was being torn away. She was pulled, twisting, toward the inferno that had once been the oak. She choked from the pain of her splintered rib. Heat licked at her. She screamed as fire kissed her skin. Her tulle gown blazed at the hem. The flames were green, unnatural, cold.

Hands gripped her then, pulling her from the flames and flinging her away. She hit the ground, twisted up in a tangle of charred tulle.

As Reiko backed away, Jack stood before the supernatural fire. Shapes moved toward him—tall, spindly things with the wings of dragons, their faces masked because their terrible beauty would shatter the souls of anyone who looked upon them.

"*Jack!*" Her voice tearing, Finn scrambled up.

Christie, pushing through the fleeing Fatas, yelled a warning.

Finn whirled to find Reiko standing with the black knife against Sylvie's throat.

"Join him in that fire, Serafina." Reiko smiled. "Or I will *flay* her—"

Sylvie smashed her elbow into Reiko's face, and Reiko stumbled back with an enraged scream. Sylvie dashed forward and grabbed Finn's hand. "Stop him!"

Astonished, Finn met Sylvie's gaze, then saw Sophia Avaline and Professor Fairchild running in their direction. She turned and raced toward the fire and Jack, who smiled at her as if she were the sun.

She realized what he was going to do. "Jack . . . *no* . . ."

Then a hand glittering with ancient rings grabbed him by the shoulder and threw him aside. As Jack fell, David Ryder looked back at Reiko.

Reiko screamed, "*What are you doing?*"

David Ryder, who held her heart, smiled. "Saving us, my love."

He stepped into the fire.

Reiko raced toward her consort. Jack lunged to stop her and they whirled together. Reiko, silvery-eyed and anguished, wrapped her arms around him.

"*No!*" Finn ran toward them.

Jack closed his eyes as Reiko dragged him into the burning green.

Finn dove forward, to pull Jack out of that supernatural inferno—

Two pairs of hands dragged her back. She struggled against Christie and Sylvie, sobbing and raging as she watched the emerald fire overwhelm the oak, driving into the night the acrid odor of a burning forest, of green curling from rot. The silhouettes within the inferno crumbled. As the fire continued to burn until the oak became a tree of flames, its branches arcing outward, shimmering with leaves of green fire, Finn slid to her knees, gasping as if the heart had been torn from her.

The Fatas who remained were silent, hair and clothes fluttering in a wind flecked with soot and molten sparks. Caliban Ariel'Pan was nowhere to be seen.

Sooty, bruised, with blisters on her arms, Finn couldn't look away from the fiery tree and its halo of light. Reiko and David Ryder were gone. And Jack . . .

A tall man stepped from among the Fatas. Rowan Cruithnear, the dean of HallowHeart, glanced at Finn. Ivory totems were braided into his silver hair. He wore a gray suit and carried a cane with an onyx raven for a handle. His eyes reflected the light as he turned to the Fatas and spoke in a baritone that carried: "I've a message from the old country; a new queen has been chosen for you, and you will serve her, and obey her, and you will cease all works of mischief, malice, and mayhem . . . or you will be harmed." Cruithnear inclined his head to Professor Avaline. "Our apologies to you and yours, Sophia Avaline."

Professor Avaline and the teachers walked to Finn, Christie, and Sylvie. As Mr. Wyatt gently lifted Finn to her feet, she glimpsed the silver revolver holstered beneath his coat and, startled, met his gaze. He murmured, "It seems you rescued yourselves. And, here we were, risking violence by bringing silver and iron."

Sophia Avaline stared at Rowan Cruithnear. "Who *are* you?"

Mr. Cruithnear didn't answer. He gravely met Finn's gaze. "Miss Sullivan . . . we are sorry for your loss."

Finn couldn't speak at first. Christie and Sylvie slid their arms around her waist, flanking her, keeping her upright. She finally found her voice. "Is he really dead?"

"Yes, Finn Sullivan." It was Phouka who answered, turning to regard the Fatas. Her voice rang out, above the roar of the burning tree. "If you are Fata, you are under my protection, for I will be regent. As for these three human children, blessed by the oak, they are also protected. The *ban nathair* and the *Damh Ridire* have passed. Honor them. Their sacrifice has bought us two centuries."

She walked to the burning tree and knelt. The Fatas folded with her, heads bowed, among them the Rooks and Jack's vagabonds.

Finn stood very still, gazing at the tree that had become Jack's funeral pyre.

"Finn." Christie's voice was raw, as if he could feel the pain shattering through her. As Sylvie laid her head on Finn's shoulder, Finn watched the tree-shaped inferno while ashes swirled and the pain slicing her to pieces became almost unbearable.

She heard someone clear his throat. Her attention slid to Absalom Askew, who stood to the side, who hadn't knelt to the tree. He met her gaze. And winked.

She stared at him. She slowly returned her gaze to the tree made of shimmering green fire.

Nothing is as it seems.

And so the trick is done.

Her eyes widened as understanding and fear and fury and hope battled within her.

She strode forward, leaving Christie to call her name and Sylvie to say, "Let her say good-bye to him."

"No—*Finn!*" Sophia Avaline reached out.

Finn, avoiding her, began running toward the burning tree, past the Rooks, through the Fatas rising to their feet. She ran as if the thing called a heart made her invincible.

Someone grabbed her—and Finn stared into Phouka's silver eyes flickering with green flames.

Then Phouka released her and stepped back with a curtsy.

Finn raced toward the tree, ignoring the flames that licked out at her, singeing her gown, making her skin feel as if it were rippling. She closed her eyes and stepped into the flames before anyone running after her could stop her.

Cold tore through her. She spoke his name as her body began to incinerate, without pain, into a dream . . .

Strong hands grasped hers and pulled her back to her body, back to pain. In the burning-cold silence, someone gently spoke her name.

It woke her.

"Jack." She reached up, to pull him out—

A burning corpse-thing lashed out at them, shrieking from the flames, grasping for them. Its claws sank into Jack's shoulders, pulling him back. His gaze met hers, despairing, and she felt him begin to let go of her hands. She met the fiery thing's green gaze and said, "Reiko Fata—*Let him go.*"

The thing crumbled, and Finn fell out of the fire with Jack.

FINN OPENED HER EYES AS the fire vanished, drawn inward, leaving her unharmed, the charred remains of the oak falling away to reveal a sapling, its leaves unfurling, its trunk strong and green, tiny lights flickering among its branches.

When a hand clenched around hers, she lowered her blurred gaze from the glittering tree . . .

. . . to the bruised and sleeping young man who lay with his head in her lap, one hand, bare of any rings but the lions and their heart, twined with hers.

NATHAN RAN THROUGH THE WOODS until exhaustion crumpled him beneath a crimson-leafed rowan.

When a voice spoke his name in a gentle, winter-poisoned voice, he raised his head.

The young man before him seemed sculpted from moonlight, autumn leaves, and ice. An ivory scar etched one cheekbone. His fur-lined coat billowed around an expensive suit. One ring-glittering hand rested on the ugly head of the white beast crouched beside him. The *crom cu* bared its teeth in a nasty smile.

"Nathan Clare." The man's gentle courtesy made him all the more terrifying. He resembled a nineteenth-century aristocrat, but he was older than that and had learned to mimic humans so perfectly he could scarcely be recognized for what he truly was.

Nathan tried to curl away into the rowan tree. This death was not the one he had expected.

The white hyena at the young man's side grinned as the young man said, "Nathan Clare. You are quite abandoned."

"Please," Nathan whispered, "I didn't . . ."

"Come, lovely child." The young man leaned down, smiling like a saint, his blue wolf eyes altogether without mercy. "Come with me, such wondrous things you will see."

AUTUMN LEAVES, FLECKED WITH BLOOD, swirled where a boy had knelt, pleading for his life.

CHAPTER TWENTY

If you want your children to be intelligent, read them fairy tales. If you want them to be more intelligent, read them more fairy tales.
—ALBERT EINSTEIN

A jackal slinked through a hall where green lamps burned like tiny suns on black pillars. The jackal had been walking in this hall forever, because it had lost something it could not remember. When it heard a voice, its ears flicked up. Among the eternal odors of stone and dust there now drifted the fragrances of green things and water. The pillars stretched into trees as the creaking of branches and the whispering of leaves broke the dead silence.

Jack . . .

The hall blossomed with green light. Sunlight kissed the ground.

Jack . . .

The jackal flinched, curled back toward the darkness it had known for so long. The voice came again.

Jack. Open your eyes.

"OPEN YOUR EYES, JACK."

His lungs dragged in air. His lashes lifted. As brightness splintered into his skull, he cried out, flung an arm over his face.

"Jack . . ." Cool hands folded over his. "Open your eyes . . . it's only the sun."

He drew his arm away.

Above him, a girl's face glistened with pollen and tears and soot. Flowers were tangled in her brown hair. He lay with his head in her lap as sunlight—*sunlight*—kissed the curve of her throat, the leaves falling around them.

He smiled as he gazed at a sun-painted world he'd believed he'd never see again, and all the aches and weariness of mortality anchored him to life.

FINN LAID A HAND ON Jack's chest, over his beating heart.

They were alone now, beneath the green sapling. The Fatas had gone. Christie and Sylvie and the HallowHeart professors had returned to Drake's Chapel. Finn knew her father would soon come looking for her.

Jack touched her face, said hoarsely, "Let's go home."

She helped him to his feet. He wore only his jeans and the moth key and the locket with his friend's portrait in it. The scars and tattoos were gone, and leaves crowned his tousled hair. He didn't smell like wild roses anymore, but of blood and tears. He studied her as she nervously combed fingers through her knotted hair. He smiled. "That was very clever of you: 'Bring me her heart,' you said, knowing she'd give it to me."

Finn toed the glossy leaves. "Well, it backfired—wrong key. Jack . . . your hand." She reached out.

He raised the hand from which he'd cut the finger and wiggled all five digits. "I think the tree likes me."

"You *are* very charming."

"And devastatingly good-looking, don't forget."

She smiled. He drew closer to her. She gripped his hands tightly, waiting for a kiss. Instead, he whispered, "You could have died. Don't do anything like that again. Where are Sylvie and Christopher?"

"With Avaline and the others—turns out Avaline was just playing Reiko and her regiment."

"So . . . part of HallowHeart's staff are faery doctors. I wonder how long they've been charming their way into Fata intrigues?"

"I suspect they've been doing it for a while, because they were *very* convincing."

"*You* were very convincing." He spoke with that careless antiquity that made her insides shiver. "I've been freed from a wicked queen and saved by a diabolical schoolgirl."

"Better believe it. What will you call yourself now?"

His fingers twined firmly with hers. "My last name . . . it used to be Hawthorn."

As they walked, he took the moth key from around his neck and handed it to her. She dropped it onto a crumbling wall. She didn't look back, didn't see the key stir and flutter and take flight. "Jack Hawthorn. I like it."

AS THE SUN CONTINUED TO rise, a moth swirled through the branches of a tree where an orange-haired figure, watching Finn and Jack walk away, began to fade. A whisper followed the moth's ascent into the sky.

"*The battle is won, the serpent gone. Fling swords and armor in the air. 'Tho we spirits have done you wrong, 'tis you who have triumphed, true and fair.*"

"DID YOU HEAR SOMETHING?" FINN murmured to Jack.

"No." And he kissed her, and it was only a mortal kiss, tart as autumn apples, hot as summer sun, with nothing of the otherworld in it at all, and everything of life and love.

EPILOGUE

This is for you, these words that are true. They are your weapon, your shield, your guide. With all my love, from the other side . . .

—FROM THE JOURNAL OF LILY ROSE

Day faded.

The moth fluttered through the woods into a darker forest, where trees glittered with frost and briars latticed the snow, where a forbidding, decrepit mansion loomed, stone wolves guarding a riven stairway leading up to timber doors that belonged to a fortress.

As the last of the sun vanished, the mansion remade itself.

The broken windows glassed over and became honeyed with light from within. Crumbling stone smoothed. Music teased the air, and lamplight swept across a garden of briar roses and waxy lilies and sweet-faced statues with very dark shadows.

The moth swept to an open window, to a girl whose hair veiled her face as she whispered, *Go back. Keep my sister safe. Keep her away from the Wolf.*

The moth fluttered up, back toward the light of the true world.

GLOSSARY OF FATA TERMS

(Very loosely based on old Gaelic)

Aillidh, aingidh faodalach—lovely, wicked waif

alainn cailin—beautiful girl

amach—out

amadan—fool

ban leannan—white sweetheart

ban nathair—white serpent

caileag—girl

Cailleach Oidche—owl

coineanach—rabbit

cro—blood

crom cu—crooked dog

Damh Ridire—Stag Knight

Dubh Deamhais—Black Scissors

Dubh ubha—Black Apple

gabh I le—go, come

leanabh—child

leannan—sweetheart

luch bheag—mouse

Madadh allaid—Wolf

Marbh ean—Dead Bird

seanchaidh—storyteller

sidhe—Irish faeries

sluagh—the dead

BIBLIOGRAPHY

Visions and Beliefs in the West of Ireland, by Lady Gregory (1920)

The White Goddess, by Robert Graves (1948)

At the Bottom of the Garden, by Diane Purkiss (2000)

Classic Celtic Fairy Tales and Tales of the Celtic Otherworld, by John Matthews (1997)

The Collected Poems of W. B. Yeats

IF YOU LIKED THE STORY, HERE'S THE SOUND TRACK

"I'll Follow You into the Dark"—Death Cab for Cutie

"Tam Lin"—Fairport Convention

"A Man You Don't Meet Every Day"—The Pogues

"Breathe Me" and **"I Go to Sleep"**—Sia

"Haunted"—Jewel

"Darkside"—Kelly Clarkson

"A Thief at My Door"—Karen Elson

"Wide Awake"—Katie Perry

"Whispering"—Alex Clare

"You Are the Blood"—Sufjan Stevens

"Lucky You" and **"Deathblow"**—Deftones

"Scarborough Fair"—Sarah Brightman

"Live Like a Warrior"—Matisyahu

ABOUT THE AUTHOR

Katherine Harbour was born in Albany, New York, and now lives in Sarasota, Florida, with a tempestuous black cat named Pooka and too many books. *Thorn Jack* is her first novel.

Visit her website at www.katherineharbour.com.